THE SECRET DUKE

THE SECRET DUKE

JO BEVERLEY

THORNDIKE PRESS
A part of Gale, Cengage Learning

GALE
CENGAGE Learning

Detroit • New York • San Francisco • New Haven, Conn • Waterville, Maine • London

GALE
CENGAGE Learning™

Copyright © Jo Beverley, 2010.
Thorndike Press, a part of Gale, Cengage Learning.

Thorndike Press® Large Print Basic.
The text of this Large Print edition is unabridged.
Other aspects of the book may vary from the original edition.
Set in 16 pt. Plantin.

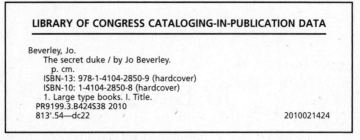

LIBRARY OF CONGRESS CATALOGING-IN-PUBLICATION DATA

Beverley, Jo.
    The secret duke / by Jo Beverley.
      p. cm.
    ISBN-13: 978-1-4104-2850-9 (hardcover)
    ISBN-10: 1-4104-2850-8 (hardcover)
    1. Large type books. I. Title.
PR9199.3.B424S38 2010
813'.54—dc22   2010021424

Published in 2010 by arrangement with NAL Signet, a member of Penguin Group (USA) Inc.

Printed in the United States of America
1 2 3 4 5 6 7 14 13 12 11 10

THE SECRET DUKE

CHAPTER 1

Dover, 1760

Laughter can take many forms, from the pure delight of a happy child to the gibber of madness. The laughter that slithered out into the dark and misty Dover night was the sound of cruel men with a victim in their clutches.

It caused the man in the street to pause.

To his left, water slapped against the wharf and wind rattled the riggings of ships. Farther out, rough water jangled a buoy bell. To his right, lanterns outside buildings were gleaming globes in the sea mist, giving only enough light for passersby to avoid the larger detritus of any port — snarls of rope, soggy bales, and broken casks leaking stinking contents.

He shook his head and moved on, but then the laughter came again, this time punctuated by one sharp word. He couldn't tell what word, but the voice sounded female.

It could be a ship's lad being teased, or a whore, well used to this rough area. No concern of his.

But then he heard a few more words. Higher pitched, but almost authoritative. Not a lad. Almost certainly not a whore. But what decent woman would be down here late on a chilly October night?

Damn it all to Hades. He'd been at sea for two cold days and nights and anticipated a fine meal and warm bed at the Compass and then home tomorrow.

He waited and heard no more.

There, whatever the commotion, it was over. But then raised jeers made him curse again and turn toward the noise. One of the misty globes probably marked the entrance to the place, but he couldn't see more than that.

As he came closer he saw only two small windows, one on either side of a cockeyed door, covered by slatted shutters that let out mean slices of tallow light. Tobacco smoke slithered out as well, along with the smell of ale, new and old, and human stink. It was a port tavern of the lowest sort, a haunt for the roughest of sailors and shore workers.

A coarse voice sneered something about tits.

The woman didn't respond.

Was unable to respond?

As he reached for the door he saw a roughly painted sign nailed above it indicating that this place rejoiced in the name the Black Rat.

"And a plague on the lot of you," muttered Captain Rose as he shouldered open the warped planked door.

He'd been right about the smoke and tallow light, and it made the room foggy, but he could see enough.

The Rat was crowded, and most of the men were still sitting on their stools and benches, drinking from pots and tankards, but they'd all turned to watch the entertainment. In the corner to his right, five men had a woman trapped. Perhaps she'd been herded there as soon as she unwisely entered.

What in Hades had she been thinking? Even at a glance he recognized youth and good birth. Her brown-and-cream-striped gown had cost a pretty penny, and her hair curled out from a dainty cap trimmed with lace. And yes, the swell behind the fichu that filled in her low bodice suggested she had fine tits. One of her captors was teasingly

9

trying to snatch away the filmy cloth, playing cat and mouse, but sure of victory.

She slapped at his hand.

The man laughed.

Rose looked around for allies, but saw no one he knew.

There was one other woman present, but she was a hard-faced forty or so and was guarding the big cask of ale. The tavern keeper or his wife, but showing no sign of interfering. She continued to fill pots and tankards as requested and take the coins. He was on his own against five, and now drinkers were beginning to notice his arrival, nudging one another and muttering.

Not surprising. He was as alien here as she. His dark suit was old-fashioned, but of excellent quality. He wore his hair loose to his shoulders and had days of beard on his chin, but these men would recognize rank and authority.

Rank and authority might help him, or it might get his throat cut. Easy enough to tip a body off the nearby quay and no one would be any the wiser. In places such as these, no one tattled.

Someone might recognize him — Captain Rose's red neckcloth and skull earrings were meant to be noticed — but that wouldn't protect him if they turned on him.

He saw neither recognition nor hostility as yet, only interest in a new actor on the stage and hope that he'd provide even more free entertainment. Rose turned his attention back to the scene in the corner. Yes, a lady. He knew by her clothes, but also by her carriage and the outrage flashing in her eyes. What — had she expected the habitués of a place like the Black Rat to be gentlemen?

Both haughty manner and generous figure were going to get her raped. Even these rascals might object to tormenting a terrified weakling, but such a bold piece would look like fair game to them, especially if she'd come in here by her own choice.

Had she been looking for this sort of adventure? Some ladies thought rough men exciting, but she'd have to be mad to sink this low, and despite an attempt at dignity, she was young. Perhaps not eighteen. Surely too young for such depravity. As a couple of the tormentors sensed something and turned to confront him, he wondered if he could use insanity to free her.

One of the two men was scarred and sinewy, but the other was an ox, all hard, beefy muscle, with a low, bony forehead. Getting the chit out of here without bloodshed wasn't going to be easy, and the blood shed could well be his own. The shorter man had slid out a long filleting knife. It would be razor sharp.

Too late to rethink now. As with any feral animals, it would be disastrous to show fear, even if his heart beat fast with it. And in truth, he couldn't abandon the foolish creature.

He strode forward, pushing his way roughly between tables. "So there you are, you dim trull!" he blasted in the voice he used to call instructions in a gale. "What in Hades do you think you're doing, wandering about down here?"

None of the tormentors moved. Nor did their victim except to stare at him. He saw then how stretched her courage was. The whites showed around her eyes. He hoped his weren't the same. *Play your part, damn you,* he thought as he assessed the danger around them.

Probably the only immediate danger was from the two who'd faced him, but at the slightest sign of fear they'd all be on him like a pack of mangy dogs. He had a pistol in his pocket, but that was only one shot. He had a blade too, but he didn't fool himself that he'd win a knife fight, and to show either weapon now would indicate fear.

There was no way out of this but through

it, so he brushed past the two men as if unaware of them, grabbed her arm, and snarled, "Come on."

She instinctively pulled back, but then complied by one step. It probably looked right for a woman caught in folly by an angry husband or guardian. When Rose directed them toward the door, however, the two men moved solidly in his way.

"Yer little lady came a-visitin'," said the ox, flexing his big hands. Clearly he thought them the only weapon he needed, and he was probably right. "Reckon she's ours now."

"She's my wife," Rose said in a weary tone he hoped would get some sympathy, "and half out of her wits, as you can see. Let us be."

"I don't mind if she's a knock in the cradle," said the man with the knife, "as long as she's got big tits." He showed dirty, broken teeth. "We want to see her tits."

Ah, hell.

"I think not," Rose said, and moved his left hand to his right wrist, then turned it, holding a knife.

The method usually impressed his foes, for he kept the knife in a cunning sheath on his right forearm so that its appearance seemed magical. In that moment of distraction, he took his pistol out of his right pocket. He was left-handed, but moderately ambidextrous, and the pistol was small and specially made so he could easily cock it one-handed. Too small for distance work, but it'd stop a man at this range.

The shorter man eyed the weapons through slitted eyes, wary but assessing his chances. The ox chewed the cud, clearly wishing he were grinding someone between his teeth.

Would they stop him again? He tested the situation by moving a step to the side. The two men moved to block him.

The knife man said to the others, "Come on, mates. He's one man, and a fribbly type, from the look of those weapons. Call that a knife! Let's get him!"

The group stirred but was undecided.

Rose raised the pistol to point directly at the knife man's left eye. "You die first."

Into the frozen silence, a voice rose at the back of the room. An elderly voice, but strong. "That's Captain Rose, lads. Don't know as I'd take him on, m'self."

Most of the room turned toward the speaker, but not the two dangerous men. Captain Rose kept his eyes on them.

"A flower?" sneered the knife man. "I'll pluck his pretty petals for him."

His companions sniggered, but they shifted like wet sand, uncertain.

"Captain Rose of the *Black Swan*," the same helpful voice called. "Broke the arm of the last man to pull a knife on him."

The three other villains backed away a bit. Rose had no idea who the speaker was, but silently thanked him, though he hoped he wouldn't have to live up to the billing.

Captain Rose and his ship, the *Black Swan,* were well-known along this stretch of the south coast. Most of the time the *Swan* engaged in general trade, but sometimes she sailed off on illicit business across the Channel. He'd made sure that people along the coast knew the *Black Swan*'s business didn't benefit the French, especially during the recent war. Even the lowest Kentish sea rat wouldn't take kindly to anyone who favored their ancient enemy.

All the local people knew Captain Rose of the *Black Swan* was a loyal Englishman and a good seaman, but he was known for other things as well. For enjoying a fist-fight, and yes, for objecting to anyone drawing a weapon on him.

But there were two Captain Roses, and he was the other one.

He was the Duke of Ithorne, known to his friends as Thorn.

The other Captain Rose was Caleb, his illegitimate half brother.

Thorn was as good a seaman as Caleb, and perhaps even better, but he had no taste for meaningless fighting and little skill in a brawl. Other than that, Caleb and he were as close in appearance as two peas in a pod. The slight differences in their features were masked by dark stubble that sometimes became a beard. To make the illusion complete, Captain Rose wore distinctive clothes — an old-fashioned black frock coat and a scarlet neckcloth — and an earring in the form of a skull with ruby eyes.

People generally saw what they expected to see, so the outward trappings meant that the man inside was Captain Rose of the *Black Swan.*

Most of the time, Caleb was master of the *Swan,* but that being the case, his reputation stuck to Captain Rose, who was generally known as a gregarious womanizer and fearless brawler. He leapt into a fistfight with glee, especially when he'd been drinking, and then afterward drank cheerfully with his opponents — as long as they'd not pulled a weapon on him. He took knives as a personal affront and would leave the offender in pieces. Perhaps Caleb's reputation would tip the scales here.

"I'm Rose, right enough, so heed the man and get out of my way."

The ox's brow lowered. "Ye're still only one."

"One of one can be more than one of another."

The ox stared, baffled.

A nearby man said, "I've 'eard of Captain Rose, but never that he was married."

"Not quite blessed by the church," Thorn admitted.

Amid laughter one of the wary brutes sneered, "For that sort of lay, I'd pick a sweeter-natured 'un."

"Perhaps I enjoy a wench with spirit," he parried.

"Spicy in bed as well, is she?"

"Exceedingly." He tossed it out simply to annoy the idiotic cause of this mess, but then recognized his mistake. New interest stirred in the room as a whole.

A pot flew by, spraying ale, and thunked into the side of the knife man's head. He cried out, put hand to head, staggered, and then collapsed to his knees.

"Hey, that was my pot, woman," someone protested, but weakly.

Thorn was cursing himself. That conversation had been a distraction and he'd fallen for it, but she'd kept her wits about her. He stepped back until he was by her side. "Good aim, ma'am."

"Thank you, sir," she said tightly, "but I have no more ammunition within reach."

He passed her his pistol. "It's cocked, so be careful."

She took it, but as if she'd never handled a gun before.

"Point it upward," he said hastily. "We wouldn't want to kill anyone. Not by accident, at least," he added deliberately.

Finally the men were backing away. Clearly the sight of a gun in the hands of a woman was more frightening than the same gun in a man's, especially when the woman had no idea what to do with it.

Thorn fought laughter, praying the girl wouldn't shoot anyone by accident, especially him. Just perhaps, however, the tide was turning in his favor. The knife man was still glazed. She'd hit him well. The ox seemed truly bovine without him.

He dug in his breeches pocket, feeling the coins there. What was the right amount for the situation? He didn't want to inflame new greed, but he wanted to offer enough to get them out of here. He took out a silver sixpence and tossed it to the man who'd lost his drink.

"Thank'ee, sir!" the man said with a gap-toothed grin.

Thorn took out a crown and held it up to one of the other bully boys. "Ransom?"

The man hesitated a moment and then snatched the five-shilling piece. "Right you are, Captain! Worth it, I reckon, to see such a good throw. I'd get that pistol off her, though, and fast."

"Excellent advice."

He retrieved his pistol from her trembling hands and uncocked it, but he kept it out. The room was still crowded, its mood still uncertain. They could be grabbed, tripped, even stabbed before they reached the door. Money alone might be cause. Women were cheap and silver was rare.

Was he thinking too much, assuming too much hazard, as his friends sometimes accused him of doing? How did one not think in a situation like this? Thinking wasn't creating a path out of here, however, and the knife man was beginning to struggle to his feet. Nearby faces were unreadable and could easily conceal a murderous interest in the contents of his pockets. . . .

Then the church bell began to toll.

Everyone's interest shifted. It was too late for any service.

"The French?" someone muttered, and others picked it up.

19

Men stood, pushing back stools and benches. Some clattered over. From ancient times, church bells had called the men of the Kent coast to repel invasion. Despite the recent treaty of peace, no one down here, just twenty miles from Calais, trusted the French.

To Thorn, it sounded more like the tolling for a death than an alarm sounded at invasion, but why toll a death so late at night?

Then someone burst in, crying, "The king's dead! George the Second's dead! Took a seizure this morning. Stone-cold dead, he is!"

Good God.

This was his moment, however. "God save the new king, then!" he bellowed. "The ale's on me. Drink up, lads, drink up, and toast young George the Third!"

As everyone turned to push toward the barrel, he grabbed the girl's arm again. When she fought him, he snapped, "Don't be a fool!"

"My cloak!" She gasped.

He saw it puddled on the floor and let her pick it up and swing it on before putting an arm around her and bullying their way toward the door of the chaotic Rat.

He was met there by a hard-eyed man, hand out. The tavern keeper. No time for haggling. Thorn took a half guinea out of his secret pocket and passed it over. The man actually smiled and nodded his head. "Thank'ee, sir. And God bless the king, indeed. It'll be mighty strange to have a new 'un."

"Exceedingly." Thorn glanced around for the man who'd helped by revealing his identity and was winked at by an elderly man puffing peaceably on his pipe. He took the risk of going over to slip him a guinea.

The man slid it into a pocket, nodding with dignity. "God bless you, sir!"

"And you."

Then he had the girl outside. He hurried her down the quay until they were lost in the misty darkness. Thorn blessed the growing crowd. When he'd entered the Rat, this area had been almost deserted, but now people were spilling out of buildings and perhaps coming from other areas of town to exclaim together over the news.

The immediate danger was over, but what in Hades was he to do with this woman? Especially now, in this extraordinary moment.

The old king had reigned for thirty-three years, as long as many here had memories, including himself. The king's eldest son, Frederick, had died some years back, so the

21

new monarch was poor Fred's son, George, a man younger than Thorn himself and under the thumb of his mother and his noble tutor, the Earl of Bute.

Chaos threatened and he needed to travel to London with all speed, but he had a reckless, stubborn millstone around his neck. She'd gathered her cloak around her and pulled up the hood against the damp chill, so he could see little of her face until she peered out at him.

In a flat voice, she said, "You're going to abandon me now."

A pretty plea would work better, my girl. But pretty pleas didn't seem to be her style, to rapacious rascals or impatient rescuers. Part of him admired that.

Or were her words simple cunning, making it hard to act that way? He deeply disliked being manipulated, and he was offended that she'd imagine he would abandon a young lady in this area at all, never mind on a night like this.

"You'd better come to my inn with me," he said shortly. "It's not far and we can sort out your problem there."

"I doubt you'll find it so easy."

"You'd rather I didn't try? Then walk away."

He sensed her flinch. "No, I'm sorry. It's

just . . . difficult."

"I don't doubt it." He put an arm around her to guide her through the growing crowd. She resisted for a moment, but then showed some sense. The mood was merry at the moment. Clearly celebrating the new reign was preferable to mourning the old, but it involved drink, a lot of drink, so this could soon become a riot.

"What were you doing in the Rat?" he asked.

"Is that the place's name? How appropriate."

"Well?" he demanded.

"I . . ." But then she turned and flung her arms around his neck, pressing hard against him. He instinctively put his arms around her, but then he grasped her wrists to pull her off. Devil take it, was this an extremely contrived attempt to compromise him into marriage?

"No," she whispered desperately, clinging to his coat. "Please!"

Good God. He'd heard of women driven mad with promiscuous desire. Was this a case? Was that her purpose down here on the quay? He couldn't deny a touch of excited curiosity, so he kissed her parted lips.

23

She became an icy statue, her lips closing tight.

Not, alas, driven mad with promiscuous desire. Not even pretending enthusiasm in the hope of hooking his interest. That left only one explanation.

"Who are you hiding from?" he whispered.

She relaxed a little. "Two men walking down the street."

The butterfly movements of her lips against his were surprisingly enticing, but not, it would seem, to her. He realized she wasn't interested in him at all.

How novel.

CHAPTER 2

Pretending to kiss, he turned them, looking around. With such a crowd it should be impossible to spot her problem, but the two men stood out by being sober and purposeful. They were working their way through the crowd without obvious impatience, but steadily. One was cloaked, one not, and both wore three-cornered hats. They could be anything from upper servants to lords.

Still holding her close, lips touching, he asked, "Are you the villain or are they?"

She stiffened. "They, of course."

"Not emissaries of your family, seeking to return you to your home?"

"Absolutely not."

"It would be unwise to make a dupe of me."

In almost a snarl, she muttered, "I wish I could tell you to go to the devil and take those men with you."

Thorn chuckled. He couldn't help it. "It

looks as if it's me or them, sweetheart. Better, perhaps, the devil you do not know?"

She audibly inhaled, but agreed with a brusque, "Very well."

He chuckled again. Dammit, but he liked the wench, for her blunt acceptance of the inevitable if nothing else. But her unwomanly nature had probably thrown her into this situation and could easily make things worse. Whoever she was, whatever her situation, she should have stayed safe at home.

They moved on, but he kept an eye on the men. One ducked into a tavern while the other remained outside, scanning the crowd. Thorn regretted that he was tall, for even as he tried to drift them on the tide of people toward his inn, he and the girl must stand out. The hunters were looking for a woman alone, however, and one in quality clothing. Wise of her to hide that frivolous cap.

But then he realized they might be distinctive simply by being sober and purposeful, just as the hunters were.

When a drunken sailor collapsed against them, staggering them both, Thorn relieved the man of his tankard. The sailor contemplated his empty hand with bewildered, crossed eyes and then bonelessly collapsed onto a coil of rope. Thorn waved the tankard and staggered onward, joining in a raucous rendering of a very dirty ditty.

"What are you doing?" she protested.

"Hiding. Act as drunk as everyone else."

"I —"

Someone nearby began a ragged attempt at the newly popular song "God Save the King."

God save our gracious king,
Long live our noble king,
God save the king . . .

Thorn joined in, deliberately as out of tune as he could manage, weaving and staggering. All of a sudden his companion staggered along with him, joining in the song in a vile nasal whine. Laughing, he swirled her in for a true kiss, catching her lips parted, touching tongues.

She jerked back.

"Drunk, remember," he said, grinning.

"I am not drunk," she spat at him, but still swaying as if she were. "I, sir, have never been drunk."

"Poor creature. What a dull life."

"Some of us can have pleasure without wine."

"You must show me how," he said, watching the men join company and move closer in their search. "But for now, giggle."

"Giggle?"

He leaned closer and nipped her ear.

She let out a yip, but then managed to turn it into a creditable drunken shriek. She also kicked his shin. He wasn't wearing boots and her shoes were solid. He staggered in truth, but kept a firm hold on her so she almost lost her footing entirely.

When she gained her balance he gave her a hard slap on the rear. She whirled on him. "You . . . !"

Fortunately blind rage made her sound like a fishwife, but they were a center of attention now, with men and women calling encouragement to one or the other. Thorn thought he'd ruined everything, but then he saw that the hunters had dismissed this uproar as nothing to do with them and moved on past.

He turned back — to encounter her hand on his cheek. Her hit was feeble, so he just shook his head at her, grabbed her wrist, and dragged her onward. "I'll deal with you, my girl, when we're back home," he announced loudly.

The crowd cheered them off, then returned to their revels, and soon they were free of the throng. He moved quickly into what shadows he could find, and then plunged down a narrow lane that would lead him to the back of the Compass Inn.

"Clear for now," he said softly to the woman, "but they'll be at the Rat soon, and there they'll hear the whole story."

She was still seething — it came off her like heat — but she said, "Then they'll learn I'm with Captain Rose."

"Good girl," he said, impressed by her quick understanding and irritated to be a step behind her. "And someone will know where Captain Rose always stays."

She pulled back. "We must go elsewhere!"

He tugged her onward. "My horse is at the Compass, and my other possessions. But we can be free of Dover in a quarter hour, and then you can explain all of this. Here we are."

A couple of grooms were in the stable yard, one walking a heated horse and the other carrying a bucket. They knew him, but were surprised to see him approaching the inn from the back, especially with a woman.

"Can I do something for you, Captain?" the one with the bucket asked.

"Aye, the news of the king's death changes my plans. I need my horse, and a pillion pad for the lady."

"Aye, sir," the man said, but with a sharp

look at the lady in question.

Thorn looked at her too, but her hood still concealed her. Was she from Dover and fearful of being recognized? Or was she a well-known villain — a pickpocket or cut-purse, or even one of the sort to entice innocent young women into brothels?

He couldn't believe it. She was too young and, though clever, not cunning or hard.

"It'll be a few minutes," he said. "Do you need some food and drink before we leave?"

"No, thank you." But then she asked, "Where are you taking me?"

She tried to make it a bold demand, but fear trembled beneath her tone. If he was any judge, she was a gently bred young lady in serious trouble, which was a mess in too many ways to count. He needed to travel with all speed to London, but he accepted the inevitable.

"Within reason, I'll take you where you need to go."

"Near Maidstone, then."

"A fair distance from here."

"Yes."

"So how did you come here?"

"By coach."

He had a feeling they could play question and answer all night, and in truth he didn't want any more of her story than he needed to get her off his hands in a way his conscience could accept.

Maidstone, then. It was en route to London, but alone he'd have made a stop before then at his home for a change of clothing and his traveling chariot, in which he could catch some sleep on the journey.

"Is there nowhere closer?" he asked.

"No."

"If we ride through the night, we might not get to Maidstone before morning, especially two to a horse. If you haven't been missed by now, you will be by then."

"Yes."

He wanted to shake her, and concerns about marriage plots were stirring again, but how could this young woman have staged that situation in the Rat on the off chance that he would pass by and decide to rescue her?

If she found out later who he was, however, she might try to take advantage of it. If they traveled overnight, she might claim to be compromised. Yet he couldn't abandon her, and it would take too much time to hire a coach and a maid to play chaperone. A coach would make tracking them child's play.

Devil take it, he was hungry. He'd expected to be peacefully at his supper now.

A boy came out of the stables pushing a barrow of soiled hay. Thorn called, "Run inside and get my bags, lad, and tell Green I'll settle my account later. Get some quick food and drink too. A pie and ale, perhaps. Be speedy now."

"Aye, aye, Captain!" The boy ran off.

"Are you really a captain?" his millstone asked.

"Yes."

"Of what?"

"Of a ship called the *Black Swan.* What's your name?"

She hesitated long enough for him to know she was going to lie. "Persephone," she said.

"Stolen away to the underworld? You don't want to share my food for fear of being trapped with me for six months of the year?"

Her reply was a blistering silence.

He considered the implications of Persephone, carried off by Hades, lord of the underworld. Though modern versions of the story glossed over such matters, Persephone had presumably been raped by the dark lord. Had this girl suffered the same fate?

He dismissed that. It seemed clear that her misadventure was recent and fresh. If she'd been vilely used she'd have to show

32

some sign of it.

"A little gratitude would be appropriate," he pointed out.

"I do thank you. I'll thank you all the more if you prove honest."

"The man in the inn had it right. You can't be accused of being honeyed. So if those men aren't after your sweet charms, why are they in grim pursuit?"

She turned her head away, a hooded, cloaked mystery. "Because I escaped from them."

"They had you prisoner?"

"Yes."

"Why?"

"I don't know."

"Come now, you must. Are you a rich heiress?"

"No."

"And you haven't escaped from jail?"

"No."

"So they took you from your home, and you all innocent of any sin?"

Her response to that was resolute silence.

Tiresome chit. He ignored her and put his mind to getting her to Maidstone and off his hands.

She had two men hunting her with serious intent. If those men came here, the grooms would probably help him in a fight, but he'd rather avoid violence entirely. He was a healthy, active man who'd engaged in some dangerous endeavors at sea, but he had no experience with this unwelcome knight-errantry, and the less bother the better with a well-bred young lady's reputation at risk.

"How old are you?" he asked.

"A lot older than I was a few days ago."

An interesting response suggesting a truly drastic disaster, but here at last was the groom leading out his horse and the lad with his food. He was followed by another boy staggering under the weight of the saddlebags. Along with changes of clothing, they contained his horse pistols and a couple of books.

He sent the bags over to be loaded on the horse and took the basket of pasties and tankard of ale, giving both lads a penny.

"And if any strangers come around," he told them, "you don't know what I'm doing or where I am."

"Aye, aye, Captain!"

He turned to the cloaked figure. "I assume I can't tempt you to some pie?"

"No, thank you."

He shrugged and took a big bite of the steak-and-kidney as he went to give the same instructions to the groom and pass over larger coins.

"May I have some ale?"

He turned to find she'd followed. He passed her the tankard. She sipped, as women were wont to, but sipped quite a few times.

"Are you going to explain your situation?" he asked.

"Not if I can avoid it."

"You don't think I deserve to know?"

"No."

"Might it not be useful for me to know," he asked, teeth gritting, "so I can keep you safe?"

"I don't see how it would make any difference."

"One example. Will those men expect you to head for Maidstone?"

He thought he'd catch her out there, but she said, "No," so simply that she must have considered that problem. For all her faults, the girl could think.

Before he could say anything else he heard a noise and instantly knew what it was — footsteps crunching on the back lane that wasn't commonly used by pedestrians.

He jerked his head in the direction of the stables. She was there ahead of him, standing back pressed to the wood just inside the doorway. He joined her, praying the grooms would realize what to do.

"You, there!"

"Sir?" asked a groom in perfect vague surprise.

"I'm looking for a Captain Rose. Do you know him?" A gentleman's voice, but perhaps only just.

"Captain Rose, sir?" said the groom slowly. "Everyone knows Captain Rose hereabouts."

"Is he here?"

"Here, sir? Not as I can see, sir."

Thorn grinned. It was going to be all right. He looked at his damsel in distress and sobered. Her hood had slipped back, and even in the dim light he could see that she was staring straight ahead, tense with dread. She had a profile that suggested she might be pretty in better circumstances.

"I mean nearby," snarled the hunter's voice.

A dangerous and perhaps desperate man. Thorn wished he had one of his big pistols, but they were in his bags.

"He's staying at the Compass sure enough, sir," said the groom. "Always does. But he's likely on his ship, sir."

"Which is?"

"The *Black Swan,* sir. Anchored out, most likely."

"So you haven't seen him in the last hour?"

Thorn tensed, wondering if the man would give a flat-out lie.

"Nay, sir, not him."

The groom doubtless expected a guinea for the lie, and he'd get it.

But then the man said, "Whose horse is that?"

After a moment the groom said, "Colonel Truscott's, sir, though what business it is of yours I don't know, and I'd better walk him, the colonel not being here yet. His lady fusses."

Hooves told of a moving horse.

The man spoke again, presumably to his companion. "Go in and ask for Rose. And for this Truscott. Shame to keep the horse waiting."

Damn. He was smelling a rat.

Thorn eased his knife free and took the risk of touching the woman. She started, but made no noise as she turned her head to him, eyes wide with fear. He held up the knife for her to see, and then put the hilt in her hand. Heaven knew whether she could use it, but it was something.

He took out his pocket pistol, but didn't cock it yet. The noise would be audible. Too late to realize that they should have gone farther into the stable, where there'd be some possibility of hiding.

But then he realized that only one man was outside now.

He could probably sneak out and kill him.

But he knew he couldn't. Not in cold blood without even being certain of his villainy. Perhaps not in cold blood even then. If he threatened the man with the pistol and the man wasn't cowed, he wasn't certain he could fire.

Damn him for a ditherer . . .

But then the man walked in — the cloaked one.

He looked forward before looking to the side, giving Thorn a second to prepare. When their eyes met, Thorn already had the pistol pointing at his head.

"On the floor," he said, cocking it. "Face-down."

The man was heavily built and probably about forty. The hanging lantern by the door gave just enough light to show a hard mouth and a heavy jaw. After a snarling moment, he obeyed.

But now what? Both men must be prevented from following their escape, and the other would be back soon. Then Persephone grabbed a leather strap draped over a stall. "Put your hands together at the back," she ordered.

"This won't work," the man growled, but then coughed, probably on a throatful of chaff.

"Just do it, or I'll stick this knife into you."

Thorn believed her, and perhaps the man did too. He put his wrists together and she tied them. It didn't look like much of a knot, but it would hold for a short while.

"Coxy?" The nasal drawl meant the other man was back. "Where did m'friend go?"

"Didn't notice, sir," said the groom. "Busy walking the horse."

"I'm in here!" yelled the man on the floor. "But watch out!"

"You really should have reversed those," said Thorn, fighting laughter at the absurdity of this, for the second man had walked in to meet the pistol. He was younger and quite handsome, but his expression had turned vicious.

"Join your friend."

With a similar snarling anger, the man obeyed.

"To your bounden duty, wench," Captain Rose said blithely.

With a frosty look, she said, "Why don't you give me the pistol? I'm sure a sea captain can tie them up more securely."

"True enough." He put the cocked pistol

carefully into her hand. At least she didn't immediately pull the trigger. There were a number of innocent horses at risk.

He found a length of thin rope and set to securing villain number two. He then retied Coxy, making a good job of it, hoping the wench appreciated his skill with knots.

He rose at last and turned for her approval.

She was gone.

Seized by a third villain?

But then he heard hooves.

He ran out, but saw the tail of his horse disappearing at speed down the lane. He swore long and vividly. "Why the devil did you let her have my horse?" he demanded of the groom.

The man backed away. "She said as you wanted her to ride for help, Captain. Seemed likely enough, begging your pardon."

"Get me another one. Any."

The man worked fast, but it took five minutes before Thorn mounted.

"But what about those men, Captain?" the groom asked anxiously, nodding toward the stables.

"Let them loose in a few minutes, but don't let them have a horse. If they give you any trouble, tell everyone that they're attempting to abduct a nobleman's sister and deserve to hang."

It might even be true.

"And make sure they know that if Captain Rose hears of them troubling the lady any more, they're dead."

The bound men would hear that for themselves. She didn't deserve protection, but he had to offer it.

He considered riding at speed along the London road, but he didn't think that cunning wench would take a straight route. She probably never had any intention of going to Maidstone. He made some inquiries nearby. A woman on a horse at night would be rare enough.

Those not celebrating the new reign were in bed, however, so he had only two sightings, neither of which led him to her. He suspected they were deliberate feints. Damnation, she wouldn't get away with this. He wasn't finished with her yet, and how did she expect to survive out alone at night on a stolen horse?

He'd delayed as much as he could, however. He turned the horse toward Ithorne Castle, annoyed, concerned, but reluctantly admiring as well. Such a resolute wench intrigued him, and he wanted to know her story.

41

But the king was dead.

Long live the king, and he needed to be in London to seize this moment.

The new king was young and hesitant, and those at court would already be jostling for influence. Some already had an advantage. The Marquess of Rothgar, for example, had been cultivating the young man for years, playing the respectful mentor rather than the parent or tutor. The Dark Marquess had a reputation for omniscience. It was as if he'd known this day would come unexpectedly soon.

But he and his like wouldn't have the field to themselves.

A shave and fashionable elegance, and on to London at all speed.

The Duke of Ithorne had rank and power above most, and must be at court to use it at this crucial moment.

CHAPTER 3

"A carriage! I wonder who it can be?"

Bella Barstowe ignored her sister's speculation. Lucinda wouldn't expect a response,
and the visitor would not be for Bella. Nothing at Carscourt was ever for the penitential
sinner except the meanest bed and board.
All the same, tedium made even tiny things
interesting, and as she continued to embroi-
der a violet in the corner of a handkerchief,
Bella listened for any indication of who the
arrival might be.

A neighbor? No, Lucinda was at the
window now and would recognize a neighbor's carriage.

A guest? There'd been no preparations,
and guests were rare here now that the only
residents were Lucinda and their brother,
Sir Augustus. Lucinda was both silly and
sour, and Augustus was a sanctimonious
prig who in any case was often away on

43

business of various kinds.

As for Bella, she was the black sheep of the family, and if it had been possible to wall her up in a cell in this day and age, that would be her fate. As it was, she was confined at Carscourt by lack of even a penny of her own. She'd thought of stealing to fund her escape, thought of it many times, but she was sure first her father and now Augustus would enjoy seeing her in court and transported, even hanged.

Bella bit her lip against tears. She hadn't wanted her father's love, but she had hoped for justice, or even mercy, up to the day he died.

As for her brother, she didn't care a featherweight whether Augustus loved her or even liked her. She disliked him, and had done so all her life. But his coldness came closer to hatred, and she had no idea why. She could only think it was because he thought her shame cast a shadow on his spotless reputation.

He, like everyone else, believed she'd run away with a man four years ago and then been forced to flee back home, ruined, when she was abandoned. She'd then made her situation worse by refusing the husband hastily found for her.

Reason for anger. Reason for disgust,

especially in a person who put such store in virtue and propriety.

But hatred?

Four years ago she'd thought her incarceration a temporary penance, that even if her family didn't think her worthy of a normal life, they'd tire of being her jailers. But instead, the terms of her imprisonment had grown harsher.

Her father had not only deprived her of money — he'd forbidden her to order anything without permission. She'd been expected to beg for new gowns and stays, and even for shoes or gloves. Before her abduction she'd adored pretty garments in the latest style, and so they'd expected her to grovel, but some spirit lacking in her before her abduction had broken free to require that she never, ever beg.

She'd learned to patch and mend her clothing, and to pretend to be happy with the result. As for shoes and gloves, as she rarely went anywhere, they hardly mattered.

After a while, that same dogged spirit insisted that if she had to repair her clothing, she would learn to do it well. From mending, she'd progressed to refurbishing, and then to improving garments with needle lace and embroidery. Rather than beg for supplies, she'd scavenged. The attics of Carscourt held a century's worth of castoffs, both faded furnishings and discarded fashion. She'd unraveled material and unpicked threads, often also finding beads, braid, and lace.

Her family had found her desperate devices satisfying, so Bella had hidden her growing enjoyment of her treasure hunting and ingenuity. Pretty, frivolous Bella Barstowe, the greatest flirt in Oxfordshire, would never enjoy such lowly and tedious tasks.

Somehow, Augustus had realized. When he'd become head of the family, he'd had the house cleared of most of what he called "rubbish," and locked up the rest. Over the past year, Bella had become miserable enough to satisfy even his warped soul.

"I hear voices," Lucinda declared, rushing to the mirror to check her cap. "Augustus is bringing someone here!"

Did she imagine the guest might be a suitor? At twenty-six, Lucinda was past her last hopes, but here she was, eyes bright, color high.

Bella devoutly wished Lucinda would marry. That would have to create a change in her own situation, for she couldn't be left here alone. It would be a dangerous roll of the dice, but at this point the gates of hell would be tempting, if only because they would take her away from Carscourt.

The door opened and Augustus ushered in a rotund, cloaked gentleman. He quickly closed the door behind him. It was April, but still cool apart from the few rooms that had a fire.

Bella's bedchamber was not, of course, one of those. Under Augustus's rule, she hadn't had a fire even in the depths of winter. She'd been tempted to start burning furniture.

Henry, the first footman, had come in behind. He helped the visitor to unwind a long, thick scarf and shed his cloak, revealing a genial gray-haired gentleman with a drip at the end of his nose. As Henry carried the items away, the guest dug out a handkerchief and blew.

Lucinda had risen excitedly, but Bella was still seated.

"Stand up, Isabella!" Augustus commanded.

Someone of his saintly reputation should be thin, but though not fat, Augustus was always slightly puffy, and he had a small mouth that pulled in so tightly when he disapproved that it looked like the mouth of a tight-drawn purse.

As Bella stood, he added, "I apologize,

47

Mr. Clatterford, but as you can see, she is not quite as we might wish."

Bella struggled to keep an impassive face as she desperately assessed a new and unexpected danger. Was this Clatterford a doctor, come to poke and bleed her? That had happened four years ago, when she'd refused to cover her shame by marrying Squire Thoroughgood, but Dr. Symons was a local man, and had been willing to go only so far in "restoring her health" and had refused to declare her insane. That threat too had been held over her back then, as they'd all tried to force her into that horrible marriage.

In her fury of outraged innocence, and still believing in her charmed life, she'd refused and refused and refused. As the years had passed she'd often thought that even marriage to a coarse man of unsavory reputation might be preferable to this interminable nonexistence. After all, a husband might die.

The visitor was looking at her kindly, but could she trust that?

Was Clatterford the keeper of an institution for the insane?

"I think Miss Isabella Barstowe was simply absorbed in her needlework," he said, coming over to look at the handkerchief she still held. "Very pretty. Your great-grandmother showed me some pieces you sent her as gifts."

"You knew Lady Raddall?" The ancient lady had proved to be Bella's only friend in the world. With Bella confined at Carscourt and Lady Raddall fixed in Tunbridge Wells, too old to travel, they'd not met since the scandal, but from the first Lady Raddall had sent frequent, supportive letters. When she'd learned that Bella's father opened and censored all Bella's correspondence, she'd sent such a blistering objection even he had quailed.

Breaking the seal on one of Lady Raddall's letters had been one of Bella's few delights, now sadly gone.

"I was so sorry to hear of her death," she said.

"Bella," her brother protested. "She was a hundred years old!"

"No reason not to grieve her death," Bella retorted. To Mr. Clatterford, she said, "I hope she didn't suffer."

"Only from some fear that she would not reach her century, Miss Isabella. Once she had that, she simply drifted away, smiling." His eyes twinkled. "She ordered a clear statement of her achievement engraved on her headstone. In case, she said, some passersby could not do subtraction."

Bella chuckled before she could help it, and it felt like cracking a sealed box. "That sounds just like her. Her mind was still young."

Lucinda cleared her throat, and Bella was dragged back to reality. Still at Carscourt. Still a penitential prisoner. There would be a price to pay for a moment of pleasure.

Augustus frostily made the formal introductions, adding, "Mr. Clatterford has made the long journey from Tunbridge Wells on some business arising from our great-grandmother's death. The will?" he asked, gesturing the guest to a chair and sitting himself.

Ah, Bella thought, sitting down again. That would interest her brother. For some reason, there was never enough money here.

"I have wondered why we heard nothing sooner," Augustus was saying, "though of course all will have gone to her grandson, the current Lord Raddall."

Clatterford settled in a chair near the fire, rubbing his hands close to the heat. "Lord Raddall no longer has the obligation to pay the dowager's jointure, sir, which is a substantial benefit. It was made generous by Lady Raddall's husband, for it was a great love match, you know, but even he could not have expected that it would have to be paid for so long. Forty years a widow. Remarkable."

"And a considerable burden on the estate," said Augustus with feeling.

He openly resented the quarterly amounts he was obliged to pay to their mother, who would persist in staying alive and had also removed herself to the coast instead of staying at Carscourt, where a good part of her jointure could be held back to cover her keep. Bella didn't blame her mother for escaping Carscourt as soon as she could, though she wished she'd attempted some rescue of herself. Lady Barstowe, of course, had also believed that Bella was an unrepentant sinner and liar and, truth to tell, had never been a fond mother to any of her children.

Clatterford turned to fully face Augustus. "The will contained a number of other bequests to faithful servants and friends, sir, and also to a charitable institution in Tunbridge Wells for aged gentlewomen. The remainder, however, is left to her great-granddaughter" — he turned not to Lucinda, but to Bella — "Isabella Clara Barstowe."

"What!" The explosion came simultaneously from Augustus and Lucinda, drowning Bella's gasp.

"Impossible," Augustus snapped. "I will not allow it."

"My dear sir, you have no power to forbid it, or to control the money in any way. Miss Isabella is of age."

Bella's birthday had been two weeks ago, but without money or any place of refuge in the world, she hadn't imagined it could make a difference.

Mr. Clatterford's demeanor was calm, but Bella caught the hint of a twinkle. He was enjoying himself, and so, all of a sudden, was she. Augustus looked as if he might choke to death. She was careful to try to stay blank, however. She could hardly believe in freedom, and if this failed, the consequences would be terrible.

"Augustus!" Lucinda shrieked, shooting to her feet, her neglected needlework spilling to the carpet. "This can't be possible. I won't have it. That . . . that . . . strumpet shall not have a large dowry when I am stuck without enough money to get a husband!"

"Your portion's enough to get one if you had looks and temperament," Augustus snapped, then turned on the solicitor. "I will contest this."

"You have no grounds, sir." Clatterford,

unlike Augustus, had risen out of courtesy when Lucinda surged to her feet. "Moreover, Lady Raddall left precise instructions for this moment, which I, as executor, am obliged to carry out. Unless Miss Isabella herself objects, she is to leave Carscourt with me within the hour."

The awful silence was broken by the door opening and Henry returning with a tea tray. Augustus snapped, "Get out!"

Henry, wide-eyed, went.

The short break had given Bella time to think, but her brain still felt scrambled and unable to make sense of it all. She was afraid to believe.

Augustus rose now and came to loom over her. "Leave here with this man and you will never return."

As a threat, it had the opposite effect. Bella leapt to her feet, thinking, *Oh, please let it be so!*

Lucinda spoke acidly. "I would have thought, Isabella, that you would have learned the folly of running off with strange men. What do you know of this . . . this Clatterford?"

That was a knife aimed at the heart, but for Bella it might as well have been made of wax. Her great-grandmother had mentioned Mr. Clatterford on a number of occasions.

What an excellent solicitor he was. How well he managed her affairs. How trustworthy and kind. His charming family, which included five grandchildren. Had she been preparing Bella for this moment, but indirectly?

Why not tell her outright?

Of course, Lady Raddall hadn't known when she would die, and she might not have been certain that her letters were given to Bella unopened. She might have feared that Augustus would find a way to foil her plan.

Bella's mind was still throwing up cautions, however. Never to return meant that Augustus would cast her out, would disown her. If this plan failed, she would have no refuge anywhere. . . .

"You see," Augustus sneered, "she's wit-addled. I really cannot permit her to leave my roof."

Bella snapped to awareness, and to the only possible decision.

"It's not wit-addled to consider a serious decision, brother, but I've done so and I'm leaving. I will collect what I want to take."

She picked up her needlework and headed for the door, stomach in turmoil, braced for Augustus to physically prevent her. He moved as if to do just that, reaching out his hand that looked more like a claw. He'd

been set upon in London a few years back
and injured. It was unfortunate, but for
some reason he'd added that to her catalog
of sins.

She found the courage to meet his eyes,
to offer a direct challenge. Even if this
proved disastrous, this moment was worth
it. He glared at her, his puffy face so red he
looked as if he might literally explode.

Bella stepped around his claw and hurried
out, but as soon as she'd closed the door
she leaned against a wall, shivering, and not
from the cold. She could hear Augustus and
Lucinda berating Clatterford. Their fury
proved this was real. The doors of her prison
had opened, and even if they led to hell, she
was going through them.

She raced along the corridor toward her
bedchamber, but then halted and ran down
the servants' stairs to the kitchen. She interrupted an excited discussion, and the subject was clear.

They all stared at her, wide-eyed and
wary. She was sure they were worried that
she'd demand something of them that
would get them into trouble. They'd always
been in an awkward position, with her being one of the family but deprived of nearly
all comforts. Most had been here before her

disgrace, and old patterns of behavior died hard.

"I'm leaving," she said to them. "Immediately. I need some valises or a small trunk. I used to have some. . . ."

After a long moment, the housekeeper said, "I hope you're going somewhere better, Miss Bella."

She saw that they were worried about her, and had to blink away tears. "Oh, yes! I've been left some money. . . ." She realized she had no idea how much, but it didn't matter. "I must leave immediately."

They all looked at her anxiously. Then Henry said, "I know where your trunk is, miss. I'll bring it to your room."

Lucinda's lady's maid bit her lip, but in the end didn't offer help. It was Jane, the housemaid, who tossed her head and said, "I'll come and help you, miss."

In her room, Bella took everything out of the clothespress and chest of drawers. A pitiful collection, but too much for the small trunk and hardly worth the bother. Despite the labor that had gone into these garments, she dearly hoped she'd soon own better.

How much money had she inherited? As Lady Raddall had expected her to leave Carscourt, it had to be enough to scrimp by on, but her jointure had died with her. How much more could there be? Would the inheritance cover indulgences? New stays, silk stockings, ribbons, perfumed soap . . . ?

Bella dreamed of shops as she and Jane packed all her underclothes, and two of her four made-over gowns.

The last things to go into the trunk were the thick bundles of letters from her great-grandmother, including their enclosures.

Once Lady Raddall had heard that Bella was receiving her letters unopened, she'd begun to sometimes enclose another — a letter from someone called Lady Fowler, who claimed to be trying to reform aristocratic society by revealing its sins.

The woman's mad, Lady Raddall had written. *I can't imagine what good she thinks she'll do by spreading tales of misbehavior in high places, but her letters are vastly amusing, especially to those of us unable to visit Town. Though sadly today's rascals rarely hold a candle to the ones of my youth, a few show promise. The Marquess of Ashart is toothsome, and comes to the Wells now and then to visit his great-aunts. The Earl of Huntersdown's a charming rascal. Men like those are another reason to read these letters, my dear. One day you'll be free of your cage, but it's a wicked world, and some of the wickedness comes in a pretty package. I'd not have you fall into its traps again.*

Bella had not in fact run away with handsome Simon Naiscourt, but she'd agreed to a tryst with him, and that had been her doom.

At first, Bella had been shocked rather than amused by Lady Fowler's letters. She'd thought herself so worldly-wise, but of course that had been folly at seventeen. She'd certainly been ignorant of some of the sins Lady Fowler detailed, and did think it wrong that they were common among peers and Parliament. There were even cases among the high clergy.

Lady Fowler also raged against the injustice of the law that gave women so few rights and gave men domination over them. Bella felt one in spirit with the lady on that. She realized she might now be able to donate some small amount to Lady Fowler's Fund for the Moral Reform of London Society.

She kissed the last bundle of Lady Raddall's letters, sending thanks to the dear lady, and put them with her other packed belongings.

"There," she said, rising to close and lock the trunk.

A glance at the clock showed that over half an hour had passed, and Bella was suddenly terrified that her brother and sister might have managed to talk Mr. Clatterford out of his plan. She put her hat on top of her plain cap and jabbed in a long pin, grabbed her thin cloak and darned gloves, and rushed back to the little drawing room.

She found Mr. Clatterford alone, enjoying tea and scones. He beamed at her. "Ready? Excellent." He rose, patting butter from his lips with a napkin. "Sir Augustus and your sister had business elsewhere, but I think we can dispense with the farewells, eh?"

"Happily," Bella said, still catching her breath. She had to ask. "It is true?"

"Your money? Yes, my dear."

Heart thumping, Bella asked, "How much?"

"The estate is still being settled, but the total is in the range of fifteen thousand pounds. Your family were so overcome by that, they had to stagger away to recover."

Bella wanted to laugh, but she didn't think she dared even smile until she was outside. Until she was off the Carscourt estate, in fact.

When the door opened, she spun in alarm, and then closed her eyes in relief. "Here's Henry with your clothes, Mr. Clatterford. Do let us go!"

Mr. Clatterford reswathed himself. When

they left, Henry winked at Bella. She did smile a little then, and whispered, "Thank you. If you or Jane suffers for this, you must contact Mr. Clatterford in Tunbridge Wells. We will help."

They hurried downstairs and out. Henry and the groom got Bella's trunk into the boot, and Bella climbed inside.

She was wound tight now, dreadfully afraid that Augustus would think of some way to stop this. She didn't know why he was so ferociously set on continuing the oppression begun by their father, but he was. Lucinda would simply be having a fit.

Mr. Clatterford climbed into the carriage. Bella watched the door for Augustus. The solicitor took the opposite seat, the one with the back to the horses.

"Oh, no, sir," Bella said, rising to exchange. "Let me . . ."

"Age before beauty?" he said. "If you don't object, may I sit beside you, Miss Isabella? I confess, I do not care to ride with my back to the horses, but I see no reason either of us should."

They both settled, and the carriage moved off.

Bella watched the front door as long as she could. It remained firmly shut, and irrationally that started to worry her. She'd rather see Augustus shaking his fist at her than not know where he was, what he was doing.

Finally she could see the door no more. She looked forward, trying to believe. "I don't know how to thank you, Mr. Clatterford."

He patted her hand. "No need, no need. I apologize for not being here on your birthday, as Lady Raddall wished, but we had extensive rains that made the roads very difficult, and I didn't think it wise."

"It's a long journey, sir."

"Not too long when the roads are dry, but the weather is unseasonable. I detect that Carscourt has not replenished the hot bricks in here. We'll see to that once we've traveled a few miles."

Bella was used to being chilly, but warm bricks would be delightful. A warm cloak would be even more so. She'd had one once. Perhaps she would again?

Pretty clothes and pretty shoes, assemblies and balls. Even attentive swains . . . It was as if four years were sliding away.

Carscourt didn't have gates, but the extent of the estate was marked by pillars. Bella watched them pass. The first mark of freedom, but they were still in an area full of Augustus's tenants.

Soon they were rolling down the street of the village of Cars Green. Only yesterday, a trip here would have felt like liberty, but now Bella felt still within prison. To be dragged back now would break her, she knew. She glanced at Mr. Clatterford, wondering if he could be part of some elaborate trick. . . .

A shout made her stiffen in terror.

The carriage stopped. She should have known escape was impossible.

CHAPTER 4

The groom opened the door. "There's a woman here wants to speak to you, miss."

Bella looked out, heart still hammering, trying to place the fat village woman. She wore a scarf around her head and was clutching a bundle.

"It's Mistress Gussage, Miss Bella," she said. "Peg Oaks as was! I was a schoolroom maid when you was young, and then I married Gussage, the assistant gamekeeper."

Bella remembered her, but was still bewildered. Was the bundle a gift?

"Yes, of course. What can I do for you, Mistress Gussage?"

The seamed face contorted in something between a smile and a grimace, and then the woman blurted, "Can I come with you, Miss Bella? It's not right you going off with a man on your own. Not after . . ." She definitely grimaced then. "Not that I ever thought . . . And I've no one now Bill's gone, see. Never had any chicks, marrying late as I did. And I'd like to see a bit of the world."

Bella was nonplussed, and looked to Mr. Clatterford for guidance.

"If the woman's suitable, it's an excellent idea," he said. "We certainly wouldn't want to give even crumbs for scandal."

Bella could imagine it: Augustus in some way turning her departure into wickedness and using it against her. She remembered Peg Oaks as a kind, cheerful, and energetic worker.

"Come in, then, Mistress Gussage. We'll sort out your baggage later. And thank you."

The woman beamed, climbed the steps, and squeezed through the doorway to collapse on the opposite seat. "As for baggage, I'm stout, but not this stout, miss." She was still catching her breath. "I'm carrying most of my clothes on my body."

Mr. Clatterford commanded the coach to go on, and it did, picking up speed, thank heavens.

"Are you quite sure, Mistress Gussage?" Bella asked.

"Call me Peg, miss, and yes, I'm sure. I'm no fine lady and I've never been five miles from Cars Green, but I may have some simple skills that'll help you."

"But how did you know I was leaving?"

"It's all around the village by now, miss. Babs, the scullery maid, ran down with the news. As soon as I heard, I thought as it wasn't right, you going off alone with a strange man." She gave Clatterford a look.

He smiled at her. "Very right, ma'am, and you are very welcome. But we are going far from here. The journey to Tunbridge Wells will take two days."

Peg Gussage looked like someone who'd marched thoughtlessly into a lion's den, but she said, "Quite sure, sir. I have little to fill my days now, and I meant it when I said I'd like to see a bit of the world before I die."

"Very well. And if you do decide to return home at some point, of course I or Miss Barstowe will arrange that for you. For now, if you are to be Miss Barstowe's maid companion, we must consider your wages and perquisites."

His suggestions left Peg slack-jawed, but she nodded vigorously.

Bella realized she was smiling, a true smile at last. She was deeply thankful Peg was with them, but she especially relished being able to make someone so happy with a quite modest amount of money.

She didn't have much experience of money. At seventeen she'd had her pin money, but all her bills for gowns and such had gone directly to her father. Since then, she'd had no money at all. However, she was sure that anyone could live comfortably on the interest of fifteen thousand pounds.

They did stop at an inn for hot bricks, and then again to change horses, but they spoke little. Bella had questions, but she'd been raised not to speak of money and such matters in front of the servants. For now she was content simply to travel farther and farther from Carscourt.

Eventually, however, thoughts of her future became insistent.

Did she want to go to Tunbridge Wells?

Once, the answer would have been yes, for her great-grandmother would have been there, but now, she wasn't sure. It was a fashionable watering place, and that frightened her. Bella Barstowe might have been freed from prison, but she was still trapped by her reputation. She could be shunned.

When she'd persisted in her refusal to marry Squire Thoroughgood, her father had ceased to keep her scandal secret. No one had believed her protestations of innocence, and she couldn't truly blame them, for her story was very thin.

She'd had to admit that she'd made a tryst with a man, a man merely passing through the area whom she'd met once at an assembly. It had been foolish, but she'd been foolish at seventeen and so confident of her safety.

She hadn't gone off in a carriage with him willingly, however. She'd been carried off by force to a low sort of tavern, where she'd been kept locked in a room for two days. "Simon Naiscourt" — she suspected the name was false — and his older accomplice, who had seemed to be in charge, had told her she was being held for ransom. They'd promised that no harm would come to her, but that if she tried to scream or shout, they'd bind and gag her.

She'd been afraid, but certain her father would pay the ransom and she'd soon be free. Her father would be furious and probably confine her to the house for weeks for the tryst, but he was frequently furious at her for what he called her flighty, foolish ways. Sitting in the dismal, dirty room she had thought he might be right.

The reason no one had believed her account was that her father had never seen a ransom demand. Instead he'd received a letter from Simon explaining that he and Bella were in love and were running away to Scotland to marry.

She'd never been able to make sense of

that. Her captors had been so impatient, so frustrated at the lack of response. But her father had shown her Simon's letter.

She'd not known about the letter until her return, however, so when her captors had tired of waiting and forced her south with them, she'd been able to think only that her father had decided to punish her by letting her reap the consequences of her folly for a while. It had been hard to believe — he was strict and stern, but she'd never have thought him capable of such callousness — but the only alternative was that he'd abandoned her entirely, and that was inconceivable. She'd continued to expect rescue at every moment.

In the end, she'd had to rescue herself.

With the help of Captain Rose.

There was a person she hadn't allowed herself to think about for years. For some ridiculous reason, in the early months of her imprisonment she'd imagined him rushing to her rescue. Idiocy. If he had rushed to Carscourt it would have been to demand her arrest for horse stealing.

She'd soon ceased dreaming all foolish dreams, and now was not a time to return to them. She needed a home, but there'd be no more balls and assemblies for disgraced Bella Barstowe.

■ ■ ■ ■

When they stopped for the night, she and
Peg Gussage shared one room, Peg all aflus-
ter. "My, my, I've never stayed at an inn
before, Miss Bella. What a fine bed! And
here's another beneath it for me. My, my,"
she repeated as she rolled it out.

Bella had been used to sharing her bed
with her personal maid when she had one,
but was glad of the truckle. She was grateful to have Peg Gussage as companion, but
wasn't quite ready to share a bed with her.

She deliberately asked for supper to be
served in their room, because she also
wasn't ready to discuss her future with Mr.
Clatterford. As they ate soup, she asked,
"Do you mind where we live, Peg?"

"Me, ma'am? No. Anywhere's new to me.
This is delicious soup. So rich."

Bella smiled. There was something to be
said for a companion so pleased with everything. A lot to be said.

"Mr. Clatterford expects me to go to Tunbridge Wells, where my great-grandmother
lived. It's also where he has his business.
But I want somewhere quieter."

Peg spread butter thickly onto fresh bread.
"Why, miss?"

"I didn't run off with that man, Peg, but no one in the neighborhood believes me, and it's not surprising. Silly Bella Barstowe ran off with a charming rascal and was discarded once her virtue was gone. She then multiplied her shame by refusing a decent marriage."

"Squire Thoroughgood," Peg muttered in disgust. "Thoroughly bad, in the opinion of most!"

"So I gather, but most people seem to think that any marriage is better than none for a ruined woman, and once I made it clear my refusal was absolute, my father allowed the story to spread around the area. From there, it could have gone anywhere by letter."

"But four years ago, miss. It'll all be forgotten."

"I wish I could believe that." Bella remembered her cooling soup and drank some. "It could be particularly remembered in Tunbridge Wells, however, because of my connection to Lady Raddall. She may even have spoken of it to friends. In outrage, I'm sure, but will people remember that, or just remember the shame?"

Peg pulled a face. "Happen you're right, miss, but then what about your older sister? The one as married."

"Athena?" Bella considered it, but only for a moment.

Athena lived near Maidstone, and it was to her she'd fled from Dover. Athena might want to take her in, for she had a sense of duty, but her husband saw Bella Barstowe as a destructive influence on his young daughters. Even if Athena persuaded him they should offer her shelter, she would be seen as a sinner and expected to be grateful and penitent all her days.

She couldn't speak of such matters to a servant, so she simply said, "No, it wouldn't do." She finished her soup, trying to find some possibility.

It seemed a bold notion, but she wanted independence. Years of imprisonment made the slightest hint of confinement unbearable, but was freedom possible for a young lady of twenty-one?

Could she seem older, and even a different person, free of scandal?

"Perhaps I'll take a new name," she said, testing the idea on Peg. "And live in a quiet place, far from fashionable circles. A village, perhaps, where I can be mistress of my life at last, but far from curious eyes."

Peg snorted. "If you want to avoid curious eyes, miss, don't go to a village. There's nothing the gossips like more than someone new to pick over. And the better sort as can read and write, they're soon writing to their cronies everywhere asking why a pretty young woman might be hiding herself away in a village, no matter what name you use."

"Oh, you're correct, of course. But then what am I to do?"

"Go to a town, miss. People don't notice so much in a town."

A startling thought struck. "Why not the Town? London. Anyone could go unnoticed there."

"London! Lawks, Miss Bella, I'd bust me stays to go to London. I might even see the king. Such a lovely young man, they say. And his dear, sweet little babies."

Bella fought laughter. "I'm not planning a fashionable life, Peg."

"That's a shame, then, but it won't bother me. Where would we live, though?"

Bella was at a loss, but then an odd notion popped into her head. Could she help Lady Fowler not just with a donation, but with actual work? She knew that some women did help like that by writing out copies of the letter and by other tasks.

"There's a Lady Fowler . . ." she said hesitantly.

"A lady, miss? That sounds suitable."

"Perhaps not. Lady Fowler is a social

reformer, Peg."

"What's one of those?"

"She wants to put right things that are wrong."

Peg poured herself more tea and added four lumps of sugar. "That seems good, miss. More tea?"

Bella agreed. "I think Lady Fowler is frowned upon in the highest circles. She writes a letter every two months and sends it to many people around the country. In it, she details wrongdoing among the aristocracy. She encourages her recipients to spread the word so as to bring about change."

Peg's eyes were huge. "How many letters?" she asked.

That was a question Bella had never asked. "I'm not sure. I think over a hundred."

"All that writing. What a wonder she must be!"

Bella was fighting not to laugh. "She only writes the original. She has helpers to copy it. I would become one of them."

"Oh," said Peg. "If that's what you want to do, miss. But I'm no use at that. I can write a bit, but it's hard work."

"I wouldn't expect you to do that, Peg, especially when it could be dangerous. Lady

Fowler is merely sending letters, but some of the content must offend powerful people."

Peg chewed. "Then why do you want to do it, miss?"

"Because Lady Fowler also urges changes in the law to protect women from male tyranny."

"Ah, I see, miss." Peg took another slice of bread and butter, then added a slice of cheese.

Bella thought Peg would soon be round as a tub without extra layers of clothes, but she was enjoying her servant's appreciation of these treats. For her own part, she was considering the complications Peg brought.

Some of Lady Fowler's helpers lived in her house, and she might have asked to do that, but she could hardly take a servant there. What was more, those resident ladies were the neediest, the ones left by fathers or husbands without enough money to survive. She couldn't take a place.

She'd have to set up her own home somewhere nearby, with Peg as her housekeeper. That was a daunting task, but having a plan made her feel much steadier. Again, she tested it on Peg, who said, "If you can have your own home, miss, why bother with this Lady Fowler?"

"To support the work."

Peg merely shrugged, but Bella accepted that her question had been a good one. The honest answer was that she was afraid to be in the world without acquaintances of any kind. Once she'd known and been known by half the county, and even had friends. Fair-weather friends, however, for none had attempted to support her in adversity.

Peg was chewing thoughtfully. "If it's what you want, Miss Bella, but it's not as it should be for a pretty young lady. You should be dancing and flirting and preparing to marry. Naughty of you to run off with a man, but —"

"Peg, I didn't!" Bella should have realized that even the villagers would believe that story. "Oh, Peg . . . I was abducted. Snatched when out in the grounds."

She told her story, but without hope. Why should Peg believe her when no one else had? As always, she skipped over Captain Rose. Another mysterious gentleman would only make matters worse.

At the end, Peg said, "Well, and it's a sad business, miss, but it's over now, so you put it out of your mind."

"I wish I could, but you must see it means I can't resume my place in society. So I will devote my time and some of my money to noble work. But if you don't want to be connected to such things, I'll arrange for you to return home."

Peg considered for only a moment. "I'm not giving up my adventure so soon, Miss Bella, and from the sounds of it, you'll need someone to look after you."

Bella reached over to cover a work-worn hand. "Thank you, Peg. You don't know what that means to me."

"Reckon I do, miss. It's not good to be alone in the world, especially for a woman. But it's for my own benefit too. So we'll live in London, will we? Where?"

Peg was cheerfully confident that Bella knew what she was doing, but Bella had hardly made a decision in her life more serious than the trimming for a bonnet. She was sure independence was what her great-grandmother had in mind, however, so she had best grasp this rare opportunity or she'd never be able to face Lady Raddall in heaven.

She tried to sound more knowledgeable than she was. "I'll rent rooms in Soho — that's where Lady Fowler's house is. You will take care of things there while I assist Lady Fowler in her work."

"Very well, miss."

The wages of a cook-housekeeper should

probably be more than the amounts fixed by Mr. Clatterford for a lady's maid, but Bella didn't know what would be right, especially in London. She didn't know how they would manage things such as the purchase of food, fuel, and anything else they needed.

In fact, she knew nothing!

Very well, she did need some help. Tomorrow she'd discuss all this with Mr. Clatterford. She settled in bed, hoping for a sound sleep, but the mattress was lumpy, and after such a day, her mind roiled. She replayed the glorious moment when she'd received the news, but she also tumbled wildly amidst fears and doubts.

London! She'd been there, but only for escorted visits to fashionable spots and entertainments, and that in the last reign. She remembered how the bell tolling the king's death had helped them escape from the Black Rat. . . .

She pushed that out of her mind.

Augustus made much of the new propriety at court, the boring prig. How he'd enjoyed lecturing her, both before and after the scandal. Enough of Augustus. Another subject to lock out of her mind.

Except that she still worried about what he'd do. Could he still claim she was mad, and lock her away? Clatterford had said no, but she couldn't entirely dismiss the fear. All the more reason to take a new name and alter her appearance.

To be a new person, with no scandal attached, and no fear of her family.

She needed a new name. What would serve? Harriet, Sophronia, Jane, Margaret . . . They all felt too strange. Something close to Bella, then. Isabella was her real name, and Arabella was too close to that. Clarabella was too frivolous.

Bell . . . Bell . . . Bellona! The goddess of war.

She liked that.

Her new surname should be something equally warlike.

Bellona Sword? Hardly.

Bellona Cannon? No.

Bellona Gunn . . .

Bellona Flint . . .

Oh, yes, Bellona Flint. Hard, sharp, and a necessary part of murderous weapons.

Tomorrow she'd find out from Mr. Clatterford what she should do to become Bellona Flint, and what else she need do to protect herself.

The solicitor was most unhappy with her plans. He tried to persuade her that she would be completely safe in Tunbridge Wells, and would soon be accepted in the best society. When Bella expressed her doubts, however, he deflated. "But you are so young, my dear. I cannot condone your setting up your own establishment."

Bella almost shivered at standing up to authority, but she did it. "As I understand it, Mr. Clatterford, you have no more power to condone my choices than my brother has."

"Oh, dear, oh, dear . . ."

At Clatterford's insistence, they were taking breakfast together, leaving Peg to eat alone.

"But London," he protested, his meal hardly touched. "I will not be on hand to advise you."

"I regret that, sir, but surely you could arrange some other trustworthy solicitor."

"But you are still too young to live alone. Only just twenty-one."

Bella didn't want to tell him about Lady Fowler, for he'd have to object. "I have Peg, and I know London a little. I intend to live quietly, and to claim to be older than my years. With sober dress and manner, I won't attract attention. I intend to make myself unattractive as well. I took part in a play once in the role of a witch. I still remember how to make my skin sallow and stick on a wart."

There were some more "oh, dears" and protests, but Bella stood her ground, and in the end he said, "I see you are determined, and I can't deny that your story is known in Lady Raddall's circle. As you surmised, she did speak of it, being much agitated over your situation." He buttered some bread, remarking, "I see the dear lady was correct. She said you were as strong-minded as she."

"Did she?" Bella asked, surprised. "I was the epitome of frivolity when we met for the last time."

"You met through your correspondence, my dear." He ate a piece of ham, still looking unhappy, and then fixed her with a stern look. "If you are determined on your rash plan, I must warn you about men." When Bella looked a question, he said, "Fortune hunters, my dear. There will be men — sometimes handsome, pleasing men — who will seek to marry you for your money."

Bella laughed dryly. "I assure you, sir, I have learned my lesson about pleasing scoundrels."

"You may not recognize the scoundrel in them."

"I'll be very wary, I promise. But are you saying I can never marry?" Bella was surprised to find some romantic yearnings still lurked deep inside.

"No, no, only that you must be careful. Do not marry in haste, and especially without trusts and settlements. Be wary of love, for it traps many a lady — and some gentlemen too — into folly. A clever rascal might claim that sensible precautions deny your love, and thus urge a hasty marriage, even an elopement. Pay attention, young lady." He pointed his fork at her. "That is the absolute mark of a bad man. As is any attempt to seduce you into the sort of behavior that would trap you by its natural consequences."

Bella blushed, but she nodded. "Yes, I see that, and I thank you. I will certainly follow your advice. But I am still set on my plan of establishing myself quietly in Town. Will you take me to London and set me up there in comfort and safety?"

He sighed. "You are very like Lady Raddall. Yes, Miss Flint, reluctantly, I will."

CHAPTER 5

Rothgar Abbey, August 1764

"How we suffer for our friends," said the Duke of Ithorne, gathered late at night with his cousin Robin, Earl of Huntersdown, and his foster brother, Christian, Major Lord Grandiston.

"I give you elegant surroundings," said Robin, gesturing at his bedchamber. "Fine brandy" — he raised his glass — "and the very best company."

"In the lair of the Dark Marquess," Thorne replied.

"Rothgar hasn't poisoned you yet. And your stiff-necked hostility must tempt him at times."

"I'm sure the devil knows slow-acting poisons."

Robin gave him a warning look, and Thorn raised an apologetic hand. It was the eve of his cousin Robin's wedding to the lady he adored, and no time for rancor.

Thorn would much rather the lady were not the Dark Marquess's daughter, but if Robin wasn't deterred by Petra's being a bastard Italian Catholic, a cousin's discomfort with her sire was hardly likely to weigh with him.

He was a disgusting example of love's insanity.

"I hereby ban all talk of politics," Christian declared from where he lounged like a panther, all blond, muscular elegance. He'd been as lithe as Robin when he'd sailed off with the army at sixteen, and even now Thorn was sometimes surprised by his physique. It had been a true shock to see him on his first return, five years older, strongly muscled and accustomed to command and killing.

Robin and Thorn were cousins and had known each other from the cradle. Christian and Thorn had been inseparable for six wonderful years.

Thorn had always been an orphan in effect. He was an only child born after his father's death, and two years later his mother had wed a Frenchman and moved to that country. By his father's will, she hadn't been allowed to take him out of the country, so his upbringing had rested with guardians and trustees.

He'd been ten when they'd decided he

should have a companion of his own station. At first, Thorn had been wary of the cheerfully energetic invader who cared not a scrap for higher learning, political geography, or the philosophy of princes. Instead even as a boy Christian had been a genius at anything physical, especially mischief.

Thorn had soon been swept along, farther than his guardians had ever intended. Riding had gone from exercise to daredevil contests. Christian had drawn him into inventive games that involved climbing trees and crossing streams on rickety makeshift bridges, not to mention bows and arrows and a cleverly devised ballista. His taste for warfare should have been obvious from the first.

Christian had no particular interest in sailing, but his sudden desire to play pirates on the Ithorne lake had led to the purchase of Thorn's first small boat, and thus eventually to the *Black Swan* and all it had brought. Grand years, and when Robin came on one of his frequent visits, they'd been a triumvirate of trouble.

Then Christian had developed that feverish desire to join the army and fight Britain's enemies. Robin had been the one to protest most fiercely, but Thorn had been the one most hurt. He hadn't tried to stop the plan, but he might have if he'd realized that war would take Christian to Canada, and they'd be together again only twice in ten years. It probably hadn't truly mattered. Soon Thorn had been obliged to devote most of his time to ducal matters.

"You really are feeling grim, aren't you?" Robin said.

"He's too mired in duties," Christian said.

"Believe it or not, I find my responsibilities satisfying, and just as worthwhile as battles."

Damn the sharp tone of that.

"Then why the *Black Swan*?" Christian asked.

"He's simply odd," Robin said, refilling glasses, and trying to lighten the tone. "Hence the name."

"A black swan's more than odd — it's impossible," Thorn said, following his lead. "Like a masquerading duke. Did I ever tell you about the time I rescued a damsel in distress and she stole my horse?" He knew he hadn't, so it served to pass over the awkward moment.

The other two laughed, but Christian said, "Lucky escape. Look what happened to Robin when he gave in to knight-errantry."

"All that is good," said Robin, with that sickening lover's smile.

"Except the matter of a thousand guineas to the Fowl Fund," Thorn reminded him.

"Don't remind me," Robin groaned.

"Payment due on marriage."

Robin looked at them both. "You wouldn't simply forget about that vow, would you?"

"My Lord Huntersdown," Thorn said with extreme astonishment, "you cannot possibly be suggesting anything so dishonorable. I have my copy with me." He produced it from his pocket.

"You devil!"

Thorn slowly unfolded his copy of the paper that they'd all signed four years ago. It had been one of Christian's rare visits to England, and they'd celebrated by going out on the *Black Swan,* enjoying their alter egos. He'd been Captain Rose, of course. Playing off their own names, Robin had been Lieutenant Sparrow, and Christian, Pagan the Pirate.

They'd devised those personas as lads on the lake, but not used them when they'd taken to the sea. That had been in a gaff-rigged lugger under the real command of an old salt called Harry Jenkins. Thorn had instantly been snared by the sea, however, and commissioned a swift, carvel-built cutter, and learned the skills necessary to be her master. By the time she was ready to launch, she'd seemed such a miraculous escape he'd named her the *Black Swan.*

He'd sailed her for pleasure and for trade, but hadn't been able to escape often, so it had pained him to know she lay idle so much of the time. The discovery of Caleb, almost his twin and with some seafaring skills, had been the final key. Thorn's foster brother, Christian, had encountered Caleb working as mate of a coastal boat out of a port in Massachusetts, and been struck by his almost twinlike resemblance.

He'd soon discovered that Caleb Rose and his mother had arrived in America when Caleb was just a lad, and had claimed their origins as Kent. Knowing the reputation of the late Duke of Ithorne, and considering the name Rose in relation to Thorn, Christian had come to a conclusion, and written to Thorn about the situation.

Thorn had soon been able to find out the rest, for the story of Mary Fukes and her child was well-known in Stowting. His father had provided a modest income for the two of them, but when the boy had proved to have such a strong likeness to the young duke, Thorn's trustees had threatened to stop the allowance if Mary did not take the boy to America.

In simple fairness, Thorn had sent a letter, care of Christian, telling Caleb he was free to return home without risk to his allowance, and had even increased it. It was only in meeting Caleb that the idea of a shared identity had occurred to him.

Despite the differences in their rank and education, they understood each other well, and Caleb was clearly clever and ambitious. It hadn't taken long for him to learn the additional skills to be the master of the *Black Swan,* but he'd also learned the changes in manner and ways of speech that made it possible for Thorn to step into his shoes.

For nearly a year, the Duke of Ithorne had sailed alongside Captain Rose, making it clear that they were two different people, but then they'd begun the substitutions. They would meet at the Black Swan Inn in Stowting. After a while, both would leave, but they would have switched identities. Caleb did not attempt to play the duke beyond that. He would journey away from the coast, where the presence of two Captain Roses wouldn't be marked.

As far as the local people were concerned, the Duke of Ithorne had generously given mastery of the *Swan* to his bastard half brother, Caleb Rose.

Thorn had known Caleb occasionally engaged in the smuggling trade — nearly every ship on the Kentish coast did — but he'd kept clear of it until the war.

Then Thorn had seized the sanctioned opportunity for adventure. His swift nighttime journeys across the Channel had been presented as smuggling, but he'd been carrying spies and messages for the government. As soon as Christian heard about that, he'd insisted on joining in the fun despite his healing wound, and so Robin had gone along too.

Good times.

Dangerous times, but still memorably good. Danger did add spice to life.

Back on land, safe and mellow on fine French cognac, Thorn had complained of the pressure on him to marry. The other two had fully sympathized, and Robin had come up with the idea of their all taking a vow not to marry before they turned thirty, with the penalty for failure completely intolerable.

It had taken a drunken hour or two to come up with the most intolerable penalty of all — giving money to a cause they detested.

Thorn cleared his throat for effect. "Dated the third day of January, the year of the Lord 1760. 'Be it resolved that young men should never marry. Therefore, we stalwart bachelors do hereby decree a penalty to be paid by any of us who succumb to that unholy state from this day forth until he achieve the age of thirty. The penalty for failure shall be one thousand guineas donated to Lady Fowler's Fund for the Moral Reform of London Society.' "

Robin looked at him, completely serious. "I can't. Truly, I can't. The woman's insane! It's a mere trifle that she wants to ban all drinking, dancing, and card playing, but now she has her claws into Petra. I suppose it's a mild scandal for Rothgar to have sired a daughter when he was sixteen, but the way the Fowler woman slides around the subject you'd think incest is involved. Then there's his cruelty to his wife."

"What?"

"Rothgar showed me Fowler's latest screed. He's vile for forcing his wife to accept such a scandal beneath her roof. As if Diana cared for that."

"Rothgar subscribes to the Fowler letter?" Thorn asked, surprised.

"Of course he does. Or someone does on his behalf. Knowing everything is one of his skills."

Thorn wished he'd thought of doing the same thing. "If the woman's after the Dark Marquess's wife and daughter, her days are numbered. And I will applaud."

"I'd like to call her out. Pity she's a woman, and an old one at that."

"Only in her forties, I think," Christian said.

"But unwell," said Robin. "It's said her husband gave her the pox. Enough to make any woman bitter."

Thorn shook his head. "Softhearted as always."

"Not softhearted enough to give her a thousand guineas. On top of the rest, she's now spewing some dangerous political rants. Think what she could do with so much money. Of your kindness, dear souls, may I not give the money to some other cause? A foundling home. A hundred almshouses. Anything!"

"She is dangerous," Christian agreed, clearly not as drunk as he'd seemed. "Her letters used to be merely a source of amusement, but as Robin says, now she preaches violent action. She and her followers have become a matter of concern."

"Ah."

Major Lord Grandiston was now in the Horse Guards, who provided escort for the monarch and were generally involved in matters of his safety.

Remembering that turned Thorn's mind

in another direction. "Do you know the king's stand on masquerades? I've heard him denounce them, but he attended that one Rothgar held last year."

"And almost fell to an assassin," Robin said.

Christian grimaced. "Embarrassing for all concerned, I gather."

"Not for Rothgar. He had the opportunity to nobly put his body between assassin and king."

"If you're suggesting he staged it," said Robin, "don't. The assassin died."

"What's one death here or there?"

Robin rolled his eyes and poured more brandy.

"I have an interest in such matters," Thorn said to Christian, cradling his glass. "I'm the host of the Olympian Revels this year, and it would suit me for the king to attend."

Christian raised a hand. "I'm not the man for subtle courtly machinations. I can suggest only that if he does attend, he'll have guards in costumes."

"That won't be difficult. Traditionally the men dress according to their position — members of Parliament in senatorial togas and military gentlemen in armor of roughly classical design."

"Real weapons?" Christian asked.

"No. But if some are on official duty . . ."

"Satisfactory."

But Robin said, "I doubt he'll attend. The revels are somewhat notorious, and I'm not aware of him attending any thus far. The previous king, of course, delighted in them."

"Mine will be suitable for the most delicate sensibilities," Thorn said.

The other two stared at him.

He smiled. "I merely mean no costumes that expose truly unsuitable parts, and no open orgy."

His friends still stared.

"You fear I will be unforgivably dull? There will be some additions. Theater people to play guests of the livelier sort."

"Ingenious," said Robin. "What would the revels be if bored ladies and gentlemen had no one to flirt with, and perhaps do more? But your hirelings will keep it out of sight. Pity I won't be there to witness the attempt."

"I will," said Christian. "Even if the king doesn't attend, I won't miss this modern miracle."

"Why won't you attend?" Thorn asked Robin.

"Petra's with child. We'll be living quietly for a while."

From what he knew of the imminent

Countess of Huntersdown, Thorn wondered about that, but he didn't raise doubts.

Christian asked, "Why a tame revel? Hardly in your style."

"Perhaps I'm adjusting my style." Thorn didn't want even Christian and Robin probing his plans, however, so he waved the paper still in his hand. "Lady Fowler? I agree it's regrettable, but a vow is a vow, especially when it requires us to pay not just for the folly of marriage, but for the folly of framing such a vow in the first place."

Robin rose to snatch the paper from Thorn's hand to reread it. "There's nothing in here about how I pay."

"True. What do you have in mind?"

"Anonymity. It's one thing to give her the money, but another for her to know it comes from me. She'd probably blast it around the world in her plaguey letter. Perhaps even claim it as proof that her accusations were correct."

"She would, wouldn't she? Very well, I'll funnel it. I have so many lawyers and bankers concerned with my affairs, Lady Fowler will never know where the money comes from."

"Thank you, thank you, thank you, beloved cousin." Robin took a stiff drink of brandy. Then he smiled. "Good practice for when you fall. Odds on you're next."

Christian laughed, but Thorn said, "You might be right."

"What?" Christian exploded. "Thorn, Thorn, think of another thousand guineas to the Fowl Fund."

But Robin asked, "You're in love?" with all the bright excitement of the new convert.

"No. And having watched you over the past little while, it seems a contagion much to be avoided." He sipped his brandy. "There was an incident on the *Swan* a month ago. Simple mischance in a storm, but it could have been the end of me. I am the last of my line."

"But it's the only pleasure you have," Christian protested.

"Not true, but yes, being master of the *Black Swan* is an important part of me. I've given it up for now. One or, better, two boys in the nursery and I'd be free again."

"Do you know how long that could take?" Christian asked.

"I believe I'm tolerably competent at arithmetic."

"Three or more years away from the *Black Swan*? You can't do it."

"I can do anything I set my mind to."

"You should marry," Robin said. "No, I'm

not speaking as the besotted lover. You need a family, and the only way to truly have one is to make your own. Anyway, it'll shake up your orderly life beyond reformation."

"There's nothing wrong with my orderly life," Thorn said, keeping tight rein on his temper. "And I'll be cast into turmoil only if I fall in love. I intend to make a rational marriage to someone perfectly suited to the burden of being a duchess."

"You're not serious, are you?" Christian asked.

"I doubt I have the temperament for mad passion."

"Yes, you do. I've seen you on the *Swan*."

"A ship might be female, but she's not a woman."

"But the fire's in you. It'll flare one day."

"What about you?" Thorn demanded. "You're a veritable inferno."

"And can burn freely. With a clutch of brothers, I carry no responsibility at all."

Robin raised his glass. "To the fact that one of us is completely free!"

They all drank and another fractious moment passed, but it was time to end this. Thorn captured the decanter before Robin could top up glasses again. "You have to be coherent tomorrow."

"Today," said Christian, standing and

stretching. "It's gone one. Get to bed, Robin, or you'll disappoint your bride."

"Never happened yet," Robin said, smiling blissfully, but they took their leave.

As they walked down the corridor, Christian said, "He's happy."

"Yes."

They'd arrived at Thorn's room, and Christian followed him in. Thorn's valet slipped away.

"Why are you so antagonistic toward Lord Rothgar?"

It was a serious question, so Thorn considered his answer. "He holds too much power, especially in his influence with the king. Someone, perhaps many, need to provide a counterbalance, and I have the advantage of outranking him."

"You'd be safer getting your thrills on the *Black Swan*."

"Go away," Thorn said, and Christian did

His valet returned to help him undress.

"Do you think I'm looking for trouble, seph?"

The valet was ten years older than Th a quiet, steady man who'd dressed since Thorn was fourteen and had attending court and other fashi events. They had no secrets.

Or rather, very few.

"Perhaps a little restless these days, sir. Since you decided not to go to sea."

"I have been aware of the imbalances at court for longer than that." As Thorn put on his robe, he asked, "Should I marry?"

"Only when you want to, sir."

"And if I never want to?"

"The world won't end if the Ithorne title does, sir."

"Sacrilege! I do want it, you know."

Robin was correct that the draw was family. He had been thinking of looking closely at one of Christian's sisters, for he was fond of that large brood, but he couldn't do that. They should all marry for love, not convenience.

"I need a wife to manage my homes and be hostess when I entertain," Thorn said, aware of arguing with himself. "Someone to buy jewelry for and have it stay in the family. Someone to bear healthy children to carry on the line."

Children to teach to sail on the lake. Who'd play pirates and Robin Hood . . .

"All in good time, sir. You'll find the right woman."

"I hope so," Thorn said, and yawned. "It vould be hell on earth to marry the wrong ne."

CHAPTER 6

Ithorne House, London, September 1764

"Here you are, ma'am." The nervous maid indicated a plain door at the end of a short, whitewashed servants' corridor. "Brings you out near some bedchambers, ma'am, and they're not properly open to the guests. But turn to your right and you'll soon find company."

The maid was gone thirty, but turned her fingers together in her apron like an anxious child. "If you're caught, you won't say as it was me let you in, will you, ma'am? I do what I can for Lady Fowler, but I need my place. And this isn't so bad a house, really. The duke keeps his sin elsewhere. It's just drink here, and gaming. . . ."

Bella touched the woman's arm. "I'll never let slip that anyone in this house assisted me. Return to your duties now, and forget all about me. And thank you."

The maid bobbed a curtsy and scuttled

away. Though Bella had no intention of scuttling, she faced the door with some of the maid's fears. She had invaded the home of a nobleman — a duke, even. What was the penalty for that? To make it worse, in moments she was going to invade a select gathering of the highest in the land.

She shivered at the thought.

Lady Fowler had received a letter from the maid, distressed that the duke was to host the Olympian Revels, an annual and wicked masked ball for the London elite. The servants would be forced to wear indecent garments. What was she to do?

Lady Fowler had seen a prime opportunity to hunt for the vilest secrets of those who ruled the country and made its laws. The maid must provide a way in for one of her flock. But which? The eventual, unwilling choice had been Bella — or rather, Bellona Flint.

Bella had achieved her original plan. She had assumed the persona of Bellona Flint — plain, severe, with eyebrows that met in the middle and a small wart on her nose. She'd rented a small house close to Lady Fowler's and spent her days at Lady Fowler's house copying the Fowler letter and being useful in any way she could. Over five months, however, she'd become disenchanted with the lady, her coterie, and her work.

Lady Fowler, poor woman, had been given an unfortunate disease by her husband. It was destroying her health so that she was now almost bedridden, and perhaps was affecting her brain. Her letter had degenerated into a scandal sheet, but now flirted with danger in radical political rants. Many of her flock were distressed, but they were timid birds, unable to protest. Bella was not timid, but she hadn't known what to do. She'd begun to think of leaving.

Now, facing this door into danger, she wished she'd already done so. Failing that, she wished she'd found a way to outmaneuver the Drummond sisters.

These recent arrivals were birds of a different feather. The Irish sisters, Helena and Olivia Drummond, had beaks and claws, and were full of ideas for dramatic action. They'd already organized a noisy protest outside one of Madame Cornelys's Venetian masquerades, and the throwing of ink on the legs of an actress playing a breeches part. On reading the maid's letter, they'd immediately embraced the idea of invading the revels, assuming Olivia would play the role.

Bella had been so alarmed at what they

might do that she'd offered to take on the task herself, but she'd forgotten her Bellona Flint persona. Olivia and Helena, both handsome in a bold way, had scoffed at her ability to act appropriately, which had led to a fiery argument. Bella had finally produced a trump card — experience of a fashionable masquerade.

When she'd arrived at Lady Fowler's, she'd kept her Bellona Flint story as close to her own as possible, omitting only the abduction and adding a few years to her age. Bellona was from a gentry family, but had been mistreated when she refused a foul husband of her father's choosing. She'd been rescued by a modest inheritance from an elderly relative.

Thus she could truthfully claim to have attended two fashionable masquerades, once as Betsy, a dairy maid, and the other time as Queen Eleanor of Castile. She knew how to behave — how to act her part and talk to others as if they were their character. Lady Fowler had awarded her the victory.

What she hadn't realized was that at the Olympian Revels, everyone dressed in classical style. Politicians wore togas, and military men wore Greek or Roman armor. Married ladies dressed as matrons or goddesses, but the unmarried should be scantily dressed nymphs.

If she'd understood that, she might never have fought for the role, but having done so, she'd lacked the courage to back out. She certainly couldn't lose her nerve now. She touched her full black wig and face-concealing mask for comfort. No one would ever know this scandalous creature was her.

A nymph's costume, by custom, was only a light, sleeveless robe. She'd insisted on wearing her shift beneath, but it had been necessary to cut off the sleeves. Her upper arms had never before been exposed to public gaze.

Nor had her toes. She'd wanted to wear stockings, but with delicate Grecian sandals, it had been clear it wouldn't do. To make the situation worse, the eye was drawn to her toes by sparkling stars on the sandal straps.

Lady Fowler or the Drummonds — she wasn't sure which — had decreed that she would be Kelano, one of the Pleiades, nymphs turned into stars after a rapacious attack by the god Orion.

"A living symbol," Lady Fowler had declared in her overly dramatic style, "of the cruelty of men!"

Thus Bella had stars on her sandals, on the dark blue girdle that gathered her white robe, and in her wig. The latter caused her no qualm, but she regretted the ones near her naked toes.

Praying there would be others even more scantily dressed, she put her hand on the latch and opened the door to the corridor a crack. She wasn't nervous solely because of her costume. She was invading a nobleman's house. Given the draconian unfairness of the laws protecting the nobility, she could probably hang for it.

She straightened her spine and peered out. Here was the ducal world. The gleaming corridor floor held a carpet runner, and the walls were painted a delicate green and hung with watercolor landscapes.

For a moment she wondered if she were in the wrong house. The Duke of Ithorne was a rake, but here was no lewdness or coarse taste. When she considered the faint sounds from elsewhere in the mansion, she was equally puzzled. She heard lively music, but no shrieks or wild laughter, yet people had been arriving for over an hour.

There could be no mistake, however, so she touched her mask again and stepped out into the corridor, closing the door behind her. She walked toward the music, and as she drew closer, she recognized a dance tune. Before she knew it, she was dancing a few steps down the carpeted corridor. It had been so long since she'd danced, and she had loved it so.

She stopped.

None of that, Bella. You're here on serious business.

She walked on, and now she heard voices and laughter, but still of the type she'd expect at an elegant assembly, not an orgy. She turned a corner and halted at the first sight of invited guests, heart suddenly hammering. She made herself move on toward the two groups, taking comfort from the fact that, yes, some of the nymphs ahead were dressed as scandalously as she.

Again, however, these people seemed to be engaged in harmless conversation. In the first group, three men in classical armor spoke with a matron and a shy nymph. Probably mother and daughter. In the second, two men in togas flirted with two bolder nymphs, but their behavior was quite within the bounds.

Seeing those nymphs, Bella wondered if she'd be caught out by being too well covered. One young lady had mere ribbons to cover her shoulders and her gown scarce covered her knees! One ankle was circled by what looked like diamonds, which seemed much more scandalous than stars on toes.

As she walked toward the first group, Bella surreptitiously raised her gown by pulling some fabric up over her belt. A quick glance told her six inches of her right leg showed. She conquered the urge to tug the skirt back down.

The soldiers and the modest ladies seemed to be talking of everyday matters — the state of the streets and the weather. Then one man mentioned John Wilkes.

She would rather not have been reminded of Wilkes. Last year he'd been imprisoned for creating an edition of the *North Briton* newspaper that criticized the king. He'd escaped the law only by fleeing the country. Now, under the influence of the Drummonds, Lady Fowler had used part of a startling donation of a thousand guineas to purchase a printing press. She said she would use it to print her letters so they could be freely distributed in London.

That was worrying enough, especially given its inflammatory content these days, but Bella feared that the Drummond sisters had more dangerous plans. They were managing to weave England's tyrannical rule of Ireland in among rants about the legal oppression of women, and that came close to treason. If they used the press to print on that subject, the poor sheep of the

Fowler flock were likely to end up like lambs to the slaughter.

Sheep or birds, equally vulnerable . . .

"Alone, fair nymph? Pray, join us."

Heart pounding again, Bella turned to face a toga'd gentleman. "Alas, sir, I am obliged elsewhere."

"What else could constrain a nymph at the revels? Pray, grant us the pleasure of your company."

The other man endorsed that, but the two nymphs clearly didn't favor a rival.

"Perhaps I wish to be obliged elsewhere," Bella said lightly. "Please excuse me, sirs."

She walked on, braced to be pulled back, perhaps accused of being an imposter. When that didn't happen, she relaxed a little. No one there had been suspicious, so her manner must have been appropriate.

She approached another cluster of people cautiously, but apart from glances, they paid her no attention. They too seemed to be discussing serious political matters. She caught reference to Greville, Newcastle, and the French ambassador.

She knew this event was supposed to be an opportunity for the great to meet and negotiate beyond the constraints of traditional rivalries and entrenched enmities, but she was surprised to find it so. It certainly wouldn't serve her purpose.

There was still time for it to become wild.

Bella turned another corner and was relieved to blend with livelier company. All was movement and lightness here, and she could pass through the mobile crowd with casual interactions. It was clear that many of the guests recognized one another, but some were playing the masquerade game and trying to guess the character another person portrayed.

A number of gentlemen tried to guess her identity, inviting her to pause with them and attempting to flirt. It was all in good humor, however, and she responded with a tease about their toga or armor and moved on. Yes, she could do this. She remembered how.

Her spirits began to match those around her. Her smile came more easily, the music danced in her mind . . . and then she realized she was glowing at male appreciation. They called her pretty and lovely, and admired her stars. . . .

They do not appreciate you, she told herself. *They are ogling your painted lips, false hair, and lewd costume.* All the same, the mood swept her back to her stolen youth and she liked it too much. It would be hard to return to her dull life after this, but what choice did she have?

She arrived at the center of the house, at a crowded grand landing above a magnificent staircase of gleaming wood and gilded metal. Above, she could just make out a richly plastered ceiling with a central painting, but little light reached there.

Instead, the hall below was lit to draw the eye, making it a stage onto which new arrivals stepped. She eased to the front of the crowd to get a better view, and was instantly assailed by noise, perfumes, and sweat, both from around her and from below.

She looked down, wondering if the duke was in the hall, greeting the most important guests. What costume would he wear? A senatorial toga, perhaps with an emperor's laurel wreath? She saw some of those, and even gilded ones.

Yes, the haughty duke would dress like that.

She hoped this invasion might lead to more information about the Duke of Ithorne, because she had a particular interest in him. She was worried about that extraordinary donation of a thousand guineas, and she'd asked Mr. Brownley, the London solicitor engaged for her by Mr. Clatterford, to try to find the source. He'd had great difficulty, for clearly the source didn't want to be uncovered, but some connection at a law firm that did a great deal of work for the dukedom of Ithorne had let slip that he knew of the matter. Now why would a young, rakish duke give such a sum to the Fowler Fund? For no good purpose, she was sure.

Had he hoped it would tempt Lady Fowler to dangerous folly? That seemed extraordinarily devious, but such had been the result. Lady Fowler was now convinced that she had powerful secret supporters and, under the influence of the Drummonds, was devising more grandiose plans by the day.

To make matters worse, for months now she'd been attacking the Marquess of Rothgar in her letters, which had to be the height of folly, even if he had foisted a bastard daughter on his wife and society.

Would the man they called the Dark Marquess be here tonight, perhaps dressed all in black? Another term applied to him was the Eminence Noir — the black power behind the throne. The term came from France, apparently, where there had once been L'Eminence Rouge — the red power, or Cardinal Richelieu.

Lord Rothgar frightened Bella more than the king did, for he knew no rules or laws. From what she knew of him, he did whatever he liked and his vengeance was swift.

Yes, she must leave Lady Fowler's. Must find some other life.

None of the men below seemed right for Lord Rothgar or the duke, though both would be hard to detect. She'd seen either only a few times and at a distance. Both were tall and had dark hair when it was unpowdered. The marquess was ten years older than the duke.

As she searched, she noticed that the arriving guests looked up and around and exclaimed with pleasure. Bella decided to go down to see the scene as they saw it.

It wasn't easy to go against the flow, and sometimes she had to brush too closely against people. Sometimes against men, who smiled and teased. One tried to compel her upstairs with him, but released her as soon as she protested.

She became hot and flustered, however. She wished some costumes didn't leave muscular arms exposed to brush her naked ones. She wished the crowd didn't occasionally press her completely against a hard body, or hard armor.

She'd forgotten the sense of men when close like this. Perhaps she'd never known it. Not like this, so informally.

Except once.

Four years ago. Dover. Wrapped in the arms of a man in the midst of a drunken crowd. Kissed in a drunken crowd. Standing in that stable close by a man's side, terrified of being caught, of the fate hanging over her, but aware of him there. Powerfully, physically aware in a way she'd never forgotten.

And he'd been fully dressed, as had she.

She pushed free of the end of the stairs and stepped into space, sucking in breaths as if she'd been drowning. Drowning in male scent and power.

She was still in the midst of a crowd, but not in contact with anyone anymore. No man had an excuse to press against her, thank the gods. She strolled toward the front door, and then turned, to see the scene as it presented to people entering the house in the normal way.

Ah.

She'd never been to Italy, but this was as she thought it would be. Illusory stone walls were broken by painted windows and balconies that showed people painted so cunningly that they could almost be alive. The dark cloth that had obscured some of her view from above gave the impression of a starry night sky. She became aware of smells. She couldn't identify them, but herbs and other aromas suggested a foreign land.

"Absurd, isn't it?"

Bella started and turned to face the speaker — a young man in peasant clothing. He wore a knee-length tunic of undyed homespun over brown leggings. He had dark stubble on his chin, unkempt grayish hair, and his mask was merely a rag wrapped around his eyes that left only a narrow gap.

For a moment she thought him an impudent servant, but the voice had not been a servant's voice. Clearly he was a gentleman, and one who took bold liberties with the limits of the costumes here to come as a Roman slave.

He was waiting for her response, perhaps wondering at her silence.

She chose rapidly between jaded and appreciative and preferred honesty. "I think it's lovely. I wonder if it truly resembles Italy."

"As a theater set resembles anything. But you think Ithorne's done a tolerable job?"

"I doubt the noble duke actually did anything."

Her companion chuckled. "How true. 'Here, minion, do this. Hence serf and do that.' "

His tone told her he was a kindred spirit

in dislike of the idle rich.

He seemed to notice the same thing about her. "Clearly we're companion souls," he said. "Come dance with me."

It might be taken as a request, but instead of offering his hand for her to take, he grasped hers and drew her back toward the stairs.

After an instinctive resistance, Bella went. She needed to be unobtrusive here until later, when the wickedness should begin, and a lady with a partner would be less notable than one alone. She couldn't deny that she'd also love to dance again, just once. It had been so long.

As she'd thought, when she had an escort other men didn't bother her. A lady should be able to go around unescorted and free from insult, but her heart wasn't in outrage at the moment. In truth, her heart was in disarray.

No, not her heart. She wasn't falling in love, but she was teetering on some brink, and all because a strong, masculine hand captured hers. How long had it been since a man had held her hand, both of them ungloved, skin-to-skin?

Four years, she supposed, at some country dance. Or perhaps when Coxy and Naiscourt had forced her into a coach.

"What angers you, sweet nymph?" her companion asked.

Bella realized they'd reached the top of the stairs and she was frowning. He mustn't think her unusual in any way, so she quickly smiled. "Only the crush, sir, and hence the delay at reaching the ballroom. I do enjoy dancing."

He glanced at the crowd blocking their way. "Shall I command a parting of the ways?"

"Are you Moses, then? You do wear a slavish costume."

"Merely a poor goatherd allowed off my solitary peak to play. But if we were to pretend all these inconvenient people were goats, I might know how to manage them."

"Goats? At the Olympian Revels?"

"Aristocratic goats are still goats. Only hear them bleat."

Bella had to chuckle. "Lud, sir! I fear you'll come to a dire end."

"Sent back to my mountain? Or forced to flee the country, like poor old Wilkes? Never fear: I'm not foolish enough to put my disrespectful thoughts into print. Are you?"

Bella gulped. Had she been caught so easily? "What disrespectful thoughts would I have?" she managed.

"About idle Ithorne, for one. He probably

has a dungeon deep below for insolence like that."

"More than likely. I hear he's a rake of the lowest degree."

He smiled. "A duke is never low, sweet nymph."

"Perhaps not in this life."

"Ah, you anticipate when we shall all be divided into sheep and goats. Unfair to goats, don't you think, to make them devil bait?"

"Very," she agreed, enjoying the harmless banter more than was wise. Lady Fowler's house was sadly lacking in wit. "You promised me dancing, sir. Are you not a man of your word?"

Oh, that was the old Bella Barstowe, all impatience and demands.

"Come, let me herd you, then." He put an arm around her and steered forward. Bella felt powerless, as if he had captured her will as well as her waist.

As if she'd go anywhere at his direction.

Like a mindless goat.

No man had ever put his arm around her in such a commanding way, and she felt the lack of her usual layers of clothing. As if by some magic he created enough space for them to pass, she almost felt as if his bare arm lay against her bare skin.

Be he of high or low degree, she'd fallen in with a rascal who didn't know the meaning of restraint. A wise woman would spurn him, but she did so want to dance.

They plunged through the throng into the ballroom.

It too was decorated to look like marble and pillars, though there'd been no attempt to hide the painted and gilded ceiling, glittering in the light of hundreds of candles. Down the center of the long room, a line of costumed guests danced to the tune "The Lady of May."

He moved them to one side so others could enter, and Bella found the strength to free herself from his arm.

He allowed it, his interesting mouth curled in humor. "Which nymph are you, my lovely one? By your stars I would guess one of the Pleiades. Stars at your toes too," he remarked, in a tone that made Bella's naked toes curl.

"Kelano," she said quickly. "Do you have a name, goatherd?"

"I'm too lowly to be named. Ebony hair," he remarked, boldly touching a long curl on her shoulder. "That could indicate Kelano the harpy, dark and clawed."

How could a touch on a wig make her shudder?

"Or Kelano of the Amazons," she pointed out, brushing his hand away. She'd researched her name. "Beware, sir. I may have a concealed bow and arrow."

"Perhaps I should search you. In case of danger to my goats."

"I think not!"

He reached out to touch the cloth covering her right shoulder, and for a moment she thought he might actually attempt it. But then he sighed. "Alas, nor do I. But you come as a mystery within a puzzle, Kelano, wrapped in a many-layered disguise. I must know more. But the night is young and there's time."

"Time?" she asked, trying not to sound breathless. She'd met some bold men when she was young, but never anyone like this. Though her breathing felt shallow, Bella was thrilled down to her starry toes. He was flirting with her in a most deliciously wicked way. And she was flirting back.

How long had it been?

Four years.

Aeons.

"Time to peel away layers until we arrive at truth," he said.

"Yours as well as mine?" It was an instinctive riposte, meant to repel, but he grinned and she realized her provocative riposte was very foolish.

"Of course," he said. "Shall we begin?" Again an invading touch, but this time a quick finger down her side.

"No," she said, stepping back, but coming up against a wall behind her.

"We could find a quieter spot. . . ."

Bella felt her eyes widen. He was proposing just the sort of scandal she'd come here to expose. And she, disastrously, was tempted!

"Dancing first," she said quickly.

Later she'd slip away from him.

"Kelano the wise." But then his smile became full of anticipation. "A slower pace does lead to greater pleasure, does it not? Come."

This time he did hold out his hand rather than compel her. Bella knew wise Kelano would find an excuse to escape now, but she put hers into his.

"You truly do enjoy dancing, don't you?"

As she was bouncing on her feet in time to the music, Bella didn't attempt to deny it, and she ran with him to join the end of the line to weave into the longways dance. Soon she was lost in the patterns of the steps.

As they met in the middle and turned, he said, "I think I might know you."

Despite a stab of panic, Bella smiled, but when she whirled off to turn with the next gentleman, her alarmed mind hunted through danger.

Could the goatherd be someone she'd known four years ago? She was certain he wasn't any of her country neighbors, and what London beau would remember her from a passing moment? And yet . . . and yet she realized there was something vaguely familiar about him.

Where?

When?

Stubbled cheeks seemed part of it, and that was a rare detail among gentlemen. . . .

She couldn't pin it down, but it nibbled at the back of her mind even as she smiled and flirted with other gentlemen. Recognition could be disastrous.

Was he recognizing Bella Barstowe or Bellona Flint? She couldn't imagine how anyone could recognize Bellona in this costume, especially as Bellona didn't mix with society at all.

"And who are you, pretty maid?"

Bella started and stared at the man she was mindlessly partnering. She gathered her wits to give the conventional response. "That's for you to guess, sir."

"Melia," he suggested.

She had no idea who Melia was, but shook her head and danced on, wondering why she hadn't given that conventional answer to the goatherd. Instead, she'd told him her name, just as she'd gone where he took her. He was a very dangerous man, and he thought he recognized her. As soon as the dance ended, she must elude him.

For now, she stole glances at him, assessing the danger.

Frequently, their eyes met.

Why was he watching her? Was he too puzzling over this sense of familiarity?

Was he part of Lady Fowler's reforming circle? No. The few men who supported her were clergymen and scholars. The goatherd was too wicked by far. Only see him flirt with every woman he passed in the dance. Of course, she was doing the same, but all in a noble cause.

She noted with regret the reactions of the targets of his flirtation — rendered silly, every one of them, young to old. She'd heard of men who could turn a woman's wits to water, and now she'd met a specimen.

And been turned silly herself for a while.

No more of that. She attended to her partners and looked for scandal. There were certainly partners she'd like to pillory, such as the fleshy senator who squeezed too close in the dance, or the stick-thin one who took an excuse to poke at her breast. Or this hairy one with moist lips who was sweating so profusely that his toga was damp.

No, that was unkind, for the room was very hot. The long windows stood open, but even though it was September it was unseasonably warm and she felt no cool breeze. When she returned to dance with the goatherd, she said, "It's so hot in here." She saw the wicked spark in his eyes and hastily deflected a suggestive remark. "A blessing that we're all lightly dressed. Perhaps this costume should become the fashion for dancing. Imagine this heat in layers of petticoats and silk."

"Or a suit of embroidered velvet," he agreed.

"On a goatherd?" she teased.

"Do goddesses sweat?" he tossed back.

"But I am a nymph. . . ."

"And nymphs are notoriously naughty."

"And goatherds are . . ." But she could think of nothing to say.

"Goats are lecherous," he offered helpfully. "Perhaps it's contagious. Oh, dear," he added, squeezing her hand slightly, "we're contaging."

"Then you'll have spread lechery throughout the whole body of dancers, sir. Which, on reflection, would be rather like giving a rash to a leper colony."

"Kelano! You shock me. But if you are hot . . ."

He deftly slipped them out of the dance and through open doors onto the lamplit terrace. It was cooler — on her sweat-damp skin almost cold — but a fire of alarm rushed through her.

She turned back toward the room, but he said, "Cold?" and picked up something from a bench. He swirled a large shawl around her shoulders, capturing her and pulling her toward him.

She tried to brace her hands on his chest to hold him off but she was too late. A moment ago she'd been dancing, and now here she was, trapped against his scantily clad body.

"Playing hot and cold?" he asked.

"Playing the goat? Release me."

He chuckled and then he kissed her. A quick kiss at first, but in moments one arm came around her and his other hand cradled her head. He kissed her again, deeply and with skill, teasing her mouth open so she felt his tongue on hers.

She tried to resist, but a starved piece of her, the part that had danced and flirted

once, and yes, even kissed on dark terraces
a time or two, sprang to terrifying life. She'd
been kissed and enjoyed being kissed, but
she'd never been kissed like this before.
Never felt quite like this before.

So endangered.

So seared.

No!

She twisted her head and pushed fiercely
away.

He allowed it, but he was smiling, eyes
glittering, and he'd captured the ends of the
shawl again, snaring her.

"Let me go!"

She intended a demand, but breathless-
ness made it more of a gasp. She knew she
was feverishly awaiting his dramatic response.

He released the corners of the cloth.

She gathered it around her to conceal bare
arms and shoulders — and disappointment.
"You shouldn't have done that."

"Then you shouldn't have come to the
revels."

"Is that the sort of event this is, then?
Where young ladies are attacked for playing
a part?"

"It's the way of any masquerade, if the
lady too wishes to play."

"I did not —"

"If my kiss offended, I apologize, but you did not seem powerfully offended, my very sweet and tasty nymph."

Bella swallowed, innate honesty forcing her to admit that he was right, and the wicked, foolish parts of her wanted to fall into his arms again.

She found the strength to unwrap herself, and dropped the shawl back on the bench with what she hoped was a casual air. "After our brief diversion, slave, I must return to more elevated circles."

"Don't trust the senators and gods. For all their august glitter, they're men just like me. If you're the sort of innocent you imply, you will wish me to return you safely to your party."

It was a challenge, as deft as a blade between the ribs, and she remembered his remark about recognition. What did he suspect? She tried to read the subtleties of his expression, but out here the lamplight was dim, doubtless by design.

"If I allow that," she said, "you would know who I am."

"Know a person by the company she keeps? Intriguing. You think you can remain eternally unidentified?"

"I can try."

That mouth, that sensuous mouth, curved

in a true smile, creating brackets in his lean cheeks. "I will find out, you know."

Bella wanted to return that smile, but she raised her chin. "I doubt it."

"It's merely a matter of when. I already feel I know you."

"And I doubt that."

"Are you a provincial, then, new to Town?"

"You'll tease no more information from me, slave." She was in danger, however, the longer she dallied here, so she said, "And now, farewell," and slipped back into the ballroom.

Praying he wouldn't pursue, she wove quickly straight through the line of dancers, ignoring objections. When she reached the far door, she glanced back. Part of her hoped he was close behind, about to capture her again, sweep her again into yet more wicked folly, but most of her was wiser.

She felt a pang of disappointment, however, to see him still in the doorway to the terrace, having lost all interest. He was talking to a gray-haired man in a simple robe.

There, see, you idiot. That encounter, that kiss, meant nothing to him. And of course she'd never truly thought otherwise. She felt able to linger a moment, puzzled by his sober, intent manner.

She remembered that she'd wondered if

he too was an invader. In that case she'd think him talking to a conspirator, perhaps plotting to harm someone. Were the two men planning to kill the duke, or set fire to the house? She should do something to stop that.

Then he looked across the room, straight at her. She'd swear his masked eyes widened. Had he understood her thinking? Frightened in a new way, she turned to leave the room, but a group of people were pushing in and she had to step aside.

She shot a quick glance back at the goatherd.

He hadn't moved, but he was still looking at her.

Bella turned again to flee, but now she saw some people were staring at her. Directly at her. Their masks concealed their expressions, but their intensity seemed almost hungry.

Had she been recognized as an interloper? Were they about to tear her apart?

One woman looked her up and down, lip curling. Lud, had the wretched man disturbed her gown and left her indecent? Bella looked down at herself. All was in order, even the stars on her toes, but something was amiss, and she didn't know what. Almost blind with panic, Bella slipped through a gap in the crowd and hurried off to her right, trying not to look like a criminal fleeing justice. She had no idea where she was going. She prayed only to find a quiet place to collect herself.

Then she heard the hiss: "Scandalous!"

Bella flinched as if stabbed, but when she looked around no one was looking at her. Three Grecian goddesses were half whispering in the way of people sharing gossip, and smiling with glee at a reputation to shred.

Bella checked around again, but no one else was nearby.

Her heart rate was settling and her mind clearing. Perhaps she wasn't in imminent danger of any kind. And scandal was what she was here for.

She bent down as if she needed to adjust a strap on her sandal, listening to the whispers.

"In flagrante delicto, dearest. Absolutely!"

"But who?"

"Grandiston, I heard."

A titter. "Then no wonder. So very, very virile in that ancient armor . . ."

Grandiston? The name was vaguely familiar, but Bella couldn't place it. Was he important enough to be meat for Lady Fowler's letter? And who was the woman?

One of the women must have asked the

same thing.

"Psyche Jessingham."

Bella knew that name, because Lady Jessingham's adulterous liaison with Ithorne had been talked about at Lady Fowler's, but not included in the Fowler letter. Lady Fowler had been forced into marriage when young with a disgusting older man and she had compassion for other women who suffered the same fate, even if they sinned.

Lady Jessingham was a widow now, but Lady Fowler kept to her policy, even though she would like to expose Ithorne for not marrying the woman whose reputation he'd tarnished.

"Psyche and Grandiston?"

The voices dropped, and Bella strained to hear. Would Lady Fowler still refuse to use scandal concerning that lady?

"She never did learn discretion," one said. "So what exactly was seen?"

More murmurs, then, "Very disheveled," the informative one said with meaning. "Gown ripped down the front . . ."

Bella suddenly realized the three matrons were looking at her, eyes cold.

She gave a weak smile and hurried away, catching just one more word. "Rothgar . . ."

Lud! Had the great marquess also been involved? Her time with Lady Fowler had introduced her to some scandalous knowledge, and she now knew that men sometimes shared one unfortunate woman. That would definitely be a story for the letter. But, oh, Lord Rothgar's poor wife, large with child, and already having been forced to accept his adult bastard daughter into her home.

She must learn more. Where was this scandalous Grandiston encounter taking place?

CHAPTER 7

Thorn moved through the throng as quickly as he could without showing urgency, for most people here recognized him and he didn't want to start any alarm. He also masked his anger, but he was furious with himself. He was going to be too late to avert disaster because he'd neglected his duty. Instead of monitoring the event and keeping an eye on the king, he'd slipped off to play with an enchanting Amazon nymph on the terrace.

He'd had to let Kelano slip away unidentified, dammit, but this wasn't a wasps' nest he could ignore. Christian had been caught in one of the private rooms of the house with some woman, and caught by Psyche Jessingham, of all people. She thought she could buy Christian as a husband, so she'd scream this to the heavens.

He supposed he should give Christian some credit for using a distant room for his

131

liaison, but he'd have his guts anyway. What had he been thinking? He was already embroiled with three troublesome women. In addition to the rapacious Psyche, he'd made a foolish marriage at sixteen to a Yorkshire girl who went by the inauspicious name of Dorcas Froggatt. He'd thought her dead, but recently learned she was alive. In searching for her in hope of an annulment, he'd fallen in love with a Mistress Hunter, but she'd fled him on finding that he was a married man.

To add insult to all this, the warning message he'd received on leaving the terrace had come courtesy of Rothgar.

Thorn was ready to grab a Chinese vase off the nearby table and hurl it at a wall.

"Sir."

Thorn whirled to find a Roman soldier looking ready to make an arrest. "You are asked for," the man said sternly.

Thorn cursed, but silently. He couldn't ignore a summons from the king. He turned back toward the revels.

George had chosen to wear a plain toga, attempting to be one of the people. He failed, of course. Everyone knew better than to bow or curtsy or give any other sign of recognition, but that was difficult for people trained to court ways from the cradle.

Thorn only just managed not to bow as he said, "I gather there has been a small contretemps, sir. I apologize."

"Very naughty," said the king, yet he seemed in good humor. "But a married couple, what?"

Married? Thorn hid surprise and inclined his head in acknowledgment of worldly wisdom. "The powers of marital affection, sir."

"Which I understand, as I am so blessed, what? May I hope you as happy soon, Ithorne? A noble line, and you the sole remainder, what?"

The king's habit of tacking "what" onto the end of nearly everything he said made Thorn want to throttle him, but at the moment he merely wanted to escape this conversation and discover the extent of the problem.

"I seek to be as happy as you, sir," he said, "and thus I'm making a careful choice."

"Let your friends pick, what? As I did."

And had complained of Charlotte of Mecklenburg-Strelitz's looks and manner, Thorn remembered. At the time, George had been taken with pretty Sarah Lennox. But the king and queen did seem a truly fond couple now, which gave support to his own intent to make a rational marriage.

"I will take your advice, sir. But for now, if you will excuse me . . ."

Waved away, Thorn returned to his original direction, considering the implication of the warning message having come from Rothgar. Had he set up this scandal and then made sure that the king knew, hoping the king would blame the host?

Thorn considered his contest with Rothgar purely political, but would the Dark Marquess be willing to use any means to diminish a challenge to his power?

He saw his serious-minded secretary, Overstone, approaching, uncomfortable in a toga, and paused for more news.

"According to tattle, sir, Lord Rothgar has diluted the scandal by claiming the couple is married. It is believed by some, but stridently denied by Lady Jessingham, who is voicing a very low opinion of the lady. Shall I support the marriage story, sir?"

Thorn thought quickly. "Not yet, but don't deny it, either. Be soothing."

Thorn hurried along a quiet corridor, braced for any level of disaster.

What he discovered was simply astonishing. Christian had indeed been caught in a passionate encounter, but the woman was his wife, the Dorcas Froggatt he was seeking to escape through annulment. Peculiar to be caught in a compromising situation then, except that she was also that Mistress Kat Hunter whom Christian had fallen in love with.

Love! There was nothing worse for ruining a man's life, especially when Dorcas, Kat, or whoever she might be was accusing Christian of compromising her to force her to hold to the marriage.

Whatever the truth of the tangled web at the end of a long night, Thorn found himself committed to going to Malloren House on the morrow to meet with Rothgar and plead his foster brother's case.

For Rothgar, damn him, was in the very middle of the whole incident. Christian's wife, it turned out, was a Yorkshire friend of his marchioness, and a guest at Malloren House. Rothgar had brought her to the revels, knowing the whole truth. He claimed a benign intent, but Thorn had to doubt that. The incident could have resulted in Thorn suffering embarrassing scandal and royal displeasure.

However, if Rothgar had deliberately used Christian as a weapon, political rivalry could shift to outright, personal war.

Only when he finally found his bed, with the sky showing predawn light, did Thorn's mind return to Kelano.

Perhaps she'd been a Harpy after all, and had caused this all by casting a curse on him.

Bella had returned to her small rented house in a sedan chair as clocks struck three. Her two young maidservants greeted her as if she'd just escaped a pit of snakes. They could be right.

"Oh, miss!" Annie Yelland gasped, still waif thin despite months of good food. "We were so afraid for you."

"All that wickedness!" declared her sister, Kitty, who'd filled out to become a buxom beauty on the same diet.

When Bella had rescued them, they'd seemed more similar — thin, pale, and frightened. Kitty, the older sister, was an inch taller than Annie, but still not tall, and her hair was red squirrel to Annie's brown mouse. Annie had better skin and larger brown eyes.

"Was it 'orribly shocking?" Kitty prompted.

"In general, no," Bella said, stretching the truth a bit. She didn't want to encourage Kitty's taste for scandal.

She'd rather not have involved the girls in the matter at all, but she'd needed to dress here and return here. Kitty was learning to

136

be a lady's maid, while Annie was learning to be a cook, but what one knew, the other did, and whenever possible they were together. If Kitty needed to mend something of Bella's, she took her sewing basket to the kitchen instead of staying in Bella's bedchamber, as she really should.

Here they were, together again, when it was only Kitty's job to wait up and help Bella undress. Bella could and would give Kitty permission to sleep in, as she would rise late herself, but Peg Gussage would need Annie in the kitchen at first light. No point in making an issue of it now. Perhaps Annie would learn by experience.

Bella went up to her bedroom with Kitty while Annie hurried to the kitchen for hot washing water. Kitty insisted on helping Bella undress, though a shift and loose gown hardly needed assistance. Annie arrived with the jug of water and filled the china bowl behind the dressing screen. Bella washed in water at exactly the best temperature, but at that point she insisted that they both go to bed.

The sisters were treasures, and she was very fortunate.

She'd arrived in London with just Peg, and rented this house. Peg would be cook and housekeeper, but she'd needed a kitchen maid and at least one housemaid as well as someone to do the rougher work, a man or a boy. Both Peg and Bella preferred the latter to be a sturdy boy rather than a man, if he was to live in. Aware of her own good fortune, she'd decided to attempt charitable selections.

The workhouse had been heart-wrenching, and she'd discovered that most of the inhabitants were elderly or infants, for healthy children were sent out to work as young as six. She'd spotted one robust-looking lad, however, on a mattress in the middle of the day.

"You don't want 'im, ma'am," the supervisor said, pulling the grimy blanket off the boy, who looked to be about ten. "We found 'im good work at a stables, but 'e got 'imself injured and won't 'eal. The rot'll creep up and kill him sooner or later."

Bella had feared that was true, but the boy's sad eyes had touched her, and apart from his swollen, suppurating leg, he looked strong. Fearing she was a softhearted fool, she'd asked his name — Ed Grange — and then hired a cart to carry him to her house. The cart had been necessary because she couldn't imagine how to get him and his leg into a coach, but he was also filthy and probably infested.

Peg Gussage had been appalled, and yes, had called Bella a softhearted fool, but she'd set to work with baths, good food, and country nostrums.

The sick lad had made finding maids even more urgent, so Bella had spread word through Lady Fowler's supporters and spoken to the vicar of Saint Anne's Church. It had been the latter who'd told her of the sad case of the Yelland sisters.

"They lived with their widowed father, Miss Flint. A coal heaver, but a worthy man. He perhaps protected them too much, for his own comfort and theirs. If they had learned a trade, or gone into service, they would be in better condition now. Last winter, he fell and broke his back. The girls tended to him with loving care, but he died six weeks ago and the modest funeral took the last of his money. Annie and Kitty kept their situation from everyone, even me, for they were terrified of the workhouse. And with reason, with reason."

"Indeed," Bella said. "How old are they?"

"They say that Kitty is sixteen and Annie fifteen, but often such people aren't sure. Too old for most charities, you see, and as I said, untrained. But they've kept house for their father, and I know of no illness or weakness. With a little kindness and ample food, they will soon be hearty workers, and they are good girls."

Knowing a more sensible woman would have ignored the case, Bella visited the girls in their tiny house. It was neat and clean, but had clearly been stripped of anything they could sell, and the girls were thin and pale. She'd be bringing more work home, not helping hands, but she could no more abandon the Yelland sisters than she'd been able to leave Ed Grange to die in the workhouse.

Taking the name Bellona Flint had not made her harder, and her imprisonment at Carscourt seemed to have left her with a softness toward the unfortunate unknown to the Bella of four years ago.

Despite their frailty, the sisters had set to work eagerly, perhaps thinking that if they slacked they'd be thrown out. Within days Ed too was doing all the work he could from his mattress in the kitchen, and in a week he was hobbling around on a crutch. Now they were all robust hard workers and Bella gave thanks every day.

She was already planning to do more for all of them.

Annie would make a good cook, and Kitty an adequate lady's maid, but Bella was reaching higher. They were both clever girls

140

and she'd already taught them and Ed to read, write, and do arithmetic. If Bella were to set them up in a business in a few years' time, they could be independent women, just as she was.

A cake shop, perhaps, which also sold and served tea. Or a haberdashery. Anything that would free them of the need to take a husband. Her time with Lady Fowler had convinced her that the dangers of marriage far outweighed any advantages for many women, but also that to be single without family or income was a dire fate.

At least Ed's life was easy to arrange. He needed only an apprenticeship.

Bella emerged in her nightgown and looked longingly at her bed. She sat at her desk instead to dutifully record the events of the night. Alas, the scandal had proved disappointing, and in any case was no secret. The whole masquerade had been gossiping about Lord Grandiston and his wife, for it seemed the marriage itself had been a secret.

She'd observed little else other than drunkenness and looseness.

She'd heard that the king had been present, but only after he'd left. She would keep that to herself in any case, for Lady Fowler saw him as the epitome of virtue, her hope for a reformed nation. The poor lady's mind seemed already strained. To discover she was wrong there might cause a fit.

Bella worried the tip of her quill, frowning over Lady Fowler. It was time to leave that circle, but where would she go? The idea of being alone in the world terrified her. She also hesitated to abandon the weaker members of the flock to Lady Fowler's erratic moods and the Drummond sisters' radical tendencies.

She rubbed her head, trying to focus on the page, but neither her eyes nor her mind cooperated. In fact her mind tried to wander to a wicked goatherd, a lamplit terrace, and astonishing kisses. . . .

She stood up, shaking herself. She, above all women, should be impervious to the seductive charms of a rascal.

She circled the warming pan around the bed, removed it, and climbed in while the warmth lingered. Perfect. She snuggled down, turning her mind away from folly. It slid toward another sort of foolishness — distant memories, revived tonight.

Her last masquerade ball. A much smaller affair at Vextable Manor not far from Carscourt. Everyone had known everyone, but they'd all pretended not to and acted their parts. She'd slipped away with . . .

Oh, who had it been? Tom Fitzmanners or Clifford Speke? Probably Tom, as she remembered the favored gentleman had been only a few years older than herself and rather nervous at finding himself alone with a young lady and invited to kiss her. He'd certainly been clumsy about it.

She chuckled at that memory. What a wicked minx she'd been.

Above all back then, she'd loved to dance.

They'd danced so much — at parties and assemblies, but sometimes impromptu at one house or another, furniture pushed back, carpet rolled up, and someone playing a harpsichord or virginals.

Four long years without dancing, without flirting, without the lightest kiss, and she'd not realized how much she'd missed it. Until tonight.

Had she panicked because the goatherd was wicked, or because of her own feverish response? A response that had sprung with teeth and claws out of starvation.

She didn't want to give away her freedom in marriage, but she couldn't deny that she wanted a man. A young, handsome, skillfully wicked man.

She rolled over and buried her head in her pillow as if she could bury all such foolishness, but her mind wasn't smothered and whirled back over the whole annihilating experience.

His eyes, capturing hers just as that silky shawl snared her, drawing her tight against his long, hard, hot body with so little clothing between them.

His mouth hot and in control of hers. Nothing at all like Tom Fitzmanners.

But a little like Captain Rose.

She rolled onto her back to stare up into darkness. She'd forgotten that kiss. That too had been stolen, but there was no other connection, so why feel as if there were?

Perhaps because of dark stubble. The goatherd had been unshaven because he was pretending to be a peasant; Captain Rose because he was one. Not a peasant, but not of the rank to attend the Olympian Revels.

They had one other thing in common: if she'd been foolish enough to fall in with either man's plans, he'd have ruined her.

No danger of that. She punched her pillow into a better shape. There was no place for rakish folly in Bellona Flint's life, and it was best that it remain so.

CHAPTER 8

After such a late night, Bella rose later than usual and sat dozily at breakfast. She went over her time at the revels again, desperately seeking some juicy tidbit to take to Lady Fowler's. The Drummond sisters would make hay of her failure.

But fail she did, so she decided that she might as well get the unpleasant errand over with. She quickly dressed in one of Bellona's dull, practical garments, quashing down foolish regret for a flimsy gown and an even more foolish regret over the way men had responded to her in that guise.

She needed no help to dress, for she still wore the homemade jumps instead of a corset, but she allowed Kitty to practice her trade. As usual, Kitty pulled a face over the unboned jumps, so as usual, Bella tried to convince her of the advantage of simple dress.

"There," she said, "neatly dressed in

145

minutes. What a deal of time most women waste on clothing. And on hair."

Kitty said, "Yes, miss," but with disapproval. Both Kitty and Annie thought anything less than fully boned stays indecent.

Kitty wasn't any happier about Bella's need to look older and plainer, and always turned away while Bella applied the cream to her face that turned her sallow, and the darker one that made her eyes sunken.

Bella shrugged and stuck on the small wart on her nose, and then she pulled her hair up tight and hid it beneath a plain mobcap.

She'd been doing this for months now and hadn't minded, but now she gazed in the mirror and pulled a face at Bellona Flint. Last night she'd been herself. She'd been pretty. Men's eyes had told her so. . . .

And only see where it might have led. As she pinned on a small flat hat, she said, "There. I have no further need to think of my hair all day long. Which leaves time for more important, more useful matters. I hope you're continuing with your reading, Kitty."

Kitty turned back from tidying the bed. "Yes, miss. I'm halfway through *Pilgrim's Progress* and there's very few words I don't know. I have written them down." She pulled a paper out of her pocket.

"Excellent," Bella said, rising. "I'll go over them with you as soon as I get home. I need to go to Lady Fowler's immediately."

"What cloak, miss?"

Bella glanced at the window and saw gray sky. That suited her mood. "The brown wool, Kitty."

She put on her leather shoes and turned toward the door.

"Excuse me, ma'am."

Bella turned back. "Yes, Kitty?"

"What am I to do with the costume, ma'am?"

Burn it, leapt into Bella's mind with a ferocity to make her flinch. Rejecting that and all it implied, she said, "Oh, pack it away somewhere. One never knows. . . ."

She hurried on her way, trying not to think why she'd reacted like that, and failing. Because she knew that for her the costume represented flaming temptation.

She'd rather not face Peg today, but she always left through the kitchen, so anything else would be like waving a banner.

As usual, Peg gave her appearance a jaundiced look, but she asked, "What was the duke's house like, then? Very grand?" She was beating something in a bowl.

"Of course."

Peg refused even to pretend a lack of interest in the grand and their ways. She often walked to the Queen's House in hopes of seeing Their Majesties out strolling, and sometimes came home happy. Bella couldn't starve her of details like this.

"The arrangement of the house was most impressive. Pillars, ruins, the effect of a square with balconies above as if of people's houses. Having never been to Italy, I'm not sure how accurate it was, but other guests seemed impressed."

"Oh, I wish I could have seen that."

"But it was only for the rich and grand," Bella pointed out. "In a just world, it would be open to lesser folk, at least before or after."

She expected agreement, but Peg said, "I don't know about that, dear. Boots all over the good floors and carpets. Dirty hands on the curtains."

"More work for the servants, you mean." But Bella wouldn't be defeated. "They could put down cloths, and keep people away from curtains."

"Then it wouldn't be the same, would it?"

"Very well, next time I invade such an event, I'll take you with me."

"Lawks, you won't!" Peg exclaimed. "I'd

not leave my room dressed as you were. You did stay safe?" she asked with a worried look.

Bella picked a raisin from a bowl and split it to take out the seed. "Completely. Though any number of men made improper proposals."

"Of course they did, pretty as you are. Any suitable?"

"Peg! I was an interloper. Anyway, you know I've no interest in men, and especially not in marriage." Bella chewed and swallowed the raisin.

"I do know, and it's a proper shame."

"Just because you had a good husband doesn't mean they're all that way."

"Oh, how you do go on. Off you go to your clucking hens."

"Oh, how you do go on," Bella tossed back at her, and left the kitchen.

At Lady Fowler's it went much as she'd expected. The Grandistons' behavior had been scandalous, for there seemed general agreement that they'd been caught intimately entwined and with Lady Grandiston's costume seriously disarranged, but their being married made such matters of little use.

"I did wonder about Lady Jessingham,"

Bella said, trying to find something of value. "Apparently she had expectations of Grandiston, not knowing he was married. As he's the Duke of Ithorne's foster brother, perhaps . . . well . . ."

"Well?" asked Lady Fowler.

She lay on her chaise before the fire in her bedchamber. She hardly left the room, which was kept unpleasantly warm. There was also a distressing smell. Strong-faced Helena Drummond, the older sister, sat on a stool nearby, the fire catching lights in her thick red hair. Bella gave her credit for fortitude.

Bella still blushed to speak of such things. "Perhaps they shared her."

Two other attendant ladies gasped.

Mary Evesham had been reading aloud when Bella arrived. A few letters lay in her lap. They would be from Lady Fowler's supporters. Mary was a recent arrival — a curate's middle-aged sister left destitute when he died. Bella rather liked the quiet woman, whom she thought of excellent understanding, and who often had a twinkle of humor in her eyes.

The other lady was Celia Pottersby, a thin, bitter widow who never revealed what had caused her bitterness.

In a corner, stocky Agnes Hoover sat sewing. She had been Lady Fowler's maid for thirty years. She hardly spoke a word to anyone, but she watched and listened, and often looked as if she disapproved of everything. She was truly devoted to her mistress, however, and treated her as tenderly as a mother.

"They probably were sharing her," said Helena Drummond with a sneer, "and in the same bed, but you've no proof, Bellona. In any case, this digging up of dirt doesn't serve the real cause."

"Then why did you propose the invasion of the revels?" Bella demanded.

"To invade a duke's house," Helena said with a greedy smile. "That could have presented many possibilities."

What on earth had the Drummonds planned?

"Did you enjoy it, dear Bellona?"

Helena's malicious look made Bella realize that the Drummonds thought she would have been horrified by playing such a part. So should she have been, as Bellona.

"It was dreadful," she said with a shudder, "but I hope I am always willing to make sacrifices for the cause."

"Dear, dear Bellona!" Lady Fowler exclaimed, holding out a bony hand.

Bella took it gently, feeling the thinness of

the skin. "I'm sorry to have failed, ma'am."

"We cannot win every battle. Sit by me as we listen to Mary. Such a soothing voice."

The stool was set too close to the fire. Sweat was already forming on Bella's face, and the poor dying lady did smell of decay.

"Alas, ma'am, I have a small emergency at my house. One of my maids . . . I will try to return later."

She escaped, feeling guilty about those trapped in Lady Fowler's house by poverty, but very relieved when she achieved fresh air again.

Thorn greeted his valet and the day sourly. Damn the Olympian Revels and all involved in them, including himself. Joseph moved quietly around the room, as always sensitive to his master's mood. At the moment, Thorn found that annoying too.

"Breakfast," he said, climbing out of the huge ducal bed. It had been his father's, and why the man had wanted bulbous carvings on all surfaces, he had no idea, having never known him. At least the carvings weren't obscene. Though that wouldn't have been particularly surprising.

A hard-drinking, hard-gaming, hard-riding rake — that had been the second Duke of Ithorne, and Thorn was glad never to have known him. He wished some of the reputation didn't cling to the title. He was no saint, but he wasn't as far gone as some assumed, and today he needed every scrap of dignity.

He went into his dressing room and used the shower he'd had installed there, copying a design sometimes used on ships. He enjoyed a bath, especially the large Grecian one in the basement, and especially with female company, but the shower was efficient.

He stood in the wide, thigh-deep basin and pulled the chain to release some water. Exactly the right temperature, of course, just off cold. He washed, including his hair, which still had the coating of gray powder Joseph had applied to disguise his hair color for his goatherd persona.

That had been fun for a while. Until everything had gone to hell.

Damn Christian, and damn his cold-hearted, newly discovered wife. But it was Psyche Jessingham he wanted to consign to the deepest regions of hell. She'd stalked Christian in hope of catching him out and succeeded, much good would it do her. Had the woman really expected to use scandal to force him to marry her?

He stepped into the warm towel Joseph

held and dried himself. He combed his hair, put on his banyan robe, and then sat to be shaved. Stubble was a useful attribute, especially the dark sort he grew rapidly. As the impeccable Duke of Ithorne, he was shaved twice a day. As Captain Rose, he let it grow, sometimes into a beard. It quite changed his looks, as had a day's stubble on the goatherd.

All the same, most people had known him. He'd been mischievously tempted to ask his half brother to come and attend. He and Caleb could have played some amusing deceptions. Alas, there was no amusement left in all this.

After breakfast he chose his dress carefully, armoring himself for a visit to Malloren House, where he'd be the petitioner in Rothgar's lair, but must not seem in the slightest way inferior.

Damn it all to Hades.

"What shall I do with this, sir?"

Thorn glanced over to see Joseph had a spray of silver stars in his hand.

"Where did they come from?"

"They were snagged in the cloth of your costume, sir."

Kelano.

He should tell the valet to throw them on the fire. They were mere tinsel and not worth a sixpence. Instead he said, "Put them on the dressing table. I may be able to return them."

Joseph did so with noticeable impassivity.

The valet was right, Thorn admitted as he left his room. Keeping such trinkets was never wise. The ornament might lead him to Kelano, whoever and wherever she might be, but she was doubtless a temptation best forgotten.

The next day Bella was reluctant to visit Lady Fowler's house. She lingered over her breakfast and the newspaper, pretending that she was hunting for hints of wicked behavior. As she looked briefly over the short advertisements, a name caught her eye. Then she read the whole short announcement:

Kelano,
I have your stars. Leave word as to when I may return them to you at the Goat in Pall Mall.
— Orion Hunt

It couldn't be coincidence. She'd lost her spray of stars at the masquerade, probably when embracing the goatherd, but returning her ornament would not be all he had in mind. The name Orion Hunt was a warning. Orion had been the god who hunted the Pleiades with wicked intent.

But she read the brief message again, tempted.

She was drawn to folly not just by spicy memories, but because it would be escape from everything else in her life. Escape from Bellona Flint. A return to that fairy-tale world that was so different from Lady Fowler's circle.

If she were to meet him, how could she do so and remain safe?

Kitty came in. "Oh, I thought you'd be done with your breakfast, miss."

Bella realized she was nibbling on a piece of dry toast. "I am," she said, rising from the table.

Kitty cleared the breakfast dishes, but was clearly still troubled. It turned out, however, that Bella's actions weren't the only concern. As the maid handed her the fichu, she said, "Miss, I've something to tell you. . . ."

Bella turned, alerted by Kitty's hesitant, anxious tone. *Oh, no.* She couldn't help looking at her maid's waistline.

"Miss!" Kitty exclaimed. "I never would. And nor would Annie."

"No, no, I'm sure not. I'm sorry. You sounded so . . . Never mind. What do you need to tell me, Kitty?"

The girl bit her lip and swallowed, then blurted out, "Me and Annie, miss. We want to get married."

Bella stared, almost saying that sisters couldn't marry each other, but her blank mind managed a sensible question, "Marry whom?"

"Alfred Hotchkins and Zebediah Rolls, miss."

A to Z, Bella thought dazedly, struggling for a response. "But, Kitty, you and Annie are very young."

"Seventeen and nineteen, miss, and Fred and Zeb are a bit older. They're cousins, see."

Bella didn't see at all. "Where did you meet them?"

"At church, miss, years ago. They're good lads. Honest, hard workers." Kitty's fingers were mangling her apron.

"You don't need my permission, Kitty."

"Don't we? Then whose do we need?"

Bella realized she didn't know, but other thoughts were tumbling in now that the shock was thinning. "Kitty, Kitty, have you thought? You don't truly want to be married. I can set you and your sister up in a business. There's no necessity . . ."

The maid's eyes widened. "Oh, I do want

to marry, miss! And so does Annie, just as much."

"But why? Think, Kitty, of the way the law puts us under the domination of a husband. Anything you earn will belong to him. He will be able to dictate where you live and what you do. The law will not defend you if he beats you." Bella didn't feel able to raise the subject of a husband's rights in the marriage bed and the danger of disease.

Kitty's brows were furrowed as if Bella spoke a foreign language. "I won't be working, will I, miss? Not for wages, and where would I live other than with him?"

"You might want to flee if he beats you."

"I doubt he would, miss, but if Fred did mistreat me, the women of the parish would see, all right, starting with his gran. A fierce lady is Granny Rolls. He'd be running to me for protection," she said with a saucy grin.

Bella stared. Women joining together to oppose the cruelty of men. Was it possible?

"And anyway, miss, I love Fred, and Annie loves Zeb, and love doesn't ask, does it? It tells."

Insanity! Bella wanted to exclaim, but she was too staggered.

"I need to meet these young men," she

158

said, aware of the absurdity of her words. She was only a couple of years older than Kitty, and was neither girl's guardian, but she had to try to protect them from this folly.

Perhaps it would be a long time before the couples could afford to marry.

"Do Fred and Zeb have a trade?"

"Oh, yes, miss! They're cousins, see, and their fathers have a coach-making business that'll be the lads' one day, so they're well set, and as Zeb's mother's dead, and Fred's is a bit of an invalid because of an illness she took a year back, they need help in the house."

"In other words, all these men want is free servants! Don't you see that?"

Kitty giggled, then quickly stifled it with her hands, but her eyes were full of amusement. Bella's cheeks heated. The girl was laughing at her!

Kitty sobered. "Oh, I'm ever so sorry, miss, but . . ." Her lips quivered again. "It'd be a lot simpler to hire a housekeeper, wouldn't it? It's us they want, miss, which is why the lads broached the matter again."

"Again?"

"Fred asked me over a year ago, miss, but with Father as he was, I couldn't, and I didn't know when I could, so I sent him off as if I didn't want him at all. So when times were hard, I couldn't ask for help, could I? Ever so cross about that, he is. But now we've sorted everything out."

Bella sighed. "I don't approve, Kitty, for I've seen many examples of the sufferings women endure in marriage, but I cannot prevent it if you're set on it. Please don't rush, however."

"Oh, we'd never leave you in the lurch, miss! Don't you worry."

Bella decided Lady Fowler's might be a haven after all, and hurried off there. It wasn't, however, and she made an excuse to leave at two o'clock. As she walked the two streets home, she accepted that part of her impulse to meet Orion Hunt grew out of Kitty's startling news.

If her maids could dally with young men, so could she!

As soon as she was home, she asked, "Kitty, do you know how I could quickly acquire a new gown?"

"Quickly, ma'am? I'd think you'd have to go to a rag shop. I mean, where used clothes are sold. They're not all rags. It's just what people call them."

"Really? Where do the clothes come from?"

"Servants, mostly, miss. Ladies often give

160

their maids their castoffs, and the gowns aren't always something the maid could or would use, so they sell them to a rag shop."

"Am I being unkind by not having castoffs for you?" Bella asked.

Kitty smiled. "You could never be unkind to me, miss. Not after what you did for me and Annie."

"I found two treasures, that is all. Do you know a rag shop? A good one."

"Good, miss? What sort of gown do you want?"

Bella considered. "One suitable for Kelano by day. I'll wear that wig too. Can you style it to go under a hat?"

"Yes, miss, I think so." But Kitty looked worried. "Oh, miss, whatever are you up to now?"

Bella swiveled to smile at her. "Just another little adventure." She hurried on before Kitty could ask more. "I won't be able to wear a mask, but I don't want to be recognized as either Bellona Flint or Bella Barstowe." She turned back to consider herself in the mirror. "I'll darken my brows again to match the hair, and redden my lips and cheeks. I think that will do. My features aren't distinctive. So, can you discover a suitable rag shop? And without telling Mistress Gussage. She'd worry."

"She'd give you a piece of her mind, and perhaps she should. You're not doing anything dangerous, are you, miss?"

"No, truly. I mislaid something at the Olympian Revels and want to retrieve it."

"Oh, miss! Are you sure that's wise, miss? What if you're recognized?"

"Hence the disguise," Bella said, facing her maid and speaking firmly. "So please let me know when you discover the right place to purchase my new gown."

Kitty ran off, which gave Bella time to rethink, but she blocked caution. For months now she'd been content to be hidden and safe, but the masquerade had cracked something, had opened a door. She could not resist walking through.

Kitty soon returned with the name of a place from a maid in a nearby house, and they went off together to explore.

They found Lowell Lane, a narrow side street, and walked along seeking Mistress Moray's, Dressmakers, a better label than "rag shop," and apparently the lady paid top price for fine goods and was clever at making over and refurbishing her stock. They arrived at the place, which was identified by a painted sign between the green-painted door and a narrow, rectangular window. A mobcapped woman could be seen sewing by what little light she had there.

When Bella went in, a bell tinkled on the door and the woman rose, putting aside her work and removing spectacles. She was middle-aged and solid, with shrewd eyes that noted Bella's dull garments and speculated. She bobbed a curtsy and asked how she could help them.

Looking down the long, narrow room, which was lined with shelves of clothing and smelled of old sweat and perfumes, Bella sensed a ghostly presence of former owners.

Perhaps that was why she felt ill at ease. She'd not purchased anything fashionable in five years, and before then she'd gone to a mantua maker, chosen a design and fabric, returned for fittings and all such bother. She had no idea how to go on here.

"I need a fashionable day gown, ma'am. What do you have that will fit?"

The woman eyed her again, then said, "Come with me," and led the way briskly to some shelves to the right. "This is a very nice gown, and likely in your size."

She took down something brown and spread it on the central table. It was a gown much like the one Bella was wearing, though of finer cloth and lower in the neckline.

"My apologies, Mistress Moray. I didn't make myself clear. I want a pretty, fashionable gown."

Mistress Moray looked surprised, but then her eyes twinkled. "And so you should, ma'am, young as you are."

She surveyed the shelves, then went to a different one and took down a cream dress sprigged with pink flowers to spread on the table. "Pale, I know, for London wear, ma'am, but it is made of the best cotton and can be laundered. It came to me quite soiled, but I've had it washed."

Bella raised it against herself to check the length, but also to sniff at it. A very pleasant smell, thank heavens. She fingered the gown as if testing the quality of the cloth, but really because it was so pretty.

Perhaps dangerously so. What would become of her if she dressed like this again?

"That'll look lovely on you, miss," Kitty encouraged.

The shop owner had gone to another shelf and she returned with a deep pink cloak. "Wear this capuchin with it, ma'am, and you'll be as pretty as could be."

"Ooh, that's just the right color for your skin, miss," Kitty exclaimed. "Can my mistress try on the gown?" she demanded.

Bella hid amusement at this grand air.

"Yes, of course. Come with me."

The dressing room was at the back of the house and lit only by a small, high window. Bella took off her gown and put on the new one. It was a little loose in the waist and a little tight in the bodice, but it would do. Except for one thing — the exposed vee from shoulder to waist in the front that exposed her jumps and shift.

Kitty immediately left to demand stays and a stomacher.

Secondhand stays?

Once she'd owned three pairs of stays, each custom-made and covered with pretty cloth. Two had been covered with fine embroidered linen, but her evening stays had been covered in silk.

During her four years of incarceration, they'd begun to wear out and she'd had to mend them, trapping whalebone that tried to escape and putting new edging where it frayed. All part of surviving her father's attempts to break her spirit. How it had infuriated him, as had her refusal to cover her shame with marriage.

His fury had been sweet reward on its own, but the result had been a battle of wills between two people who would never bend — and, she now realized, the forging of a new person she still didn't fully understand.

Kitty returned, triumphant. "Here we go, miss. Now we'll have you decent!"

"Now you'll have me uncomfortable, you mean," Bella grumbled, but she shed the gown and went through the tedious business of putting on stays, having to straighten her shoulders and stand taller. Had she perhaps begun to slouch?

Kitty pinned a cream stomacher on the front, and Bella put the gown on.

Bella Barstowe, she thought to her fly-specked reflection. *It's been a long time since we met.*

Kitty added the pretty, hooded cloak, and a straw hat trimmed with pink apple blossoms. It suited so well, Bella wondered if clever Mistress Moray had done the trimming while they'd struggled with the stays.

"Yes," Bella said. "It will do. It will do very well."

She put on her own clothes again and went to pay. The sum was so modest, she almost protested, but she didn't want to draw too much attention to herself. Instead she purchased the brown and another blue-and-white-striped gown without even trying them on. She added two more stomachers, another hat, a fur muff and a pair of silk shoes that were pure indulgence. Whatever her life was to become, she doubted she'd be dancing in fine company.

Mistress Moray was obviously thrilled by the purchases, and Bella realized that she hadn't used her money for charitable purposes. She'd thought Lady Fowler's work was benevolent enough, but now that felt tainted by her doubts about the woman and her mission.

As they walked home, Bella said, "Kitty, you and Annie must visit Mistress Moray and choose an outfit each."

"Oh, Miss Barstowe. Thank you. Such pretty things as were there."

Bella smiled at the girl. "Consider it in lieu of the castoffs you don't get from me."

Kitty smiled back, but then asked, "What does 'loo' mean?"

"In lieu. It's French for 'instead.' "

"Oh." Bella saw her mouth it. No doubt soon Kitty would find an excuse to use her new word. She felt a pang for her futile ambitions for the girl, for she was very clever. But what was the use of being a clever woman in this world? She'd be a clever wife and mother, which would be good, but she wouldn't have any need of French.

Back at the house they experimented with the disguise. Kitty dressed the wig up while Bella painted her face. Then Bella put on the whole outfit and considered herself in the mirror.

No one who knew Bella Barstowe five years ago would recognize her, but . . .

"Could anyone recognize me as Bellona Flint?" she asked.

"I can't see how, miss, not with the wig and paint. Truly. I think you could walk by any of them at Lady Fowler's house and they'd not know you."

"Excellent." Bella took it all off, then went to her desk. Now to send a message to the goatherd.

But goats are lecherous, she remembered. She must be careful, especially with someone who called himself Orion Hunt. That meant she couldn't allow for a reply.

She wrote: *Kelano will meet Orion to retrieve her stars at noon tomorrow.*

If he had any notion of a nighttime tryst, he'd be disappointed. Bella had no intention of plunging so deeply into danger, even if she couldn't resist dipping her toe into the pool. She was deathly tired of being serious and sober, and she wanted to meet the goatherd again very, very much. To banter with him, flirt with him, and perhaps, yes, kiss him again.

To be a pretty young woman again.

To be Bella.

CHAPTER 9

Bella approached the Goat the next day with butterflies inside. Some were excitement, but others fluttered a warning. Peg might have guessed the real nature of the meeting, but if so, she'd not protested. Peg approved of anything that took Bella away from Flint and Fowler. She also completely supported Annie's and Kitty's marriages, and was busy planning their wedding breakfast.

Bella stopped to frown at the narrow, three-story inn, losing her nerve. Her whole life was spinning out of control again, and coming here could only make it worse. The goatherd was bound to see it as encouragement, perhaps even as her agreeing to a wicked liaison.

She couldn't turn back now, however, without being eaten up by curiosity.

She gathered herself and walked confidently toward the Goat.

It wasn't as large or as busy as the nearby Star and Garter, but it showed no sign of being a sink of depravity, and the people going in and out looked respectable. Bella touched her face, pointlessly trying to assure herself that her dark brows and reddened cheeks and lips were in place, and then walked through the door.

"I am here to visit Mr. Hunt," she told a manservant, with as much sangfroid as she could muster. She saw the look he gave her, and realized that he took her for a whore. She almost protested, but that would only draw attention to herself. Instead she was grateful to hurry after him down a corridor to a door.

He knocked. A voice said, "Enter."

The servant opened the door. Heart thundering, Bella went in. She heard the door close behind her, but was staring at the man who awaited her.

A footman. In livery and powder. A masked footman to boot. The mask was in the Venetian style and made to resemble an animal — in this case, a goat. It covered only the top half of his face, but the nose jutted out to shadow the mouth and jaw.

A footman, though?

She'd liked the idea that the goatherd wasn't one of the elite, that he might even have been an interloper like herself, but a gentleman. To tryst with such a one was adventurous. To tryst with an upstart foot-man was merely tawdry.

"My stars?" she demanded coolly.

He silently gestured to a cardboard box on the table close to him.

"A mute goat?" she queried, going forward cautiously.

"Perhaps simply frugal with words."

She paused, assessing the voice. The mask muffled it, but as at the revels, she detected no trace of a lower accent. Not a footman.

"Why the disguise?" she asked.

"I could ask the same of you."

"I'm not in disguise," she lied, satisfied to have scored her point. He hadn't denied the disguise.

"You usually paint so heavily?" he asked.

"It's fashionable. For men as well as women."

"Most especially for those who seek to hide the ravages of time. Are you really so old, Kelano?" When she didn't answer, he shrugged. "I grant you, court makes its demands, and both men and women wear painted masks for that performance."

And you go to court, Bella thought. It rang through the way he spoke about it, but also, now that she thought of it, in his stance. A good footman stood tall, but this man had the easy elegance of high birth, of being trained in deportment from his first steps.

That made him especially dangerous. He was here in disguise to ruin a silly young thing.

"If you please, sir, move away from the table."

"Why?"

"It would be foolish for me to go so close to you."

"Then why," he asked, amused, "are you here?"

"To retrieve my stars."

"They are tinsel and paste and not even worth a shilling."

"Perhaps I have a fondness for them."

"Try another excuse."

"I don't have to try anything," she said tartly, and found the willpower to turn and walk to the door.

"Kelano."

The word stopped her, and she turned back.

"I harbor hopes that you came in order to meet me again."

Bella considered him. It was true, after all, and something did hum in the air between them. Something special.

"Perhaps I did," she admitted. "But I have

encountered not goatherd but goat."

"And I have encountered not nymph but Harpy. Why the paint?"

"I could hardly come here as myself, likely to be recognized."

"Ah. So you would be recognized in your natural form."

"Anyone can be recognized anywhere, if only by their shoemaker."

"I suspect shoemakers remember only feet. You're not willing to trust me with your name?"

"No more than you are willing to trust me with yours." But Bella was struggling not to smile. It had been so long, so long, since she'd crossed verbal swords with a quick-witted man.

"You came here to meet Orion Hunt," he said.

"A person no more real than Kelano. Why did you seek this meeting?"

"I wished to encounter you again, but I've failed. This isn't you."

"Nor was Kelano."

"But closer, I think."

"What of you?" she demanded. "Which is closer to the truth, goatherd or goatish footman?"

Even in the shadow of the goat's nose she could see the smile. "The goatherd, I assure you, but I could hardly walk through London in that costume."

The image tempted her to smile back. "What need had you to disguise yourself?"

"What need had you?"

"I told you. A lady alone, meeting a gentleman. If it became known, I could be ruined. Would you be ruined if anyone discovered you were here with me?"

He picked up the box. "That would depend on your definition of ruined. Such a discovery could ruin my life."

"How?"

"If you come from a respectable family, I might be compelled to marry you."

That caused an extraordinary jolt of sensations that Bella had no time to analyze, for he came forward and offered the box.

She snatched it, feeling like a nervous bird offered a seed.

Her wariness was justified. He caught her left wrist, trapping her. Wild sensations shot along her arm, and some thrilled her, but for the most part she was afraid. She pulled back. "Let me go."

"In a moment."

At his tone, Bella shivered head to toe. "Don't, please. . . ."

"I won't hurt you. I merely want a reward. A kiss would be a fair fee for the return of your trinket, but alas, my mask means it can only be on your hand." His voice had deepened so that it seemed to hum over her skin, making Bella aware even of the air she inhaled. "You will permit?" he asked, almost in a whisper.

He didn't wait for her answer — she remembered that about him — but switched his hold and slowly raised her gloved fingers.

Again, she noted courtly grace, and it was as dangerous as a sword sliding out of a scabbard. Her goatherd was no footman, and had definitely not been an interloper at the Olympian Revels. He was one of the powerful. If she fled this room screaming, her clothes half torn off her, it would all be hushed up.

She had no family to protest or protect her. She was alone in the world and for the first time completely aware of the danger of that. What a fool she'd been to come here!

She tried to pull her fingers free, but he had her trapped as he brought her hand beneath the mask, into the goat's maw.

Watching her, his eyes glittered.

Enjoying her fear?

Bella made herself relax. She even managed a slight smile. "I remember that goats don't eat meat."

Perhaps those eyes truly smiled, and then

she felt teeth on her fingertips. The jolt was visceral, deeply disturbing.

Yes, he smiled. She could imagine his grinning mouth, her fingertips between his teeth.

His teeth released her and she felt the pressure of his lips on the back of her fingers. She should scarcely be able to feel it through leather, but she shuddered deep inside, where she still churned.

And not with fear.

"I wish . . ." How had that escaped her?

"You wish what, bright star?"

As prosaically as she could, she said, "I wish I knew who you are."

He lowered her hand, but kept control of it. "If you tell me, I'll tell you."

"Why would it be difficult for you?"

"Why would it be difficult for you?"

"Everything is more difficult for a woman." Bella pulled her hand free and was embarrassed to find his grip had not been compelling after all. She took a step away.

"Perhaps not quite everything. Women, for example, are not required to fight."

"But suffer just as much if caught up in warfare."

He inclined his head. "A wife is not personally responsible for her debts. Are you married?"

The question was slid in so deftly that Bella almost answered. Instead she said, "Does it matter?"

"An angry husband might call me out. Another danger."

"An angry husband would horsewhip a footman. Or even murder him with society's blessing."

"Is our world as wild as that?"

"Yes."

"You might be correct, but a clever husband would wait a little and dispatch me secretly. He'd probably beat his errant wife. Are you an errant wife, Kelano?"

Bella frantically sought the right answer. Would claiming to be married provide protection, or would being unmarried be safer, because then she might be someone he might be forced to marry?

And why was the idea of being forced to marry this man so shockingly enticing?

"What of you?" she demanded sharply, taking another step backward toward the door. "Are you married?"

"No, but please don't think me inexperienced in the necessary skills."

"Not for a single moment, sir." Bella's face went so hot she feared her paint would melt.

He only smiled. "Thank you. I lay all my experience at your feet, my star. If not today, will you meet me again?"

"No! And I certainly would never meet you at night."

"A word of warning, sweet nymph: night is not necessary for sin."

Bella knew her eyes had widened. Knew she should run away. Now. Yet she seemed glued. Rooted.

"You would enjoy my sinful skills, Kelano. That is a promise."

Bella took another step back and came up against something. She hoped it was the door. "I would never be so foolish," she said, groping behind her for the handle.

"Yet you are here. Did you truly come to retrieve a few pennies' worth of ornament?" When she had no reply, he smiled. "If you return tomorrow at noon, I will be here awaiting you. As will be the bed."

He gestured toward it with courtly grace and an extraordinarily beautiful hand. The strength of that hand shook her conviction that he was an aristocrat, but everything else about it said wealth and pampered high birth. . . .

Temptation almost drowned her, but the very power of the danger threw her into a panic that allowed her to break free. Unwilling to take her eyes from danger for a moment, she found the handle, pressed it and escaped.

Bella ran down the corridor, but managed to halt before turning into the entrance hall. To run through it would be to invite seizure as a thief, but her heart was galloping even if her feet weren't. She looked back, fearing pursuit, but the corridor was empty.

She hurried, but attempting to hide her urgency, and emerged onto Pall Mall, alert for lurking danger there. Might he have people on guard?

Once outside, she looked around, fearing some sort of trap or pursuit, but no one stopped her, so she turned into a side street and paused a moment to collect herself.

She'd escaped. That man didn't know who she was, and she certainly wouldn't return tomorrow. Strength allowing. She'd thought she'd encountered attractive men, and even some wickedly appealing ones, but she'd never encountered anyone like him. At the revels and again today he seemed able to overcome her will, to entrance her like a fey prince.

Her steps sped as she hurried home, hurried back to the safety of Bellona Flint, whom no man would attempt to seduce into a sin-drenched daytime bed. She was still clutching the box. She tossed it in the gutter to see it immediately snatched by a street

179

urchin who appeared out of a crevice and darted back again like a spider.

Bella pitied the child, but there were so many like him. She realized she hated London. She hated its dirt, its overwhelming mass of people, many of them penniless, its politics and scheming. . . .

A man called out something lewd, and she realized she was near St. James's Street, where men had their clubs. She turned again, trying to get her bearings for Soho, looking around for a hackney cab or chair stand. She knocked against a man, or he knocked against her. She flinched away, but he was already stepping back, bowing slightly in apology.

Bella nodded to the fashionably dressed gentleman, but then stared. She knew that rough-skinned, pockmarked face. "You!" she exclaimed.

He retreated even more. "Ma'am?"

Bella opened and shut her mouth, fighting for coherent speech. On top of everything else today, this.

"You," she said again, low and fierce now. "You stole me from Carscourt and carried me to Dover." She stepped forward, the question that had tormented her for years boiling out of her. "Why? Why!"

As she advanced, he retreated, hissing,

180

"Not so loud, dammit."

Bella stopped, aware of people nearby pausing to pay attention. She no more wanted attention than he did, but she wanted answers — she wanted to know why her life was such a disaster — and it seemed fate had placed answers before her. Perhaps she should be afraid of Coxy, but at this moment she felt like a wolf with prey in its sights. All the same, she tried to relax, to look as if this were some sort of normal conversation.

"What a surprise to encounter you, sir," she said.

He also relaxed, looking her up and down with a sneer, as if he were the wolf. "I heard you'd fled your family, Miss Barstowe. I confess to being pleased to see a Barstowe brought low."

He too thought her a whore, but she couldn't care for that. "If I am, it is your doing, you worm. Tell me why you abducted me."

"Why should I?"

Bella stepped closer. "Because if you don't, I will throw a scene here that will never be forgotten. I will ruin you just as effectively as you ruined me."

He saw the wolf now. He said, "You wouldn't. . . ." But his eyes shifted around to see who was nearby.

"I will," Bella said. "What have I to lose?"

"You want to know?" he snarled. "I'll tell you then, and willingly, but not here."

"If you imagine I would go anywhere with you . . ."

"Not private," he muttered, looking around again, "but just walk with me. And try to look less like a clawed Harpy."

Bella laughed at that, a harsh laugh, but she turned and walked down the street, attempting a normal air for those who were curious. Her heart had been pounding for so long she felt light-headed, but one clear thought obsessed her: in a moment, she'd know. It wouldn't repair anything — nothing could — but she would know.

"It was your brother's doing, Miss Barstowe."

Bella stopped to glare at him. "Don't lie to me."

" 'Pon my word, it's the truth. The cause of your ruin was Augustus Barstowe, now Sir Augustus Barstowe, pillar of the community."

Bella walked on, struggling with the idea. "What could he have to do with you?"

"Everything. He lost a great deal of money to me at cards. And refused to pay."

Bella managed not to stop, but she scoffed.

"Saint Augustus? Gaming? You must think me a complete fool."

"He hoodwinked you too, did he? Believe me or not, as you like."

In a day of extraordinary things, here was another, but for some reason she believed this hated man. Looking fiercely ahead, she said, "Tell me."

CHAPTER 10

"Your brother lost money to me and refused to pay. Do you know that gaming debts are not legally collectible?"

"I didn't."

"You see why I had to take measures. I threatened to tell your father. That usually works with young men one way or another. Your brother insisted that even if informed, your father would never pay gaming debts, and that he simply didn't have the funds. A sneaky specimen, your brother. He pointed out that if I told his father about his gaming, Sir Edwin would stop his allowance, which would make it even less possible for him to pay, and also that his father was a stern magistrate who might bring charges against me for illegal dice games. In effect, he claimed there was nothing I could do, and smirked about it."

"That," said Bella, "I can believe. But . . . gaming. I had no idea. I don't think anyone did. Or does now. Does he still play?"

"He's an addict, Miss Barstowe, so yes, he plays. He avoids me, however, and I him."

Bella walked on, trying to absorb this extraordinarily different view of reality. Augustus had always been the virtuous one, grieving sorrowfully over every little sin of his sisters, but especially over Bella's, because she was the one who wasn't afraid of him.

Clearly she should have been.

To imagine him a secret gamester was difficult, and yet it fit with her deeper knowledge of him and his heartlessness.

"But why did you punish me?" she asked.

"Not punishment, Miss Barstowe. Trade. I'm not a man to be brushed aside, but inquiries revealed that your brother had told the truth about your father. Sir Edwin was so opposed to gaming that he'd see his son known as a man who didn't pay his gaming debts rather than give me a penny."

"Then why didn't you ruin Augustus instead of me?" Bella demanded.

"Because that wouldn't have produced my money. Abducting you, I thought, would."

"I think you're mad."

"Bad, Miss Barstowe, but not mad, except in thinking that any parent would pay the fairly modest sum of six hundred guineas to

185

have their daughter safely returned to them."

"The ransom amount," she said. "But how did Augustus contrive to lose so much?"

"Very easily. As I said, a quite minor debt at the gaming tables."

Bella knew that was true, for gaming losses lay beneath some of the tragic stories that came Lady Fowler's way. Men had lost their entire fortunes in a night. She'd always had trouble believing it, but apparently she was a victim of gaming herself.

"So you abducted me to get the ransom? Why, then, did my family know nothing of a ransom? They were convinced that I'd run off with a man and been abandoned."

"There, I made a serious miscalculation," Coxy said. "I used your brother as my intermediary."

"Augustus knew of this plan?"

"Miss Barstowe, he was the designer of it. He told us where to make the assignation, and he was to find the note left there, and give it to your father. I assumed your brother would see that the plan served his interests. Instead, he destroyed it and said nothing."

Bella stopped to stare at him. "He did what?"

The man met her eyes, and though he was

a hard-bitten, wretched individual, she saw truth. She also understood why he was telling her this. Even after all these years, he was still angry over the way Augustus had twisted his plan.

Anger churned in her too, and more than anger. Her innards lurched with revulsion, and she covered her mouth, fearing to be sick. She realized they were on a quieter street now with no one about, but she wasn't afraid. She was too consumed with horror and fury.

"Dear heavens, why? I never liked Augustus and he never liked me, but . . . how could he abandon me to such a fate?"

"He's never explained his actions to me, Miss Barstowe. At the time, he convinced me that he'd delivered the note and your father had torn it up, which is why I was compelled to act on the alternative and carry you south with a mind to selling you."

Bella turned her back to stare at black railings in front of a brick house. "I can't believe you. No one can be so vile. More likely that he gave the letter to Father, and Father refused to pay."

"Your father was that callous? But even if so, why did your father treat you as he did when you returned?"

Bella swallowed acid bile. "Guilt?"

But she didn't believe it. She'd disliked her father for his rigid morality and unforgiving nature, but he would never have done anything so obviously wrong. He'd have punished her for her folly in agreeing to a clandestine meeting, and done his best to have her abductors hanged, but he would have paid her ransom.

Augustus.

Augustus had left her to her ruin. She remembered the way he'd treated her all the years of her confinement, as if he were the long-suffering saint and she the dreadful sinner. She'd learned that he'd even cast her leaving Carscourt in the worst possible light, letting slip to neighbors that his poor sister had run off with another man. She wanted to wrench one of the spear-tipped railings free and drive it through his rotten heart.

She turned back, eyeing the man beside her. "I'm to believe that you let him get away with this? That you never received your money?"

He smiled, showing a broken tooth. "I see you understand me, Miss Barstowe. Your brother paid me when your father died."

"You waited for three years after my escape? When you could have gone to my father with the whole story? Which would have exonerated me!"

"You were never my concern, and Sir Edwin was not a man I wanted to tangle with. In addition, I'd been warned off."

"By Augustus?"

A curled lip showed he had the same opinion of that. "By your rescuer. Captain Rose left a message telling me to leave you alone. I learned that he too was not a man to tangle with."

Captain Rose. The hazy image of Bella's nightmares and her dreams. A tall, dark man in an old-fashioned frock coat, a scarlet neckcloth, and with a skull for an earring. A man who had produced knife and pistol as if by magic, and faced down five murderous wretches, not to mention Coxy.

She'd long since locked away that period of her life, but how extraordinary that he'd tried to protect her, even after she'd stolen his horse.

Thinking it through, she turned back. "Did you have anything to do with my brother's broken hand?"

A sour smiled twisted Coxy's lips. "I have a reputation to protect. He had an unpleasant encounter with some ruffians one night."

Bella remembered when Augustus had been attacked and had his purse stolen.

She'd still been protesting her innocence and refusing to marry Squire Thoroughgood when Augustus had returned from a visit to London with a bruised face and a broken left hand. The bones hadn't healed straight, creating that slightly clawlike appearance. He'd turned even more vicious toward her then, though he'd cloaked it in sanctimonious condemnation.

"After that," the man said, "he was positively eager to pay me a small amount every month, and as I said, he paid the whole amount with interest when he inherited. It was a pleasant surprise to have to wait only three years to be done with it all. Did your father truly die of an intestinal rupture?"

Bella stared at him. "You think . . . ?"

"I merely wonder. When a death is so very convenient . . ."

She put a hand to her mouth, finally accepting the full horror of it all.

Augustus was a gamester.

He had always known she was innocent.

He had always known that her plight was entirely his fault, and yet he'd been so harsh to her.

And he might have killed their father. That was mere speculation, but after what she'd learned it seemed possible.

When her brother had inherited, he could

have set her free. Instead, he'd tightened her restrictions, and she now saw why. It had been spite, because he held her responsible for his pain and deformity.

She turned to ask another question, but the man — Coxy — had gone. She saw him in the distance, pausing to speak to some other gentleman. She could pursue and make the threatened scene, but he was no longer her worst enemy.

Her worst enemy, the cause of her destruction, was her brother, Augustus.

She hurried home, the ramifications swirling in her mind, then halted when she saw a new horror. Augustus planned to marry, and to marry a sweet, young innocent.

Peg received news from a friend in Cars Green, and the latest letter had been all to do with Sir Augustus's wooing of Miss Langham from Hobden Hall. Bella had felt uncomfortable with the idea, but only because her brother was cold. It would be a good marriage for Miss Langham in the world's eyes, for her father was a newcomer to gentry circles, having made money in trade. Fine imported leathers, Bella thought.

When Bella had been seventeen, Charlotte had still been in the schoolroom, but she'd attended some casual social affairs with her parents. She'd seemed shy, quiet, and eager to please, and even now she couldn't be older than eighteen.

She saw a rank of sedan chairs and summoned one. As it carried her back to her Soho house, she made herself consider that Coxy had been lying, but his casual honesty about his own villainy made him credible, and his version of events did make sense. Even her father, harsh and rigid though he had been, would not have left his daughter in the hands of bad men for lack of six hundred guineas.

On the other hand, Augustus would go to desperate measures to hide his sins. If Father had found out, Augustus, not she, would have ended up limited to Carscourt without a penny of his own. Their father might not have told everyone in the neighborhood the nature of his heir's sin, but everyone would know it had to be terrible. Word would spread and he'd never be able to claim moral superiority again.

Why he should care so desperately about that, she had no idea, but he did. Some men lived easily with scandalous reputations — like the Duke of Ithorne, for example, and his cousin, the Earl of Huntersdown. The Marquess of Rothgar and his family were the same, and it wasn't simply a matter of high rank. They didn't care what lesser mortals thought of them.

Augustus wasn't of that type. Without his moral superiority, he'd be naked. For the first time, she appreciated the rakes for their lack of hypocrisy. Her brother, her vile, deceiving, hypocrite of a brother, was a far worse man.

And she was going to have to do something about him. She was going to have to prevent the marriage, but it couldn't stop there. He must never ruin another young life.

But how?

She was home. She climbed out of the chair, paid the men, and entered the house, brushing by Kitty's anxious questions.

Kitty pursued. "But where are the stars, miss?"

Bella came fully to the present. Stars? "Oh, the ornament. Ah. I threw it away. It was crushed."

Because she'd been in such a panic about Orion.

Orion Hunt, whoever he was, was nothing.

"Shall I try to find them, miss?"

"What? That trinket? No. Stop chattering, Kitty. I need to think. Tea in my room, now."

Bella hurried upstairs, unpinning both hat and wig as she went.

When she glanced in the mirror, she realized that Coxy would never have recognized her if she'd not accosted him, but she didn't regret the encounter. At long last she knew the truth.

No wonder he'd sneered at her. The red of her lips and the dark of her brows had smudged. She grabbed a cloth and tried to wipe it all off, but her attention was still fixed on Augustus and the necessity of action.

As she cooled and came back to reality, she flinched from that; she couldn't live with this knowledge and do nothing.

She wished she had the courage to simply kill him. She did own a pistol, and knew how to use it.

Buying the pistol had been one of her first acts when she'd been set free. She'd always remembered the feeling of holding the gun back in the Black Rat. She hadn't known how to use it then, and it had been heavy and awkward in her hands, but she'd felt its power. She'd seen the way rough, dangerous men backed away when she was armed, and she'd wanted that power again.

It had taken courage to visit the very masculine world of a gunsmith's and buy a pistol. Probably Bella Barstowe couldn't have done it, but Bellona Flint could. She'd arranged for private lessons early in the morning at an establishment where men practiced their shooting. She returned every week to fire a few shots, and she kept her pistol in perfect order. She would never be so wantonly vulnerable again.

She doubted she could kill anyone, even Augustus, however, especially in cold blood.

She attacked the face paint anew, remembering what Coxy had said about Captain Rose. How astonishing that he'd done his best to protect her.

He'd affected her life in so many ways. First by rescuing a stranger, then by showing her the power of a gun. He'd worked with her as a partner in the stables, trusting her to do the right thing.

Perhaps without that time with him, she might not have found the resolution to refuse an intolerable marriage. Without the seeds sown then, she might not have had the strength to build a new life.

If only he were here now to strengthen her again . . .

She laughed at herself. As well wish for Oberon the Fairy King.

Kitty came in with the tea tray. "Why, miss, whatever's the matter?"

Bella smoothed her expression. "Nothing, Kitty, except this paint. It won't come off."

"You need hot water and soap, miss. I'll fetch it."

Kitty left, and Bella stared blindly at her own reflection. . . .

Could Clatterford help her? She knew he'd be as outraged as she at the story, but was it something the law could address? Even if they could find Coxy again, they'd never get him to testify in court. Given that, she'd better not mention it at all, for she feared she'd have to break some laws before the deed was complete.

She wanted to ruin Augustus as he had ruined her. She sat up straighter. Could that be her revenge? Simply revealing that he was a gamester might be shriveling enough for a man such as him. It wouldn't completely satisfy the ferocious anger inside her, but it would damage her brother's reputation and save Charlotte Langham.

How to achieve even that, however?

Lady Fowler might include his shame in her letter if there was proof. If not, perhaps Bella could circulate her own account of his sins. But first she needed proof, and she had no idea how to get it.

Where did men play dice and cards away from the eyes of people who knew them? She wished she'd forced such details out of Coxy. How could someone like herself — a young, inexperienced woman — invade such a place and then expose what went on to public scorn?

She remembered Captain Rose. Now, there was a man who doubtless knew. He was probably a gamester himself and knew all about a gamester's haunts, but she viewed her mind's path with alarm. No, she couldn't go to Dover in search of a man she'd met so briefly four years ago.

She saw no other plan, however, and she must do something or go mad.

As soon as she accepted the plan, an amazing calm settled around her. It brought a certainty she'd experienced only once before — when she'd decided she must escape from that room in Dover at all costs.

That had gone against her instinct to wait to be rescued and she'd had to overcome a powerful fear of climbing down so far, but she'd done it, and it had definitely been for the best.

Because of the help of Captain Rose.

She poured herself tea and drank it, making clear plans.

She must leave as soon as possible. Her purpose did not allow for delay.

She thought it took about twelve hours to travel to Dover, but it was a good road with frequent coaches, some of which traveled through the night. She would do that and be there tomorrow.

She suddenly remembered the Goat and the goatherd who might return tomorrow, full of lascivious hopes. All the more reason to leave Town, though he and his tempting ways had shrunk to a speck of importance beside her need to ruin Augustus.

Was her brother also a seducer of innocents? A drunkard? Now that she knew of one vice, she suspected there were many others.

Kitty came in with the hot water.

"Pack for me, Kitty. I'm going to Dover."

Kitty almost dropped the jug. "Dover, miss?"

"Yes, Dover, and as soon as may be. Have Annie purchase me an inside seat on the earliest possible fly."

"Just you, miss?"

Bella was caught off guard. A lady would take her maid on such a journey, but she didn't want Kitty with her. The girl would worry, and Bella would worry about her. This enterprise could be dangerous.

"Just me," she said firmly. "I'll be perfectly safe on a public coach, and there'll be inn servants to assist me as necessary. Many women travel alone that way."

"Not ladies of your status, miss."

"My status is not so very high."

As she'd hoped, Kitty didn't feel sure enough of her ground to argue.

"I'll clean my face while you pack, and I'm going as Bella, not Bellona. I'll travel in one of Bellona's gowns because they're practical, but pack the ones we bought from Mistress Moray."

"And the stays, miss?" Kitty asked hopefully.

"And the stays," Bella conceded, pretending a sigh.

She had to wear stays and more fashionable gowns, because Captain Rose would expect someone similar to the young lady he'd rescued, but she couldn't regret it. A few short months ago she'd scurried into hiding as Bellona Flint, fearing casual recognition, but also wanting to look plain and older so as to fit in with Lady Fowler's set. As Kelano she'd had a taste of being herself, and it had changed everything. Bellona felt like a prison, but Bella felt like a pair of comfortable shoes after a time in ones that pinched.

She realized something else.

Bella, not Bellona, should wreak havoc on Sir Augustus Barstowe.

Augustus.

The cause of all her troubles, and with

not a scrap of shame or compassion in him.

Bella Barstowe would see him in hell — she swore it — even if she had to join him there.

Thorn had taken off his mask as soon as the mysterious Kelano left, and put it in a valise, which he was now carrying home, simply another footman on an errand. In the livery of dark blue with silver braid, and wearing a powdered wig, he was virtually invisible in fashionable London, and being invisible was a luxury.

He sometimes played the footman simply to escape for an hour or so from being the damned Duke of Ithorne. Captain Rose was a better escape, but he hadn't put on that disguise in months now. He wasn't sure how long he could hold out.

He had gone out on the *Black Swan,* but as the owner, the duke, he'd had to be rather distant with men he drank and rollicked with as Rose. It wasn't the same.

Thorn watched a flock of grubby lads race by, involved in some game that made sense to them alone. He didn't envy them, but he wished he'd had a time when he hadn't been a duke.

Even George, king of England, had known childhood and youth without the ultimate burden, but there'd been no such mercy for Thorn. His earliest memories involved people saying, "Come along to bed, Your Grace," or "Drink your milk, Your Grace."

He shrugged. As with the king, there was no escape save death. He only prayed there were no titles and ranks in heaven.

A wench with dark hair made him pause, but of course it wasn't Kelano.

Who knew why one woman sparked desire in a man whilst another — as pretty, as charming, as alluring — did not? He knew only that it happened, and he hadn't been able to get Kelano out of his mind. He wasn't sure if he'd hoped this encounter would end in bed, or cure him of a passing folly, but it had done neither. Her clever resistance only made the chase more interesting.

He should have set people to watch and follow, but he'd assumed they'd either come to good terms and she'd reveal her true self, or he'd find her charms vanished by daylight. Now she was tangling his mind, and would do so until he'd solved the mystery.

A foolish young woman aware of walking into a trap, but with wit and steel beyond her years. Would she return tomorrow? Would he? She could be setting a very clever marriage trap. Nearly everyone at the revels had either instantly known his identity or been told.

Wiser to let her slip away.

He entered his mansion by the back door, as a footman should, and snatched a jam tart from the kitchen table as he passed by. His pastry cook shouted and waved a fist, but then recognized him. The man still shook his head.

Thorn went up the back stairs and through the plain door to the luxurious ducal realm. In his rooms he stripped off the wig and livery and Joseph took charge of it.

"It went well, sir?" Joseph asked.

"Neither well nor not well," Thorn said carelessly, running his comb through his hair.

Joseph passed him a fresh shirt. He was not a chatterer, but was a very good listener.

"She was less light and flighty than at the revels," Thorn said as he fastened the five buttons. "I admit to disappointment."

"Perhaps she simply wanted her trinket back, sir." Joseph held out brown breeches.

"It's a nothing and she treated it as such. On reflection, however, I don't dislike her restraint. It makes the game much more interesting."

"Always, sir," said the valet, reflecting Thorn's slight smile, but adding, "As long as it's not a dangerous game."

"The dangerous ones are the best sort," Thorn protested with a grin, "but I'm trying to be good."

He was soon dressed for a time of working, in plain waistcoat and jacket.

As he slid on the ducal signet ring, Thorn decided that yes, he was pleased Kelano hadn't proved to be a strumpet. Lovers were easy to find. Intriguing, quick-witted challenges were scarce. He would return tomorrow.

Joseph produced a soft, lace-edged cravat. "You haven't discovered who she was, sir?"

"No." Thorn tied it and fixed it with a plain gold pin. "She wasn't any lady on the list, but people bring friends who happen to be in Town, as long as they're of high enough station."

He tied his hair back with a simple ribbon, remembering his exchange with Kelano about face paint. He was glad no looming court visit required him to use any now.

"Some men bring lowborn ladies, of course, but they keep close to them. I wondered at the time if she was one of the theater group, but they have no knowledge of her."

He surveyed himself in the mirror to be

sure nothing was out of place, and approved.

"She's a mystery, Joseph, and I intend to enjoy her, but the work is doubtless piling up and I must return to harness."

CHAPTER 11

The long journey on a full coach gave Bella time to think.

Tangling with Captain Rose was rash, but she knew no one else who might help her. And yes, she admitted, he had lived in her memory as a rescuing hero. If he proved to be a villain, she had her pistol in the small valise tucked by her feet.

No one on the coach was talkative, but they did exchange occasional comments, especially at the short, hurried breaks at inns. Bella was surprised to find that she felt odd as herself — as a soberly dressed young lady — and sometimes slipped into being Bellona, offending others.

As darkness fell, she accepted that she hated living a lie, and she particularly hated being Bellona Flint. Poor Bellona. She'd created her, and now she was going to kill her. She'd cut her connection with Lady Fowler and leave the rented house, and she and Peg would find a new home, honestly.

Sleepless darkness brought doubts, however, and she began to toy with a new identity. Someone more true to herself, but free of danger of scandal.

No. It was as if she became a little fainter, a little more smudged, with each deception. See, she no longer knew who Bella Barstowe was.

Was she the confident, flirtatious girl who'd been snatched from Carscourt so long ago?

Was she the locked-in person she'd become to survive her incarceration?

Had she become sour Bellona Flint?

No, never that.

Was she Kelano of the revels, the foolish woman who'd gone to an assignation with a man she knew to be intent on seduction? Or was that the old Bella revived, as flighty as they'd all accused her of being?

Perhaps she dozed a little, squashed in the middle between a heavyset man and a plump woman, for she woke with a start, prompted by a memory.

The stable lad at the Crown and Anchor!

She was so jolted that she was surprised no one else jerked with alarm. All was quiet, however, so she settled back. Remembering.

When they'd arrived in Dover, her captors

had callously told her their plan — to take her to Paris and sell her to a brothel. She'd fainted, and when she'd come to her senses, she'd been locked in a bedchamber at an inn. Finally, she'd accepted that no one was going to come to her aid.

The only blessing was that her passivity on the journey had blunted her captors' watchfulness. They'd locked her in, but the room had a window. It was on an upper floor, but Bella had been ready to attempt the climb, reasoning that a broken leg would bring her help, and death might truly be preferable to her fate.

She was saved from both by a passing boy. He came along the alley below, whistling and carrying a bucket, so she attracted his attention. When he gaped up at her, she softly asked if he could find a ladder. When he continued to gape, she took off her silver cross and chain and dangled it, promising it would be his if he helped her.

He stared up and said, "Are you a princess?"

Bella almost told the truth, but a fable might work better with a youth. "Yes. And I've been captured by a wicked monster who's disguised himself as a man. He could return at any moment. Please help me!"

The lad dropped his bucket and raced off,

to return struggling with a long ladder. It wasn't at all what she'd hoped for. It was a very crude affair — only cross sticks fixed to a pole. She was desperate enough to ignore that, and in any case, what did it matter? She'd never attempted to climb up or down a ladder of any kind.

It was even more frightening than she'd expected. She wouldn't have done it if the alternative hadn't been far, far worse. She wriggled her legs out over the sill, feeling for a rung and clutching to the wooden frame for dear life. Her skirts snagged on the rough wood. She was going to be a ragged mess to add to her troubles.

Finally she had a foot on a rung, but it still took every scrap of her courage to let go of the sill and trust to the wobbly pole. It creaked and swayed as she fumbled her way down, fragile rung by fragile rung.

Once on the ground she'd had to lean against the wall to recover, but she'd pulled herself together. She'd escaped, but she must get far away from the Crown and Anchor.

She'd given the lad the silver cross and chain, and it was that memory that had shocked her so. She'd worried that he'd be accused of stealing it, so she'd promised that if he kept it safe she'd return and give him the price of it. And she'd forgotten.

Everything that had happened afterward had wiped him from her mind, but he could have been transported, even hanged, in the past four years!

What a wretch she was. With all her troubles, she could have asked Lady Raddall to attend to the matter. It was a kind of debt, left unpaid, making her almost as bad as Augustus.

One thing was sure: her first act in Dover, before making the slightest inquiry about Captain Rose, must be to try to find that lad. Had he given her a name?

Her mind was blank, but then she remembered — she thought she remembered — Billy. It was a start, and she would find him, or she deserved no good fortune at all.

She dozed off again, but only fitfully, and dawn found her fully awake if weary, and ready for more plans. A young, unaccompanied lady needed a story to tell, especially if she were going to dally in an inn for days.

This wasn't the same as being someone else. It was merely a device.

She would use her own name, but be a governess waiting for a party due to arrive from France. Her dull Bellona gowns would support that role, as would the plainer rag-shop one. Alas, there'd be no wearing of the pretty sprigged print for a while, but it had been complete folly to bring it.

By the time the coach drew up at the Ship Inn, she was ready for her part, but she hadn't forgotten her duty to the boy who'd helped her.

She waited for her valise to be taken out of the boot, intending to ask for a room at the Ship, but when she heard another passenger ask about the Compass, she revised her plans.

The Compass was where Captain Rose had taken her, and he'd clearly been a familiar guest. As a guest there, she'd be ideally situated to learn more about him. She didn't expect Captain Rose to be at the Compass now, for he had a ship to sail, but that would suit her perfectly. She intended to find out all she could about him and make a sensible decision about whether to ask his help, and the Compass was the place for that.

A man loaded her small trunk into a cart and set off. Following behind, Bella felt almost light-headed with lack of sleep, but the sea air, made crisp by a slight September chill, woke her up. She began to enjoy being Bella Barstowe, independent and purposeful.

As she drew close to the Compass, however, her new confidence began to fail her. She'd never gone into an inn alone before. Well, she'd entered the Goat — and been taken for a whore!

Clocks struck and she realized it was noon. Was Orion Hunt waiting at the Goat? How would he react when Kelano didn't arrive? She must hope he'd lose interest. There'd be no more folly like that.

"Ma'am?"

She realized the man with her luggage was looking at her oddly, as if he feared her wits were awry. She squared her shoulders and walked on. No one could think her a whore this time, in her Bellona gown and with her hair drawn back tightly beneath cap and hat.

So it proved. She was given a room without quibble. It was a small room that looked out into a narrow alley, but what else could a governess expect? At least the maid promptly brought a jug of hot water and seemed eager to be of service.

Bella washed and unpacked, but she left the pistol case in her small valise. The maid might look in a drawer. She longed to crawl into the bed, but she must find Billy, so she set out for the Crown and Anchor. She didn't want to enter the inn, for there might be someone who could recognize the girl who'd arrived with two men. Heaven alone knew what the people there had thought of it all, but it wouldn't be to the credit of reputation. In any case, as she wanted a stable boy, she entered the busy coaching yard and caught a middle-aged man's attention.

"Billy Jakes, ma'am? Left two years ago to work for Sir Muncy Hexton, out Litten way. He do something wrong, ma'am?"

"Not at all. I was asked to give a message to him."

"A message?" said the man, much surprised, but then a laden coach rolled in and he hurried away.

Bella too hurried away before anyone grew suspicious.. Suspicious of what, she wasn't sure. But she was feeling furtive.

Memory had her retracing her flight that night, which brought her to the busy quay. She walked close to the buildings, where it was quieter, looking for the Black Rat, but she didn't see it. Perhaps it had become the Red Cock, or the Jolly Tar.

The area was as rough and pungent as she remembered, but freshened by a brisk sea breeze and sunshine, as it hadn't been that night. There'd been a mist, she remembered, cold on the skin and rendering everything ghostly.

She'd not have entered the Rat if she'd

seen it by daylight, but she'd known her captors were in pursuit and ducked into a hiding spot. . . .

Such folly. But what else could she have done?

She turned her back on the buildings and her memories to look at the boats filling the harbor. Was one the *Black Swan*? She hoped not.

Would it be painted black?

She strained to read names. The *Dotty Philips*. The *Kentish Hope*. The *Singing Willie*.

She walked on, but when she saw the harbormaster's office, she went in and asked if they kept lists of ships in the harbor. A busy clerk pointed her to two large slates on the wall on which names were written. She went over and saw one was for arrivals and one for departures. The *Black Swan* wasn't on either.

Better so, she told herself. She needed to learn a lot more about Captain Rose before making any decision. There was a saying that revenge was a dish best eaten cold. At first, right after her encounter with Coxy, she'd have gulped it down scalding hot, but she was more in control of herself now. She would have her revenge, but she would not destroy herself in the process. It must all be carefully worked out.

She returned to the Compass, considering going immediately in search of Billy Jakes, but early or not, she was simply too tired. She went up to her room and surrendered to the bed.

She slept through to the early morning. Very early. It was hardly dawn when she woke, so she didn't try to summon a servant, even though the fire had died and the room was chilly. She bundled herself in the coverlet and sat to make notes on her plans.

Her pen hung idle for a moment as she contemplated how perfect it would be if Augustus died. Dead, he could never hurt anyone again.

Alas, from cowardice or morality, she couldn't make it so. It would be wonderful to hear that he'd broken his neck, but she couldn't push him off a cliff, or even hire someone to do it.

The door opened and a scruffily dressed girl crept in. She started to see Bella awake, her bucket of coals clattering. "Oh, beggin' your pardon, miss! I've come to get the fire going."

"Please do," Bella said with a smile.

The girl hurried to the fireplace, head down as if she were trying to hide inside her large mobcap.

When the flames were licking, Bella said,

214

"Is it too early for hot water and breakfast?"

The girl's eyes were huge. "I'll tell 'em, miss. Won't be too long, I'm sure, miss. Got to go now, miss."

She backed out of the room, clearly unaccustomed to actually encountering an awake guest, poor thing, and perhaps not much over ten.

Perhaps there were useful things she could do for young girls forced into work, though that one probably thought herself fortunate to have employment.

Bella looked at her blank sheet of paper, despairing of her dithering mind. There were people at Lady Fowler's who were so sure of themselves. Lady Fowler herself, the Drummond sisters, and even sour Hortensia Sprott. At least the matter of Billy Jakes might be simple.

She dipped her pen and wrote: *Find out how far away Litten is and hire carriage if necessary.* There. A start.

Next she must tackle the subject of Captain Rose.

She dipped the pen again and wrote: *Stir gossip about R.*

She would learn about Captain Rose, his character and activities, from the servants here.

She dipped her pen and added: *Enjoy*

peaceful solitude and time to think.

This was the first time in her life that she'd been alone, with no one in authority over her, no one dependent on her, and no pressures or obligations. When she was dressed quietly, men were unlikely to pester her or even notice her. Who was more unobtrusive than a soberly dressed governess?

It was all a blessed relief.

When the hot water arrived, brought by a more senior maid, Bella established her reputation as a gossip by engaging her in general talk. She discovered Louisa had worked at the Compass for five years, first as an undermaid and then as she was now, and liked her place here.

How strange to think that Louisa had been here in 1760. Had there been any gossip among the servants about the goings-on in the stables? It would be unsafe to raise that question, however.

When Louisa returned with breakfast, Bella had her assist with the stays as a way of keeping her there a little longer.

Was Dover particularly busy at the moment?

Did the Compass have any notable guests?

Were there dangerous smugglers or pirates hereabouts?

The name Captain Rose never came up.

Before the maid left, Bella asked her about the distance to Litten and the weather forecast.

Three miles, and the day would be clear but crisp.

Bella told her she'd need a one-horse chair after breakfast, and when she went downstairs it was waiting for her. Armed with precise directions to Sir Muncy Hexton's house, where Billy Jakes worked, she set off, hoping she retained her ability to drive a simple carriage.

The horse was steady, needing little guidance, so her skills weren't challenged. As they ambled along country roads, the journey became another pleasant escape. This was so different from crowded London, and she was bothered by nothing more than the occasional bird or animal, and a few other travelers who merely exchanged good-days.

There were tranquil places in the world, and ordinary people living good, ordinary lives. It was easy to forget that.

She was a little sad when she arrived at her destination.

The modest manor house lay on the edge of the village of Litten Gorling, fronting the village street. A high wall ran backward along a lane, and Bella took that direction, seeking the stables. The lane followed the wall in a turn to the left, with laden orchards on her right and harvested fields beyond.

Ahead of her lay a stable block. She drove in, and when a young man ran out to hold her horse, Bella asked, "Are you Billy Jakes?"

He'd grown tall and filled out, but it had to be him.

He glanced at her warily, but nodded. "I am, ma'am. Can I help you?"

Bella climbed down unaided. "I'm wondering if you still have my silver cross and chain, Billy. No matter if you don't, but if you do, I'll keep my promise at last and exchange it for coin."

He stared at her and color touched his cheeks. "You're safe then, miss. Ma'am. I always wondered. Me talking that nonsense about princesses. Yes, I've your silver still." He looked troubled. "Do you truly want it back? I've thought of giving it to my Anne. We're courting," he added shyly, but with such a lovely smile that Bella envied his sweetheart. "I've not done so yet because her father'd want to know where I got it."

"You'd rather keep it than have the coin?"

"I know it's foolish, ma'am, but it's so pretty, and I still think of you as my princess. And now Anne's my princess. She deserves pretty things."

Bella felt almost tearful. "Then she should have it. What if I were to speak to Anne's father and tell him it was a reward for a great service?"

A big grin spread. "That'd be grand, ma'am! And if he accepted that as truth, no one else would question it."

"Then tell me where to find him."

"No need of that, ma'am, for here he is, coming to see what's going on. He's the head groom, ma'am. Mr. Bickleby."

Bella turned and saw a sinewy, grizzled-haired man whose queue was thin because the top of his head was completely bald.

"What's this then, Billy?" he demanded. "Why're you keeping the lady talking?"

Bella smiled. "Mr. Bickleby, please don't be angry with Billy. It is I who have kept him in conversation. In fact, I came here to speak with him."

Spiky brows lowered. "What's he done, then?"

"Been a hero," Bella said firmly.

The man bridled back. "What?"

"Perhaps I could speak to you in private, Mr. Bickleby, while Billy waters my horse?"

After some suspicious glances, the man led her into a small room. "Well, then, what's all this about, ma'am?"

Bella told him a very brief and edited version of her story. "I regret the delay in returning, but Billy did me a great service and I would be happy for him to have the chain and cross as reward and to give it to your daughter."

The man pulled another face, but he was nodding. "Aye, she'd like that. And she likes him. They're both young, but both have a steady head, and Billy's a good, honest worker."

"You may tell the story if you must, Mr. Bickleby, but I would rather my name not be attached to it."

"No trouble about that, ma'am. None of anyone else's business if I say I'm satisfied about it."

"Excellent. Thank you."

Bella turned to go, but the man said, "Are you in more trouble, ma'am?"

She turned back, stiffening.

"Begging your pardon, ma'am, but you're not that many years older than Billy and Anne, I reckon, and here you are, alone."

Bella knew he meant well, but his concern seemed to threaten her freedom. "I'm in no trouble, Mr. Bickleby, but I thank you for your kindness."

"As you say, ma'am. But it's not good to be alone, for man nor maid."

Bella almost objected again, but then she said, "No, it isn't. But sometimes it is our fate."

He looked skeptical, but didn't persist. Bella went back to where Billy was walking her horse. "All's well."

His face shone with happiness. A trite phrase, but Bella hadn't seen the effect before.

When had she ever felt so gloriously happy?

And when, if ever, would she?

She drove out back toward Dover with her vision blurred by idiotic tears. They turned into fuel for her anger at Augustus, however. By now, she might have loved and been loved by a good man if not for her vile brother.

She returned to Dover as the sun was setting, wishing Captain Rose were at the Compass, so she might be able to set out upon vengeance immediately.

When Louise came up with her supper, Bella asked — idly, she hoped — about new guests.

Only two families. Of course Captain Rose hadn't turned up.

As she drank soup and ate grilled cheese, Bella considered. She wanted to find out about Captain Rose, and she didn't want to return to her uncomfortable Bellona life in London.

She could extend her stay here to at least a week, but she'd need occupation. This might be a pleasant escape from her normal life, but she didn't like idleness, so she'd buy some cambric and make handkerchiefs. Perhaps she would give them as farewell gifts to the ladies at Lady Fowler's.

Before she went to bed, she wrote a letter to Peg, telling her all was well and not to expect a return within the week. The next morning she walked to the shops and purchased a book to read and some cambric and thread. She had her small needlework case with her, and over her years at Carscourt the simple matter of hemming handkerchiefs had become soothing.

She had another purpose as well: it gave her occupation as she sat in the small parlor provided for the use of guests. The parlor lay off the front hall, warmed by a fire and containing a few chairs and a desk at which guests could write letters.

A newspaper was placed there every day, and Bella read it, but it was always one or two days old, and the news seemed from a distant world. She tried to avoid items she'd once have noted for Lady Fowler. That part of her life was definitely over, but she did see a small section to do with the revels, informing the reader that Lord and Lady G——n were happily reconciled and en route for his lordship's family home in Devon. Bella felt happy for them, and pleased that the Fowler letter wouldn't attempt to exaggerate what had clearly been a minor drama.

One day the words "His Grace, the Duke of Ithorne" leapt out at her, but it was merely a notice that he'd attended a meeting of the patrons of the smallpox hospital. Doubtless that was something he did only out of a sense of noblesse oblige, but it made her think a little better of him.

Most of the time, she sat with her needlework and listened to comings and goings and occasional snippets of conversation. Bella enjoyed her little window on a passing world, and even heard snatches of drama — missed sailings, lost luggage, and even a case of terror of the sea — but nothing about Captain Rose.

By the third day she had a small pile of handkerchiefs and was wearying of the diversion when she heard someone say, ". . . the *Black Swan*."

She stilled, straining to hear more. She thought it was the innkeeper who replied, but he said only, "Rain comin' in."

Bella hastily folded her needlework and left the room as if returning to her own. To her annoyance, the innkeeper was already alone, but she seized the moment.

"Did I hear mention of a black swan?" she said lightly. "Does such a thing exist?"

The innkeeper bowed with cursory courtesy. "Not at all, ma'am, but perhaps that's why the name appeals to many. There are inns with the name, and even a ship."

"A ship?" Bella asked.

"Probably more than one, but there's a local version. There's a painting of it over there, ma'am." He indicated a picture on the wall.

The walls of the entrance hall were almost covered by paintings of ships, but Bella had paid them no particular attention. Now she went to look at the one indicated, but it was simply a ship to her.

"Is it famous then," she asked, "to have its portrait painted?"

The man chuckled. "Not particularly, ma'am, but I had an artist staying here a while back who couldn't pay his bill, so I provided canvas and paints and he made the pictures for me of local ships. The *Black Swan*'s master is always asking to buy that one, but I like it."

"You know him, then?" she asked, trying

to sound as if she made idle conversation, but with a thumping heart.

"He stays here when he's in town, ma'am. Now, if you'll excuse me . . ." He was off to deal with another guest before Bella could glean any more.

She lingered, pretending to study the painting but listening to a new conversation. Neither told her anything new.

Frustrated, she put on her sturdy hooded cloak and went for a walk in the blustery wind before the threatened rain arrived. She could see the building clouds, and as it was not yet noon, once the rain arrived, it would probably settle in for the day.

She took a direction away from the docks, where buildings provided a little protection from the wind, and then turned away from the main streets with their shops and inns into residential streets.

She passed old cottages and newer terraces and saw women engaged in all the daily work of looking after home and family. She paused to watch a smith beat metal into a curve for some purpose, and later saw men laying bricks for a new house.

All around her, people were busy with ordinary life. Did she have any hope of an ordinary life? She'd taken that for granted once — that she would marry, have children, and run her household. In one wild turn of the cards, it had been stolen from her, and even destroying Augustus's reputation wouldn't restore her own.

As a church bell began to ring noon, the first rain splattered. Bella turned to return to the inn, but she had to pause when a small but merry wedding party spilled out of a church onto the street, tossing grains of wheat at the blushing couple. Despite the spitting rain, the newlyweds laughed and looked into each other's eyes as if stars truly twinkled there.

The party raced off, anxious to reach shelter before their best clothes got wet, but Bella followed more slowly, tears mingling with rain.

Bella finally accepted that she wanted, desperately wanted, to marry.

With a modest fortune, even she could buy herself a husband, but she doubted he would be a choice specimen. For heaven's sake, she'd suffered four years of imprisonment rather than make a bad marriage, and many of the women she'd met at Lady Fowler's were testaments to the destructive power of the institution. Even Clara Ormond, who'd had a happy marriage, had been left in poverty by her husband's fecklessness.

Yet the longing wouldn't die.

She thought of Kitty and Annie, whose eyes shone. And Peg with her sweet memories. And Billy Jakes.

She wanted a good husband, a home, and children.

Once she would have imagined a manor house, or even aspired to a great estate. Now a modest house would suffice if it held a dear companion. There would be a cozy drawing room where she could sit and sew as her husband read aloud to her. There were children in her dream house too, but in her vision, they were tucked in their beds for the night.

There was nothing grand about this. Nothing to thrust her into embarrassing attention or demand courage. Simply comfort and loving security.

She was jerked out of her idyll by a heavy splash of rain on her face.

See, even the heavens wept at her ambitions!

She ran into a cake shop to take tea and hope the rain passed, but at one of the small tables a couple was holding hands, staring entranced into each other's eyes.

Bella turned and walked out to trudge back to the Compass, grateful for the rain that hid her leaking tears. As she approached she glared up at the dripping inn sign. Why couldn't the compass there tell her which direction to take for better days?

She went in, and was standing in the hall, wondering what to do with her sodden cloak, when the outside door burst open and wet men flooded into the hall. Noisy men, smelly men, chattering, laughing, calling out to one another and sometimes shaking off rain like dogs.

Bella pressed back against the wall, wishing they weren't between her and the stairs.

"Pounce! Pounce!" a man yelled. "Where are you, you blackguard? The *Black Swan*'s in, and we're all famished!"

Bella no longer noticed discomfort. She searched for the bellowing man. For Captain Rose?

Then a ruddy-faced, black-haired, beefy man yelled again. "Ho, the Compass! Where is everybody? Here's good men dry as a witch's —"

He stopped because he saw Bella.

He turned ruddier. ". . . broomstick . . ." He trailed off. "Boys, boys, there's a lady present!"

Now they were all staring at her, rough men looking like uneasy schoolboys. Bella scanned them, seeking Captain Rose. Tall, dark . . .

Three servants and Mr. Pounce hurried in to take charge. The crew was herded into the dining room and the innkeeper turned to her. "Your pardon, Miss Barstowe. No offense meant. How wet you are. I'll have someone take your cloak for drying. May I have your dinner sent up to your room?"

Bella glanced toward the dining room, now packed with men from the *Black Swan,* but the innkeeper would never allow her to eat there, so as she surrendered her cloak, she accepted the inevitable.

"Yes, thank you. I gather those men are from the ship we talked of earlier. The *Black Swan.*"

"The very one, ma'am." He was already turning away to pass her cloak to a servant.

Bella asked a blunt question. "Is one of those men her master?"

He looked back. "Captain Rose, ma'am?" He was understandably puzzled by her interest, but didn't seem suspicious.

"I've heard a little about him. Is he the yelling man?"

Bella didn't think so, but perhaps five years had distorted her memories that much.

"No, ma'am. That's Pudsy Galt, the bo-sun. I'll have your dinner in your room in a trice."

He hurried away and Bella heard the meaning. She was to go to her room and stay there, and not harbor any foolish, romantic thoughts about Captain Rose of the *Black Swan*. She lingered a moment longer, listening, but the men's voices were a cacophony and she could pick out nothing useful.

She went up to her room, mind whirling. Even if Captain Rose wasn't in the dining room, he must now be in Dover. He might still stay here as he had before. Which meant she might soon have her chance.

Suddenly her knees were shaking so much she had to sit down.

Wanting to encounter Captain Rose was very different from the imminent prospect of it, especially when he was connected to a bunch of dirty, raucous men who were doubtless now becoming drunk.

CHAPTER 12

She opened her door a crack and heard the growing volume of noise. Louise was coming with her dinner tray, so Bella hastily closed the door again and retreated to a chair.

The maid came in, put down the tray, and laid out the dishes. "There's a decanter of claret, ma'am, with Mr. Pounce's compliments, on account of the disturbance below."

She was keen to rush away, but Bella said, "Are those men staying here?"

"Bless you, no, ma'am. They'll be off to other amusements." A dimple was an indication of the sort of amusements. "They generally come here for their first meal ashore, though. Captain Rose pays for it."

"How generous."

A wide smile now. "Oh, he is, ma'am. He always stays here when he's in Dover, and always remembers the servants kindly."

Before Bella could ask another question, she added, "I have to go, ma'am," and whipped out, closing the door firmly behind her.

After a few moments, Bella opened it again, hoping she'd hear a voice she remembered. Then she sat to her dinner and tried to eat.

She wouldn't have believed it possible, but the men below became noisier, and their deep-voiced revels were sometimes interrupted by feminine squeals — ones that didn't sound at all protesting. She wondered if Louise's voice was among them.

She knew she should be disgusted, but an unfortunate part of her was envious. She didn't want to be an inn servant romping with rough sailors, but she wanted the high spirits of a celebration and, yes, the company of appreciative men.

The claret was very welcome.

Then came a sudden cry of, "Cap'n! Cap'n!" and a thumping of tankards on tables.

A new voice called, "Are they treating you well, lads?"

"Aye!"

"Then give me a jug of ale and a plump wench. I've some catching up to do!"

Laughter poured up to Bella's room like a flood.

She sat there, eyes wide. That was Captain Rose?

That voice didn't fit her memory at all! And the image conjured by his words fit even less. A jug of ale and a plump wench?

It made perfect sense, however, for the sort of man he must be. She'd clearly embroidered brief memories into whole new cloth.

She refilled her glass and drank deep.

This Captain Rose was probably more likely to aid her in illegal acts, but she didn't think he would be at all trustworthy. Strangely, she was still certain that back in 1760 she would have been able to trust him.

She frowned at her empty glass. That was foolish, because she hadn't trusted him. She'd stolen his horse and ridden off alone — which in itself had been terrifying — because she hadn't trusted his intentions.

Clearly she'd been right.

His arrival downstairs didn't calm the affair. Instead, it grew wilder. Soon the men were all singing what sounded like a common tavern song, thumping and banging the rhythm, one strong baritone in the lead. Bella knew it was good that she couldn't make out the words.

Her glass was full again, so she sipped, considering the new reality.

It wasn't surprising that she'd built Rose into a chivalrous hero. Back then, even after all that had happened, she'd still been able to dream of a man dashing in on a noble steed to carry her away from imprisonment and torment.

Now it would seem she had a more likely case — a rough sea captain who enjoyed ale and wenches — but a man who was generous to his men and to servants, and whom people in general seemed to think well of.

She hadn't invented the way he'd reacted so quickly and bravely to the dangerous men in the Black Rat, or the fear his very name had stirred there.

He was still a man capable of daring action, and that was what she needed.

Probably.

She'd have the night to think about it. He always stayed here, so she'd speak with him on the morrow. She reached for the decanter, and realized it was empty. No wonder her head felt a little strange.

She stood, swaying slightly, and went to close the door. There was nothing more to learn that way. She considered the chair by the fire and the book on the table beside it, but instead went to the bed and lay down.

Oh, dear. She'd left the door unlocked so Louise could return for her dinner dishes, but probably she was busy with the jollity downstairs. . . .

She really should bolt her door before she fell asleep.

She should get up, undress, and wash — but it was so much easier to simply lie here. . . .

She didn't know how much time had passed before she heard footsteps coming along the corridor. Not a servant's careful tread but confident, hard boots. She forced herself upright. What had she been thinking, leaving her door unlocked in an inn full of drunken ruffians?

She was halfway off the bed when the boots passed. A moment later, a door close by on her right slammed.

Was that Captain Rose?

Bella sat looking to her right as if she could see through walls. If he was there, he'd be there tomorrow. But then quicker steps hurried past and a door opened. She caught some words. ". . . your horse, Captain . . ."

Horse? Did that mean he was leaving?

She stood, swaying slightly. If he was leaving, this could be her only chance. Her only chance to meet the man, talk to him, assess him.

If she had the courage.

Steps passed again. The servant going away.

Heart pounding, throat dry, she checked herself in the mirror. Some hair was straggling out from her cap. She tidied it away. She tried to smooth creases out of her brown gown, newly aware of how little it flattered her.

"And a very good thing too," she muttered to her reflection. "The last thing we want is to appeal in that way to a sailor new to shore."

That thought made her hesitate again, but she set her jaw, put on her shoes, opened the door, and peered out. The corridor was deserted, and below all was still. The crew had gone on to their other amusements.

She wondered why Captain Rose wasn't with them. Lud, might he have brought his amusement upstairs with him? She thought she'd heard only one set of footsteps, but a woman's softer shoes might not have made much noise.

Or he might have carried her. . . .

For some reason, that image stirred her ridiculous longings again.

If he had a woman with him, she'd hear

something at his door. Talk, laughter, something.

She closed her door and then crept along to listen at the next. She couldn't hear sounds in that room, and she thought the slamming door had been a bit farther along. Behind the next door, she did hear movement, and then a muffled curse.

A man's voice, and not loving.

She listened awhile longer and heard only a thump.

She gathered her courage and knocked. It was a very timid knock. Perhaps he didn't even hear it. She knocked firmly.

"Come in, damn you!"

Heavens, he'd wake the whole house and she'd be found here like this!

She opened the door, slipped in and closed it, then turned to face Captain Rose.

Her jaw dropped. He was undressed down to his breeches. His chest and lower legs were bare.

He blinked as if to clear his sight. "Who the devil are you?"

Bella licked her lips. "Isabella Barstowe."

He blinked again, his brow furrowing. "Did I send for you?"

He didn't recognize her, but why should he? She wasn't sure she'd have recognized him if not for the ruby-eyed skull dangling from his ear. It had to be him, however. Tall; dark hair loose to his shoulders; stubble — though this time it was close to a true beard. Carelessly flung on the bed lay his shirt, a black waistcoat, frock coat, and bloodred cravat.

His chest was a great deal broader than she'd expected, but what did she know of men's chests?

"Well?" he barked, frowning now.

"No, sir, you didn't send for me. I wished to speak with you."

"Not a good time, Miss Barstowe." He turned to the washstand, picked up a cloth, soaped it, and started to wash.

Bella stared, mouth agape. She'd intended a conversation that would reveal the sort of man he was, but perhaps his actions spoke more clearly. He was an oaf.

All the better to assist in a brother's destruction, though . . .

"I'm Persephone," she blurted.

He turned to look at her, scrubbing the cloth over his muscular chest. Bella's eyes followed the cloth and saw his right shoulder.

Saw dark marks. When it moved on, the marks became clear — a tattoo of a black swan.

"Persephone who?"

She dragged her eyes up again.

His eyes were brown, but she hadn't been able to see eye color four years ago.

Perhaps the difference she sensed between then and now was that then he'd been sober and now he was not. He wasn't rolling drunk, but something in the careful way he spoke told her he was half-sozzled.

"I stole your horse," she prompted.

He blinked again, but then his eyes widened. "Oh, that! Have you come to pay for it?"

"What? No. I mean, yes. I mean . . . I wish you would put some clothes on!"

"I have some clothes on," he said with the hint of a grin, "and you did barge in here uninvited." He picked up the discarded shirt, however, and pulled it over his head. "Now, Miss Barstowe, horse thief, why are you here?"

Bella did her best to collect her wits. "Captain Rose, we can talk later, when you're . . . recovered, but I feared you'd leave before I could speak to you tomorrow. I need your help." He seemed unimpressed, so she added, "Or rather, I need to hire you."

"It's business, is it?" he said in a slightly more interested tone. "I can give you a few minutes." He gestured to a chair. "Please,

239

ma'am, be seated."

Bella perched on the hard chair, hoping it would make her feel more in control. He sat in the other, leaning back and stretching out his long legs. Long legs bare from the breeches down. With dark hair on them.

She wasn't in control at all, and this whole idea now seemed insane. She rose to leave, but he said, "If we're to do business, we should settle debts first. The horse?"

"It was returned to you. I owe you nothing."

"What if I didn't get it back?"

She studied him warily. He was playing with her, but was he lying?

"You didn't? I arranged for it to be left at an inn near Maidstone, and word sent to the Compass."

"Then perhaps whoever you trusted with the message decided to simply keep the horse."

Bella wanted to smash something. Had nothing gone right during that time?

She'd left the horse at the inn because she didn't want to arrive at her brother-in-law's house on a stolen horse. During the long, slow ride she'd come up with a story. She claimed to have escaped earlier, just south of London, and to have traveled a short distance by cart.

Once alone with Athena she'd told her the truth and begged her to send the guinea to the inn to have the horse returned. Athena had promised she would, but Athena was afraid to cross her husband. Perhaps she'd gone straight to him.

Sir Watson Ashton wouldn't have paid, especially with proof that Bella had lied. Athena had already had to persuade him not to turn Bella from the door.

"How much was that horse worth?" she asked tightly.

"Hard to remember after so long . . ."

He was delaying, keeping her here.

She edged toward the door. "Then I will leave you to your . . ." She waved feebly toward the washstand. "You can give me an account later."

"Not so fast." He was past her and blocking the door before she could react.

Bella stepped away from him, hand to hammering heart. "I'll scream."

"You'd have to explain how you came to be in my room."

"Let me pass."

He leaned against the door and folded his arms. "You came to hire me. For what?"

Bella tightened her lips.

"As a lover?"

Bella jerked backward. "Absolutely not!"

He grinned, running his eyes coarsely over her. "Pity."

Ridiculously, amid fear and fury Bella felt a little spark of pleasure from that.

Was she so starved for male appreciation? *Yes.*

"So why did you come here?" he demanded with an implacability that told her she'd have to give him some story he could believe. She pieced it together with skill driven by desperation.

"I . . . I had a chance encounter with one of the men who abducted me."

"Go on."

"He told me that you'd threatened retaliation if he did anything more to harm me. I was grateful. That made me think of your horse. That I couldn't be sure it had been returned to you. So I came to see."

"Hiring me?" he prompted.

He was damnably persistent. "I've changed my mind on that."

"One sensible decision. You traveled here alone? How old are you?"

"That, sir, is none of your business. Get out of my way."

He merely cocked his head. "Persephone. She's the one who was stolen into the underworld and escaped, but had to return for a sixmonth in the year. Is this your underworld? And I'm your Pluto?" He grinned again, and it was a taunt. "Those stories of gods and goddesses. They call them classics, but it's all disguises and false identities used to do wicked mischief." With a sudden change of tone, all humor gone, he asked, "What mischief brought you here, Persephone?"

Bella caught her breath. He thought she might be a danger to him. He was, after all, some sort of smuggler.

"I mean you no harm, Captain. I promise you."

"But you might cause it anyway."

She began to wonder if she might be in real peril here. If he might actually murder her because he saw a threat. She'd heard horrific stories of smugglers' cruelty, and the skull's ruby eyes seemed to flicker by candlelight.

He straightened, however, and stepped away from the door. "Your time's up. I'll be back in two days, maybe three. If what you want from me is important enough, be here when I return and we'll talk again. Perhaps it'll make more sense when we're both sober."

Bella blushed that her state had been obvious, but she was focused on the possibility of escape. She worked her way to the door, keeping her eyes on him, and as much distance between them as possible.

"Will you be here?" he asked.

Door already an inch open, she met his flat eyes. "I don't know."

He nodded as if that, at least, made sense. "I'm changeable as the sea, Miss Barstowe, sometimes rough, sometimes gallant, but on my word, unless you harm me or mine, you're safe from me."

Bella studied him, hearing truth but finding it hard to believe. But when he began to take his shirt off again, she whipped around the door and raced back to her room. Once inside, she shot the bolt and leaned there, heart pounding.

She should return to London on the morrow and forget all about Captain Rose. He wasn't the gallant hero she'd created in her mind.

She wasn't entirely sure she would, and could make no sense of her own reasons.

Thorn broke the swan seal and read the note from Caleb.

Now here's a turnup. A female confronted me in my room at the Compass calling herself Persephone. She seemed half-drunk and not at all clear, and I had little patience with her, especially when she said she wasn't interested in my bed. Then she said she'd stolen my horse and I remembered you telling that story. I grew curious.

I kept her talking, but didn't learn much. She'd come because she wanted something, though. She spoke of hiring me. She might be in trouble again. Gave the name Miss Barstowe.

In the end, I decided it was for you to deal with, so I told her I had urgent business, which was true enough — a wench elsewhere. I told her that if she really wanted to speak to me, she should wait three days. That should give you time to get here if you're interested. I'll lie low, but give me the word and I'll go back in three days and scare her off.

Caleb

Thorn put down the letter, very thoughtful.

"*Ee-oo-ah.*"

He looked down at the meowing cat in the basket, her two kittens greedily attached, as seemed constantly to be the case.

"You're doubtless correct, Tabitha, but it's unignorable, you know."

"*Ah-oo.*"

245

"You're only concerned about the fate of yourself and offspring if I come to an untimely end. Remember, you're Christian's cat."

Tabitha spat, and Thorn laughed. Christian and his wife had acquired the strange cat in their adventures, but Tabitha had taken him in dislike. That was why he'd asked Thorn to care for her for a while, with the strange comment, "She won't talk to me."

Oddly enough, as soon as Christian left, the cat had begun to make its strange, speechlike noises. They made no sense, of course, but the cat did seem to recognize Christian's name.

"Very well," Thorn said, "you're Caro's cat. They are happily together now, however, so you'll have to tolerate him."

The cat put out a paw and hooked down the lid of her basket. The ultimate disapproval. But that would imply that she did understand English, which had to be impossible.

An intriguing creature. She was a strange breed mostly found on the Isle of Man, hence called Manx. The cats had little or no tail and large hindquarters that looked like those of a rabbit, leading to speculation that they resulted from a mating of a cat and a rabbit. In Thorn's opinion, if that were true, they must have very strange cats and rabbits on the Isle of Man.

In Christian's adventures with Caro, they'd spun a wild story of the cats being from Hesse and bred to hunt ferocious rabbits there. The myth of the cat-rabbit of Hesse was delightful, but Thorn was more interested in establishing the truth, and now that he had temporary custody, he'd invited scientists to study the matter. There were currently two warring camps on the subject, and a search was under way for more specimens.

Thorn had installed his feline guests in his private study in a velvet-lined basket, and assigned a page to attend to them. They were pampered beyond belief, but Tabby, as Caro had named her, still felt free to complain. She'd learned to close her basket as a snub, but the one attempt on his part to fasten the lid down to prevent wandering had led to ferocious violence accompanied by what appeared to be cursing worthy of the lowest sailor.

Thorn had accepted that he'd finally been cowed by a female, and chosen to be amused. He'd given her the more dignified name of Tabitha and appointed her the resident Delphic oracle. After all, that oracle had supposedly been hard to interpret.

"To go or not to go, that is the question," he orated to the closed lid. "Do you think Mr. Shakespeare understood how apposite some of his words would remain, centuries after his death?"

The lid rose a little, but Tabitha gave no opinion.

"Barstowe. Do we know a Barstowe?"

"Aa-oo."

"No, I didn't think so either. A false name? And what could she want, so many years later?"

Tabitha rose up so the lid fell backward. One of her kittens scrambled out. She took its ruff in her mouth and dumped the creature back in again. Thorn knew from experience that this game could continue for a long time. Tabitha had only two surviving kittens, and one was like her, while the other was normal, which also fascinated the scientists. The normal kitten was adventurous, whilst the Manx one was timorous, and whether that was significant, Thorn had no idea.

When Christian had foisted the creatures on him, the kittens were nameless, so Thorn had named them. The normal, bold one was black, so he'd named him Sable. The gray Manx kitten was plump and warier, so he'd

irreverently called him after the king —
Georgie.

Tabitha retrieved Sable again and yawned.

"Exhaustion or boredom, my lady? Shall I
import mice? Or rabbits?"

"Ee-oh-ar-oo!"

An appropriate response to a private joke.

"My apologies, of course not. But give me
your wisdom. Has Miss Barstowe learned
that Captain Rose is sometimes the Duke
of Ithorne and set out to demand marriage
because of our adventure four years before?"

The noise the cat made sounded amus-
ingly like a snort.

"Why else would she suddenly remember
me? I am perplexed."

"O-er-o."

"Ah, of course. Thank you." Thorn rang
the bell on his desk, struggling again with
the idea that the cat might actually understand language. That sequence of sounds
came only when summoning his long-
suffering secretary would be wise. Perhaps
he should devise some experiments.

A footman came in. "Overstone, if you
please."

When the rotund young man entered,
Thorn said, "Barstowe. A lady of between
twenty and twenty-three."

"I can make inquiries, sir."

249

Sable escaped again. Tabitha picked the kitten up and carried it to Thorn's desk. She leapt up, her large hindquarters making it exceptionally easy, and put the kitten down. Then she leapt off again and went for a stroll.

"Child minder?" Thorn asked in disbelief. His secretary made a peculiar noise that might be choked laughter. "You exceed yourself, madam." But Thorn rescued the tiny adventurer from danger of ink, or the inkwell from danger of kitten.

Needle claws pricked as Sable explored his hand. Thorn realized he was smiling. "Very well, I like your spirit, mite."

He waved Overstone off to his research and conducted a language experiment. Georgie, as usual, was peering over the edge of the basket, mewling, but scared to venture away.

Thorn said, "Why not bring your other babe up here?"

Tabitha made a sound that was completely indecipherable, but didn't do as she was asked.

"And that tells me nothing," Thorn noted as Sable began a fearless progress up his sleeve.

Suddenly sorry for the timid kitten, he went and picked it up. Georgie wailed. Tabitha turned, but she merely watched, slit eyed.

"Your mother also thinks you should be more venturesome," he said, returning to his desk and putting the kitten down there.

Tabitha leapt up again to hover.

"I wonder if human infants are as complicated," Thorn asked. "But your two remind me a little of Christian and myself. I wasn't timid, precisely, but I was more . . . careful before he came. You really should mellow toward him, you know. He's a good man. Better than I, for he's straightforward."

He put a quill pen in front of Georgie, who batted at it tentatively. Sable raced down Thorn's arm to leap on the pen in predatory fashion. But Georgie held his ground.

"Admirable," Thorn told him. "Don't let the jackanapes run all over you." As the kittens were now a tangled ball, either in affection or competition, his advice came too late.

With what sounded like a sigh, Tabitha plucked one from the melee and went off to deposit it in the basket. It was Sable.

"Won't work. He'll be out of there in a trice." But Tabitha turned back and hissed at the escaping kitten, and Sable slid back into the basket.

"Discipline. Excellent. I believe I'll install you as nursery governess if I ever find a suitable wife. Now, what would Christian do about Bella Barstowe?"

Tabitha had her mouth full of Georgie, but she shot Thorn a look.

"True. He would race off to discover all. It's what he did. But look at the chaos that resulted."

Tabitha was putting Georgie in the basket, but Thorn didn't need her wisdom. "In the end, it won him the woman he loves."

"Ai-ee-u?"

"Of course not. Bella Barstowe? But I have to know the end of that story."

"Ar-o-o."

"Very well, I'm desperate to escape for a few days. No harm to it. There's nothing of importance at hand, and even if I've forbidden myself the *Black Swan,* this gives me an excuse to be Captain Rose."

Thorn summoned Joseph and set him to packing for the captain, then checked his more personal commitments to be sure nothing would be neglected. He wrote quick letters to Christian in Devon and Robin in Huntingdonshire. Robin had made him promise that he'd always let him know when he was becoming his alter ego.

When Thorn had asked why, Robin said,

"So that I can worry about you."

"Wouldn't it be better not to know?"

"Then I'd have to worry all the time."

So many people worried about him, and he wished they wouldn't.

Overstone returned with a sheet of notes. "There are a number of Barstowe families, sir, with and without an E. Oxfordshire, Shropshire, Hampshire, Lincolnshire. I will require a little more time."

"Don't look so pained. I don't expect Rothgar-like omniscience."

The secretary said, "Thank you, sir," but he looked as if Thorn had insulted him with low expectations. He'd look more pained in a moment.

"I'm going to Ithorne. Order my traveling chariot to be ready in an hour, and send a groom immediately with this for the Black Swan Inn at Stowting."

His secretary did look as if he'd suddenly felt a boil in a very tender spot. He knew a message to Stowting probably meant Thorn was about to become Captain Rose. It seemed Tabitha might too. She hissed.

Thorn wrote quickly. By the time he folded the letter, Overstone was ready to drip hot wax so Thorn could impress his seal. Not his ducal crest, but the image of a black swan.

"Sir . . ."

"If there's any matter needing my attention over the next few days, you have an hour to present it."

"Very well, sir."

After a struggle, Thorn added, "I won't be going to sea."

Overstone didn't say, *Thank God,* but the sentiment clearly showed on his face. He couldn't understand Thorn's need for another life, especially one that involved rough living and occasional danger.

Thorn, on the other hand, felt excitement dancing through his veins. He wouldn't want to be Captain Rose all the time, but his adventures in that persona were precious flights of freedom.

"God bless Miss Barstowe," he said to Tabitha, "husband hunter or not."

He dealt with a few papers, but then all was ready for his departure. Feeling slightly foolish, he said farewell to the cats. Tabitha glared and closed the lid of her basket.

"I've left orders for your tenderest care," Thorn protested.

"Ee-o-uar-sss."

Now that sounded alarmingly like a dismal prognostication followed by a curse.

CHAPTER 13

Bella woke the next morning feeling slightly unwell. Even if she did decide to return to London, she couldn't face it today. She soon convinced herself that Captain Rose had proved not to be truly dreadful, and it would be only sensible to stay and talk to the man when he wasn't in his cups.

That talk, however, would take place in a safer spot than a bedchamber. In the parlor downstairs. Yes, that would be safe.

With this plan in mind, however, she definitely needed to learn more about him, so she asked Louise to help her wash her hair. It was impossible to have a conversation while washing her hair over a basin, but when the maid began to work a comb through the tangles, Bella started on her subject.

"I encountered Captain Rose in the corridor last night. A very handsome man."

"That he is, ma'am." In the mirror, Bella

could see the twitch of a wicked grin on the maid's face.

Bella sighed. "But a bad man, I fear."

"That he is too, ma'am." But then the maid said, "No, not bad. But bold, and with wicked ways."

"Does he live here in Dover when not on his ship?"

"A few miles inland, miss."

"Is he married?"

"Not him!"

"Do many sea captains marry?"

"A fair number, miss."

"It must be strange, being married to a man who's often away."

"Be a blessing with some of 'em, I reckon, ma'am. There, why don't you sit afore the fire to dry it faster."

Bella moved, silently agreeing with the maid's words about husbands. Lady Fowler would definitely have preferred to have her husband away most of the time.

"I suppose Captain Rose has been going to sea since he was a lad," she said, as she raised her hair to let the heat get underneath.

"Such a pretty color, your hair, miss. Catches the fire so lovely, it does."

Bella chuckled. "I hope it doesn't catch fire."

"No risk of that, ma'am." Louise set to tidying things away, and Bella was trying to think how to rephrase her question, but the maid answered.

"Captain Rose only came here about eight years ago, miss, though he's Kentish-born. Raised in America, he was, see, but returned to his mother's village and not long after he became master of the Duke of Ithorne's ship."

Bella started so sharply that the maid hurried over. "Did you burn yourself, ma'am?"

"No, no. I just . . . A duke. How amazing. How did that happen?"

And what did it mean for her plans? The link between this adventure and her London life seemed ominous.

She saw Louise wrinkle her brow as if uncertain how much to share.

"Do tell me," Bella urged.

"I suppose it's no secret around here, but I hope you won't be shocked, miss. You see, Captain Rose is the duke's illegitimate brother. They're so alike there's no denying it, which is apparently why the lad and his mother were sent away when he was young. Then some friend of the duke's met Caleb — that's his name — and was so shocked by the resemblance he arranged a meeting."

"It's like a play," Bella marveled. "What

happened?"

"The duke could have been harsh about such an obvious scandal, but he wasn't. When Captain Rose — well, he wasn't a captain then — said he wanted to return to his mother's village, His Grace made no objection. And when the duke learned he was a sailor and had risen to bosun on a trading ship, he trained him to be master of the *Black Swan.*"

"How generous."

"Indeed it was, miss, but then the duke's an orphan, or as good as. Perhaps he was glad to find a brother, even one from the wrong side of the blanket." She gathered up the wet towel and the slop bucket. "I should go and see if I'm needed elsewhere, miss."

"Yes, of course. Thank you."

Bella hardly noticed her leave, she was so absorbed in the extraordinary information. Captain Rose — the Duke of Ithorne's illegitimate brother, and supposedly almost identical!

She'd seen the duke only from a distance. He certainly had the same dark hair and a similar tall build, but beyond that they seemed completely different. One was elegant and haughty, almost sleek. The other was handsome but rough-hewn. Earthy.

What did this mean, however, this absurd

coincidence? Did it put her in danger?

As she combed out her hair she decided it wasn't quite such a coincidence after all.

The duke's seat was in Kent, and only about ten miles from here. If his father had sired a bastard, why not on a local woman? Apart from the early displacement across the Atlantic — and that made sense — why shouldn't the bastard son end up here, and why shouldn't the duke employ him on his ship? Was it odd that a duke owned a ship? She had no idea.

The coincidence was that she'd encountered Captain Rose here in 1760 and in 1764 slipped into the duke's London house because of her work with Lady Fowler. Those were two separate events that happened to have a link, as when one met a stranger and in talking discovered a person both knew.

Should this affect her plans?

No. She rose from the fire and went to sit before the mirror. Even if Captain Rose regularly reported all his doings to his august patron, the name Miss Barstowe would mean nothing to the duke.

The next two days crept by and gave Bella too much time to dither. At one moment she was determined to stay and speak to

Captain Rose. At the next she was ready to take a coach for London and forget about him. She still wanted her revenge on Augustus, however, and had no other notion how to achieve it.

Coarse though Captain Rose was, she felt sure he'd relish exposing a worm like Augustus, and would do it with gusto.

She purchased more material and thread and desperately sewed more handkerchiefs.

She was in her room, considering another day's wait without enthusiasm, when Louise came to say that Captain Rose was below and asking to speak to her. The maid was clearly full of questions, and Bella feared she blushed. She had no acceptable explanation, so she didn't attempt one.

"I'll be down in a moment, Louise," she said. As soon as the maid left, she hurried to the mirror to check her appearance. For this encounter, she must be neat, clean, and sober.

A matter of business, that was all.

She took a few steadying breaths and then left her room and went downstairs. At the bend in the stairs she saw him, and something made her pause. Surprise, perhaps, though why, she didn't know.

He was standing with his back to her, fully dressed in his old-fashioned style, but with tall riding boots. She much preferred the modern coat with the skirts cut close to the body, but on him the fuller style looked almost elegant.

Elegant?

Not a word she'd have attached to the man she'd spoken with the other night. Of course, he'd been scantily dressed and drunk.

He turned and looked up.

Bella continued on her way down, wishing her heart weren't suddenly pounding with nervousness. She'd asked, begged, for this meeting, and now that she'd achieved it, she must be the one in control.

When she reached the hall she curtsied and spoke coolly. "So, you are returned, Captain."

He bowed in much the same manner. "As you see, Miss Barstowe."

"And in good time."

"Dastardly to keep a lady waiting."

Through this meaningless exchange, Bella almost felt she was talking to a different person — a more reserved and formidable one. Did drink alter a person as much as that?

"It's a pleasant day," he said. "Would you care to walk?"

Bella hesitated over that. She'd expected

to take him into the parlor, but she realized that would be safe only with the door open. She might have matters to discuss that weren't for other ears.

To be with him with the door closed would be folly, especially after their last encounter.

His brow rose at her silence.

Conducting this interview outside, in public, would be an excellent thing. Bella curtsied again. "I'll go for my outer clothing, Captain."

She hurried upstairs, certain that he was studying her just as keenly as she'd studied him. With lascivious intent?

She realized for the first time that he might have an odd impression of Bella Barstowe. Four years ago she'd told him as little as she could, so he knew she'd been pursued by bad men, but not why. He might well think she'd tumbled into that predicament more willingly, perhaps with sinful intent.

No wonder he'd made a coarse suggestion the other night.

Her hands turned unsteady as she pinned on her hat, and she fumbled with her cloak and gloves. If there were a horse at hand, she might have mounted it and fled, but she wouldn't allow such weakness.

A short while with him, out on a public

street. There was no danger in that, and he still might be exactly the man she needed to help her destroy Augustus.

Thorn waited for Miss Barstowe's return, fascinated by what he'd seen of her.

She dressed more plainly than four years ago — her gown approached dowdy — and had changed rather more than he'd have expected in that time. He vaguely remembered a pretty girl, and she'd become a good-looking woman who could perhaps be beautiful if relaxed and happy, but she seemed hard and wary. Perhaps that was understandable after her terrible experience.

He felt a strange need to make her relaxed and happy and find out.

She certainly had lovely hair. He hadn't noticed the color four years ago in muted light. Now she kept it tucked away under an unbecoming cap, but the escaping wisps had been an auburn that came close to bronze, a shade that looked particularly well against her creamy complexion. . . .

He caught himself. He was not interested in Bella Barstowe in that way. Bad enough that he had a strange obsession with Kelano — who had not returned to the Goat, wise nymph. To his benefit too. She was far too tempting for his sanity, and his purpose now was to find the perfect, suitable wife.

That was an excellent reason not to be here, involved with Bella Barstowe, who'd doubtless ended up in trouble four years ago through folly and loose behavior.

He should leave and return to his proper sphere, but she was coming back downstairs in an equally dull heavy wool cloak, a small plain hat on her capped hair. Anything farther from a cunning seductress was hard to imagine. The innkeeper, Pounce, had told him she claimed to be a governess. Unlikely for the spirited young lady he remembered, but not many governesses came to their role by choice.

She walked toward him, trying very hard to be calm and composed, but he saw nervousness beneath, and now she did look her age. So why was she here? What had driven her to accost Caleb in his room? If she was afraid of Captain Rose, why had she patiently waited for him to return?

Sighing at his own folly, he knew he must learn all, and help her again if necessary.

He offered his arm. She hesitated, but then took it, and he led her out of the inn and into the breezy street. He hoped she'd speak first, for Caleb's account of their meeting had been too brief, but she'd turned mute. Clouds were gathering, and to his experienced eye, rain was on the way, so he broke the silence.

"Let us resume our conversation, Miss Barstowe. Or perhaps you could repeat it. I was a little hampered a few nights ago in my ability to understand. You came to Dover to pay me for my horse?"

She met his eyes then, with remarkable directness. "I made arrangements for it to be returned to you, sir."

"If I dispute that?"

Her lips tightened, which was a shame, because in their looser state they were luscious. Not too wide — he always distrusted a wide mouth — but generously full.

Much like the lips of Kelano. He hadn't been aware of such a strong preference. . . .

"If you truly didn't get your horse back, Captain, I'll pay you its value. Have you calculated that?"

"Fifty guineas," he said.

"Fifty guineas?"

"It was a good horse."

"Not that good," she snapped.

Thorn had to fight laughter, and he was delighted that her fighting spirit hadn't been crushed. "I'm adding something for hire and inconvenience. Well?"

She stopped, pulling her hand free so as

to face him fully. "Is that your condition for continuing this conversation?"

"Always best to set sail with a clean hull."

"Whatever that means. Very well, sir. I'll pay you fifty guineas, but only because I do owe you something for the inconvenience and for rescuing me. Thank you."

She snapped out the last words, meeting his eyes, chin up, head tilted slightly to the right. He recognized the frightened, spirited girl, but was surprised to feel a poignant sympathy, as if they had been more to each other than was true.

"I was honored to be of service, Miss Barstowe," he said, and meant it.

They walked on, but then the wind rose off the sea, carrying moisture, dust, and fallen leaves that made her grab her hat and turn away from the worst of it.

"Perhaps we should return to the Compass," she said.

Warning bells sounded. "To your room? Rather compromising, don't you think? Or is that your purpose? You did invade my bedchamber."

She stared at him in disbelief. "You imagine I'd want to trick you into marriage, Captain Rose? Why?"

Even though Thorn knew she was referring to a sea captain, the sheer novelty of her attitude made him want to grin with delight.

"Forgive me," he said. "Complete idiocy. But you did come to my bedchamber. . . ."

Her color had risen. "Because I thought you might leave immediately. I explained that."

But Caleb hadn't. This conversation was like a maze, and danger could lurk at its heart. He'd escaped marriage traps all his adult life and wouldn't be caught by the likes of Bella Barstowe.

"In my experience, Miss Barstowe, the only time a woman is willing to dance attendance on a man is when she has marriage in mind. Or occasionally marital pleasures."

"You are disgusting," she said, blue eyes flashing with anger. She walked away, heels sharp on the cobblestones.

He should let her go, but he'd suddenly had an astonishing notion. He caught up with her. "What a temperamental wench you are."

"I am not," she said between her teeth, eyes fixed ahead, "temperamental. Or a wench. Please do not pester me, Captain Rose."

She marched on. He kept pace, studying her.

Bronze hair, not black. Complexion clear of any paint.

But the voice and mannerisms, especially when annoyed . . .

Could Bella Barstowe be Kelano? How? Why?

Did she know he was Ithorne?

That could make this into a very clever wedding trap.

She suddenly stopped and turned to face him. "Do I have to scream?"

If so, she was playing a very deep game.

"Would it do any good?" he countered. "The people at the Compass know you left with me willingly, and we've been in sight of others all along. We still are, and as I'm known here, I believe my reputation is more at risk than yours."

Her chin went up and her lips pressed together. "Ridiculous."

Oh, yes, Kelano. He felt sure of it.

"Is it?" he asked, racing through all the possible permutations of this. "You did burst into my bedchamber unannounced."

Her color was mostly anger, but it was still pretty. There were advantages to lack of paint, especially for a lady with such an excellent complexion. Despite the blush, she still met his eyes. "As you remember, I was of a mind to hire you. And not, I assure you, for . . . for . . .”

He rescued her. “Then what do you want of me?” he asked. “There are any number of people who'd like to catch me in an illegal activity.”

Her color calmed a little, and then she nodded. “I see. I suppose a smuggler must fear the law.”

“I'm no more a smuggler, Miss Barstowe, than you're a wench.”

“If you so insist.”

“But then,” he teased, “you are a wench.”

Her eyes flashed again, but there was humor in them now.

“Whatever you are, Captain Rose, I'm not part of a plot against you, but I can see why you might think so. Given that, I'm surprised you will not leave me be. Good-bye, sir.”

She walked off again, not angrily, but firmly.

Having a woman walk away from him, twice, was a novelty. Or more than twice? Kelano had also rejected him. Twice.

Fighting a smile, he caught up and kept pace. “But you have some urgent need of me, Miss Barstowe. You seized the opportunity to speak to me. When I didn't have time to delay, you waited here, twiddling your thumbs. . . .”

"I never twiddle my thumbs."

"Then what did you do these past days?"

"I sewed handkerchiefs."

"Neatly?"

"Perfectly."

"What a model of domesticity!"

And unlikely for both the girl he'd rescued and Kelano. Was he building a wild story out of nothing? Even if so, there was her youth, her need, and her urgency. He couldn't abandon her.

"Tell me what you think I can do," he said, as persuasively as he could. She made no response. "Devil take it, Miss Barstowe, governess or not, you're too young to be venturing out alone, especially to make assignations with dangerous men."

That brought a response. She whirled to face him. "Do not presume to order me about, sir! And in any case, such a guardian would be to protect me from dangerous men like you."

She actually poked a gloved finger into his chest.

"Touché," he said, smiling, "in both senses of the word."

A number of people were watching. Dover would be abuzz over this for days: over a young lady berating Captain Rose and getting away with it.

He added to the story by stepping back to sweep a bow. "My dear Miss Barstowe, I apologize for all my many faults, but please believe me, at the moment I'm willing to be your most humble servant. So why not tell me your problem so we can see what I can do to help."

CHAPTER 14

Bella's fiery infuriation fizzled into a kind of quiver. Was it the bow — so elegant and courtly? Or eyes that seemed sympathetic, and truly interested — in her?

And in this light his eyes seemed hazel rather than brown.

Changeable as the sea. That was how he'd described himself, and it was clearly true, but how could she cope with such a man? She needed to escape this bramble patch she'd wantonly walked into, but she felt already entangled. Trapped.

"Is your problem a vile man, Miss Barstowe? Perhaps the same one who caused you to be in the Black Rat four years ago?"

"How do you know that?" she asked, appalled.

He raised a soothing hand. "Simple deduction. Something caused you to come to me. The only connection between us is that brief incident years ago. Have those men attempted to harm you again?"

Bella tried to gather her wits. His explanation made sense, and yet his guess seemed uncanny. "No, they haven't harmed me. You warned them off, for which I truly thank you."

"How do you know that?" Now he seemed startled.

Bella realized people were eyeing them with interest and walked on. There was no reason not to tell him this part.

"One of them told me. The older one, called Coxy. I recently encountered him in London, completely by accident. I was so shocked to see him that I felt no fear. I demanded to know the reason for it all."

"Forcefully, I'm sure," he murmured. "You didn't know why you ended up in the Black Rat?"

"You did?" she asked in horror. Had he been part of the plot all along?

He raised a hand. "That wasn't my meaning. I assumed back then that you understood everything, but chose not to tell me. Is Barstowe your real name?"

"Yes."

"Unwise, perhaps, to be using it here?"

A dry laugh escaped. "As a result of what happened four years ago, Bella Barstowe is ruined. There's no more harm to be done."

"Tell me what happened." He sounded both serious and sympathetic, which was tempting as the apple in Eden, but Bella didn't obey. This man was dangerous as the serpent.

"I can't compel you," he said, "but sometimes telling a tale helps to clarify the mind, and I was present for some of the story. I'm naturally curious about the rest."

Put that way it was hard to deny him, though she didn't relish reliving the story. "I was snatched from my father's estate," she said.

"How was that possible? They invaded the gardens?"

"Are ladies only allowed to stroll in the gardens? I was some distance from the house" — she added a lie — "collecting wildflowers to press for my collection."

"First handkerchiefs and now a pressed-flower collection," he said, clearly not believing any of it. "And your maid?"

"I didn't take her," Bella admitted.

"An assignation?"

The last thing Bella wanted was a revealing blush, but she felt the heat in her cheeks. "Very well. I had arranged to meet a new admirer. And yes, it was foolish, but how was I to suspect that he was part of such a plan?"

"What happened?"

His sympathetic tone drew more from her, and soon, walking briskly through the chilly air, she found herself telling him all. As she came to the end, to the vile fate she'd faced, she could hardly get the words out. After her time with Lady Fowler, she knew more about the darkest side of brothels.

He took her gloved hands, offering firm comfort. "You escaped," he said, as if she needed the reminder.

Perhaps she did, for it almost broke her control.

"Why wait until then, though?" he asked. "Why not escape earlier if you were able?"

His calm questions pulled her out of the dark, and perhaps the brisk, damp wind helped to scour her mind. "I was closely guarded at first. One of them was always with me except at night, and they always made sure my room was secure."

"You didn't try to get help from others along the way? Innkeepers, other travelers?"

"No. They threatened me, but . . . It may seem odd, but I was still very worried about the story getting out, and sure my father would deliver the ransom. But even if he didn't . . . I think I assumed they would give up and release me."

"You were very young and had lived a

protected life. When did you change?"

"When we arrived in Dover and I learned their plan. By then, thank God, they'd grown careless, misled by my passivity. They locked my room at the Crown and Anchor that night, but there was a window."

"Good girl."

At the approval, she looked up to see a warm smile in his eyes. She smiled back, realizing that she had done something remarkable back then. She told him about Billy Jakes, and about finding him in Litten.

"Does he have good employment?" he asked.

"Yes, why?"

"I could help him if he needed it."

"I don't think he wants to go to sea, but thank you for your kindness. He seems well set up at Sir Muncy's place, and is soon to marry the head groom's daughter."

He nodded. "So you escaped the inn. How did you end up in the Black Rat?"

"Sheer stupidity," she confessed. "I was scurrying through the streets of Dover, afraid and in a panic. I had no money. I knew no one here. I decided to go to the church and ask the vicar for help, but then I saw my captors, already searching, so I slipped inside the nearest public building. I knew it would be a rough place, but I could never have imagined what happened there." She looked up. "Please do let me thank you again for rescuing me. You risked your life."

"Devil a bit," he said cheerfully. "Once those men gathered their wits they'd have realized they didn't want that much trouble, even over such a pretty morsel as you."

Bella looked ahead, again stupidly warmed by a casual compliment. But then she realized that this time, it wasn't so much the compliment as the man paying it. Much to her surprise, she liked Captain Rose. Wisely or not, she wasn't the least bit afraid of him. She even felt he could be a friend.

She'd felt completely different the other night in his room.

How odd.

"So you rode off on my horse and returned where?" he prompted. "Maidstone?"

"To my sister's house near there. She took me home."

"To the father who failed to ransom you. Was he so vile?"

She hadn't told him about the switched notes because she hadn't been sure whether to broach her plan. Her reasons for hesitation were different now — he might think her unnatural, unwomanly, to want revenge.

"The ransom note was never found," she said.

"Another failed agent, as with my horse?"

She gave a short, bitter laugh. "Indeed. Except that this failed agent was the cause of all the trouble." It would not be held back. "It was my brother, Augustus," she said, hearing a hiss in her words.

"What did he do? Lose the ransom note?"

"Deliberately. And then he substituted one that seemed to be from my lover, announcing our plan to run off and sin. And," she added grimly, "after all it was his plan in the first place!"

"Ah, gaming debts, I assume."

"How —" But she broke off with a sigh. "Is it so common for men to lose huge sums at the tables?"

"Common enough, though it doesn't usually lead to such a complicated drama. Gaming debts aren't claimable by law, you see."

"Coxy said that."

"I'm sure he knows all about it," he remarked. "Thus, there are other ways to make losers pay. If the gaming is among gentlemen, then any defaulter will be ostracized. Fear of that usually makes them find the money. If they can't, they blow their brains out or abscond to a foreign land."

"If only Augustus had chosen either of those."

"Miss Barstowe, I like your spirit."

Bella laughed and she did truly feel lighter. Because of his admiration.

The streets were now almost deserted as the weather grew more ominous, but it didn't seem to bother him, and she certainly didn't want to end this meeting.

"Coxy seemed a gentleman," she said, but then added, "more or less."

"There's a distressing number of more-or-lessians about. From our brief acquaintance I'd say he was less."

"You're probably correct, because he wasn't able to use the threat of exposing Augustus to other gentlemen to squeeze the money out of him." Bella considered her plan. Though misty, it involved catching Augustus in the act and shaming him. She, however, had the advantage of not wanting money. Shame would be enough. "Where do men like that gamble?" she asked.

"Usually a gaming club, more generally called a hell. But why would your brother play in such places rather than in better circles?"

Bella answered without hesitation. "Because he had to preserve his pristine reputation, especially from our father, who detested gaming above almost anything." She clutched her hat against a gust of wind, looking up at him. "Can a person conceal his identity in hell?"

His eyes smiled. "Too profound a theological question for me, Miss Barstowe, but in a hell, he could give a false name. As long as he played with coin, no questions would be asked."

Bella considered that. "But he ran into debt."

"Which meant the men he played with accepted his vowels."

"Vowels?"

"A written promise to pay, abbreviated to IOU."

"So a fortune could be lost, a family ruined, by a few letters on a piece of paper?"

"Yes, sadly that can be the case."

"Tragically," she said, thinking of Hortensia Sprott, left in poverty by a father's vowels. That fueled her desire to expose her brother. Perhaps she could expose others at the same time and prevent some future suffering.

"Coxy took Augustus's promise to pay," she said, "so he must have felt sure he would get his money. Why?"

"We can't be sure, but is your brother clever?"

"No."

"Then he probably thought he was concealed by a false name, but was in fact known by all the sharps."

"Sharps?" she asked.

"Men, occasionally women, who make their living at the tables. They're usually highly skilled players, but they'll cheat if they need to, and do it skillfully enough that many a pigeon will never know they were plucked."

"A pigeon," Bella said with relish, able to let go of her hat, though she didn't trust the calm. She smiled at her companion. "I like the thought of Augustus as a pigeon, especially a plucked one."

"And baked in a pie," he said, eyes twinkling. But then he came to a halt and asked, "Is that your purpose?"

Bella searched his features, but in the end she had to act on instinct. "Yes."

"How?"

"By exposing his addiction to gaming."

His brows rose. "And you came to a sea captain for help. Why?"

Put like that, it was ridiculous. Bella could hardly confess that he'd been her mythical hero for four years.

"Because I know no one else who might be able to help," she said. "You've already educated me about gamesters."

"That doesn't mean I am one."

"But you do know how to deal with dangerous men. I'm sure you have knife and pistol with you now."

His smile was wry. "True. Very well, Miss Barstowe, let us consider the matter. Without commitment," he warned. "When pressed for payment, why did your brother come up with such a wicked plan? Why not confess to your father? It's the usual way. The father berates the son, but pays up for the honor of the family."

Bella shook her head. "Father would have done more than berate. He'd have stopped Augustus's allowance and imprisoned him at Carscourt."

She managed not to say, *As he did me.*

"Then why didn't Coxy go directly to your father, threatening to expose your brother as one who doesn't pay his debts of honor? I'd say he was gentleman enough to make that threat credible."

"Debts of honor?" Bella scoffed. "Pigeon droppings, more likely."

"Very apt, and thus they are called. But why didn't the sharp take that route?"

"He didn't say, but I can guess. Any inquiries around the area would have told him what Father was like. Stern, rigid, and unforgiving. He'd punish Augustus, but he wouldn't pay. He'd think shame was his just deserts."

As with me.

"What's more, he was a magistrate. He would have found some crime to lay against a sharp and inflicted the worst punishment he could. Lud! Augustus has that position now, making judgments about poor unfortunates from the magistrates' bench, when he's a worse sinner than all of them."

"The poor unfortunates are there for a reason."

"I hope you never end up facing him."

For some reason, he smiled, as if seeing a prospect he relished.

"So the sharp is balked," he said, "and abducts you so that the ransom will pay the debt."

"At Augustus's suggestion," Bella reminded him.

"I don't forget that. I'm puzzled that he didn't let the plan go ahead. Your father pays the ransom. Any anger falls on your head for wandering too far afield. His debt is paid."

"Do you doubt my story?" Bella demanded, hurt. "I have no proof."

"I believe you believe it."

"What purpose could Coxy have in weaving it?"

"None, it would seem, but I would like to

understand your brother's plan."

"He's never liked me, so perhaps my fate wouldn't weigh with him." Even to Bella that didn't seem enough. "He's always been selfish. But yes, it's hard to think he abandoned me to such a fate."

Rain splashed her cheek, and it almost felt like a tear.

Captain Rose moved them to a more sheltered spot, frowning at the darkening clouds. "We should get back to the Compass, but let me speculate. Unfortunately I occasionally meet such men — weak and utterly selfish, and therefore always afraid. He probably intended the plan to go through, but then he began to wonder if the sharp had told you of his part, carelessly or out of spite. Or if you'd overheard something. His imagination would paint the worst outcome. If you never returned home, you could never expose him."

"That's monstrous!"

"But he is, isn't he?"

Bella covered her mouth, but she knew it was exactly the right word. That knowledge had driven her here, to this desperate association. She'd simply not worked through the damning details.

"Your dear Augustus must have been very, very frightened when you returned home."

Bella had never thought of that. "So that's why he was so vicious!"

"How?"

Bella shook her head. "Petty things, but wearing. It doesn't matter."

"I doubt that," he said, but a gust of wet wind caused him to shield her. "Back to the Compass. So you returned, were not believed, and were imprisoned. Not unreasonable treatment of a daughter who had apparently run off with a lover and been gone for days, though some families would attempt to conceal the incident, or cover it with a marriage."

"They tried the latter. I refused."

"Why?"

She turned narrow eyes on him. "Would you marry a foul harpy twenty years your senior who would always regard you as a penitent, never to be given any freedom to sin again?"

"Hard to imagine the situation, but no, Miss Barstowe, I wouldn't. Do you know the amount of your brother's debts?"

"Six hundred."

"A modest amount to cause such mayhem."

"Modest! Smuggling must be a very profitable business."

"It is, but I am not a smuggler. Or rarely,"

he amended. But then the rain swept in suddenly, in a drenching downpour. He put an arm around her and hurried her toward a building. "The Crown and Anchor. They'll serve us tea."

Bella was having to run to keep up with him. "It's where I was held!" she reminded him. "Someone might recognize me."

"Let them," he said, with a flash of grinning teeth.

Bella laughed. For the joy of running. For a man's strong arm. For the delight of the confident grin. When had she last been so carefree?

As they dashed into the inn she thought, *At the masquerade. With the goatherd. Slipping out onto the balcony for naughty kisses.*

And Captain Rose was the Duke of Ithorne's bastard brother.

She stood stunned by the thought. Had this man, shaking water off his three-cornered hat, been at the revels, disguised as a goatherd? It wasn't beyond belief.

Was that why she had become so attracted to him so quickly today?

What of the footman? Captain Rose again?

It thrilled her, but worried her at the same time. Might he recognize Kelano? What would be the consequences of that?

Images of beds rose in her mind. . . .

"What's amiss?"

Bella started out of her thoughts to find him looking at her.

"Are you still worried about someone here recognizing you after four years? I doubt I would have without prompting, but in any case, why would it matter?"

Bella didn't have to reply, because a woman marched into the hall. "Don't you go getting your wet all over my floors, Caleb Rose!"

Caleb. For some reason the biblical name didn't suit him.

"I can no more help it than a duck straight out of a stream, Aunt Ann," he protested. "Have pity on two ducks and provide tea."

"Oh, go on with you," the plump woman said, chuckling. "Sari, get some towels!" she called as she led them to a small parlor with one narrow window and four plain chairs. It was warmed by a fire, however, so Bella took off her cloak. The rain hadn't soaked through, thank goodness, so she hung it on a hook on the wall.

Captain Rose was still teasing the middle-aged innkeeper, and being treated the same, with much laughter. As Bella stripped off her gloves and held her hands out to the fire, his behavior made her smile. Surely a man must be good to be treated with such affection.

A maid came in with linen cloths, and Bella wiped the rain off her face and hat as best she could as she tried to assess similarities between goatherd and sea captain. Tall. Well built but not heavy. Stubble on the chin . . .

He turned and caught her studying him. Both maid and innkeeper had left, so they were alone, and though the door was open Bella felt a frisson of impropriety. It arose, she realized, entirely from seeing him as an ordinary man. No, not ordinary, but a man she might — she hesitated over the extraordinary notion — might marry.

He gestured to a chair near the fire. "Why don't you sit down and tell me exactly what you have in mind for your brother."

Bella took a chair on one side of the fire and he sat in the other, doing it with neat grace. It was a strange thing to note, but she remembered the way he'd lounged the other night. Graceful, but in a more animal way. The effects of drink, she supposed. She was surprised he was going to content himself with mere tea after the chilly rain.

Changeable as the sea, indeed.

He raised a brow. "You're studying me as if I'm a mystery."

"Perhaps I'm wondering how shocked

you'll be at my plan."

It was true. To propose revenge to a smuggler and scoundrel was one thing. To mention it to this man now made her nervous.

The innkeeper returned then, bringing the tea tray herself. She poured for Bella, adding milk and sugar as required, and put the cup and saucer in her hands. "There, now, ma'am, that'll warm you. And don't you let him get up to any of his tricks. I'll let you pour your own, particular as you are," she said to Captain Rose. "You behave yourself, my boy, and keep this door open."

She swept out, and as Captain Rose poured a small amount of milk into his cup, he pulled a wry face. "Clearly she feels entitled to treat me like a naughty boy."

"It's good that someone does."

His lips twitched. "Ungrateful wench."

She smiled back at him, suddenly very . . . happy. Yes, that was the word. Another unfamiliar sensation, but here in this cozy room, by a warm fire, sipping sweet tea, she felt happier than she could remember.

He poured tea into his cup and drank some. Bella realized something else.

"This is excellent tea."

"You're a connoisseur?" he asked, watching her over the rim of his cup.

"No, but I know good from bad, I think,

and I like this."

"It is a blend I like, and Aunt Ann serves it here to customers likely to appreciate it. Let's return to the punishment of Augustus the Vile. Do you have any notion how to expose his sins?"

Bella had to confess, "No. I thought of merely catching him in the act, but that wouldn't achieve much, would it?"

"He would very much dislike it."

"True. And perhaps I could spread the news." In the Fowler letter, she was thinking, but the sins of a country baronet wouldn't interest that lady. "He plans a marriage, you see, to a sweet and innocent young girl. I don't just seek revenge. I need to ruin him so he can't marry Charlotte Langham or any decent woman. So he can't hurt people anymore."

He was looking at her blankly, and she turned away. "I'm sorry. I don't know why I'm burdening you with all this. I was mad to come to Dover."

"Nonsense. As I said, I'll help you if I can, but you can't be the one to speak of your brother's sins. It would be taken as spite."

Bella looked up again and sighed. "I know. It's hopeless, isn't it?"

He offered her more tea and she accepted it. He took a second cup himself.

"Death would be the ultimate justice," he said.

She searched his features. "I couldn't kill him. Perhaps a stronger woman could, but no, I couldn't."

"Could you bring yourself to hire his killer?"

She felt pinned by his questions, as if on trial. Strangely, her principal thought was that she wouldn't want her brother's death on anyone else's conscience, but especially not on this man's.

"No," she said. Not wanting to seem weak, she added, "Death's too good for him." Abruptly, she realized it was true. "I want him to live with his penance as I did," she said, "but all life long. And I want him so thoroughly shamed that he'll have to stop being a magistrate. Stop going in decent society. So that he'll not even be able to walk down a street . . ."

The words had spilled out of her, but now she looked at him, wondering if he was disgusted.

All he said was, "He might, after some years, blow his brains out. Would that distress you?"

"No," Bella said. "I don't think it would. I'm sure that's very unchristian."

"There's nothing wrong in wanting just

revenge on the blackguard who caused you so much pain, and yes, Miss Barstowe, I will help you if I can. After all, this matter touches me. I was entangled with your mishap, and I intend to make your brother pay. The question is, do you want to be involved, to be present, or will you be satisfied that it has been done?"

Bella put down her cup and saucer, dazed by the choice. Her desire for retribution had been powerful, but her vision of it had been very misty. It still was, but the question he'd posed was startlingly clear.

She inhaled, but then said, "If possible, I would like to be involved. And yes, to be present. But . . ."

He raised a hand, smiling. "No need for buts until we know what's involved. Does your brother live mostly in the country or in Town?"

"In the country. In Oxfordshire. He visits London occasionally, but rarely."

"Interesting. London offers more anonymity."

"I think he used to go more, but he was set upon by ruffians and has avoided the place since except for business. Oh, that was Coxy's work. His retribution."

"A coward," he said. "As I thought. But if I know the country, no matter how devious your brother is, some people will know his vices and his haunts. It's in Oxfordshire that we'll find information and a plan."

"Oxfordshire," Bella said, intending to say that she could not return there, especially not to the area around Carscourt. But that would be where the plan would have to take place.

"Where is your home now?" he asked.

Bella had to think quickly about how much to tell him, for she didn't want him to know about Bellona or Lady Fowler. His opinion of her mattered too much. But she had to admit to some home.

"London," she said. "Soho."

"Alone?" he asked, brows raised.

"With an elderly relative. Her offer of a home allowed me to escape."

"She allows you great freedom."

What could she say but, "Yes."

"Then we should travel to London together. I have business there, as it happens, and we can discuss matters further en route."

Business with your half brother, the duke? That connection still worried Bella, but His Grace the Duke of Ithorne could not magically discover that his half brother was consorting with a woman who'd invaded his revels, and who was an associate of Lady Fowler.

"We won't be able to discuss such matters in front of other passengers," she objected.

"We'll travel by post."

He said it so calmly, as if it were not outrageous at all. Not long ago, travel with a strange man in a private carriage would have seemed impossibly scandalous. Now, with him, it was irresistible.

With this colleague, this conspirator.

This friend.

This man who might be and become more — especially in a private carriage.

"Very well," Bella said, as calmly as she was able. "An early start?"

"Before dawn, if you're willing."

"Of course. As this is my business, Captain Rose, you must allow me to pay for the chaise." It would stretch her income to the full.

"Nonsense. I would be traveling to London anyway."

Relieved, Bella graciously acceded, and they rose to make their sedate way back to the Compass.

Inside, however, Bella was all nerves and excitement.

This morning her driving purpose had been to get revenge on Augustus and prevent him from ever hurting others. She still wanted that, but now she felt on the road to something much more alluring.

Discovering more about this intriguingly changeable man.

Thorn escorted Bella Barstowe to her room at the Compass, aware of danger, and that it was irresistible. The danger presented by an intriguing and desirable woman.

Kelano of the Pleiades, but Kelano the Amazon too, willing to fight for justice. Kelano the harpy, the agent of his destruction? Danger did add savor to life, but he couldn't imagine Bella in that guise.

Tempting her to travel with him was setting the stage for disaster, however. She'd scoffed at the idea of wanting to be compromised into marrying a sea captain, but if she discovered he was a duke she might see things differently. The astonishing thing was, that didn't deter him. After avoiding traps all his adult life, he seemed now willing to shrug at one.

There was something between them. Something he'd experienced only rarely, and never with a young, single woman. She felt it too. He could tell.

It had been there at the revels, and again at the Goat, even though she'd been so wary then. It had been the reason she'd fled, and the reason he'd returned, against his better judgment, the next day.

The reason he'd felt sharp disappointment when she hadn't come to the tryst.

The reason he was going to travel with her tomorrow and, with or without her, destroy her brother.

He wished he could sweep her suffering away, and restore to her all that she'd lost, but that was impossible, even for the Duke of Ithorne. As Duke of Ithorne, however, he had a thousand ways to destroy her brother without involving her at all.

His rational side knew that would be best. He should return her to her home in London and compel her to stay there in safety. She deserved to be part of it, though, to witness justice done, and he'd give her that, at least.

CHAPTER 15

They set out before dawn by chaise to London, as planned. When Bella saw four horses pulling the light post chaise, she was fervently glad she'd allowed him to pay for it all. Sea captains must be wealthier than she'd thought.

In the night her thoughts had turned to marriage.

Once, not long ago, she'd been sure it was folly for a woman to marry if she had the means to stay single, but that certainty had proved a brittle shell, easily cracked — by happy lovers, and by a man who could just possibly be a good husband.

He was handsome, but that weighed little. More important, he was kind, considerate, and could laugh with his aunt, an innkeeper. Physically, he stirred her, and in the night she'd remembered that kiss from long ago, spinning into dreams and fancies that combined goatherd, footman, and dashing, heroic Captain Rose, all wrapped up as an ideal husband.

And now it appeared he was also rich.

Even so, such a marriage would once have been low for Bella Barstowe, but that Bella might as well be dead. She was never going to marry a country gentleman, and certainly not achieve her youthful dream of wedding a lord with a grand estate and a house in Town. She was never even going to be accepted back into any version of the society into which she'd been born.

So why not become Mistress Rose?

Her betraying nighttime mind had spun out images of life in one of the Dover cottages, of his kind and loving arms, and of children. Of neighbors and respect. Of shopping and cooking . . .

Even a nighttime vision had stuttered there, for she didn't know how to cook. Then she'd realized that Peg might want to come with her, and that she could find replacements for Annie and Kitty.

Servants meant she'd had to adjust her neat cottage to something a little larger. Captain Rose was a captain, after all, and half brother to a duke. The duke might visit. She'd added a modest drawing room and dining room and furnished all with a degree of elegance. That had required a footman, but that had toppled her into memory of the Goat, and a bed, and into very different imaginings that had made her blush when they'd met this morning.

She'd heard him casually explaining to the innkeeper that he'd brought word to Miss Barstowe requiring her to return to London and that he was offering her transportation. She hadn't even thought of how it would look here, but if there was any possibility of her dreams becoming true, that was important. She'd made sure to look both dull and distant.

Now they were traveling at speed, and Bella was discovering that a chaise was very small when shared with a large man, especially one whose presence seemed particularly powerful.

She took refuge in rational thought. She had had some rational thoughts in the night, and now she raised a problem.

"I'm nervous about being recognized near my home. I'm still a scandal there. Even the people who are kindly disposed to me still think I ran off with a man, so it would be disastrous to be found out there with you."

He nodded. "In addition, any word of you in the area might alert your brother and make him behave cautiously. It really would be wiser if you remained in London and left this to me."

He was right, but Bella absolutely didn't want that.

"I think I can disguise myself," she told him, not mentioning her experience at it. "A wig and some face paint will do, as we don't venture too close to Carscourt. I can arrange the disguise overnight at my home in London."

Kelano's dark wig. A light touch with Bellona's sallow face.

He frowned slightly, and she thought he might try to insist that she stay behind, but then he shrugged. "As you will."

"What of you, sir? Your dress will be very remarkable in Oxfordshire."

He smiled down at his black frock coat. "I like to be remarked upon, but to be less so I need only dress in tedious modern style."

"And remove the skull from your ear?" Bella suggested, hearing and liking her own teasing tone.

"Must I?" he complained, eyes twinkling.

"I fear so." He reached up and unhooked it, and then offered it to her. "I give you charge of it."

Bella took it, saying, "A skull . . ." and thinking, *If only you gave me charge of your heart.* Even so, she closed her hand over it, resolved to keep it safe.

"Why do you wear it?" she asked. "It makes you seem a pirate."

"Because it amuses me. And because sometimes it's useful to be remarkable."

"As at the Black Rat," she remembered.

"Indeed. Now, if you truly wish to come to Oxfordshire with me, we have another problem. We will be an unusual couple, and we don't want to make people speculate about us."

Bella looked a question.

"We look nothing alike, so claiming to be brother and sister would be doubted, but we're too close in age for any other innocent explanation." After a moment, he added, "The only solution that occurs to me is that we pretend to be married."

Bella almost jumped in her seat. "Absolutely not!"

It would sound like outrage, but it drove too close to her dreams.

"No impropriety, I assure you, but how else are we to present ourselves?"

He was right, and Bella was calming down, but it still felt too dangerous in so many ways. "Half brother and sister," she suggested.

He raised a brow and she grimaced. She knew country ways. Even though it was possible, it wouldn't be believed.

"I'm sorry if the idea distresses you, but if you want to come with me, I see no choice. Any peculiarity will draw attention, which makes it more likely that you will be identified. And if I may be blunt, you say yourself that you've no reputation to lose."

Bella flinched, but it was true. She had no reputation left.

Which meant she was suited to be no man's wife.

All her pretty dreams faded away. She fought not to show any trace of her pain and said, "Very well," with a shrug. It made her all the more determined to ruin Augustus as he had ruined her.

He inclined his head. "Then may I call you Bella?"

It was a crumb, but she took it. "I suppose that would be appropriate. . . ." But then she said, "No, you can't. Using my real name anywhere near Carscourt might trigger recognition."

"So it might. Sharp wits, indeed," he approved. Another crumb. "How shall I address you then?"

"Conventionally. 'Wife,' or 'Mistress Rose.' "

How painful this pretense was going to be, but she would choose it over the alternative — saying farewell to him in London and probably never being alone with him again.

"If we're to be so conventional, you should be a prim young wife." He lazily assessed her. "Your clothes fit that role, but your liveliness doesn't. Perhaps spectacles." Bella had started again, for spectacles were part of Bellona. "With plain glass, of course," he explained.

She had to say, "Where would I find such things?"

"I'll procure some for you. And a ring, of course."

Worse and worse. Bella rubbed the third finger of her left hand. "That feels wrong."

"All in a good cause," he said, so casually she could have hit him.

"Travel gives me a headache," she lied. "May we talk later?"

He agreed, of course, which left Bella at peace with her misery. She turned toward the window and tried to pretend he wasn't there.

She had to come out of her megrims, of course, so she allowed that a pause for tea while the horses were changed had revived her. Put simply, she had a gift — stolen time with this man. She would make the most of it, which meant she wanted to find out more about him.

Once they were under way again, she asked, "So what is your business in London, sir? To do with a ship?"

"With cargo. It will take little time."

"And your ship? The *Black Swan*? It doesn't need you?"

"She — ships are always female — is being careened. Having her bottom scraped," he added with twitching lips.

Bella managed not to react, but she wanted to giggle. Instead, she drew him out about ships and the sea.

Sometime later she found she was talking about herself, but safely, about her area of Oxfordshire. About the geography, agriculture, and industry. She was ashamed of her ignorance and had to confess to being a poor student.

"Being more interested in sneaking out to meet young men on the far reaches of the estate," he said.

"But not until I was at least fifteen, I assure you, sir. Before that I merely daydreamed my way through my lessons."

"Dreaming of meeting young men on the far reaches of the estate."

"No. I dreamed of meeting young men at parties, balls, and assemblies. In London, even. At court." She smiled at her youthful folly. "And being adored by all, of course."

"How many of your dreams came true?" Thorn asked, trying not to startle her out of honest reminiscences. He wanted to know all about Bella Barstowe.

"Some did," she said. "I began to attend local assemblies at sixteen, and went to London in the winter of 1760."

"When George the Second was still alive?"

"Yes. I was presented to him. Very abrupt, but I think he teased me. I wasn't sure, because his German accent was so strong. I gather our new king has no accent at all."

"Having been born and raised in England."

She smiled at him. "Strange for that to be strange."

"Isn't it?"

"Perhaps we should allow no monarch on the throne not born here."

"An astonishing and possibly treasonous notion!"

"Isn't it?" she tossed at him, mischievously repeating his phrase.

It was as if she blossomed before his eyes, not from a bud, but from a thistle into a flower. Not a rose. Something bolder. Perhaps a poppy. Vivid red and dancing in the breeze. That should be her destiny, not whatever drab existence she made do with now.

"Why are you looking at me like that?" she demanded.

"I was revising England's history under your new rules." He risked a diversion to what interested him. "Have you ever attended a masquerade?"

She blushed again. Very prettily. "Why ask that?"

"Mere curiosity."

"Then yes, I have, occasionally."

"Do you enjoy them?"

She was wary of the direction of his questions. Interesting.

But she answered, "Yes."

"What was your favorite costume?"

"What was yours?" she countered.

He thought of the goatherd's homespun, but said, "A pirate. And you?"

"A medieval queen."

"Weren't you young for the part?"

"Everyone is young for a while, even queens."

"True. Many a princess has been married into queendom at a young age. And to a foreign country."

"Another example of the injustices visited on women," she pointed out.

" 'Struth, are you truly of that stamp?"

"Don't you think I have reason?"

He remembered her story. "Yes, yes, you

306

do. Let's return to our plans. Who are the notable people in the eastern part of Oxfordshire?"

Thorn listened, but he was distracted by visions of Bella Barstowe at sixteen, delighting in parties, assemblies, and balls. Dressed as a young queen at a masquerade. Her figure, he remembered, had ripened young. That had been her problem in the Black Rat, that and her refusal to be cowed.

She would have been bold at sixteen, but not very foolish. A girl with a mind and sharp wits, relishing the game but, as she'd said, knowing the limits. She'd probably already had suitors and been on the road to a desirable husband and a happy life.

Until her brother stole that from her.

Surely there was some way to return her to that road. She was still young, and still pretty, but chained by a shredded reputation. Her revenge wouldn't restore it. . . .

Unless her brother could be compelled to tell the truth.

He wouldn't suggest that to her yet. He didn't want to raise her hopes. But restoring her to her rightful station was now his prime purpose in this enterprise.

Of course, he could also always raise her above her station. He could make her a duchess.

Perhaps he twitched, for she looked a question at him. What had she been talking about? Local hunting? He was saved by the coach turning in for a change of horses. He leapt down to speak to the postilions.

What a ridiculous idea. Bella would have no more idea of how to be a duchess than would a fledgling chicken.

Bella watched him leave, dismayed. What had she said?

Something about her parents. That they weren't affectionate, but that she and her sisters and brother had seen little of them.

Had that disgusted him because matters were arranged differently in simpler households? Her throat ached at more evidence of the social gulf between them. She didn't mind it, but perhaps she was too formed by her own life to be a sea captain's wife.

When he returned and the coach set off again, she remained silent, but he said, "You were speaking of your childhood, I think. Were there servants who took gentle care of you?"

She wished she could tell him all about Peg, but that would lead to other matters, so she mentioned her briefly along with others and then asked, "Were your parents loving?"

Immediately, she winced. He'd been born the bastard son of the duke, and at some point sent to live far away because he and the duke's legitimate son looked too much alike. No wonder he said, "No," rather shortly. Perhaps that was also why he seemed cautious about what he said next.

He talked of childhood games and then turned the conversation back to her. "I feel certain you were drawn to your parents' attention now and then by naughtiness."

Bella had to chuckle. "Painfully so, but I learned to keep to the safer side of their tolerance, or perhaps they simply wearied of me. My older sisters behaved exactly as they should."

That led to talk about Athena in Maidstone, and then to memories of the Black Rat, and every word, every connection, drew her deeper into emotions that could only lead to pain.

"Do you still have your knife?" she asked.

He extended his right hand and she saw the hilt appear at his wrist. He slid it free with his left hand. Left-handed. She hadn't noticed that before, either. Every detail was precious. She told him about her pistol and why she'd purchased it, and took it out to show him.

By the time they drew close to London,

the long journey had passed in far-ranging conversation that seemed to flow easily, even though she knew he was keeping secrets. She couldn't complain when she was keeping more.

As the coach rattled on cobblestoned streets she dreaded even a brief return to her life of lies and was tempted to tell him all about Lady Fowler and ask his advice. It was doubtless as well that he returned to the subject of her brother.

"I'll make inquiries in London about hells in your area of Oxfordshire. I don't suppose you know of any?"

The words slipped out. "My hells there were of a completely different order."

He touched her hand, looking somberly into her eyes. "We will make him pay."

They'd both removed their gloves, and she felt the comforting warmth. Then he curled his long fingers around hers, intensifying something that was more than physical heat. Something that made it much harder not to reveal the follies of her heart.

She stared at the carriage floor, probably looking bashful and even afraid, but trying desperately to reveal nothing.

He raised her hand to his lips, which made her eyes fly to his.

"I solemnly pledge to avenge you," he

said, and kissed her knuckles.

The carriage seemed extremely small now. It would take only the tiniest movement to be close enough to kiss.

He relaxed away from her, and she came to her senses. Clearly that sort of kiss hadn't been on his mind at all.

They sank into silence until they arrived at the George Inn, where they would leave the carriage.

Bella hoped he would allow her to go off alone in a sedan chair, but of course he didn't. As he escorted her to her house she fretted that he'd expect to go inside. How could she explain its being her own house, staffed by her own servants?

He didn't attempt to enter, however, but simply waited until she'd unlocked the door. She looked back and waved.

He bowed in that wonderfully elegant way he had, looking darkly mysterious in the flaring light of the linkboy's torch.

The house was dark and silent, and she hoped to slip up to her bedroom unnoticed, but a mobcapped head peered over the rail of the upper landing, illuminated by a quivering candle. Kitty seemed to have a poker in her hand. But then she ran downstairs, in danger of tripping on her nightgown and breaking her neck.

"Oh, miss! Praise the Lord, you're safe!"

CHAPTER 16

Bella suffered a suffocating hug and then broke free. "I'm completely safe," she lied. "I wrote to say as much."

"But you've been gone so long! Oh, I'm sorry, miss. I know I shouldn't. But we've been so worried."

Bella sighed. "I'm sorry, Kitty, but I have important matters in hand, and I'll be away again in the morning. So let me get to bed now."

"Away again?" Kitty's lips trembled as if she'd cry. But she pulled herself together. "As you say, miss. But I'll go and get you some hot water. There's a fire in your room, miss. We've been expecting you back every day."

She was off before Bella could protest, and in truth she'd like to wash after the long journey. She climbed wearily upstairs, rather daunted by the thought of another day's travel tomorrow.

Even with Captain Rose.

Caleb.

For some reason, she couldn't think of him as Caleb.

Better not to think about him at all.

Easier not to breathe, she accepted as she unpinned her hat and took off her cap. She reached in to empty her pockets — and came up with an ivory skull with ruby eyes.

She considered it as if it were a magical head that might speak wisdom, but then wrapped it in a handkerchief and returned it to the pocket for safety.

Thorn walked to his house through the dark and dangerous streets of London with only the linkboy as company. He needed to think.

Bella Barstowe as his duchess. Ridiculous, but once thought, the idea had put down roots.

He'd met every woman considered suitable to be his wife and none had more than a superficial appeal. He'd been able to look ahead and see only tedium with each. Tolerable tedium, as long as she had her life and he had his, but nothing more.

Many were pretty and some were beauties, but he wasn't looking for an ornament.

Most were well trained to run great households, take their place at court, and mingle with the powerful. That was definitely a consideration, but now he wondered why. At the moment his households ran without a duchess.

The eligible young ladies understood court as fully as they understood fashion and frivolity, but learning court protocol would require merely intelligence and application, and he was sure Bella had both. What was more, she had been presented years ago — as a provincial visitor, not as a natural part of that world, but it wouldn't be completely strange to her.

Which left . . . her reputation.

It was an impediment, for people could be cruel, especially to those they saw as intruders, and many would be bitter at her snatching the prize. On the other hand, in the highest circles many were more tolerant of peccadilloes than in gentry circles, and his ducal cloak could cover most flaws.

Robin and Christian would accept her, which was a start.

No, the real start would be to tell Bella who he was before this situation became disastrously snarled.

But he didn't want to do that yet.

As he approached Ithorne House, he grimaced at himself. It was like the plot of a foolish play, but he wanted to see if he could woo and win Bella Barstowe as a simple sea captain, not as the Duke of Ithorne.

Bella took down her hair, trying not to remember the touch of their bare hands and his lips on her knuckles. Trying not to remember the kiss that had never been.

She shook herself and undressed down to stays and shift, then took the pins out of her hair. She was brushing it when Kitty came in, Annie trailing along with the warming pan, but her eager look made it clear she'd mostly come to satisfy herself that indeed Bella was home and safe.

Bella had Kitty get her out of the stays, then shooed them both off to bed.

Alone, she stripped to her bare skin and washed off sweat and dust. As she wiped the soapy cloth around her breasts, she remembered when she'd burst into his bedchamber as he'd been washing.

Washing his muscular chest . . .

A strange sensation made her look down. Her nipples were sticking out. She passed the cloth over them and started at the sensation, at the heat sweeping through her body. Where was he now? Was he washing as she was? She circled the cloth, imagining him doing the same.

She jerked, shivered, and tossed down the

cloth. She hurried into her nightgown and into the bed, but she expected her unruly mind to disturb her sleep again. But the next thing she knew Kitty was shaking her awake.

"There's a package come, miss, so I thought I'd better wake you up."

Bella sat up, rubbing her gritty eyes. "A package? What time is it?"

"Nearly nine, miss."

Bella sat up sharply. She'd said she'd be ready to travel on by ten. "Water, breakfast. And bring out all those items I bought at the rag shop." She took the box Kitty was holding. "And scissors to cut this string."

In moments she had the box open. It contained blond hair. She warily picked it up and realized it was a wig. She unfolded the note beneath.

Strong writing, but just a little untutored, as one would expect.

My dear Miss Barstowe,
  I will be at your house at ten in the morning with a chaise. You mentioned a wig, but do you have one?
                         Your servant,
                         Captain Rose

She did have a wig, of course, but this

mousy blond was much better than the dramatic black. And, she suddenly realized, if Captain Rose had been the goatherd, he might recognize it. A narrow escape.

She climbed out of bed, washed, and put on her shift and stockings. Rebelling against traveling in stays, she put on a pair of her light jumps. If that spoiled the lie of her gown, so be it. Kitty had spread out all her gowns.

Should she wear the pretty one she'd worn to go to the Goat? No, again, he might recognize it. Very well, the more sober brown again. It was practical for dusty travel.

She would take the other, though. There might come a day when it wouldn't matter that he might recognize it.

She sat at her dressing table to brush and pin up her hair. When she fixed the blond wig on top, it was quite convincing. It was already arranged in a neat, quiet style that would never attract attention.

Demure.

Depressing, really, and it made her skin pallid.

"There's something else in this box, miss," Kitty said. "Another pair of spectacles."

Bellona wore half-moon spectacles, but these were perfect circles, and when Bella

318

put them on they gave her an owlish look to add to her demure pallor. The disguise would work, though. Even if she met someone who'd known Bella Barstowe four years ago, this pale, plain creature wouldn't stir suspicion.

She put on the dull brown dress, then added a plain cap and one of Bellona Flint's dull brown hats. Once she'd added her dull brown cloak, she'd looked such an antidote everyone would be surprised that Captain Rose had married her.

"All in the cause," she muttered, turning. "Is my trunk packed?"

Kitty was fighting tears. "Oh, miss, what are you doing? Can't I come with you? It isn't right. You're going off with some man!"

"Yes, I am, but if I were running off to be wicked, I wouldn't dress like this, would I? Don't be silly. And keep all this to yourself."

She saw it was nearly ten and went below to talk to Peg. She'd rather slip away, but that would hurt Peg, who was already punching viciously at a mound of dough.

"You're leaping into folly again, aren't you?"

"I never leapt into folly before," Bella retorted.

"Yes, you did. Many a time. You only got into trouble once. And I grant that wasn't your fault, but if you'd not been off wandering . . ."

Bella let the complaints run past her until they were exhausted; then she sent Annie off on an errand and quietly told Peg what she'd learned, and what she had planned.

"Sir Augustus!" Peg exclaimed, but then she said, "Not that I'm surprised, and that's the truth. A sneaky child, and then there was talk later."

"About what?" Bella asked, suddenly very interested.

Peg gave her a narrow look.

"Yes, I'm probably going to take some risks. But if you can tell me where Augustus goes to game, it will be less risky."

Peg pounded the dough a few more times. "There's a place in Upstone. The Old Oak Inn. It services men, but there's other stuff goes on, and kept very quiet. But you don't want to be going there."

"Yes, I do. Don't worry. I'll have an escort."

Bella said it mischievously, and got the expected response. Almost. Peg spluttered, but then compressed her lips and took her feelings out on the dough.

"You'll murder that," Bella said.

"Shows what you know about making bread. You'll do what you do. I knows that."

"I will be safe," Bella said gently. "I'll be with the gentleman who rescued me all those years ago."

"That Captain Rose? But you said he was a pirate!"

Annie came back then and squeaked with alarm.

"No such thing," Bella said. "He's not even a smuggler." *Most of the time,* she added to herself. "But he feels offended against because he was embroiled in the situation, so he's willing to help me." Peg needed distraction, or she still might attempt to stop Bella's plans. "And when I come back, there will be changes."

"Changes?" Peg asked suspiciously.

"For the better. I intend to leave Lady Fowler's flock."

"Well, thank the good God for that. Where'll we go, then?"

"I don't know. Perhaps you should choose. Think about it while I'm gone. Oh, there's the door."

Bella ran off before Peg could make any more objections.

She opened the door herself, to find Captain Rose waiting outside with a chaise.

His brows shot up and he smiled. "Even better than I hoped. I doubt I'd have recognized you without warning."

"I suppose it's something that I don't normally look appalling."

He chuckled. "Not quite enough to make infants scream. Are you ready?"

He carried her trunk out to the chaise and stowed it in the boot. Bella carried her small valise into the carriage with her. She took her seat, looking curiously at the basket on the floor. Food for the journey?

He entered and the postilions set the four horses into motion. If the basket contained food, it was still alive.

"Did I hear a squeak?" she asked warily.

"Perhaps. I have devised a plan to explain our lingering in one area, and also wandering around alert for dens of iniquity. We will be seeking cat-rabbits of Hesse."

Bella wrinkled her brow at him. "Are you making sense?"

"Perfect sense," he said, eyes bright now with amusement. "A case has recently come to light of a creature that might be a cross between a cat and a rabbit. The scientific community is in a furor about it, especially about whether it is possible. A very eminent gentleman whose name we will never divulge has sent out agents around the nation to discover any other examples."

"Half cat, half rabbit? Which half is which?"

He laughed, looking ridiculously young. "What a delightful question! One that no one has yet posed. Generally the front end is cat, the back end mostly rabbit. Big haunches and little or no tail."

"You're serious," she said.

"Completely."

"Why Hesse?" Bella asked, still suspecting he was playing her for a fool.

"Because the original specimen is said to have come from there. Where it is the terror of the infamous Hessian fanged rabbit."

"Captain Rose, I do not appreciate your indulging in nonsense at a time like this."

"Miss Barstowe, I am relating honestly the story I have been told. On my honor. And here as evidence is the cat." He picked up the basket and put it on his knee.

"You've brought a cat?"

"Three." When he raised the lid, she saw a lushly padded interior and a dark cat. Then she saw the two separate tiny bundles.

"Oh," she said, automatically reaching out.

The cat hissed, and she pulled her hand back.

"Manners, Tabitha," he chided.

The cat said, *"Eee-ah!"* It did not sound apologetic.

"You will see," he said, "that a cat-rabbit of Hesse talks. With time, you will understand her perfectly."

"Will I, indeed? What does '*eee-ah!*' mean, then?"

"Unsuitable for a lady's ears. A human lady, that is."

"I'm not surprised she's upset. Cats with very young kittens don't like to be disturbed."

"So you would think, but she insisted."

"Insisted?" Bella asked, looking at him narrowly. "If you are going to taunt me for the rest of the journey, this will become very tiresome."

"I speak nothing but the truth," he protested. "Whether she's taken a dislike to the lad appointed to care for her or fancied a journey, she was most vociferous on the subject of coming with us."

"She's your cat?" Bella asked, completely confused.

"Oh, no. Not at all. She belongs to a family connection."

"In London."

"In London," he agreed. He seemed to be daring her to ask more questions, and she would have except that she could guess.

She wouldn't have thought the Duke of Ithorne interested in odd cats, but noblemen had their eccentricities. He must have spent the night at his brother's house.

It was another blow against her impossible dreams. A man who moved comfortably at the highest levels of society could never marry someone like herself. She'd thought she'd reconciled herself to that, but a new pang showed the work was not quite complete. Perhaps his charming whimsy about the cat had undermined it.

The kittens stirred and clambered over their mother. Then they tried to climb the walls of the basket. Captain Rose put his hand nearby, and one scrambled onto his fingers, mewling and licking. The other hovered, thinking about it.

Mother cat watched, but she didn't hiss at him.

"They're different, aren't they?" Bella asked.

"Yes. One's a cat-rabbit, but the other seems all cat."

"How is that possible?"

"That's what fascinates the scientists, but if we assume Tabitha is the result of a mating of cat with rabbit, and that her own . . . er, partner was a tomcat, then it might make sense. In the strange way these things work, one offspring could be all cat and the other part rabbit."

Bella was blushing a little, for this wasn't the sort of subject a lady discussed, especially with a gentleman, but she was fascinated. "What of the other kittens?"

"Alas, only two survived, and the careless person in charge at the time didn't preserve the bodies."

"It would have been a strange thing to do."

"Not with a little forethought," he said seriously, making her chuckle.

"Do you always think so far ahead?"

"I try to. For example, I have remembered your wedding ring." He dug his free hand into a pocket and produced a little cloth pouch, offering it to her.

Bella stiffened, but he said, "It really is the only way."

She opened it and found a plain wedding ring. "It doesn't look new."

"It shouldn't, should it?"

It really wasn't such a terrible thing, Bella told herself. She pulled off her left glove and put on the ring. It was just a little tight. *So he's not infallible,* she thought, with some satisfaction, but other thoughts were squirming in. About real rings . . .

She pushed them away and took out the handkerchief that contained his earring. He had his hair tied back, and she saw he wore a plain gold hoop there now. "You'd better take your skull back," she said.

"What?" He looked at her, startled, but

then smiled. "Keep it."

That was rather indefinite, but Bella returned it to her pocket. It was as if she had custody of a little bit of him, which was particularly poignant as she watched the kittens explore his hand, and his gentle way with them.

She wanted charge of all of him, but it would never be.

"Upstone," she said, too abruptly, in her need to break the moment.

"Upstone?" he asked.

She quickly reported what Peg had said, though she credited only a servant who used to live in the area. "I've thought of a problem, however," she said. "My father sat on the magistrates' bench in Upstone, so Augustus probably does too. We might encounter him there. I mean on a street, in an inn . . ."

"Not in a gaming hell or brothel," he said, returning the kittens to their mother.

"Brothel?"

"That was the implication, I believe."

Bella thought over Peg's words and blushed.

"The place sounds ideal," he said. "If he is often at the Old Oak, it could provide our opportunity."

"But how?"

He put the basket back on the floor of the swaying carriage. "We entice him into the same trap — debt. He'll be no wiser now than he was in the past."

"He has a lot more money now," she pointed out.

"Then we raise the stakes."

"Oh, how I detest gaming! What point is there, other than to ruin men and ruin their families as well?"

"Women game too, and their husbands are held responsible for their losses."

"Why?" she demanded. "Why does anyone risk money on dice and cards?"

"For the thrill of it," he said.

"The thrill of winning? That only means someone else must lose."

"Winning is a thrill, but the fear of losing is an even greater one for many. Gambling without risk is dull to them, but gaming for high enough stakes is life lived on the razor's edge."

"But why is that good?"

He just smiled.

"I see you are a gamester too."

"No," he said simply. "I do play — it can also be an amusing way to pass an evening. But I never play for stakes that could thrill me in either victory or defeat. I have other sources of that."

"Smuggling, I suppose."

He sighed. "You will persist. The sea, my dear, the sea. Now, there's a mistress that will feed us fear or exaltation as the mood takes her."

As you do me, Bella thought.

And why else was she here but for the thrill of it, for the addictive power of life lived on the constant edge of something?

He was watching her. She could only pray he couldn't read her.

"Merely plunging Augustus into debt won't serve to ruin him or shame him," she said. "Not without ruining many others. My mother, my unmarried sister. All the servants and tenants. I can't do that."

"A tenderhearted avenger," he said wryly. "You complicate things. Very well, we'll have to have him discovered drunk and in the company of low, loose women. Very loose, very low women."

Bella gaped at him. "Augustus? He's too . . . too highsnooted to sink to low women."

"You think so?" He smiled. "A monkey on it."

"What?"

"I wager five hundred guineas that he already sinks to low women whenever he can, and that that's part of the appeal of the

Old Oak."

"Five hundred . . . !" Bella spluttered. "Do you have that sort of money to lose?"

"I wouldn't lose."

"You are a gamester! A sharp, even. Well, I certainly don't have that much to wager."

"Then we won't gamble on it. We'll simply do it. Think of it. Not just gaming, but whores. There'll not be enough of his reputation left intact to clothe a mouse." Then he laughed. "That put stars in your eyes. What a strange wench you are."

No, you put stars in my eyes. But the thought of Augustus naked in shame was delightful too.

The sun had set and shadows were deep when the chaise rolled into Upstone. He told the postilions to take him on to the best inn in town.

"The Hart and Hare," he said as they alighted. "We must hope they never attempted a mating."

Bella suppressed a giggle. She was given custody of the closed cat basket as he arranged rooms. When they went upstairs, however, Bella realized that he'd taken a parlor and a bedchamber.

One bedchamber.

Part of her sizzled with excitement, but

she still had her wits. "We need two bed-chambers."

"Don't turn squeamish on me now, valiant lady. We're an ordinary couple of no significant wealth. Why would we take two bed-chambers?"

"Because I snore. Or you do."

"We'd endure. People do."

Bella narrowed her eyes at him. "I am not sharing a bed with you, Captain Rose, wedding ring or no."

"It's a very big bed," he pointed out, gesturing toward it.

And reminding her vividly of the Goat. Parts of her threatened to melt.

"We can sleep mostly clothed," he coaxed. "Or you can sleep on the floor."

"That," she said, "is a gentleman's duty."

"But you're the one objecting to sharing the bed."

She threw up her hands at this outrageous way of looking at it. "What if anyone were to find out?" she demanded. "I'd be ruined."

But that, of course, was no weapon at all.

Bella paced the room, truly angry now. Clearly he'd always intended to make her his whore. Never a wife, oh, no. Not Bella Barstowe.

"You had this in mind all along," she accused, facing him.

"No, on my honor. I only thought of the detail when we arrived. It's a real concern, and you can trust me."

"Ha!"

She prowled to the bed as if she could change it by force of will. Split it into two, perhaps.

That made her pause. How odd that sharing a bedroom with a man seemed tolerable if there were separate beds. She was sliding slowly down into hell.

"It is a very large bed," he said again. "It could probably sleep five."

Bella had heard that sometimes many strangers did share a bed in an inn, and indeed, this would suit the purpose.

She turned to face him again. "Very well. But you will keep your shirt and breeches on."

He inclined his head. She knew he was amused and victorious, but he was doing a very good job of hiding it.

"Will you sleep in your stays?" he asked. "I don't advise it, but it's your choice."

She smiled triumphantly. "I'm not wearing any."

A slight flare in his eyes was alarming, but deliciously satisfying at the same time. She'd never known that being without stays might excite a man.

Bella. The last thing you want at this moment is to excite him!

"I'm wearing jumps," she explained, "for comfort while traveling."

"What a very sensible woman you are."

Bella turned to the mirror and removed her hat. "A woman traveling alone has to be, Captain." She considered her very long hat pin and placed it on the stand beside the bed, then turned to smile at him.

His lips were twitching. "Very sensible. Now, I should go below to down ale and talk to the locals. I hope to learn more about the Old Oak, but I can also introduce our cat story."

"What exactly is our cat story? What are we going to do with them?"

He'd opened the basket, but the kittens were fully involved with feeding.

"We will venture abroad every day to show Tabitha to the locals and ask for reports of similar strange cats."

"Or strange rabbits," she said.

He looked at her, arrested. "You really should be on the scientific team. I'm not sure anyone's thought of that. Yes, and strange rabbits. What would the combination do to a rabbit?"

"A long tail?"

"And small ears."

"And the eyes."

"Indeed, the eyes. I do hope we find a specimen. But while I'm below, I'll have a supper tray sent up to you. And something for Tabitha."

As soon as he left, the cat stirred. *"Ah-oo!"*

It was so clearly mild alarm — *What do you think you're doing?* — that Bella laughed.

"Yes, you and your babies are left in my tender care. I know little of such things, but I won't let any harm come to you."

The cat slitted its eyes at her. Then, to Bella's amusement, it managed to reach out a paw and pull the lid of the basket over itself and its babies.

"Is that a cut direct?" Bella asked of the universe.

A squawk might have been confirmation.

She chuckled, but then turned serious as she considered the bed again. Whatever Captain Rose had in mind, she had no intention of letting him have any liberties. She acknowledged her own desires, but she'd not court ruin that way.

She unpacked her small trunk until only the pistol case was left. She loaded it and put it carefully into her valise, then put the valise on the floor beside the left side of the bed, the same side that was already armed with a hat pin.

In due time she might move the gun under her pillow. That made her nervous, but as long as it wasn't cocked, it shouldn't fire. Or so she trusted.

She paced the room nervously again, but then made herself think about the important purpose here: Augustus.

How often would he visit the Old Oak? Even with the cat story, they couldn't dally here for weeks without raising far too many questions. She glared in the direction she thought Carscourt should be, longing to go there immediately and simply choke Augustus until he went purple in the face.

She realized her fists were clenched and relaxed them. She'd dug crimson arcs into her palms.

She considered the wedding ring, and ridiculously, tears blurred her vision. Why had she never known how much she would want to be married once she found the right man?

A maid came in with a tray and set out a simple meal on the table. There was an extra dish with pieces of meat on it. "This is for the cat," she said, looking around.

"Place it by the basket, thank you," Bella answered.

The maid did so and left. The basket remained shut.

"I think that's called cutting off your nose to spite your face," Bella said to the basket, and settled in to enjoy her meal, but thoughts of her future blunted her appetite.

Marriage was an easy and proper way to assume a new identity. She wouldn't be able to marry Captain Rose, but perhaps some other, simpler man could be tempted by her money. An honest, trustworthy, kind man, who would give her his name.

Bella . . . Pennyworth, bookseller's wife, would have no connection at all with Bella Barstowe of Carscourt, and even less to Bellona Flint.

That vision should provide hope for the future, but it felt as appealing as cold suet pudding.

She'd eaten only half her meal, but she opened the door and called for a servant. As soon as one came, she had the dishes taken away, noting that the cat had sneaked out to eat its food undetected. The basket was closed again.

Even a cat rejected Bella Barstowe, and it seemed her "husband" would spend the whole night carousing downstairs. Clearly her virtue was not threatened at all.

Thoroughly depressed, she demanded hot water in the bedchamber.

When it came, she locked the door to the

parlor and the other to the corridor, and prepared for bed. She took off her gown and jumps. She thought about removing her petticoat. It was bulky, but she had to keep it on or she'd be in only her shift, which was less covering than her nightgown.

She thought about her nightgown. It rose up to the neck and fell to the floor. The sleeves were full-length. But a nightgown was a nightgown, and she couldn't share a bed with a man when in her nightgown.

She took off her stockings and then unpinned the wig and let down her hair. She brushed it, plaited it, and then went to glare at the bed.

She drew the curtains all around it. Perhaps he'd take that as a hint.

She listened at the adjoining door. Nothing. She quickly unlocked both doors, then scrambled into the dark tent of the bed.

She realized that she'd left the candle lit, but so be it.

She pulled the covers up to her nose and lay on the very edge of the side farthest from the door. Remembering the pistol, she reached down and undid the clasp of the valise.

She couldn't bring herself to put the pistol under her pillow. That felt far too dangerous. It was close, and that was a comfort, but she wasn't sure she'd get a wink of sleep.

CHAPTER 17

Thorn knocked before entering the bedchamber. There was no answer. By the guttering candle he saw the evidence of washing and the curtains drawn firmly all around the bed and smiled. She was probably clinging to the very limit of the far side as if her life depended on it.

He really should take the floor, but floors were damn hard and it made no sense. She was ruined by being here, regardless of where he slept. If it ever came to that, they were compromised in any number of ways without sharing a bed.

He trimmed the candlewick, and then went out to the parlor to request fresh water. When it came, he carried it quietly into the bedchamber and went behind the screen to wash.

He resumed his shirt as instructed, but then instead of climbing in on the near side, he picked up the candlestick and went

339

around to the far side of the bed. He parted the curtains just enough to see. There she was, right on the edge as he'd expected, but if she'd huddled under the covers at first, she'd eased them a little, exposing her head. He smiled at the plain nightcap tied beneath her chin.

He'd had many women in many beds, some briefly and some for the night, but none had worn a prim, plain cap. Was that why it seemed ridiculously erotic?

She'd plaited her bronze hair, but wisps escaped. Her lips were slightly parted, and he remembered their sweetness on the terrace at the revels. He leaned down, but then straightened, restraining himself.

Her eyelashes lay on her cheek, but they were not extraordinarily thick or long. Her brows would benefit from plucking, but they were elegantly curved. He would not resort to ogling her chin. Though it was a pretty chin, and could be firm.

He pinched out the candle, but the image of the sleeping Bella lingered in his mind as he made his way around to his side of the bed. He settled into it as carefully as he could, and hoped for sleep.

Bella awoke the next morning sniffing the air like a wary rabbit. If she'd had whiskers, they'd be twitching. She could sense the man. She could smell him, though not by any distinct aroma. She thought perhaps she could hear him breathe.

She squirmed onto her back and slid a look at him.

He was on his back too, his far arm hidden, but his nearer one out on the bedcovers between them. He seemed fast asleep.

She wanted to study him. She wanted to move closer. She found the strength to slide sideways out from beneath the covers, letting her feet down to the floor without use of the steps. Once she was out of the bed, she grabbed her clothing and crept into the next room.

She could hear the inn sounds now — wheels, hooves, and voices outside the window, and steps in the corridor. She was sure those noises had been audible from the bedchamber, but tension had deafened her. The cat's basket was open, but cat and kittens seemed asleep.

She hurried back into her clothes, and then realized that there was no mirror in this room, and her hairbrush, pins, and cap were also in the bedchamber. She left her plait as it was and went to the window to peer out. A reasonable day. Perhaps a little sunshine for their ridiculous search for cat-rabbits of Hesse.

She had to chuckle. The whole story must be a confection.

A noise to her right made her turn, startled. There was no one there. It had been a soft sound, like something light falling. After looking around, she noticed that the cat's basket was shut.

She went over and opened it. "You are very rude."

As the cat's face always scowled, it was hard to tell its feelings, but she'd swear it was scowling at her now.

"You're not even his cat. You belong to a friend of his."

The cat made a sound like *"zup!"* that Bella heard as a sneering dismissal. She lowered the lid of the basket, saying, "Have it as you will."

"Don't tell me you're talking to Tabitha as well."

Bella turned sharply, feeling caught in a misdeed. He was mostly dressed, lacking only his coat, though his hair hung loose as it had the first time she'd met him. As it had that drunken night at the Compass. And at the Olympian Revels?

"She shut the basket lid to snub me."

"Yes, she does that."

Bella was looking at the basket as they

spoke, and she saw the lid rise a little. Then it rose more as the cat stood. Tabitha kicked it back completely with one hind leg, saying, *"Ah-ee-o-ee."*

Addressing Rose, of course, and it sounded like, "How are you?"

Bella stalked into the bedroom to do her hair. *Let them commune with each other.*

When she saw her scowling face in the mirror, however, she burst into giggles. When she recovered enough, she saw Captain Rose in the mirror, smiling at her.

There was something in his face, almost a tenderness, and it made her heart flutter. Bella paid attention to her hair, untying the plait and brushing it out, for some reason tongue-tied.

When she glanced again, he was still watching, leaning against the jamb of the open door.

"Is something the matter?" she asked, not turning.

"No. I'm simply enjoying watching a woman attend to her hair."

"A novelty for you, is it?" she asked scathingly.

But he said, "Yes."

"You'll be trying to convince me you're a saint next."

"Never that. Do you need help?"

"With my hair? I doubt a man like you has the skills."

"I can tie knots."

"Which is the exact opposite of what I want."

She focused on her own reflection again, aghast at the effect he was having on her. Her heart was racing. She was sure she was flushed. It was because of the bed and the soft, sweet domesticity winding around them.

"Have you ordered breakfast?" she asked, more sharply than she'd intended.

"I'll attend to it, Your Majesty," he said, and disappeared from view.

Bella put her hand to her chest for a moment, trying to steady her heart, but when she looked in the mirror, her eyes were bright.

Stars in the eyes.

Was there any way to make her dreams come true?

She wouldn't even consider whether it would be wise to do so.

A snug house in Dover. A bedchamber much like this one, but with a smaller bed. One they would truly share.

She hastily twisted her hair and speared it with hairpins. She fixed on the wig and put the cap on top. There, that was better, but her eyes still sparkled. She put on her spectacles. They dimmed the glow a little, but not, perhaps, enough.

Why did she want to conceal it?

Hadn't he, perhaps, looked at her in a special way?

She heard someone arrive in the other room and rose. Breakfast. He must have left to order it, for she hadn't heard him shout. She smoothed down her skirts and checked her appearance once again, wishing she were a raving beauty. Wishing she were at least dressed prettily. Then she joined him.

"We have tea and chocolate," he said, gesturing for her to take a seat at the table. "If you want coffee, I'll get it for you."

"No, chocolate is perfect," Bella said, sitting. She watched him pour tea for himself. It was a clear amber and he added no milk or sugar. She also noticed a small wooden chest on the table.

"Have you brought your own tea?" she asked.

"A foible of mine."

"I'm still surprised to find you a tea drinker."

He smiled at her. "What constitutes a tea drinker?"

Daring to tease, Bella said, "A milksop?"

"Unfair to the most enchanting brew the

345

world knows, Bella. You permit that, in private?"

Bella suspected she should object for her heart's safety, but she said, "Of course. And you are Caleb?"

"Ah." He considered his teacup, then looked up. "My friends call me Thorn. From Rose, you see. Will you use that?"

She wanted to, but it felt dangerous. "I'm not sure. It seems such a . . . personal name."

"What do you call your brother?" he asked, beginning to eat ham.

"Augustus. We were never close enough for nicknames, though I certainly should have thought of an alternative." Bella took a piece of fresh, hot bread and began to butter it. "Augustus means the most high. I wonder what the opposite would be."

"Mean?" he suggested. "Shameful? Base?"

"I don't suppose there's a name that means base."

"Bastard?" he offered, then asked, "What's the matter?"

Bella looked at him, trying to decide what to say. "I understand you are a bastard. An illegitimate son of the Duke of Ithorne, and brother of the current duke."

"Ah, that." He did look uncomfortable,

but then he shrugged. "I feel no shame in it."

Bella watched him eat ham with a hearty appetite and had to believe him. "I hear the current duke has been kind to you."

"I get to sail the *Black Swan*. I don't envy him, if that's what concerns you. Hellish business, being a duke."

"Most people wouldn't think that."

"Most people have no idea what it involves."

"You say that fervently. He talks to you about his life?"

He was busy pouring himself more tea. "We are brothers."

Bella remembered her questions about the donation of a thousand guineas. "Is he a generous man?" she asked.

He looked up in surprise. "Ithorne? I'd say so."

"Does he support any particular causes?"

"Seeking a donation? For what?"

She'd triggered his curiosity, so she shrugged. "Oh, nothing like that. You probably find dukes commonplace, but to me one is an extraordinary creature."

"He's just a man, like me."

She had to chuckle. "I doubt that. He probably has ten servants to help him to dress, and four barbers to keep his face free of hair."

"He does like to be clean shaven."

"There, see. And never a hair out of place or a spot of dirt on his shining shoes."

"Exactly!" But his lips were twitching.

"I have seen him, you know," she said. "At a distance, of course. But he is always in perfect order."

"In public. He has a private face." He drank tea, watching her. "He is not so bad a fellow, Bella. Believe me."

She realized he was fond of his brother and perhaps even loved him and she was embarrassed to have poked fun. "As you say, perhaps it's not easy to have such a high station and have everyone in awe of you."

"No. Perhaps the bastard son has the best of it, so Bastard Barstowe would be far too good a name for your brother." He considered a moment. "I believe I will simply think of him as Slug."

Bella almost choked on her chocolate. "Excellent. Henceforth, he is Sir Sluggaby Barstowe."

They clinked cups, in perfect agreement, and returned to their meal.

"So how long do we have to give Sir Sluggaby his comeuppance?"

His expression altered, and she realized that she'd licked butter off her lips. "They say warm butter is injurious to health," she said nervously, "but it is so delicious."

" 'They' are invariably killjoys," he said.

"They are, aren't they?" He was still watching her and had hardly touched his food.

"Eat!" she commanded. "Would you like hard eggs, cheese . . . ?"

"Are you going to mother me?" When she looked up, he added, "Or wife me?"

She caught layers of meaning in that and her cheeks went hot. "Don't!" It had escaped without thought. "Don't," she repeated, "don't tease me in that way here, now."

"You're right. I apologize. But it is almost irresistible, Bella."

He began to eat again. Bella attended to her own food, tongue-tied.

"And," he added, "it is delightful that you leave the door open to my teasing you that way in some other time and place."

Bella looked at him, and honesty wouldn't let her dismiss the suggestion. She was leaving the door wide-open, and to pain as well, but she was willing to take the risk. For now, however, they should return to business.

"What did you learn last night?"

"The Old Oak is as reported, and a fairly discreet place. Most of the men who game there also use the women. You are disturbed by my speaking of these matters?"

"No," Bella said, "but I pity the poor women forced into that trade."

"You have a kind and thoughtful heart. No one would think such work ideal, but there will always be some women who must earn their bread, and morality aside, there are worse ways."

"No one should be forced to that," Bella protested.

"Of course not."

"I mean that no one should be so poor as to have no choice."

He sighed. "I forget you are a social reformer. Where is the money to come from to fund these women's lives?"

"I don't know. I'm sorry. It's just that I've experienced being penniless and it imprisoned me because I wasn't willing to take that road. Not everyone has food and shelter, however, and thus they are forced."

He nodded. "Perhaps we need convents."

"Convents?"

He took a piece of bread. "Convents gave women of means an honorable choice other than marriage, and poor women a refuge where they were safe from men. They also provided commanding women a place where they could rule. I think you might have made an excellent mother superior."

"I?" Bella said in surprise.

"You're young yet, but in twenty or thirty years you could cow bishops and kings. You have a natural command."

Bella laughed. "Is that truly tea, or are you drinking brandy?"

He held the cup out. "Smell."

Bella did. A slight aroma. Definitely not brandy, or any other sort of spirit. "I assure you I'm not that sort of person."

"Has no one ever followed your lead?"

"No."

But then she thought about it. Peg hadn't precisely followed, but she'd attached her fate to Bella's. Annie and Kitty had been taken in out of charity, but instantly looked to Bella for guidance. Some of the flock had turned to her with their concerns about the Drummonds, as if they expected her to be able to oppose them.

She looked at him and read his expression. "Don't be smug."

"Smug?" He laughed. "I don't think anyone has ever described me as smug before. So you do have followers. Who?"

"None of your business, and not an army. It could be weeks before Augustus visits. How long can you dally here?"

She busied herself with bread to hide her

intense interest, praying it would be a long time.

"How long can you dally?" he countered. "When does your relative return home?"

She'd forgotten that. "I'm not sure." She had to give an estimate. "Perhaps a fortnight."

"That would stretch our local inquiries," he said. "We'd best pray your brother's addiction brings him here sooner. Of course, he could have more than one haunt."

Two weeks had been too much to hope for, but Bella hoped it would be many days before Augustus needed to live on the razor's edge.

"Tonight, I need to visit the Old Oak and learn all I can there."

"It seems to me that you are doing all the interesting tasks," Bella objected.

"You want to visit a brothel?"

"No, how will it look to people here? Your wife might object."

His nonwife certainly did.

"Will you throw a scene?" he asked, interested.

"I'm more likely to throw a pot. A chamber pot, perhaps."

"Mistress Rose, you alarm me."

"Good."

"But in your service, I still must visit the Oak."

Bella could see no rational argument against it. "Very well," she muttered. "What do we do until you can sink into debauchery?"

"Search for Hessian cat-rabbits." He drank the last of his tea and rose. "I'll arrange for a vehicle. Try not to get into a fight with the cat queen of Hesse while I'm gone."

He left, and Bella looked at the closed door, fighting tears. She realized it wasn't a matter of a brothel. It was because her plan might be completed in one day.

In the past such speedy retribution would have been cause for joy, but now it meant only that their time together could soon be over.

CHAPTER 18

It had been dark when they'd arrived, but by daylight, even sullen daylight, Bella recognized Upstone and the countryside around. They drove along lanes, stopping at each farm or cottage to ask about cat-rabbits. They exhibited the specimens to the dubious, and for some reason Tabitha tolerated it. Sometimes she seemed to be reveling in the attention.

Even with the evidence, most of the farming folk expressed great doubt of any cat being interested in a rabbit in that way, and vice versa. Bella could see she and Thorn would be well remembered as those moon-mad London folk and their peculiar cat.

The kittens were enjoying the attention too, and Sable in particular often had to be returned to the fold.

In their wanderings, Bella noticed a few changes. A large elm had been struck by lightning near Pidgely, and someone had built a handsome house near Buxton Thrope. When they stopped in that village to make their cat-rabbit inquiries, they divided their efforts. There were some women gathered in gossip, and Bella went to them, while Thorn entered the inn to talk to men there.

A team, and they were a good one.

Bella casually asked how old the handsome house was, commenting upon its elegant lines. She soon learned all about it, but that wasn't her goal. She'd made an opening to ask about other notable houses in the area, and whether any might be open to visit. She was fishing for opinions about Carscourt, and about Augustus.

Carscourt was soon mentioned, and one sturdy woman muttered, "But an ugly place that is. Ugly as the hearts inside it."

Bella might agree, but she feared that picking up that stitch might make the woman turn silent. "Is it old?" she asked.

"Old, ma'am? Nay. No' but a hundred years or so."

"And has it always been in the same family?"

"The Barstowes? I dunno, ma'am."

An ancient, bird-thin woman chimed in. "They came there during Cromwell's time. Roundheads," she spat. "There was a royalist family there afore, the de Breelys, but none were left, or none that returned, so the Barstowes kept it."

That was clearly regarded as theft.

Bella had never been aware that dislike of her family went so far back, but country memories ran long. The events of the past century — the beheading of the king, the long, strict rule by Parliament when all the joyous traditions were banned, and the return of the monarchy — all were still remembered here.

"I suppose the family is thoroughly royalist now," she said, in the manner of one making peace.

"Maybe," said the first woman, "but they've still got cold, Roundhead hearts. Sir Augustus had Ellen Perkins whipped for lewd behavior, and her only a widow with her needs."

"What happened to the man?" Bella asked.

The woman gave a harsh laugh. "Fined. Ellen don't have the money to be fined, but he might have ordered her whipped anyway."

"And he put old Nathan Gotobed in the stocks for selling wares on Sunday," said another woman. "Doing no one any harm."

"They do say Sir Augustus was frothing

mad that nobody threw anything at the old man there," said a young woman with a babe on her hip.

"That's why he don't use the stocks much," said the older woman. "It's a fine or a whipping if you're up in front of Sir Augustus Barstowe."

Bella sensed a silent curse at the end of that, but the women weren't going to go that far in front of a stranger. The weight of her family's reputation lay heavily on her as she joined Thorn near the carriage.

"I really wish I could find the strength to kill him," she said.

"You've heard about him too, have you?"

"What did you hear?"

"Just general cruelty, especially against those who drink, gamble, or behave licentiously. I wonder if all magistrates are harshest on those who commit their own sins, or even the sins they wish they dared commit."

"I'd rather they took up self-flagellation," Bella said.

"Amen. He has no admirers hereabouts, but no one mentioned hypocrisy. What of the women?"

"No."

"Shame. Has anyone recognized you?"

Bella hadn't been watching for that. "I don't think so, and I don't expect it unless I encounter someone I knew well. And even there, apart from my family and the Carscourt servants, any memories would be long in the past."

"We'll avoid the area close to Carscourt, then," Thorn said, handing her up into the chair.

"The people there are less likely to talk about Augustus, in any case. They are completely dependent on him, poor souls."

They continued their progression around the fringes of Barstowe influence, asking about cat-rabbits, but also bringing up Barstowe and Carscourt whenever they could. The dislike was sometimes overt, sometimes subtle, but it was universal. It was linked to Augustus, but went back to her father, and included her sister Lucinda, whose idea of charity, apparently, was to visit the poorest and lecture them on their fecklessness. Bella had assumed Lucinda's charitable visits had included soup and warm clothing.

"I feel tainted," she said as they drove to another village. "Perhaps I'm the same beneath. Perhaps my desire for revenge is proof of it. . . ."

He put a gloved finger over her lips, drawing the placid horse to a standstill. "There is nothing warped about that."

" 'Vengeance is mine, saith the Lord'?"

" 'God helps those who help themselves.' And speaking of helping ourselves . . ."

He slid his hand to cradle her face and leaned forward to kiss her.

It was a very gentle kiss — not tentative, but respectful. Not perhaps gentle so much as tender, and it melted Bella's heart. Her lids drifted down and she sensed only warm lips. And birdsong, and the touch of a breeze, which both seemed to add to the magic of the moment.

He drew back and she opened her eyes. "Thank you," she said without thinking.

"Thank you," he said, with a sweet smile.

She'd never have expected a sweet smile from Captain Rose. "Changeable as the sea," she murmured.

"What?"

"You told me that about you. At the Compass, when we were both drunk."

He seemed blank.

Bella chuckled, feeling extraordinarily happy. "Perhaps you were drunker than you seemed."

"I must have been. And yes, I am. Changeable. I prefer to think of it as many-faceted, but perhaps I deceive myself."

"Many-faceted is like a stone. It's hard. I prefer changeable like the sea."

He laughed. "You clearly haven't encountered a hurricane." He took up the reins and they drove on.

Maybe not, thought Bella, *but I might be experiencing one now.*

Thorn tried to keep his features calm, but he was irritated with Caleb for coming up with the word "changeable" without telling him.

And that was ridiculous. In fact, he was angry because more slips like that could make Bella question whom she was with. For example, Caleb did not like tea, and thus as Captain Rose, Thorn avoided it. He'd ordered it without thinking at the Crown and Anchor, and Caleb's aunt Ann had served it, as she knew he liked it. She was Caleb's aunt and could tell them apart, but she treated them both with the same warmth.

The tea had been a mistake, however, and he might make more, and — he almost laughed aloud at the oddity of this — he was worried that if Bella realized he was the duke, he'd lose her entirely.

What a topsy-turvy world.

She seemed to have strong opinions on injustice, however, which he feared might go along with a radical dislike of the aristocracy. His challenge might not be to win her without dangling wealth and a title in front of her, but rather to win her despite those handicaps.

And he wanted to win her.

He'd enjoyed the past few days with Bella more than he could remember enjoying time spent with any other woman. A week ago he would probably have said that days with a woman would be deadly dull, especially a woman who wasn't a lover.

These days had been different, however, despite the ordinary activities — walking, traveling, eating. . . .

Sleeping in the same bed?

Kissing?

Kissing in the sweetest, gentlest way, however, that was completely new to him. Not flirtatious kisses. Not kisses as prelude to passion.

Simply kisses, which he wanted more of, for their own delights.

He feared he was going mad.

Bella was aware of the silence as they drove back to their inn, but didn't know what to make of it. She'd like to think that he was as overwhelmed by the kiss as she, but she doubted it.

She suspected he was troubled.

He was troubled, no doubt, because he

feared he'd raised expectations, and that would trouble him only if he had no intention of meeting them. It caused a pang, but not a severe one, because truly, she expected nothing else. Dreamed a little, yes, but expected, no.

At the inn she adopted a calm, mildly cheerful manner and acted as if the kiss had never happened. They went up to their room, but the silence lingered. He was uncomfortable. He wished he weren't stuck here with her.

"Perhaps we could sup downstairs?" she said. "In case we overhear anything?"

He agreed so smoothly she suspected he'd been thinking the same thing. "We should perhaps be a little cool and distant," he said, "given that I'm about to go off to a brothel."

She hated the reminder of that. "If I indulge in a screaming harangue, that could be your excuse to go to the Oak."

"So it could," he said, opening the door for her, "but perhaps you shouldn't attract quite so much attention?"

"How very frustrating," Bella said, and led the way downstairs.

They ate mostly in silence, which would have given an excellent opportunity to listen to other conversations, but the only other couple eating in the dining room was silent too.

Afterward, Bella returned to their room, bitterly aware of where he was, and vaguely aware of what he probably was doing. When she realized she was pacing the room, she made herself sit down and read for a while, but the words hardly made sense, and the candlelight strained her eyes.

Instead, she sewed, finishing some plain hemming she could almost do blind.

It gave her mind too much time to wander.

She realized that Tabitha hadn't closed the basket lid, so Bella asked, "He calls you an oracle. Are you able to give advice, or even tell the future?"

The cat made one of her incomprehensible series of sounds. Bella chose to take it as encouragement.

"I see you like him. I must warn you that sailors are notoriously unfaithful, being away so much."

The cat's answer seemed denial.

"No, no, it's true. Do you think perhaps wives don't mind too much if it happens on a distant shore? It's certainly not the same as when a husband sets up a mistress in a nearby village and all the neighbors know about it. That was the situation with Lady Fowler and others among her followers."

It was what Squire Thoroughgood had done with his first wife, heartlessly shaming her. That had been just one reason that Bella had refused the match.

"It's intriguing, isn't it?" she said to the slit-eyed cat. "What we can do and not do. For example, I would have said I could never have traveled like this with a man. A stranger, really."

Tabitha made a sound that appeared to be a sigh. Bella chose to take it as sympathy rather than boredom.

"And now he's off to a brothel. To find information, of course, but I assume he'll have to . . . to do what men do in such places." Bella realized she was scowling as much as the cat. "Of course, it's nothing to do with me."

The door opened and Bella started, but it was only the maid, come with more wood for the fire. The woman looked around. "Oh, I thought I heard voices, ma'am."

"The cat," Bella said. "It gets nervous in silence. Cat-rabbits do."

The woman looked dubiously at Tabitha, who obligingly chose that moment to rise and take one of her walks, showing her rabbitlike hind end.

"It is an odd one, and no mistake," the maid said. "Have you found any others, ma'am?"

"Not yet, no."

"Then likely there are none hereabouts, ma'am. The whole area's talking of the reward your husband's offered. Shall I bring your water yet, ma'am, and the warming pan?"

In other words, *Are you ready for bed?*

Bella realized the maid might know that Mistress Rose's husband wasn't in the inn, and might even know where he was. How mortifying, but even more so to be sitting up waiting for him to roll home.

"Yes, please," she said, and was soon preparing for bed.

She climbed up the steps and into her side of the big bed, feeling even more awkward than the night before.

That kiss had changed everything.

No, not just that. A day in his company had also turned her mind upside down.

They talked so easily, and often found amusement in the same things. There had also been some comfortable silences, but underneath, such awareness, and a powerful physical sensation whenever they were close.

She'd never experienced the like before.

She rolled onto her back. What if this were her wedding night and she were waiting for her husband?

Did she love her mythical husband? Had they been courting for weeks, months, even years, with kisses and a little more than kisses, both burning for this night?

Or was it an arranged marriage, with the two of them still almost strangers and she uncertain of how he would be? She'd heard enough snippets at Lady Fowler's to know a wedding night could be rough or considerate. Even, it seemed, clothed or unclothed.

She realized then that she'd put on her nightgown.

How had that happened?

Because the maid had spread it on the rack near the fire to be warm, as Kitty did. Her mind on other things, she'd put it on without thinking.

She should get up and change into her shift and petticoat, but she was too warm and comfortable, and after all, the plain, serviceable nightgown did cover all except her head and hands.

If this were her wedding night she might have something of finer cloth, trimmed with lace, and perhaps not fastened right up to her neck.

She was growing too warm now, and strangely restless.

She remembered those women at Lady Fowler's who had better memories, women who'd loved and enjoyed their husbands and who would smile in a sweet, sad way when they thought of them.

Those women had come to live on Lady Fowler's charity because their sweet, loving husbands had left them penniless. That was the trouble with choosing a husband. A woman needed not just a man to love and . . . and pleasure her, but one who would manage his affairs wisely, work hard, and provide for her and her children, even after death.

Thorn.

"Thorn." She said it aloud, savoring it. She was certain he was a hard worker who would manage his affairs well. He'd never leave a widow burdened with debts or unprovided for. And he would skillfully pleasure her.

Her hand wandered over her body as she wondered exactly what that pleasuring involved. Apart from kisses and embraces, she wasn't clear. She felt sure she could get infinite pleasure from kissing and embracing Thorn.

Memories rushed in, memories of that encounter when he'd been drunk. His nakedness and how it had made her feel. The brash invitation to his bed. His promise that she'd enjoy it, which she'd believed.

And again at the Goat. Another wicked invitation, and as sinfully tempting.

Put together with hot, overwhelming kisses on a terrace at Ithorne House . . .

Bella drifted into wild, unthinkable dreams. . . .

Thorn crept into the room after midnight, boots in hand, somewhat drunk but mostly unblemished. He'd gone to the Old Oak prepared to use one of the women if necessary, but he'd been glad not to have had to. A good part of the reason was the unsavory nature of the place, but the other was lying in his curtained bed.

Their bed.

He'd carried up a candle and now he took it behind the screen to undress and wash. He returned to the hearth for the water jug so thoughtfully placed there, but the fire was dead and the water cool. What else could an errant husband expect?

He cleaned his teeth and washed as thoroughly as he could, glad to get the stink of the Oak out of his nose. He'd stripped off his shirt because a clinging whore had left cheap perfume on it along with streaks of her heavy face paint.

She probably wore it to cover pox sores. It was that sort of place. They had what he wanted, however, and more than he'd hoped for. Bella would get her just retribution, and he'd have the satisfaction of providing it.

He went to his valise to find a clean shirt and put it on, then carried the candle over to her side of the bed. He carefully parted the curtains, letting in as little light as possible.

His heart somersaulted in his chest. With her plait and cap, and a nightgown frill demurely circling her neck, she looked young, and innocent in a way long lost to the girls at the Oak.

She stole his breath, but why the devil had he allowed her to come on this dangerous adventure? He'd not just allowed it; he'd encouraged it, because he'd recognized Kelano and been fiercely curious.

How had Bella Barstowe come to be at the Olympian Revels?

Again those needle pricks of suspicion stirred that this was some deeply complex plot to trick him into making her his duchess, but he couldn't believe it. Especially not after days in her company, and that sweet, inexperienced kiss.

He should send her packing for her own safety, but how? He knew her by now, and knew she wouldn't be sent away so close to triumph. If he forced the issue she might take any notion into her head and act on it.

It occurred to him that she was a combination of his friends' wives. At times calm and conventional, a perfect, tranquil companion like Caro. At times fiery, resolute, and capable of instant, extreme action like Petra.

The perfect combination.

She opened her eyes and tensed. Before he could speak, she relaxed. "Oh, it's you. What time is it?"

"Long past midnight. Go back to sleep."

But she was smiling at him, sweet and beguiling in that rosy relaxation that came out of sleep.

He leaned down and kissed her. He made sure to keep it like the last kiss, gentle and unalarming, even though her warm scent rose dangerously into his brain. He drew back, making it slow so she didn't imagine rejection and be hurt. He stepped away from the bed meaning to take the candle and go around to his side.

But then she licked her lips. And left them parted. With a sigh, he leaned down again to taste a little more.

Delicious. He put a hand to her cheek to cherish her, ran his fingers up under her cap, into her hair, wishing the cap gone and the hair loose.

She welcomed his deeper kiss, and then she gripped his upper arm, making a sound in her throat. It was faint, hesitant, but unmistakably a response. Something deep inside him stirred. Desire, yes, but more than that — a need to cherish and protect, to hold her. . . .

He was on the bed now. She'd rolled with him, onto her back. He was half over her, but the bedcovers were still between them. She was safe.

Her hand squeezed his arm again. It wasn't hot, but it burned anyway.

He released her lips to kiss her cheek, her ear, and along her jaw. "Tell me to stop," he said.

"No." But, ever sensible, she added, "Not yet."

He chuckled as he ran his finger along the frill of her nunlike nightgown. It came up to her neck as her shift didn't, but it destroyed him as her shift had not. "When should I stop?"

She was blushing deeply, but her eyes shone. "I don't know. Yet."

"Wicked wench."

He tugged the lace loose and laid the gown open down to the cleft between her breasts.

"I'm not a wench," she insisted, but her

voice was husky and her chest was rising and falling with her excited breaths.

That breathing sped when he slid a finger into the rich, warm valley between her breasts, hardly seen in the dim light, but so vivid to his senses.

"Please be a wench," he murmured. "Just for tonight."

He stroked the generous swell of the breasts on either side and then he cradled one, loving as always that sweetest of all soft weights. He was hard now and aching to be in her, but he wouldn't do that. He commanded himself, laid down the order that no matter what, he wouldn't do that. But he must have a little more.

He kissed her again, more deeply now but still carefully, enjoying her unskillful enthusiasm and her sharp reaction when he brushed a thumb over her nipple. She made a throaty sound, part alarm, part astonishment, part — he hoped — excited pleasure.

He wanted to purr, because clearly he was the first to do this to her, to summon these exquisite pleasures. He'd known it must be so, but the confirmation was like a medal, like a victory. Like a conquest.

"It's all right," he said. "It's all right. Just let me touch you there."

She shifted, and it could've been with

resistance or pleasure, but then she whispered, "Very well."

"Very well indeed." He kissed her again as he played with her, assessing her response. If she was afraid, she wouldn't respond and he'd stop.

He caught the catch in her throat as she opened her mouth more, pressed closer. Their tongues met, hers tentative but eager. He thrust with his. Her body moved in response. It was torment. It was wonderful.

He kissed her and played with her, first one breast, then the other, then slid away from her panting lips to put his mouth to a breast.

Once he had her response there, he pulled back the bedclothes at the side, raised her nightgown, and explored between her thighs, sensing, sensing, sensing her every reaction so he could stop if he must. So he could progress at the right pace, give her all possible, perfect delight.

For why else had he become skilled in these arts, if not for this? For this woman. This moment.

He'd been trained when young by skillful women, and the training had included self-control, because he had always wanted to be in control. Bella was safe here with him, and as she moved in delight, more frantically by the moment, her face showing how lost she was in that wondrous land, he smiled, complete. Then he pushed her over into the little death.

He met her in the climax kiss, catching her cries, and then slipped under the covers to hold her through the shudders of after-pleasure. He soothed her back, kissed her cheek, told her how much her pleasure had pleased him.

Some women didn't believe him. Some were even suspicious of any man wanting to bring them to climax and witness it. His own fierce pleasure in bedding a woman was delicious, but he couldn't be fully aware when he was consumed himself. Bringing a responsive woman to her peak, fully aware of every sight, sound, taste, and smell — that was a special banquet.

He could, at the right time, with the right woman, make it last a very long time. He looked forward to that with Bella one day very soon.

He smiled down at her cap. She was silent, but he didn't press her for words.

Eventually she asked, "What was that?"

"Now there's a question. Pleasure. Is that not explanation enough?"

She shifted to look at him, frowning

slightly. "But you didn't . . . enter me. Did you?"

"No."

"I don't understand."

He kissed her again. "It's too complicated to explain now. I must leave you for a little."

He went to the parlor to relieve himself, thinking of Bella while he did it. Would she mind if she knew that? He returned to the bedchamber, extinguished the candle, and then got into his side of the bed.

She made a move to be closer, but he said, "It's better if we keep apart now. Good night, Bella."

After a moment, she said, "Good night, Thorn."

He was glad she couldn't see his uncontrollable smile at hearing his intimate name from her lips here and now.

CHAPTER 19

Bella woke the next morning, touching her body. She remembered why, and stopped. But she smiled. That had been the most extraordinary experience of her life. No wonder some of the women in the Fowler flock smiled in that sweet, sad way when they remembered their improvident husbands.

Surely Thorn must be thinking of marrying her to behave in that way. She sent up a silent prayer: *Please let that be so.*

She heard the church clock strike eight and sat up carefully, not wanting to wake him. She had only dim light through the drawn bed curtains, but she could see his lashes and the thickening darkness on his chin. A few more days without shaving and it would be as dense as it had been when she'd burst into his room at the Compass.

She remembered that hair rough against her skin last night and wondered if she'd like the feel of him more or less if he were clean shaven.

She realized he must have shaved after that night. Then why not shave every day? She shrugged away that question. She didn't know the ways of men.

Her hand had reached out to touch him, to cherish him, but she drew it back. *Let him sleep.*

She eased out of the bed and restored the curtains after herself. Then she stretched and smiled. She felt wonderful. Full of some new energy, perhaps even looser in every joint. She moved the window curtains an inch to look out and saw gray and drizzle. Not a good day for cat hunting. Still, she smiled.

Someone had been in and built up the fire for the day. Bella felt a jolt of horror at being caught in a man's bed — but then she chuckled. Here, they were a married couple. It was allowed.

She smiled at the simple wedding ring, stroking it, daring to dream. . . .

A water jug had been set on the hearth, covered by a thick cloth. She carried it to the washstand and poured half into the bowl, and then returned it to the hearth to keep warm for him. She gathered a clean shift and stockings, and added her petticoat and gown, and took them all behind the screen. Then she took off the nightgown to enjoy a full wash of a body that felt subtly, delightfully different.

When she started to dress, she was reluctant to become sober, prim Mistress Rose, but she did so, pinning up her hair, and fixing the mousy wig on top.

She added the plain cap, then went into the parlor to wait for Thorn to rise. Tabitha looked up, made a sound that seemed like, *Oh, it's only you,* and went back to sleep.

Bella simply sat, her hands idle, not even thinking in any particular way, but feeling content.

Thorn emerged about half an hour later, dressed and ready for the day. Tabitha greeted him enthusiastically, and he had a short conversation with the cat. Bella watched, awash with idiotic tenderness, but also with anxiety. Was he avoiding paying any attention to her because he was regretting what had happened in the night?

When their eyes met, he smiled in a way that eased any niggling doubts.

"Good morning," she said, knowing she was blushing.

His smile deepened. "Good morning." He looked around. "Breakfast?"

Bella shot to her feet guiltily. "I should

378

have —"

"Bella. I'm merely concerned that you've been waiting for me. I don't like to think of you going hungry."

He went to the door to bellow for a servant.

"So useful to have a shipboard voice," she remarked, still smiling. She couldn't help it.

He grinned at her. "Extremely so." He went to the window. "What a miserable day, but good for making plans." He turned to her. "Your brother was at the Old Oak last week, and he visits frequently."

That reminded Bella where Thorn had been last night. She pushed the awareness away. Nothing would spoil the present.

"How does he avoid scandal?"

"There's a discreet door into some back rooms for special gentlemen, so they don't have to be seen by less sneaky men."

Bella grimaced at the thought, but she asked, "If he's a favored gentleman, won't they warn him of your inquiries?"

"I'm not such a fool. I was very discreet until I realized how much he's disliked there." He shot her a guarded look. "He's not kind."

Bella had some idea what that might mean. "He has no notion of kindness. Does that mean they might help us?"

"With pleasure. They won't regret the custom of a man like that."

"How sweet it is that he'll get his come-uppance in part because of his own foul nature. Have you devised a precise plan?"

"No." He came to stand closer to the fire, which meant closer to her. "It would be easy to expose what happens in the back rooms to the clients in the front, but I'm not sure that will be enough. We need some truly respectable people to be brought face-to-face with it."

"And they won't patronize the Old Oak. Might it take a while to discover a way to do that?" Bella asked, concealing her hope-fulness.

"It might," he agreed. "Are you sure your elderly relation won't become concerned?"

She hated lying to him, but she must. "As I said, she's visiting friends, so I'm at liberty for quite some while."

"Lucky wench."

"I am not a wench," she said, but with a smile. Which he echoed. She felt as if he'd moved closer. "What of the gaming?" she asked. "How is that done?"

"In those private back rooms. I found that convenient, as I was able to play instead of using the other services."

Bella blushed with relief and knew he saw it.

"Did you lose much?" she asked.

"How very wifely. Does it not occur that I might have won?"

He was teasing, so she smiled. "Did you?"

His lips twitched. "No, but only because I thought that wise. A losing customer is always welcome."

Their breakfast came then, and they abandoned such talk. Instead, they discussed what area to visit today in search of cat-rabbits of Hesse.

They spent another day like the last, ambling through country lanes in search of cat-rabbits. The skies were gray, but nothing could dampen Bella's spirits. The kittens were particularly restless, and she had kitten-herding duty while Thorn drove. Tabitha permitted it; in fact, she leapt down to explore, perhaps to hunt.

When she returned, Bella scolded her.

"This is your job, you know." When Sable scrambled to the edge of the carriage as if thinking of attempting the jump, she captured him again. "Can't you make them behave?"

"*Ee-ow,*" and a snort.

Bella laughed, because she was enjoying

the kittens too.

When they stopped to dine at an inn, however, Bella put the kittens in the basket and the basket on the floor of the parlor. To Tabitha, she said, "Take up your duties, mother."

Tabitha sighed, lay down, and the kittens attached themselves.

"That wasn't what I meant!" Bella protested, and found Thorn laughing at her.

He swept her into his arms for a quick but thrilling kiss, knocking her hat askew just as a maid came in to lay the table.

Bella pushed out of his arms, but all she could think of to say was, "My, my," which made her sound like a moonling.

"If you don't want to be kissed, wife, you shouldn't be so kissable."

The maid chuckled, and shot Bella a congratulatory smile. Bella turned to straighten her bonnet and saw her own pink cheeks and sparkling eyes, even behind her tilted spectacles. The maid saw a loving couple. Bella could only dream it might one day be so, but she was haunted by the knowledge that when this adventure ended, they might part.

As they rolled back to Upstone at the end of the day, it began to drizzle. Bella shut the basket on the cats and pulled up the hood of her cloak. Thorn had only his three-cornered hat to protect him.

"Should have brought a cloak," he said wryly. "Don't look so worried; I've been wetter by far than I'm likely to be today."

"Do you often encounter rough seas?"

"Better than a dead calm. Just as a temperamental woman is better than a cold one."

The question jumped out before she could stop it: "Which am I?"

He looked at her, eyes twinkling. "Neither. You, my dear, are a brisk wind on a sunlit day, filling the sails and giving the ship wings."

She stared at him. "I wish I were."

"What? A wind?"

Bella laughed the moment away. "No, I don't think I'd like that." She was saved from finding something sensible to say by sight of a rider cantering home, head down against the rain.

She expected him to pass, but he drew up. "Good day to you. You the people who've been asking about cats and rabbits?"

Bella sat frozen. It was Lord Fortescue, a friend of her father's, and still fit and alert at gone sixty. If he was suspicious of them, he'd look at her closely. Might he recognize her?

He said, "Good God!" and she braced for trouble, but he apologized. "Your pardon, ma'am, but, Ithorne . . . what are you doing here like . . ."

"Like an ordinary human being?" Thorn completed amiably. "Incognito."

"Ah." Another look at Bella, one that saw a mistress, and then his attention was all on the supposed duke. How was Thorn to handle this?

"Serious business?" Fortescue asked.

"Not at all, sir. Some peers seek foreign lands or distant stars. I seek more cat-rabbits like this one." He opened the basket.

Tabitha glared up and then hooked the lid back down over herself and her kittens.

"Deuced odd creature. Won't keep you in this rain. Where're you staying?"

"The Hart and Hare in Upstone."

"May I call on you, Ithorne? There are some matters I'd like to discuss."

Bella saw Thorn's face twitch, but he said, "Of course, sir. Sup with me tomorrow night."

They arranged the time, and Lord Fortescue touched his wet hat and rode off. All the while, Bella looked ahead, wondering why Thorn hadn't simply corrected the error.

As he set the horse into motion again, she

exploded. "What are you thinking? Bad enough to pass yourself off as your brother — I'm sure that's illegal — but to invite Lord Fortescue to dine? He might not see the differences in this weather, but across a table . . ."

"Trust me," he said calmly. "My half brother and I are very alike."

"But he's a duke and you're a sea captain. Why not simply correct him and tell him who you are?"

"At first it seemed simpler not to. I had no idea he'd seek another meeting."

Bella wiped a drip off her nose. "He wants to talk politics. You know nothing about politics."

"Don't I?"

"Not as your brother must."

"True," he said with an irritatingly cryptic smile. "I keep aware of the elements, however. The question is, should you attend?"

"No," Bella said firmly. "I want no part of it. In any case, Lord Fortescue was a friend of my father's. He paid little attention to me, but he still might recognize me."

"Ah. Very well."

"Can't you put him off?" she begged. "The law is harsh. They hang people for almost anything. I'm sure impersonating a duke is some sort of treason."

385

"Bella," he said, perhaps even laughing at her. "Trust me."

She opened the basket and said, "Can't you talk sense into him?"

The cat's eyes opened to slits for a moment, then closed again. The silent answer was clearly no.

"This could ruin my revenge," she said to the irritating man. "And if you say 'trust me' one more time, I'll . . . I'll stick my hat pin in you."

He only laughed.

They were welcomed back to the Hart and Hare with towels, roaring fires, and a hot punch. Bella made full use of all of it, but Thorn disappeared. She immediately worried that she'd offended him with her protests.

She was sitting before the fire in the parlor in dry clothing, taking comfort from a cup of hot punch, when he appeared, drying his hair with a towel. He'd removed his jacket, and wore only his waistcoat over his shirt.

"Where did you go?" she asked. "To cancel the arrangement with Lord Fortescue?"

"No." He poured some punch and sat down. "The innkeeper wanted to give me a note without your seeing it. From the Old Oak."

"You've been there? Now?" She hated the thought of him visiting the brothel again, even briefly.

"Briefly," he said with meaning. "Augustus will be here tomorrow."

He seemed pleased with the news, but Bella's stomach lurched.

Tomorrow.

This could all end tomorrow.

"So we need to make plans quickly," she said. "Excellent."

"New plans," he said, leaning forward to refill his glass. He offered her more, but she shook her head. More drink and she might burst into tears.

"Mistress Calloway, the innkeeper, had assumed that I was interested in a time when your brother would make a private visit to the Oak. But today she thought to tell me that tomorrow is the magistrates' court here in Upstone. Your brother will be here in that capacity."

"But that's of no use to us, is it?" Bella asked. "Unless he goes to the Oak afterward."

"The Oak comes to him." He drank with relish. "The three magistrates hold court here at the Hart and Hare, and stay the night afterward."

He was smiling like a cat with feathers around its mouth, but Bella was focused on something else. "He'll be at this inn? What if our paths cross? He'll recognize me!"

"Maybe not, as you are, but yes, you'll need to stay out of sight. But listen, this could be perfect for your plan. After their legal duties, the three magistrates enjoy a hearty supper and a convivial evening, which involves card play . . ."

"Ah!"

". . . and — excuse me — whoring."

"Here?" Bella asked.

"Here," he said. "In the same ground-floor room where they hold court. Mistress Calloway sends three of her women here and they enter through the window. I can't believe the inn people don't know, but they can pretend they don't. No one crosses the magistrates. They regulate all matters of trade as well as crimes, and if someone offends them, some irregularity can always be found."

"Disgusting."

"But not our current concern. The event becomes debauched, so our revelation might be as simple as opening the curtains."

Bella was imagining it all, slack jawed.

"More punch?" he offered.

She held out her glass, and then took a deep drink. "How do we open the curtains? We won't be inside the room."

"You won't be anywhere near, but I'm sure I can find an excuse to enter."

"And a way to make sure people are outside to see the scene?"

"Word can be spread. Picture it. It will be like the curtain rising in the theater. And on such a scene, such actors . . ." He smiled at her. "How your eyes sparkle."

Bella supposed they did. "Is it very bad of me? What of the other magistrates? We catch them in this trap too."

"Only if they are enjoying the same vices as your brother."

"Do we know who they are?"

"I thought you might."

Bella gasped. "Yes, of course! What am I thinking? One must be Squire Thorough-good. That's the man my father wanted me to marry."

"He's upright and righteous? That might spoil our plans."

"Neither. Oh, I suppose he's considered righteous, after a fashion, applying the law with a harsh hand, but he's known for hard drinking, and for being unfaithful to his first wife."

"How old is he?"

Bella shrugged. "Gone forty, I'd think. Why?"

"He was hardly a suitable choice for you."

She grimaced. "My father insisted I must be married, and no one was competing for the honor. Squire Thoroughgood offered to rescue me from shame. My father approved. I remember him telling me that Squire Thoroughgood was a stern man who'd know how to keep a flighty wife in line, with a whip if necessary."

His jaw was tight. "I wish your father weren't dead. I'd enjoy giving him my opinion of his conduct."

"He'd have had you thrown out."

He smiled in that grimly confident way he had sometimes. "I doubt it."

Bella supposed he'd go to such an interview with his crew beside him.

She contemplated the morrow with increased satisfaction. "If Squire Thoroughgood is caught up in Augustus's shame, I will have no objection."

"Good. Do you approve the plan?"

Bella drank more punch. "If it can be executed, yes. But the scene will have to be instantly and visually scandalous. How can we ensure that? The men playing cards won't be enough."

He took a drink, considering her. "They

roll dice. When they lose, the women take off items of clothing."

"Oh."

"When the clothing is gone, there are other penalties."

Bella decided she didn't need to know any more. "So we merely need a signal for when matters have progressed far enough."

He smiled, perhaps in accolade. "Precisely. However, it would be useful to have a few important witnesses at hand, as well as the ordinary folk. Ones not afraid of the magistrates and thus certain to spread the story far and wide." He straightened. "Fortescue! Perfect."

Bella put a hand over her eyes. "You want to involve Lord Fortescue in this outrageous plan? You're mad."

"Brilliantly so, I hope. Who better? He's tough, testy, and straitlaced, and a viscount has nothing to fear from a magistrate. He wouldn't normally concern himself with such misbehavior, but face-to-face with it, he'll bear witness."

"You sound as if you know him well."

"I've had dealings with him."

"As Captain Rose."

He looked at her blankly, as if her comment made no sense, but then said, "Trust me, Bella."

"Hat pin," she muttered.

"Turn your sharp wits to whom else we can draw in as a witness. What of the family your brother wants to marry into?"

"Langham. But Mr. Langham is merely rich. He's trying to establish his family here, so he won't want to stir trouble."

"Not even if it seems his daughter's suitor is a thorough wretch? If he sees it with his own eyes?"

Bella considered that. "Yes. Yes, then he might act. From the little I've seen of him he is a devoted father. If he learned of that possibility, he would come here to see the truth."

He nodded. "That can be arranged. Who else?" He tapped his finger on his glass as he thought. "Fortescue should be a strong witness. He detests hypocrisy. However, Langham, as you say, might not want to speak out. What of the vicar? Do you know what sort of man has the living here?"

"Oh, yes!" Bella said. "If he's still here, it's Reverend Jervingham. A roaring parson, and a son of the Earl of Moncliffe, so not prey to local influence. He's known for denouncing sinners from the pulpit, great as well as low."

"I already adore him," Thorn said with a satisfied smile. "With an audience of as many local people as we can alert, those three gentlemen should do the trick."

"As long as the magistrates do behave badly."

"According to Mistress Calloway, they always do."

"Always?"

"Your brother is a habitual sinner, Bella. We won't be catching him in one unfortunate lapse."

"No, I suppose not. But . . . but they're supposed to uphold the law!"

"Which never, of course, applies to them. So all we need is a signal. A way to know when to invade and raise the curtain."

"Why not let one of the women do that?" Bella suggested. "I suspect they would."

"And would be delighted to." His eyes twinkled. "A strong scream would give me excuse enough to rush in, don't you think?"

She twinkled back at him. "How could a gentleman do less?"

They toasted each other. It would have been a perfect moment, Bella thought, if their anticipated triumph would not signal the end of all her hopes.

For that was true. Her dreams of marriage were just that: dreams. Even with Augustus ground into the dust, she would still be ruined Bella Barstowe.

"I should return to the Oak to make the arrangements," he said. "I apologize for my apparent misbehavior."

"I will certainly have to play the sorrowful wife."

He rose and came to kiss her, tasting spice with brandy, oranges, and nutmeg. "I wouldn't go if it weren't essential," he said.

"I know."

He kissed her again. "We both know that if this were reality, you'd wrap the poker around my head."

She chuckled. "If this were reality, sir, you'd have learned to behave long ago."

He laughed softly too. "I'm sure I would."

Bella maintained her mask until he left, but then she had to dab away some tears.

The maid came in with supper for one and a dish for Tabitha. She gave Bella a pitying look, and Bella desperately wanted to assert that her "husband" would never be so disrespectful. That he had a noble purpose . . .

Oh, she was running mad, and she would keep all her attention on her revenge. That, at least, she could have.

After supper, Bella sat to sew, needing the calming effect. She'd almost finished hemming the gentleman's handkerchief she was working on, and as she set the final stitches, she decided to give it to Thorn. It was a plain handkerchief, so he would not need to feel it was special, but she'd know he had it, no matter how things were in the future.

CHAPTER 20

Thorn returned within the hour, which was a secret joy.

"What a vision," he said. "A lady sewing by candlelight."

She gave him a look. "Strong daylight is preferable. I can do this only because my fingers know the work even if I were blind-folded. Did the women agree?"

"With pleasure, as you said. He really is disliked. He pays his fees but never more, and he . . . Never mind." He sat opposite her chair. "I also learned the name of the third magistrate. Sir Newleigh Dodd. An-other nasty specimen?"

Bella searched her memory. "He must have been appointed since I left. I don't think I know him."

"He'll be from the same mold, or too weak to object. Here's the sequence. The magis-trates hold court and then dine. They're generally half-drunk when the women arrive, and fully drunk later, but tomorrow night the women will add extra spirits to their punch to speed the process. Once the activities have reached truly scandalous dimensions, one of the women will shriek and I'll rush to the rescue, with Fortescue close behind."

"What about the spectators outside?"

"Mistress Calloway's having a word with one of her customers who does a trade in wondrous nostrums. Tomorrow evening he'll offer a demonstration of a new tonic against the rheumatism that can be activated only by moonlight. That will take place in the stable yard, outside the room where the magistrates sup."

"That's very clever."

He inclined his head.

"What of the vicar?" Bella asked. "He won't come for a patent medicine."

"That will be less precise, but I've recruited the local grocer, a man called Colly Barber. Your brother had him put in the stocks for giving short measure, and he swears it was contrived because he wouldn't supply Sir Augustus Barstowe free of charge. Whatever the truth of that, he'll take a message to the vicar, summoning him here. The question is, what message?"

"Religious duty," Bella said firmly. "He'd

never ignore that. The message says that Squire Thoroughgood has taken a fit brought on by eating to excess, and is crying to confess his sins before he dies. He's corpulent, so it's believable."

"Clever, Bella. Langham will probably come if he receives an anonymous message informing him that his future son-in-law is consorting with low whores. The stage is set."

Bella ran over it all in her mind. She wanted this to work. "How will the grocer know when to take the message?"

"When he hears the scream."

She shook her head. "That will be too late. Even though the vicarage is close by, Reverend Jervingham could arrive when everything is over. What if we check for the place closest to the vicarage that can be seen from the bedchamber? I'll be in there, leaving you and Fortescue to your political supper. When I hear the scream, I'll wave a candle to signal the grocer to go, cutting his journey by half."

"As neat as your stitchery. Excellent."

Bella basked in his approval. Before she could get maudlin, she said, "Speaking of neat, shouldn't you shave if you persist in passing yourself off as the duke?"

"I'm Ithorne traveling incognito, remember? A duke can grow a beard as well as a peasant, and it serves to blur any differences in our features."

She could only sigh. "And who am I if not Mistress Rose?"

"I'm afraid you have to be Ithorne's *chère amie.*"

His mistress. But the French meant "dear friend."

He leaned forward and took her hand. "You have become a dear friend, Bella, so it's not a lie."

That almost destroyed her composure, but she managed, "And you are a true friend to me. You've taken on my cause as your own. But, my friend, may I not play a part tomorrow apart from candle waving?"

They were still hand-locked, and she would not change that.

"You should keep to your room, Bella," he said. "It could all be very unpleasant."

"Good."

"I mean, the sins could be."

"I need to see the result," she said.

"You might be recognized by any number of people."

For a moment Bella balked. "But it won't matter then. I mean, it won't ruin the plan."

"Your reputation?"

"We've dispensed with that long ago."

His hand and features tightened, almost as if he were angry, but then he said, "By all means, rush down after me, then, and play what part you wish."

"Thank you. I do believe this will work."

He raised her hand to his lips and kissed her fingers. "It will work, for it's my service to you, my lady." He freed his fingers from hers, however, and stood. "I must leave you again in order settle a few final details. Not, I promise, at the Oak."

"See that you don't," she said with teasing severity.

"I'll send someone up for your supper dishes, and with your washing water."

He left, and Bella realized he'd ordered her to bed.

How should she understand that?

When the maids had come and gone, Bella took off her gown and washed, but then she looked at the bed, wondering what to wear. Shift and petticoat, as she had the first night? Nightgown, as she had last night?

She knew what she wanted in this bed this night, but she didn't want to send too broad a hint, to make him feel he must, if he didn't want to.

Her needs were wicked, but she didn't care, for this might be their last night. Her needs weren't wicked at all. She wanted to be the true wife to Captain Rose, his help-mate and companion, keeper of his home ashore, mother of his children, and lover in his bed.

She wanted that more than anything else she could imagine.

More, even, than her revenge against Augustus.

Yes, it would seem love was selfish, for if she had to choose between marrying Thorn and stopping her brother's evil course, she'd marry Thorn and leave the world vulnerable to Augustus Sluggaby Barstowe.

She put on the nightgown. When she'd brushed out her hair, she plaited it and put on her nightcap. Then she drew the curtains around the bed and climbed into it.

It wasn't long until he entered the bedroom. She listened to the sounds beyond the curtains, trying to hear eagerness or reluctance in them, and then felt him join her in the bed. She didn't look. She didn't want him to feel he must do anything at all.

He slid over, close to her. She turned her head to look at him then and saw bare shoulders. No shirt.

Her mouth dried. They were beautiful shoulders, and even in the dim light, she could make out the tattoo — the one of a black swan that she remembered from the

Compass in Dover. She touched it, surprised to find it smooth. "Why have this done?"

"Sailors do. So their bodies will be identified if they drown."

"Don't speak of that."

"It's a reality of life on the seas." He fingered the bow that tied her cap beneath her chin. "You permit?"

Bella swallowed, not sure what she was permitting, but she said, "Yes."

He tugged it loose and then pulled her into a sitting position so he could take off her cap. Then he moved her entirely so her legs were on either side of him, so she was almost sitting in his lap, spread over him. . . .

He slid his hands behind her to undo the ribbon that held her plait in place and freed her hair, running his fingers through it. His touch against her scalp was so sweet she wondered why she'd never been aware of the possibility.

She realized that in this position she could do to him what he did to her.

She ran her fingers into his hair. "Does that feel as wonderful?"

"I hope so, for then I'm pleasing you delightfully."

Shyly, she asked, "What else can I do to please you?"

"May I open the curtains and light more candles?"

"You left a candle lit?"

"How else are we seeing?"

She laughed at her folly. "Yes, I'd like to see more. Is that too bold of me?"

"Nothing is too bold, Bellissima. Nothing."

He climbed out of her side of the bed, sweeping back the curtains to let in candle- and firelight. It gleamed on his naked torso. He wore only his linen drawers.

He'd brought a whole branch of candles into the bedroom, and now he lit them.

He'd prepared for this, which both shocked and thrilled her. Certainly he wasn't reluctant. He wasn't doing this out of obligation. That allowed her to eat up his beauty. Broad shoulders tapering down to trim waist and hips. Strong buttocks beneath fine lawn. Muscles everywhere. Sleek muscles, but powerful. She supposed a sea captain did more than simply shout commands.

He turned with the single candle, catching her ogling him, and grinned as he returned to the bed. Bella frankly appreciated the front view. The uncertain light of the wavering candle painted different contours on his chest. Different from her memories of him at the Compass. But if anything he was more beautiful.

He put the candle on the bed stand and sat before her again. "If I distress you, tell me to stop."

"I can't imagine you distressing me."

"I can. In ways you will later like."

She laughed. "That makes no sense."

He smiled. "We'll see."

He unfastened her nightgown and spread it, but he continued to pull it down her arms, down until her breasts were completely exposed. She wanted to cover them with her hands but, at the same time, didn't want to.

"Undistressed?" he asked, watching her.

"Disturbed," she managed, "but not distressed. Does the sight of my breasts please you?"

"Immensely." He leaned down and took a nipple between his lips, playing with it. Bella grew hot and tried to grip him, but her arms were trapped.

He sucked. Her body jolted.

"So responsive," he murmured, kissing and licking his way to her other breast. "You have no idea how much it pleases me to reveal these delights to you. You are, I hope, delighted?"

Bella gasped. "I do believe I am, sir, but

you have my arms trapped and I want to touch you."

He worked the nightgown all the way off her arms, freeing her, exposing her down to her hips. He ran his hands over her, then around to her back. How could she not have known how sensitive her back was? She was complete sensitivity, humming with it. She slid her hands behind him, stroked him as he was stroking her.

She remembered hair, and raised one hand into his. Her fingers played against his scalp and then down the back of his neck, understanding what he'd said about the pleasure of pleasuring.

Perhaps he purred before he lowered his lips to her breasts again.

Bella ceased thinking as she tumbled into dark, heated passion.

She emerged hungry for more. More in all ways. She kissed his chest and then the dark tattoo. She drew a nail down his skin, watching the way the line was pale and then disappeared. She played with his body, and he permitted it, simply touching her, stroking her, in ways that seemed almost idle except for the way he kept her alive with sensation, and built more desire.

Then came the time when all their bed-covers were gone, and all their clothes were gone. The room was chilly, for the fire had burned low, but they had heat enough between them.

Bella studied his manly part, the way it rose up against him so long and stiff. She touched it. So hard. So hot.

She heard his breath catch and looked at him. He smiled and closed her hand around it. "You permit?" he said.

Bella inhaled. "Do you?"

"Of course."

He put his hand over hers and moved her against him. "That pleases me, Bella, but only do what pleases you."

"I am pleased by pleasing you."

He grinned. "My view entirely. Please me, then."

There was freedom in that, but challenge too, so Bella decided to do exactly what pleased her as she explored this new experience, and it seemed to work as he'd said, and please them both. Especially when she had the pleasure of watching him in his passion, literally at her hands.

He'd thrown the sheet over himself to catch the fluid. The fluid that should enter her.

If they were married.

This, she realized, was the height or depths of sin, but she didn't care. She cradled his head and kissed him, a deeper, hotter kiss than ever before, and then he pleasured her again, and again, seeming to know how to send her to a point of destruction and then rescue her just before she died.

"I want to do that to you," she mumbled, exhausted.

"What a delightful thought," he murmured against her neck, and tucked her close against his body as she slid down into sleep.

She stirred as a clock chimed. Five times.

It was still dark. She was still held close against his glorious, naked body.

She thought of all the women who didn't seem to experience this symphony of pleasure. Perhaps she should write a book. For the wives, or the husbands?

"Your thoughts?" he murmured, a skillful hand playing on her flank.

"Only of pleasure. Why isn't it always like this?"

"You're very responsive."

"Is that why other women don't seem to experience this?"

He turned her and teased her breasts again. They were sensitive, almost sore, but he seemed to know that. His touch was soft as a feather.

"You know the intimate secrets of other women?" he asked.

Bella realized she was close to things she didn't want to talk about, but that she'd have to, and soon. There must be honesty between them. She pushed that aside for now.

"Women sometimes talk," she said. "It's clear many dislike their marriage bed."

"And sometimes that's the problem." He swept fingers lightly down her naked body to end at the sensitive rim of her behind. "For some women nakedness itself is unpleasant."

"Oh. But are all men as skillful as you at this?"

"No."

"Why not?"

He chuckled. "What interesting conversations you start, my fascinating Bella. As well ask why not all cooks produce good food."

"A matter of training?" she asked doubtfully.

"And perhaps natural talent."

She rolled to meet his smile. "I should have expected you to claim that."

"Talent and a great deal of training."

Before Bella could ask her startled question, he kissed her into silence with too much talent for her to resist.

CHAPTER 21

Bella woke late and lazily, once again physically complete. She rolled to look at Thorn, beautiful in relaxed sleep. If only that had been their wedding night, sealing them together for eternity.

As it was, she felt it should be almost the same. How was it possible for them to have done such things and part? But he might see it differently, and she was aware that he had not taken her maidenhead. Such extraordinary care.

Might it mean that he wanted to be sure that they wouldn't be tied by a child?

It hurt to think him so calculating, but in truth, it was sensible.

What did sense have to do with such things?

She knew she could scramble her wits by going around and around that, so she turned her thoughts firmly toward the day of retribution. She rose and dressed quickly and went into the parlor to take refuge in needlework. Once Thorn emerged from the bedchamber, however, she became almost shaky with awareness of him, with memories, with echoes of sensation. . . .

He smiled and kissed her, but it was a gentle kiss.

Probably that was wise.

"It's going to be hard to wait," she said, but then wasn't sure what she was referring to. He smiled, and she wasn't sure of the meaning behind that, either.

She said, "There's nothing to do until the magistrates' court is over and the men are settled to their pleasures."

"We could have breakfast," he pointed out, amused, and went to summon it.

He was all too aware of the effect he was having on her, but she couldn't be angry at him. She could never be angry at him over anything.

Bella was surprised to find herself hungry, but she supposed she'd taken a great deal of exercise in the night. If so, it hadn't tired her out. After breakfast she paced the parlor restlessly.

She suddenly turned to him. "I want to visit the court."

"Is that wise?" he asked, still drinking his tea.

"I don't know. But I want to see Augustus being a magistrate. Remind myself of how foul he is."

He considered her. "I don't suppose he'll recognize you if we stay at the back of the room, but tease some of the wig forward on your face, and wear your hat with the brim pulled forward. And the spectacles."

Huffily, she picked them up from the table. She'd never disliked wearing Bellona's pair as much as she disliked these. It could be because they were round lenses, or it could be because she hated what they did to her appearance now, with Thorn.

He smiled as if he knew. "They won't be here until the afternoon, however, so we should go hunting."

Bella didn't want to, but she had to agree. Thorn even insisted on taking a leisurely dinner at an inn some miles from Upstone, when she fretted that the magistrates might advance their plans. That something could go wrong if they weren't in the Hart and Hare.

"Patience, my dear," he said when she fumed at him. "We'll be in time, and the later we return, and the less chance of stumbling over your brother, the better."

She settled back into their pattern of stopping to ask country people about the cats.

411

Today there were no kisses, but only comfortable silences and relaxed conversation. Bella noticed how easy his manner was with farmers and farm laborers, putting everyone at their ease.

How different he must be from his haughty half brother. He was, however, just a little too fond of flirting with the women, and they were all extremely eager to flirt with him. Life married to Captain Rose would be trying at times, but she definitely wanted to attempt it.

They returned to Upstone as the clocks struck three, and by the time they approached the Hart, Bella was so highly strung she was almost bouncing. Tabitha had shut the basket on her, and Thorn was shaking his head.

"Do try to act as if this is an ordinary day."

"I should have brought a handkerchief," she muttered.

He immediately offered his.

"To sew, you idiot!"

She looked at him, appalled, but then began to giggle. His lips were twitching, and she thought they must both seem like idiots as they arrived in the yard. The place was quite busy, perhaps because of the court.

Bella hurried to their room to check that hair and hat hid part of her face, and then

412

she went with Thorn to the long room where the court was taking place.

It was the room where the magistrates would later dine, so as they entered, Bella quickly checked the windows. Two large ones. Excellent.

She looked to the far end, where the three magistrates were deciding the fate of a miscreant. Squire Thoroughgood was in the center, fatter than ever and sneering. On his right sat a fashionable man in his thirties, looking bored. That must be Sir Newleigh Dodd. On his left — on the sinister side, thought Bella — sat Augustus.

He'd put on a little weight since she'd last seen him, but managed to look pinched with superiority and disapproval, even with rounder cheeks. The case seemed to be one of destruction of property, which was serious. The young man had held a grievance against a landowner and had destroyed some fences. He was trying to deny it, but it seemed clear enough.

Once Bella would have been sure he was wicked and deserved the strictest punishment. Now she knew more about how hardship could lead to desperation.

Squire Thoroughgood imposed a fine of three guineas. Nearly everyone in the room gasped, and the young man cried, "I can't pay that!"

"Then you'll go to America to work it off," said Augustus with disgusting satisfaction. *Disgustus,* Bella thought, without the slightest amusement.

"Stay here," Thorn said. "Don't attract attention."

He rose and strolled closer to the magistrates' bench. "Gentlemen, I will pay this young man's fine."

Two pairs of eyes glared at him. Sir Newleigh merely looked like a surprised sheep.

"Who are you, sir?" Squire Thoroughgood growled. "And why seek to pervert justice in this way? In league with him, are you?"

"My name is Captain Rose, and justice requires only that the fine be paid, does it not?"

"Justice requires that a sinner be punished!" Augustus cried, slapping his hand on the table. Bella was sure he wished he had a thundering voice rather than a high-pitched one.

Thoroughgood was red in the face, but Sir Newleigh was pale, and now a highly alarmed sheep. He was staring at Thorn as if his eyes would fall out.

"Sir . . . !" He gasped. "I mean . . . Captain Rose?"

Thorn turned to face the man. Bella couldn't see his expression, but his voice was icy when he said, "That is my name, yes."

"But, but . . ."

Oh, dear heavens, the man had recognized, as he thought, the Duke of Ithorne. Again, Thorn was allowing it. Before a court. That would be perjury, wouldn't it?

Sir Newleigh was a fish now, mouth opening and shutting, but he didn't say anything more. Instead, he leaned to splutter at Augustus, "Let him pay the fine, dammit!"

Augustus was red in the chubby face. "Absolutely not. I won't have some upstart military man interfering in my court!"

"It's not your court, dammit."

Bella caught her breath at a new problem. A falling-out between the magistrates could ruin their plan!

Perhaps Thorn saw the same thing, for he spoke soothingly. "Sirs, I have no desire to interfere in the process of the law. But I believe any Christian may be charitable. I sense that this young man has learned his lesson." He took out his purse and poured out some golden coins, which he gave to the slack-jawed youth. "Be wiser in future."

With that, he bowed to the bench and returned to his place by Bella. Augustus's angry eyes followed him, so Bella kept her head down so that her hat brim hid her face.

"We'd better leave," she murmured to Thorn, "before you're overtaken with charity for the next case too."

"You're right, but I dislike this lot extremely."

As a new case started, they rose and left. Bella said, "Let's stroll around the town to remove you from temptation."

"Very well," he said, almost crossly. "But idleness, stupidity, and viciousness. What a triad."

"Sir Newleigh thought you were the duke. I was terrified that you'd confirm it! But what did he think Ithorne could do to harm him?"

"Give him the cut direct at court. Social death. Speak of him with disapproval. Make a humorous story of it all. Laughter destroys most effectively. I hope most ferociously for laughter tonight."

Bella linked arms with him. "Stop scowling. People look afraid of you."

He relaxed and smiled at her. "You're never afraid of me, are you?"

"Should I be?"

"I'm not sure."

"What does that mean?" she asked.

"I'm not sure of that either," he said.

Bella shook her head. "Dukes seem to have a revolting amount of influence. They're only men, like other men."

"Heresy!" he declared. "And not true. Their every word is attended to, their every expression watched."

"That must be very uncomfortable."

"Are you feeling sorry for Ithorne? Few would."

She looked up at him. "Before, you implied that you pitied him."

"But I don't at the moment," he said with a strangely cryptic smile. He looked around at the street. "This is very pleasant."

"It's an ordinary town."

"Not while you are here with me."

Bella met his eyes, blushing, but she had to smile. He was right: this was a perfect moment.

As they turned back toward the inn, she began to tense again with nervousness and anticipation.

"Worried?" Thorn asked.

"Only that it won't happen."

"If it doesn't, we'll try again."

That made Bella wonder if she wanted the plan to work or not.

Thorn escorted Bella to their room, but then left with the excuse of needing to check on their arrangements. In truth, he needed a moment to try to regain sanity.

Tonight, Bella would get her justice, but tomorrow he had to return to his world. Tasks and duties would be piling up. Anything could have happened in the past few days, for no one knew where to look for him. That was a degree of selfishness he'd never permitted himself before. At times over these past days, he'd felt as if he truly were Captain Rose, and had begun to spin dreams that went with that insanity. Dreams of a sea captain's life, and a simple home.

He took refuge in the taproom, sitting in a corner by himself.

He'd embarked on this enterprise to help a gallant young woman, and to punish a man who deserved it. Then he'd been seduced by the novelty of winning a woman who didn't know he was the duke, but he'd not thought through the consequences.

When had that ever happened to him before? It was as if a madness had overtaken him.

And last night, he'd almost completed their lovemaking. Out of desire, yes. Out of physical need. But because temptation deep in his mind had growled, *Then she'll be yours, will she, nil she.*

He, who'd grown so adept at avoiding

compromising situations, had almost compromised a woman into marriage.

He'd have sunk his head in his hands and groaned if not for a lifetime's awareness of being watched. Bella was falling in love with him, just as he'd hoped. Falling in love with Captain Rose, with no expectation of wealth, rank, or grandeur.

Falling in love with a lie.

"Want more, sir?" asked the barmaid — who, being swollen with pregnancy, clearly wasn't a maid at all.

He agreed. When she brought back the foaming pot, she asked, "Trouble, sir? With the wife?"

He looked at her. "Why guess that?"

She grinned, showing a missing tooth. "There's a look men get when it's a wife matter."

"Is there indeed? Different from when it's just a woman matter?"

She cocked her hip, prepared to linger and chat. "Depends on the woman too. Love-struck lads, well, they might as well have a sign around their neck announcing whether their darling is pleased with them or angry. Once a man's married, trouble with the wife's a heavier burden, 'cause he has to go home to it. And, of course, a husband don't get excited at her kindness, having won her for eternity."

"Are all husbands so careless?" Thorn asked, interested in this country philosopher.

"Most of 'em, and the wives too. We don't notice our house, either, until the roof leaks, do we?"

"A wise homeowner keeps the house in good repair."

She snorted. "Most I know wait for the leak, then fix it."

"And there," said Thorn, "we probably have a summation of all the troubles in the world."

"A what?" she asked.

"An adding up. You've put a lot of complicated things into a simple, neat statement. The question is, is my roof leaking?"

"Is your head wet?" she asked.

He chuckled. "Very apt. Yes, it is. Which roof is leaking?"

"The one over your head." She was grinning at him, thinking this a joke, but Thorn took a deep pull of ale, considering the analogy.

"Perhaps the model should be a wet floor. Is it not true that sometimes the source of a wet floor isn't immediately obvious?"

She looked around to see if anyone else required her, then sat down. "It is, sir. A puddle could be a simple spill, see, or a leak from the roof. But it could be rising from below. My uncle Aaron had wet in his barn floor all of a sudden, and it turned out a stream had moved its course. That barn had stood there fifty years, dry as dust, and there he was all of a sudden with muddy boots."

"A stream moving course. A force of nature."

"That's it, sir! He never did find out quite why, and such trouble as he had . . ."

Thorn let her chatter flow by him, taken by an image that seemed all too apposite. Some irresistible and unsuspected force had changed his life, changed it profoundly, but he'd been unaware until his boots had stuck in the mud. . . .

The church clock struck six. A few moments later, he watched through the taproom door as people left the room opposite. The court was over. The unseemly revels would begin. He had one thing he could do honestly for his lady.

A number of men came into the tap and the barmaid rose. "I have to go, sir."

He gave her a shilling. "I've enjoyed our discussion. You're a wise woman."

She colored and smiled almost shyly. "Just common sense," she said, and went back to her duties.

Common sense. Common, but rare at the same time. Especially, it would seem, in him.

Bella was sewing again to hold on to sanity when Thorn returned from wherever he'd run off to. Something was wrong; she knew it.

Her reputation? Had he suddenly remembered it?

"The court's ended," he said briskly. "The magistrates will soon begin their supper, and Fortescue will be here in a half hour."

At least they were to go ahead with the plan.

"Excellent," she said, "but it's so hard to wait. Even Tabitha has been prowling."

The cat did it again, rising from her basket to stalk around the room as if looking for prey. Sable scrambled after her and she turned and hissed.

He fled back into the basket so quickly he tripped over his paws.

Thorn went over and soothed him. "Tabitha's sensitive to atmosphere," he said. "Perhaps we should all calm down. Would you like me to read to you?"

Bella was startled and even guilty to be offered part of her dream. She knew that experiencing it would only add to the pain, but she agreed. "What books do you have with you?"

"No novels, I'm afraid." He looked through his valise. "Hume's *Essays Moral and Political* would be rather dry. *The Memoirs of the Bedford Coffee House* rather flighty, and *The Revolutions of Persia* rather alarming."

"An odd collection for a sea captain," she said. He was such a puzzling man. No, fascinating.

"Morals are never useless," he said. "A sea voyage requires amusement, and you never know; I may venture to Persia."

"Then I choose to be alarmed. Read to me of Persia."

He took out the book and sat opposite her, adjusting a candle to give better light. "Like most adventures, it's mostly tedium," he warned as he opened it at his mark. He turned a few pages and then began to read.

Bella tried not to slide back into dreams, but here they were, by the fireside in a cozy parlor, he reading to her as she sewed. It was a passage about beggars wrapped around with a philosophy of money and not very interesting, but so beautifully read. She hadn't realized before the quality of his voice. She could listen to him read anything with pleasure, and watching him at the same

time, gilded by fire and candlelight, was,
yes, idyllic.

CHAPTER 22

They were disturbed by a knock on the door. He marked the place and put the book aside. "Fortescue. I gave instructions for him to be brought up."

It began. Bella rose, kissed him quickly, and slipped into the bedchamber. He came after with the cats in their basket. "Best keep Tabitha out of this."

He kissed her before returning to the parlor. Bella stood there, fingers to her lips, heavyhearted.

"Ee-ow-ah."

For once, it didn't seem to be a complaint at Thorn's absence, but directed at Bella.

"Who do I think I am?" she speculated.

Tabitha left the basket and leapt easily up onto the windowsill to look out.

"Perhaps you should have candle duty," Bella muttered, and began to pace the room.

She stopped. The click of her heels might be heard next door, or even below, where the magistrates were. She could hear the men below quite clearly. Not their exact words, but their voices and tone. Squire Thoroughgood said something loudly and was answered by a whinnying laugh.

Augustus.

When he grew excited he always laughed in that high-pitched way.

Bella realized she'd risen to her feet as if she'd charge into action immediately. She sat, hands clenched, and waited.

The men's voices rose and fell with merriment and excitement. She heard no women's voices yet.

Though her task was simple enough for a child to do, she couldn't help but go over it: Once the woman screamed — it would be a piercing scream — she would wave the candle in the window. Colly Barber had a lantern and would signal back so she would know he'd seen it.

That was her entire part, but it should bring Reverend Jervingham. Thorn and Fortescue would rush down. They couldn't predict when Mr. Langham would arrive, but even if he didn't witness the scandal, he'd hear about it. Charlotte would be safe.

She rose again to pace. Stopped again. Realized she didn't need to wear her shoes and took them off so she could prowl. Tabitha stayed on the sill, as if on guard, but her tail twitched. The kittens, perhaps sensing danger, only peered out of the basket.

Bella listened at the door to the parlor. A calm discussion was taking place, so Fortescue was still convinced he was talking to the Duke of Ithorne.

A knock at the corridor door startled her, but it was only her supper tray and Tabitha's dish. Bella hadn't expected to be hungry, but suddenly she was. Did her body want to prepare for action? She was halfway through her steak pie when she heard the women arrive.

She pictured them scrambling over the low sill. What did whores wear to such an occasion?

Their high-pitched voices joined the men's. Another whinny from Augustus, pitched almost as high.

But then it became quieter below, with only occasional bursts of noise, perhaps marking success or disappointment. Had they started their dice game?

Bella drank some of her wine, trying to imagine exactly what was going on.

How long would it take to get to the right point?

How long would Fortescue stay?

The women's voices were sometimes

shrill, but they seemed merry.

Perhaps it was all different this time.

Perhaps the plan wouldn't work.

In that case, they'd have to stay and try again. . . .

No, she wouldn't be selfish. She'd seen Augustus abusing his power as a magistrate. She knew his character. He must be stopped now, tonight.

Then she heard a shriek, and not a merry one. Not the scream that would be the signal, but enough to make Bella want to rush to the woman's aid. She remembered her pistol and took a step toward her valise. She made herself stop. She mustn't spoil everything by impetuous action. Not this time, not even when she heard a new burst of laughter from the men.

They were cheering one another on — to do what, she hoped never to know. Not all the women's cries were of pain, and there was laughter from them as well as the men. The men's laughter, however, especially Augustus's high whinny, was vile.

Then she heard the unmistakable sound of a whip. Twice. Thrice. That brought a new kind of shriek, a begging one.

Wasn't that the signal? Why wasn't Thorn doing anything?

Then the whip again and a bloodcurdling scream.

That must be it!

Squire Thoroughgood bellowed, "Shut up, you stupid woman!" but Bella heard Thorn next door exclaim something, and then his running, booted footsteps going below.

She grabbed the candle so quickly it almost went out. She carried it carefully to the window and waved it. A lantern flickered back and then went dark again. Colly Barber was on his way.

She put on her shoes and raced after, catching up to Lord Fortescue at the bottom of the steps. Thorn was already at the downstairs parlor door.

A few men were in the hall, clearly having come out of the taproom, tankards still in hand, alerted by the scream, but unwilling to interfere.

"The magistrates." It ran around like a snake's hiss.

Outside in the street someone cried, "Murder's being done at the Hart. Murder!" That should bring everyone within earshot running.

Bella was hard-pressed not to smile with grim satisfaction.

She watched from the third stair as Thorn threw open the door, Fortescue at his back, head thrust forward to see.

From this height she could look over Thorn's shoulder and see a naked woman flat on her front on the long table amid the wreck of the magistrates' supper and some dice. Livid stripes marked her buttocks.

She saw Thoroughgood staring at Thorn, his face puce with rage.

Augustus — how blessedly perfect — Augustus was standing behind the table, his jacket gone, riding crop in hand. His jaw had dropped and seemed frozen in that position, his eyes showing white all around.

"What the devil's going on here?" Thorn bellowed in a shipboard voice, continuing on into the room. He shrugged off his coat and flung it over the woman.

She scrambled off the table, huddling into the coat, looking the perfect image of terrorized womanhood. Bella didn't miss the bright satisfaction in her eyes, however, and hoped the whores could fully play their parts.

The men in the hall were inching toward the doorway now. In a moment it would be a stampede to get a better view.

A lady really should flee to her room at this point, but Bella would not miss a scrap of this. She raced down the last few steps and seized the place just behind Fortescue.

Now she could see the complete scene, and it was almost too much for her. The three whores were naked except for some pieces of jewelry. Food and drink had spilled onto the floor, and some broken glass threatened bare feet. Perhaps that was why the three women all wore shoes, which seemed only to emphasize their complete lack of other clothing.

The room stank of food, wine, cheap perfume, and something else.

Squire Thoroughgood had risen from a chair at the head of the table and finally found his voice. "Take your rotten carcasses out of here, damn your eyes! Out! Out!"

The local people shrank back, but Thorn moved forward. "If anyone is rotten here, sir, it is you and your friends. What sort of debauch is this? What a stink."

He strode around the table to the window, pushed back the shutters, and flung it open. The people outside rushed to see.

"This is a private matter," Thoroughgood snarled, on his feet now, growing, impossibly, a deeper red. "I'll have you horse-whipped!"

Sir Newleigh, wig gone to reveal thin, pale hair, whispered, "Goody, Goody, it's . . . it's you-know-who!"

But Thoroughgood was beyond reason.

431

He leaned forward to glare even more fiercely at Thorn, his belly pressing into his messy plate. "I don't care if he's the bloody king. I don't care if it's God himself. I'll have him up for . . . for something. Tampering with the law! That's it. Tampering with the law."

"Make way, make way." A deep baritone accustomed to thundering from the pulpit parted the audience like the Red Sea. The Reverend Jervingham had arrived. Tall, robust, and with a mane of silver hair, he lacked only the beard to represent God himself. Bella ducked behind Lord Fortescue, and Fortescue backed out of God's way.

His arrival created a moment of complete silence.

Then the whores grabbed clothing from the floor to attempt to cover themselves, while Sir Newleigh's mouth opened and shut like a mechanical doll's as he tried and failed to find something to say.

Augustus, clearly lost in his own horror, moaned. He was behind the table, however, and he'd either lowered or dropped the whip.

Thoroughgood said nothing, but rage steamed all around him.

The vicar turned to him. "I was summoned to hear your confession, Squire Thoroughgood, you being in extremis. Though your health is not as bad as I feared, your soul is in an even worse state." His voice rose again to its godlike tones. "Confess, confess, you miserable sinner, before it is too late."

"Go preach to hell," Thoroughgood said, sitting down again.

Bella heard gasps behind her, but Reverend Jervingham seemed unmoved. He turned to the other two men. "Can I hope you gentlemen have an interest in avoiding the torments of hell?"

"Oh, yes, definitely . . ." said Sir Newleigh, but in a fading voice. His eyes turned up and he crumpled to the floor in a dead faint.

"Sir Augustus?" asked the voice of God.

Now Augustus was opening and shutting his mouth, but then he did find words. "Sir . . . Reverend . . . all a mistake. Terrible mistake. None of my doing. Meeting of the magistrates . . . women . . . whores . . ."

Thorn was behind Augustus and now he grabbed him by the shirt collar and hauled him backward, away from the table's concealment. Augustus's breeches were down around his knees, only his shirt keeping him decent.

"I can explain. . . ." He gasped, half choking.

"Perhaps you were preparing to be punished for your sins — is that it?" Thorn grabbed the riding crop from the floor and landed a stinging blow on Augustus's behind.

Augustus shrieked. "Stop! Stop it! How dare you . . . ?" He yelped again under another blow.

Bella covered her face, but it was to hide her thrilled delight. This was better than anything she'd ever dreamed.

Thorn let her brother go. Augustus dropped to all fours to scurry under the table like the cockroach he was.

Thorn turned toward Squire Thoroughgood.

"You wouldn't dare," the man said, but he was pale now, rather than purple. Pale with fury, however. "You might be a poxy duke, but you wouldn't dare."

"Duke . . . !"

The word skittered around behind Bella and she winced. They were back to that danger. All concern about that flew out of her head when Thoroughgood suddenly produced a pistol and pointed it at Thorn. He held it aimed on him while he used his other hand to unsteadily cock it. He was drunk, but not too drunk to kill at that range.

Why, oh, why hadn't she brought her pistol down with her?

"Don't be a fool, man," Fortescue said sharply.

"Put down that weapon!" Jervingham commanded.

Thorn had become very still, and Thoroughgood didn't seem moved by either instruction. Thorn put the crop on the table.

"I think I'll shoot you anyway," Thoroughgood sneered. "Last of your line, aren't you, Ithorne? That'll be some recompense for this."

"You'll hang," Thorn said.

"Shoot m'self first."

"By all means," Thorn said in a fine simulation of amusement. "Shoot yourself now and the whole area will be much improved."

Bella growled at him. Why enrage the man more?

When Thoroughgood raised the pistol, trying to sight on his target, she looked around for a weapon. Any weapon.

A gaping man nearby clutched a pewter tankard. She grabbed it from him. Last time she'd thrown a pot of ale, she'd hit the man's head by sheer good fortune, so she didn't aim there. She'd aim for Squire Thoroughgood's enormous middle. It should at least give Thorn a chance. Praying that the goddesses of good fortune would bless her again, she hurled the tankard with all her might.

It hit and exploded with such a bang her ears rang. No, wait! It wasn't the tankard. Smoke swirled from the powder, and plaster sprayed from the wall.

He'd fired!

She whirled to look at Thorn, but he was looking at her in astonishment, seeming unharmed. Then his eyes turned brilliant with laughter. "If we had an army of such stalwart wenches, Britain would never lose a battle!"

Thoroughgood stared at the damaged wall, finally at a loss. Bella realized that her tankard had knocked the pistol sideways.

Thorn turned to the room in general. "Attempt to commit murder, wouldn't you say? I think we need a magistrate."

Laughter began as a titter, but then swelled and spread until it was a gale. Sir Newleigh had come out of his faint but was a wreck of a man. Augustus was still hiding beneath the table.

None of the magistrates would be able to hold their heads up in this area again, and

Bella felt a tiny touch of pity — for Sir Newleigh, at least. She'd seen enough to heal her wounds and was easing away from the door when a new arrival to the inn politely asked others to make way.

Ah. It was not quite finished. Bella stayed to watch the arrival of Mr. Langham. He was a stocky, square-jawed man dressed by an excellent tailor.

He came to the doorway and looked around the room.

After a long silence, he said, "I was given to understand that a certain gentleman was here, but I see it isn't so. I'm glad of it."

"If you seek Sir Augustus Barstowe," said Reverend Jervingham, in a tone weighty with sorrow, "look under the table, sir."

From the sounds, Augustus was trying to scrabble backward, but Thorn must have pushed him forward with his boot, for suddenly his pop-eyed, chubby face came into view, cowled by the tablecloth.

He was crying.

His nose was running.

"Sir . . . I can explain. . . ."

Poor Augustus. He'd always been able to wheedle out of any sticky situation, and he hadn't yet accepted that he couldn't do that here.

Mr. Langham stared. "I very much doubt

it, sir. If you were a gentleman, I would assume you would know that you will never be welcome in my house again. But as you are not, I'll make it clear: if you ever approach my daughter in any way, you'll receive a whipping that will cast anything that's occurred here into insignificance."

He turned and walked out, jaw set so fiercely that he looked like a bulldog, paying no attention to anyone else.

Now it was over, Bella thought.

Now it was done.

She even felt a tiny bit sorry for Augustus in his complete destruction, but she remembered it was well earned and she had no regrets.

She slipped back toward the stairs. She'd have done it without notice, except that the mood was turning jolly and a number of the men congratulated her on her aim. It wasn't hard for her to demur, to say haltingly that it had been an impulse of the moment. That she had no idea what had inspired her. She was feeling slightly shaky, almost light-headed, and held tight to the banister as she went upstairs.

Once in the bedchamber she collapsed onto a chair. This dizziness must be shock. Instead of being thrilled, she felt sick.

This wasn't a happy ending. Perhaps those

other magistrates hadn't deserved shame and ridicule as Augustus had. She loathed Thoroughgood, but he was doubtless no more wicked than many other men. She hardly knew Sir Newleigh. He might be nothing more than weak.

She lowered her head into her hands, unable to think clearly. Discordant thoughts jangled in her mind.

What-ifs . . .

If-onlys . . .

What now?

Ah.

"Bella? What's amiss?"

She looked up to see Thorn's concern.

He came to kneel by her chair. "Was all that too much for you?" When she didn't reply, he asked, "Was that not what you wanted?"

His anxiety touched her soul. She'd never thought to see Captain Rose uncertain and worried. She straightened and took his hands. "Yes, of course it was. Thank you. It was magnificent."

He studied her a moment longer and then pulled her up from the chair and sat down in it. He brought her into his lap. Bella tensed for a moment, but at his gentle urging she relaxed into his arms.

"Now," he said. "Tell me what you're

really thinking."

That it's over would be the true answer now. Both her driving purpose and her time with him were over. Instead, she said, "I suspect Sir Newleigh is not a truly bad man."

"Weak involvement in sin is as vile as powerful commitment."

"Is it?"

"The consequences for the victims are the same."

"I suppose so. How are the women?"

"Cock-a-hoop. Did you expect anything else? But they too had no deep animus against Sir Newleigh. Thoroughgood and your brother were the vicious ones."

"What will happen to them now? The magistrates."

"They'll have to give up their seats on the bench."

"Is that all?"

"It's significant. Thoroughgood may bully his way on with life, but if your assessment of your brother is correct, he's finished."

"I wonder what he will do?"

"Skulk, placing the blame on everyone but himself."

"Oh, poor Lucinda!"

"The sister who lives at your old home? If she's wise, she'll move elsewhere."

Bella relaxed again. "Athena will offer her a home. Some of this dirt will stick to all of them, however."

And to me, she realized. She was now not just Bella Barstowe, but the sister of ridiculous, disgusting Augustus Barstowe. Was that being hoist with her own petard?

It tasted bitter in her mouth, but still, she didn't regret anything.

She'd stopped Augustus. She'd ended his corrupt power.

For some reason, that made Bella weep. Once she began, she couldn't stop, though she tried, choking out apologies, gathering up her skirt to mop her face. He found a handkerchief and put it into her hands, but other than that, he simply held her, rocking her slightly.

She got a grip on herself and sat up straighter to blow her nose. "I'm so sorry. It must be shock."

"When did you last cry?"

The handkerchief was the one she'd made for him. That made tears threaten again, but she pressed a dry part firmly against her eyes, commanding herself to calm.

"A long time ago," she admitted. "My family took tears as a sign of repentance, which implied guilt. So I stopped."

"Then I'm glad they flowed again," he

said, and held her closer.

That began the leaking once more and she let his voice soothe her until she heard:

". . . that harpy Lady Fowler."

"What?" Bella squeaked, trying not to leap up.

He tightened his arms. "Have you heard of her? A demented woman who's taken it as her duty to expose the evils of highborn men. If she picks up this story, it will get widely distributed, and she'll be of some use."

"Oh, yes," Bella said as her heart rate steadied a little. She could tell him there was little interest in such peccadilloes at Lady Fowler's these days, but of course she wouldn't.

"I wonder where she gets her scandals from?" he asked.

Bella felt that being so close as he said such things would reveal her secrets and pushed gently off his lap. "I must wash my face."

She went behind the screen and used the cold water there. The mirror showed her reddened eyes and nose. What a fright. She pressed the cool cloth to her eyes and then tidied her hair.

She practiced a composed smile, and then emerged. "I'm sorry for being a watering pot. Did I ruin your jacket?"

"No. My lap is still available."

And tempting.

But this was over now. When would they leave? It was late, but there was some moon. They could travel in the dark. She'd make this easy for him.

"Thank you," she said, "but I believe it's time for me to stand on my own feet. Or at least sit in my own chair." She took the one opposite him. "Our task is complete, isn't it?"

"Our part, yes. Alas, I doubt your brother has the spine to shoot himself, but as you once said, living with the world knowing the truth about him will be a form of hell. What will you do now?" he asked.

Of course he had no suggestion. No proposal.

She shrugged as if it were of no moment. "Continue as I was, living a quiet life."

"A sad waste. Do you never seek out excitement?"

There was something behind that question.

A prelude to an invitation to become his mistress. It was the best she could hope for, but she knew she couldn't do it.

"I think I've had enough excitement for a lifetime. You must need to return to your

443

ship. It's been most kind of you to spend so much time on this."

"Don't," he said.

"Don't what?"

But then he rose and turned away from her. "Dammit, you're right. This is over."

Though it had been her point, his words felt like a sword to the heart. Bella swallowed, but said, "Of course it is."

He turned and came to kneel by her again. "Bella . . . Bella, I would . . . I need to return to my life."

She took his hands, and this time she was offering comfort. "I said that, I think."

His hands tightened on hers, almost as if they clung. "I've enjoyed our time together more than I could have imagined. I have been, I think, happy in a way I don't remember before."

A tiny bud of hope began to unfurl. Did he need some encouragement? She couldn't imagine why, but perhaps being a sea captain's wife was seen as arduous.

"I . . . I believe I wouldn't mind being with you for longer. . . ."

Perhaps she would accept an invitation to be his mistress after all.

Yes, of course she would.

But his tight lips warned her before he rose and stepped back.

"Yes, you would mind. Don't argue. I can't explain. Please believe me, Bella: it isn't possible. It simply isn't possible to continue like this."

No one could doubt that. She had to look away to try to hide her pain, though she was sure she failed.

"Very well," she said at last. "I'm sure it will be for the best. Some of us aren't made for peaks of excitement." She found the courage to look at him, and even managed a slight smile, because she hoped it would ease his pain. "Having been deprived of a quiet, normal life for so long, I truly want it, and I see that you cannot provide it. I haven't known how to create it, but I think I will be able to now, with my wound lanced, drained, and able to heal."

He drew her to her feet. She hoped for a kiss on the lips, torture though it would be.

He kissed her hand. "I pray that is so. I truly only want what is best for you, Bella Barstowe. Always believe that."

He stepped away and managed a casual tone that might fool many. "I should go below to rejoin the celebration. I won't disturb you when I come up. I'll sleep on the floor in the parlor."

He took the coverlet and a pillow off the bed and left.

Bella stood there, tears flowing helplessly down her face, but she did not let herself sob until she was sure he was out of earshot.

CHAPTER 23

They left early the next morning to return to London with the excuse that the events of the night before had been a little too much for Mistress Rose's nerves. The inn-keeper was most apologetic, and from his manner he clearly believed that he'd had the Duke of Ithorne as his guest.

The general atmosphere around Upstone was decidedly jolly.

Tabitha must have felt neglected, for she seemed to be sulking, and the occasional sounds she made were almost growls.

As the coach rolled down the street some-one spotted it, and there was a spontaneous cheer. Thorn waved, grinning, but then settled back into his corner. "We'd best not return here for a while."

We.

There was no *we*.

Perhaps he realized that, for he fell into silence.

When he asked, "Would you like me to read to you?" it was a blessed relief. Events in Persia were safe.

After a while, she took over and read to him, and then they took turns. The book lasted the whole journey, until the coach drew up in front of her small house in Soho.

"What will you tell your benefactor?" he asked.

"My benefactor?" Bella asked. "Oh . . ." She couldn't lie to him. Not now. "I live here alone. With three servants, but no one else. I have a small annuity."

"Not so small," he remarked, "if you can afford this. You're young to be alone."

"My housekeeper has known me from a child, and I have a solicitor who advises me when applied to."

"But leaves you to your own mischief most of the time."

"Mischief? You know why I embarked on this adventure."

"Are you saying that other than our time together you've lived a quiet, blameless life?" There was an edge to that that might be suspicion. It stirred welcome anger.

"What are you accusing me of?"

He didn't flinch and his lips were hard. "We have been together twice, Bella — in Dover four years ago and recently. Your actions don't convince me that you spend all your time sewing handkerchiefs."

"No, I also walk in the park. I sometimes attend lectures on art and history."

His eyes demanded more.

"What?" she asked. "Tell me what you believe I've done." Had he somehow learned about Bellona and Lady Fowler? Lord, had he recognized Kelano?

She'd have thought that impossible. She'd been so changed. . . .

He shook his head, relaxing, but still disapproving. "If you live so quietly, it's wrong, Bella. Perhaps living with your sister wouldn't be as impossible as you think."

"You're being completely illogical." But he'd already left the carriage to walk around and open her door. She gathered her belongings into her valise and he lifted it out, then offered his hand.

She took it and descended, by which time Kitty had the door open, her face bright with relief.

"Thank you," Bella said to Captain Rose, dropping a curtsy, fully on her dignity. "I wish you well."

He bowed. "As I do you, Miss Barstowe." He turned to the coach and put a foot on the step. But then he turned back. "If you ever have need of me again, a note to the

Black Swan Inn in Stowting, Kent, will find me most speedily."

Then he climbed into the coach and slammed the door. It moved off, and Bella did not indulge in watching it. She walked into her house, Kitty's exclamations and questions washing over her. She climbed the stairs blindly, unpinning her hat. She'd done this before, she realized. When she'd returned from the Goat.

When she'd returned from Dover too. But then she'd had such dreams, such hopes.

She remembered the skull. She'd kept it safely in her right pocket ever since he'd said, *Keep it.* She considered it, tears falling. An excuse to write to that address in Stowting?

"Oh, miss, whatever's that?"

Bella quickly closed her hand around it and smiled for Kitty. "Nothing. I'm all right, truly. Just tired from the journey and from some exhausting days."

And nights.

Never forget the nights.

"So you're safe, miss? You did what you needed to do?"

Bella sat to unpin the wig. "Yes and yes, Kitty. I need some good strong tea, please, and then I'm going to bed."

One way to achieve peace and solitude.

"I'll just get the warming pan, then, miss."

Kitty left and Bella could let her face relax, seeing in the mirror the misery stamped into her features. She wouldn't permit it to show in front of others. The last thing she wanted was pity. She tossed aside the wig but had to stand and go to her valise for her brush.

Annie rushed in to thrust a warming pan into the bed. "Tea in a moment, miss!" she said in a gasp before running out again.

Bella brushed her hair, standing in front of the fire, watching the dancing flames. Would she ever be as alive? As alive as she had been for a few short days?

And nights.

She seemed unable to stop her mind from running over and over things. Perhaps if she allowed it, in the end it would run down like a clock. Then she would not wind it up again. It was over. Now she must decide what to do with the rest of her life. It felt like a void.

Kitty and Annie hauled in Bella's trunk between them. They put it down and left, and a moment later Kitty, somewhat flushed, returned with the tea tray.

"Here you are, miss. Hot, strong, and sweet."

She poured some, and Bella took the cup

without a saucer, cradling it in her chilled hands as she sipped. "Oh, that is good. Thank you, Kitty."

Not as subtle a taste as the tea he favored.

She'd never react to tea the same way again.

Kitty looked across from where she was hanging a fresh nightgown on the rack in front of the fire. "You do look tired, miss."

Probably a polite description, but Bella said, "I am."

"Shall I get you out of your stays now, miss, or get the hot water?"

Bella found a real smile. "I'm back to my jumps, Kitty, so the water, please."

Kitty pulled a face, but it was mostly teasing. At the door she paused and said, "There's a pile of letters in your parlor, miss. Do you want me to bring them up?"

"A pile of letters?" Bella asked, surprised.

"A couple are from Lady Fowler, miss. I couldn't help but notice that on the front."

Lord. She'd sent Lady Fowler a note to say she'd been called out of town, so what could be driving her to send letters here? Bella certainly couldn't deal with them now.

"They'll wait until tomorrow," she said, and poured herself more tea. She nibbled one of Peg's crisp biscuits. It was delicious and helped settle her mind. They'd eaten at an inn only a few hours ago, but when she thought about that, she wasn't sure how much she'd consumed. She'd been trying so hard not to show how much pain she felt.

She took off her clothes and wrapped herself in her dressing gown, forcing her mind toward her blessings.

She'd achieved her victory over Augustus.

She was a fortunate lady with an independence.

She was young, and healthy, and had friends. . . .

No, she didn't. She had two maids who would soon leave to marry. She had Peg, but though she felt almost as warmly toward her as a mother, Peg wasn't a friend. A few of the women at Lady Fowler's might be friends, but she was about to cut that connection.

Thorn. Their time together had felt like friendship, perhaps her first true friendship, and one she could never match. A woman couldn't have a male friend except in marriage, however, and it seemed they could not marry.

When the water came, she discarded her dressing gown and washed thoroughly, soaping away as much of her recent adventure as she could. Bella Barstowe must be newborn. She must make a life for herself, and this time she wouldn't run from prison to convent.

She would find a way to be truly free.

Resolved, she put on her nightgown, extinguished the candles, and went to bed.

As Thorn drove toward his house he resumed his ducal status as if putting on the ermine-trimmed robes and coronet. The more time he allowed himself away from his responsibilities, the greater the weight of them when he returned.

Having a wife to return to would make a difference.

Having Bella to return to.

But he was imagining returning to a cozy parlor, to sitting by the fireside, he reading, she sewing, sharing comfortable smiles.

His duchess would have her own suite of rooms, just as he had his. Their "parlors" would be drawing rooms, usually shared with dependents and guests. She would have a boudoir, and she would entertain her more intimate guests there. He had his study, where he did the same.

There could be days when they never met, even if under the same roof.

In Upstone he'd intended to attempt to woo Bella as the duke, perhaps simply by turning up on her doorstep and trying to explain the whole sorry mess. Now, in London, as he drew ever closer to his ducal state, the gulf between them widened.

The carriage was passing St. James's Palace, where the Duchess of Ithorne would be expected to take her turn as lady-in-waiting to the queen. Not only could he not envision Bella in that role, but the stiff-rumped little queen would never accept someone so scandalous.

Yes, Robin's and Christian's wives would accept Bella, and perhaps some others, but many wouldn't. She'd be uncomfortable and unhappy, which would infuriate him. He'd soon become a terrifying despot who took out his ill humor on innocents.

He must at least give this time before he did something that could make them both miserable for the rest of their lives.

On arrival, he put himself straight in Overstone's hands. He wanted to be drowned in work.

CHAPTER 24

There was something to be said for waking up in one's own bed in one's own house, Bella thought when she opened her eyes the next morning. A great deal to be said. Even if it would be more pleasant to wake up with someone . . .

She slammed that door.

She savored the simple pleasures of familiar sounds from the street and the way the slit of daylight drew a line on the opposite wall, and began to grieve.

She liked this house. It was just large enough for her small household, and the neighbors seemed pleasant. Bellona Flint had probably seemed too stern for friendship, but they had always exchanged a goodday and bland comments about the weather. She couldn't stay, however, because how could she explain to anyone the transformation from Bellona to Bella? How could she make a complete break from the Fowler flock when living a street away?

That reminded her of the pile of letters. She'd like to ignore them, but in the end it would be better to deal with them quickly. She rang the bell that stood at hand. Kitty soon arrived.

"You're up bright and early, miss!" she said, putting down her coal scuttle and kneeling to make up the fire. "And looking all the better for a good night's sleep. I hope you did sleep well, miss?"

"Yes," Bella said, somewhat surprised. She'd expected to lie awake, tormented by memories. "I must have been more tired than I thought."

"All that traveling, miss. Shall I bring your breakfast once this is going?"

"Yes, please. And the waiting letters."

Kitty lit the fire and watched it a moment. When she was satisfied, she rose, wiping her hands on her apron. "Very well, miss. And what gown will you want?"

Bella made a firm decision. "None of Bellona's. Bellona Flint is going to disappear."

"Very good, miss!" Kitty said fervently.

Bella chuckled. "I've been a sad trial to you, haven't I? And yes, I'll wear stays."

Kitty was grinning as she hurried away.

Bella did her best to keep her mind on simple things as she waited. For her new life she would need new gowns. Should she patronize Mistress Moray again, or visit a mantua maker? Here or elsewhere?

Perhaps she should leave London entirely. An idea crept into her mind. . . . But no, she would not move to Dover! Nor to any other port on the south coast where she might happen to encounter Captain Rose. She'd avoid the coast entirely. But apart from that, she might as well stick a pin in a map.

Breakfast was a welcome distraction. She took her first sip of chocolate and then considered the letters. All were from Lady Fowler's house but not, in fact, from the lady herself. Two were from Mary Evesham and the rest from various ladies there.

She drank more chocolate and took a bite of warm buttered bread and then broke the seal on the first letter to arrive, one of the ones from Mary Evesham. She was a curate's sister and both intelligent and wryly humorous.

My dear Miss Flint,
Your good sense is sorely missed here. Lady Fowler is most unwell. To be frank, she is sinking fast, but her mind is decomposing first, which is creating great alarm and disorder here. I myself

am atremble as to what she might do or encourage. If you are avoiding this place out of wisdom, I am reluctant to encourage you to return, but I must.

With high regard,
Mary Evesham

Bella blew out a breath. Alarming, but what exactly did it mean? Mary's term "atremble" would be her humor, but she was clearly alarmed.

She fortified herself with more chocolate and opened the next to arrive. This was from Clara Ormond, an elderly lady who was both plump and nervous, living in dread of being forced out onto the street. She was one of the ones Bella desperately wanted to help, because she was clearly unable to help herself. She'd loved a loving husband, but had no children. Her husband had suffered business losses, and when he'd died, she'd found herself penniless. She had no true interest in Lady Fowler's causes, but had simply thrown herself on the lady's mercy.

The letter was a desperate plea for Bellona to return before disaster — underlined three times — befell them all.

The next was from Celia Pottersby along the same lines but with mention of the

Drummond sisters playing on Lady Fowler's degenerating mind.

Hortensia Sprott, thin and sharp, stated bluntly, "She's mad but don't know it. The sooner she dies the better. Pray it happens before she ruins us all."

The final letter was the second from Mary.

My dear Bellona,

Out of pure selfishness I must beg you to return to us, if only for a little while. Matters are serious and I don't know what to do for the best.

I know I would serve you better by recommending that you stay away, even that you leave London completely, but I must ask you to return.

With high regard,
Mary Evesham

The letters troubled Bella deeply, but why had all these women written to her? She was the youngest among them and had no power to change anything.

Thorn had said she was a leader. She'd disagreed, but perhaps he'd been right in saying that people saw her that way. Was a leader simply someone who chose to act rather than wring their hands? And did sheep in distress look for anyone to lead them out of trouble?

She was uncomfortable with thinking of the letter writers as sheep, but even Mary, with her good sense, and Hortensia, so fierce and sharp, were penniless and dependent. That was enough to drain the courage from anyone. It had trapped her at Carscourt for four years.

All the same, Bella wanted to toss the letters in the fire and proceed with her plan to leave London. She had no duty to these women.

She buttered more bread and spread plum jam on it thickly. This situation was *nothing* to do with her, and the more disastrous it was likely to be, the less she should have to do with it.

She couldn't even put the food in her mouth.

She groaned, but accepted that she'd have to at least visit Lady Fowler's once or suffer the guilt of it all her life. Perhaps it was simply wild speculation and panic. She'd seen alarms over nothing go through the house like a fire.

In addition, she owed something to Lady Fowler herself. She had provided a refuge when Bella had needed one, and she probably was dying.

Kitty returned with the blue dress and

Bella's prettier underwear.

"Ah. I'm afraid I need one of Bellona's gowns after all. I need to make one last visit."

Kitty's face fell and Bella braced for a long argument against the action. But her dismayed comment was, "No stays then, miss."

Bella burst out laughing. "No stays. But tomorrow, I promise."

Bella had been Bellona for six months. It hadn't felt strange to her, even at first. Perhaps Bellona had been a natural fit for the frozen person who had escaped Carscourt. Now it felt a more uncomfortable disguise than Kelano or her other recent personas. As she walked to Lady Fowler's house, she feared everyone must know she wasn't who she appeared to be.

At the door she thought of knocking, because she felt she no longer belonged, but she walked in. Ellen Spencer came out of the scriptorium — the room where the flock transcribed the Fowler letter. Ellen stared, squeaked, and ran upstairs.

Bella watched her, astonished.

Then others were around her, fussing, explaining, and talking over one another so she couldn't understand a thing.

"Silence!" she commanded, and was obeyed.

Ah, yes. Bellona was back and the sheep knew their grim shepherd. She again wanted to turn and run, but she couldn't abandon them.

"The parlor," she said, and led the way. Once there, she demanded, "What's the fuss?" A dozen mouths opened. "Just one of you."

"Oh, Bellona," said Clara, dabbing at tears, "I'm so happy you're back. You'll know what to do."

She attempted an explanation, but it wandered and was often interrupted by others. Some things were clear: Lady Fowler was confined to her bed and said to be raving, but no one was permitted in her room but the Drummond sisters and Ellen Spencer.

"Why Ellen?" Bella asked. "She's not been here long."

"We don't know," said Mary Evesham, "but there was something odd about her coming here, and she seems devoted to the Drummonds. She does anything Helena or Olivia tells her."

"And now they're planning a news sheet!" Clara wailed.

"The Drummonds? They haven't used the

press before?" Bella asked, surprised.

"Olivia printed copies of Lady Fowler's most recent letter," Hortensia said. "It worked very well. Some of us took copies out and paid female street urchins to give them to ladies in the better parts of town. So as not to leave a trail back to here, you see."

Bella wrinkled her brow. "But if it was the Fowler letter, wouldn't everyone know where it came from?"

"Of course we left off the name and address," Hortensia said, sharp as a blade.

"But even so . . ." Bella abandoned any attempt to point out logic, aware of so many anxious eyes. "I gather the forces of the law have not descended, so all must be well."

Mary Evesham agreed. "We appear to be safe. But I think Lady Fowler was disappointed. I fear she actually wants to be dragged into court."

"Ah," Bella breathed. "To go down in history like John Wilkes. To be a martyr."

"I don't want to be a martyr," Clara protested. "Save us, Bellona!"

How? But Bella didn't speak the word. A leader's task, she thought, was to give at least the illusion that someone was certain and unafraid.

"You say a news sheet is planned. What

will it say?"

"We don't know," said Mary. "Some of us managed to do the typesetting of the letter, but it's slow, difficult work. It all has to be done backward. But now there's a typesetter. Mr. Smith is so very swift and accurate, but we don't know what the sheets say. They print only one to test the plate, and Olivia Drummond takes it straight to Lady Fowler."

"I fear it will be as you said, Bellona," said Celia Pottersby, a thin, pale widow who always predicted the worst. "A publication like the issue of the *North Briton* that put John Wilkes in the Tower. If he hadn't been a member of Parliament, they would have hanged him for saying such terrible things against the king. Lady Fowler is planning treason, and we'll all hang with her. . . ."

"No!" Clara gasped. "They can't! We have nothing to do with it."

"They arrested the printers of the *North Briton*," said Hortensia, who never found a fact too harsh to be faced. "And any others connected."

"They can't arrest nearly twenty respectable women," Bella said, hoping that was true. Some looked reassured, but others didn't.

"What of the typesetter?" she asked.

"Surely he can tell what words he's setting."

"With the name Smith?" asked Mary dryly. "He'll pocket his money and disappear. This is all a consequence of that thousand guineas."

"It was a curse on us," agreed Celia. "A viper planted among us by a wicked man."

Perhaps by the Duke of Ithorne, Bella thought. Her investigations had led to a legal firm that did much work for him, and he might have motive to wish Lady Fowler harm. Lady Fowler had turned viciously against the Marquess of Rothgar over the matter of his bastard daughter, and that daughter had married the Earl of Huntersdown, who was Ithorne's cousin, and apparently a friend. Huntersdown was married to that bastard daughter, so the attacks might seem doubly offensive to the duke.

Ithorne probably was angry, but how could he have dreamed up such a complex revenge? He couldn't have been able to predict the disastrous results of the grand donation.

If Ithorne had been the cause of these problems, however, Bella might have reason to appeal to Thorn. She could ask him to speak to his brother on their behalf. To appeal to his sense of justice.

Part of her leapt eagerly toward an excuse

to contact him — which meant the other part must slam that door and lock it.

How long, how long until this insanity passed?

"I'm sure the situation can't be so bad," she said to the anxious women. "It is simply necessary to keep a cool head."

Elizabeth Shutton said, "I do believe my son and daughter-in-law would benefit from my wisdom." She was a widow in her fifties who lived here almost as if it were a hotel, never attempting to do any work.

"But, Elizabeth," Clara said, "you've always said you'd be unhappy as a charity case in your old home."

"Nonsense," Elizabeth said, and swept out.

Clara looked confused, but Bella had always suspected that Mistress Shutton wasn't as short of money as she claimed. Perhaps others would find other homes more appealing than this one now. She hoped so.

She rose. "I must pay my respects to Lady Fowler."

After a long absence such a visit would be natural, but Clara gasped, Mary grimaced, and Hortensia said, "She's raving."

Celia raised a lace-trimmed handkerchief to her nose. "And the smell."

Bella braced herself and went upstairs.

Ellen Spencer was on guard, but her eyes were huge behind her spectacles. "Lady Fowler's not receiving," she said, but it came out faintly.

Bella summoned Bellona's flinty points. "Out of my way," she snapped, and swept forward.

With a gasped, "Oh, dear!" Ellen stumbled out of danger.

Bella opened the door, but stopped, hit by heat and, yes, stink. The fire burned high, and Lady Fowler was propped in a sitting position in her big bed. She was definitely close to death. Her breath rasped in and out, and her face had shrunk down almost to the bones, covered by yellowish skin.

"Who is it?" she asked in a breathy croak.

Was she blind?

"Bellona," Bella said, her voice soft with pity despite everything. This was a sad end to a sad life.

Helena Drummond rose from a chair by the bed. "Get out of here. Can't you see Lady Fowler is too ill for guests?"

"I'm no guest." Bella closed the door and walked forward.

Helena barred her way. Bella shoved her. She must have put all her fury at this situation into it, for Helena stumbled back and thumped down on the carpet.

Bella went to the bedside, hand over her nose, hoping Lady Fowler was too blind to see. Hoping the lady couldn't smell her own rot.

"Lady Fowler," she said softly, already running with sweat. "I'm sorry to find you in this state."

"Bellona? Where have you been? You did not have permission to go."

Bella smiled slightly. The old arrogance was still there. "I told you I was leaving, madam. I had family business to attend to."

"Your family cast you off."

"Even so. What can I do for you?"

A clawlike hand reached out. Bella put hers into it. The skin was hot, dry, and flaky. It felt as if it might crack or rub away.

"Help with my great work," Lady Fowler begged.

"What is it?"

"Say no more!" cried Helena, grabbing Bella and trying to pull her away from the bed. "She's a spy, ma'am. That's where she's been. Conferring with your enemies. She's only returned to prevent your great work."

Bella grabbed the bed curtains and struggled to stay where she was. "That's not true. What is this great work?"

But Lady Fowler was gasping for breath, wheezing in what air she could. Agnes Hoover, her personal maid, was at her side instantly, raising her and holding a glass to her lips. "Here, my love, my pet. Drink this." She glared up. "Get away, all of you. Leave her to die in peace."

"An excellent idea," Bella said, turning to face Helena.

"We are her handmaidens in this work," Helena said. "I never leave her side."

Bella had to give her credit for fortitude. She couldn't bear the room a moment longer and retreated to the door. She paused there. "Has a doctor been sent for?"

"There's nothing anyone can do," said Agnes, not looking away from her mistress. "I have medicines to soothe her." She did look up then, directly at Bella. "It won't be long."

She was about sixty and Bella had never seen her face without a scowl, but Bella felt Agnes was begging her to provide calm for her mistress's dying days. Another person looking to her. She left the room and inhaled a deep breath of relatively pure air. The corridor was deserted, so she took a moment to think.

She wanted nothing to do with any of this, but she couldn't abandon all these women.

She might be the youngest, but unlike all of them except the Drummonds she hadn't been beaten down by life. She also had her independent income. That was like owning a pistol when the rest of them were completely defenseless.

What to do?

Clearly Lady Fowler was beyond help, but she must also be beyond doing more harm. The Drummond sisters were the danger, but Helena, the most dangerous, had pinned herself up here. Bella wondered about that. What purpose did it serve?

Olivia had always been the one most involved with the printing press. She was probably down there now. The simplest action would be to disable the press.

Bella went down the servants' staircase. It took her first to the kitchen, where the three servants looked at her with anxious and pleading expressions. Them too?

She gave them a vague smile and continued to the room where the press had been set up. When she opened the door, a man turned. Then he stared, looking very wary.

Yes. "Mr. Smith" had no intention of being connected to this enterprise. She wondered how much he was being paid to take the risk. He was a short, thin man of about forty with brown hair. He was in shirtsleeves and wearing a leather apron.

"I'm Bellona Flint," Bella said, "one of Lady Fowler's closest confidantes. I've been away. I wanted to be sure you had everything you require."

"Yes, thank you, ma'am."

Bella nodded. "And the press is in good order?"

"Not my job. I'm the typesetter."

"Ah. I assume the type is in good order, then. I gather some of the ladies used it, and I fear they may have disordered things."

He let out a snort. "Made a pig's dinner of it and damaged some, but that'll have to be as it is. You'll have to tell the others that they need to print the first two pages now, so I can reuse the type for the next ones."

He turned back to his work. Bella watched for a moment, appreciating the lifetime of practice that enabled him to reach without looking to the correct box for each letter. Pick up the square of lead, place, and tap into place. Pick up, place, tap into place.

She went to the press, but looking at it told her nothing, and she couldn't tamper with it while the typesetter was there. She wondered what hours he worked.

She left and went up to the parlor and asked.

"He works late," Mary said.

"And arrives early," Bella guessed. "Eager to finish the work and be gone. He says someone needs to print the first two pages. Where's Olivia?"

Uneasy glances flittered around. "Out somewhere," Hortensia said. "Comes and goes as she pleases!"

No reason for any of them not to do the same, Bella thought. Did they feel imprisoned? Or as if they were in a convent, needing permission from the mother superior?

She remembered Thorn's comments about convents.

No. She wouldn't think of everything in reference to him.

"In any case," said Mary with wry meaning, "Mr. Smith insists that any printing happen at night when he's not here. Disturbs him, he says."

"I see. Then it will have to be tonight. I will return to assist." Bella needed to read what was being created here before she made any other decisions. She pulled on her gloves. "After being away, I have a number of matters to attend to, so I'll leave for a while."

"How is Lady Fowler?" asked Clara anxiously.

Bella wished she could soften it. "Close to death, I think."

The ladies gasped and moaned, and Bella thought that perhaps someone would truly mourn Lady Fowler. But then Clara asked, "What will become of us?"

"Perhaps she'll have made provision in her will?" Celia suggested anxiously.

Bella hoped so. If the flock could continue to live here, she wouldn't have to worry about them.

"She had her lawyer here about it," Mary said.

"That could be good news," Bella said.

"It could. Of course, Helena was the only one with her. . . ."

Their eyes met. Mary, like Bella, didn't trust any will made under Drummond influence. Another thing to do: write to Mr. Clatterford and seek his advice on wills made under influence.

CHAPTER 25

Thorn found it damnably difficult to concentrate, and there was much that he should focus on. Food prices had soared since the end of the war and it was causing unrest. Possible solutions were subject to intense debate, including the troublesome corn laws. The American colonies were objecting to the taxes imposed to pay for their defense against the French. The pestilential issue of John Wilkes and his treasonous edition of the *North Briton* dragged on and on. The man's flight to France hadn't ended the matter.

Overstone had prepared lengthy reports on every issue that might conceivably have importance. Provisions for the navy. Pay for the army. Agricultural improvements in Norfolk. Thorn was reading over all this when his cousin Robin walked in.

"What the devil are you doing here?" Thorn demanded.

Robin's brows went up. "Business. I did write. Hoping to stay here rather than a club, the house being unprepared." He flicked through the pile of unopened letters and pulled out one. He turned it to show that it was from him. "Been away?"

Thorn frowned at him, but really at himself. Overstone didn't open letters from friends. All the more reason for Thorn to attend to them first.

"Dover," he said.

"Playing Captain Rose again? Good." Robin took a small dog out of his pocket. It could only be described as a ball of fluff.

" 'Struth, not that," Thorn complained, but it was a joke.

Robin had acquired the papillon dog in France, and the creature considered itself an essential accessory. Robin indulged it, and took Coquette nearly everywhere, even to court.

"Tabitha," Thorn said, "don't eat the butterfly."

Tabitha looked up and closed the basket. Coquette pranced over to sniff. Robin laughed.

"I don't play when I'm Captain Rose," Thorn said. "In fact, I rarely get to play at all."

"That could change. Did you know people

are smuggling sheep to France?"

"Sheep? To France?"

Robin's smile was pure mischief. "English sheep being superior to French ones. Don't you think we should stop the trade? I'm due for a time as Lieutenant Sparrow."

"Won't your bride object?"

Robin pulled a face. "Petra's more likely to insist on coming. No," he corrected, "she's being very sensible now that she's carrying our child, but that would make her more cross at me if I went off adventuring."

"I admit to the temptation," Thorn said, leaning back. "Hunting illicit sheep in the *Black Swan*."

With Lieutenant Sparrow and Pagan the Pirate. And even Buccaneer Bella?

Thorn came to his senses and straighened. "The sheep trade will have to succeed or fail without my intervention. I'm drowning in work. What brings you to Town?"

"Rothgar."

"So he pulls your strings now, does he?"

Robin gave him a look. "I've never had the problem with him that you do."

"You don't outrank him."

"I still outrank most of England and none has become an obsession. In truth, I admire him. Don't always agree with him, but he's devilish clever and disgustingly high-minded."

"He always looks after his own interests first."

"He doesn't neglect his own interests. There's a difference. He bears you no ill will."

"Which I find rather galling."

"What? You think he should shiver in his shoes at the thought of you? Stop being a blockhead over this."

Thorn flinched under Robin's rare anger. "Let's talk about something more interesting. How's Petra?"

"No, let's not."

Robin was lighthearted to a fault, but when he took that tone, a wise man paid attention.

"What do you want? Or should it be, what does *he* want?"

"A meeting," Robin said.

"We met. We negotiated Christian's affair. We even cooperated. We meet at court and in Parliament all the time."

"You know what I mean."

Thorn picked up a paperweight, then realized he was fiddling and put it down. "Why?"

"Britain has peace and it looks likely to stick, which is lulling people into thinking all is well, but there's a deal of trouble stir-ring."

"Is that your insight or your father-in-law's?"

"You won't irritate me with that gibe. The evidence is clear, but yes, he's applied a lens that makes it clearer. The troubles in the colonies aren't going away. That Otis seems able to stir emotions, and now others follow where he leads. Their arguments are absurd, but if Britain mishandles the situation, we could lose the entire Americas to the French."

"But not if Rothgar and I man the barricades together?"

Robin rolled his eyes. "You and he are among the few powerful men not driven by self-interest. In his case, I believe it's a moral choice. In yours, I see it as more because there's nothing you want that you don't have."

Thorn worked very hard at keeping his face still, but he did say, "My freedom?"

"You have Captain Rose. Or, no, you've given it up. Is that what has you growling? Get back to sea now."

"I thought I was needed to save the kingdom from disaster."

Robin inhaled.

Thorn said, "I've given up Captain Rose

for now because I should continue the line before endangering myself again. If you want to be useful, find me the perfect wife."

"Marry one of Christian's sisters."

"He warned me off."

"What?" Robin asked, astonished.

"Months ago. He wants me to marry for love."

"So do I."

"So might I, but love doesn't come so easily to me. At least, not with the right women."

Robin became more alert. "Who's the wrong one?"

"Forget it."

"Not if you've fallen in love. Only consider. Petra isn't the 'right woman' for me, and most people would have thought Caro a bad match for the heir to an earldom."

"Petra was raised an aristocrat," Thorn said. "She navigates our world with ease, despite being a bastard Catholic foreigner. Being Rothgar's bastard helps rather than hurts. Caro was raised as gentry, and that's Christian's background, despite the earldom. She'll fit comfortably into Devon society, and with luck it'll be decades before she has to be a countess. I don't have that luxury. I need to marry a duchess."

Robin didn't immediately protest, which

was telling, but then he said, "Unless your beloved's a dairymaid, she'll learn."

"She's a dairymaid," Thorn agreed.

Robin swore at him, pleasantly.

"I'll meet Rothgar," Thorn said. "Anything to get you out of here. When and where?"

A hiss made them both turn.

They both acted.

Sable had escaped to play with a new friend, and Tabitha was about to rush to the rescue. Robin snatched his ridiculous dog out of danger, but Coquette came with a kitten clinging to her back, and Tabitha was ready for one of her mighty leaps.

Thorn grabbed the cat from the unarmed end, which meant hindquarters crushed to his chest. Robin was plucking off the kitten, which for some reason was trying to cling. Tabitha thrust with her back legs again. If Thorn hadn't let go, she might have crushed his ribs. As it was, he tumbled backward onto the carpet, and had to scramble to his feet to try to save Robin.

But Robin had dodged the first leap. He put the kitten on the carpet, Coquette held high.

Tabitha glared, tail swishing, but then she spat at his boots. She grabbed Sable by the ruff and dumped him back in the basket.

"Whew!" Robin said. "Perhaps we should

481

breed the things as warrior cats."

Thorn rubbed his sore ribs. "Only if they can attack backward. My life," he said, "is in constant disorder, and I am not pleased."

"Tell me about it?" Robin asked hopefully.

"No. Tell me when and where I'm supposed to pay homage to Rothgar."

Robin stroked the agitated dog. "You and I are invited to sup at Malloren House tonight. If convenient. If not, some other time at your convenience. But soon. There is some urgency."

"The Wilkes affair?"

"Ongoing to the point of tedium. No." Robin glanced at the door to be sure it was still closed. "The king may not be well."

That caught all Thorn's attention. "I've heard nothing."

"It's being hushed up, but he had a strange turn. News from the colonies had him nearly frothing at the mouth."

"So he lost his temper. He no longer has the power to order people beheaded on a whim."

"It wasn't temper. Or not just temper." Even though they were alone, Robin lowered his voice. "He seemed, for a very brief while, mad. There have been other signs."

Thorn paced to the window and back,

thinking through the implications. "He has sons."

"Babes."

"What happens if the king goes mad? Forced abdication?"

"A regency, more like. But who? The queen? She's very young and doesn't speak good English. The next obvious person would be the king's mother."

"Who is under the influence of Bute."

"And perhaps under him in other ways. Then there's his uncle, the Duke of Cumberland."

"No."

"No," Robin agreed. "There's no good obvious choice, which means that factions at court and in Parliament will war over it."

"Meaning the king could go stark, staring mad and no regent appointed?"

"It's possible. Or completely the wrong regent. Rothgar believes a group of trustworthy men should stand ready to act in concert if necessary."

"With him the obvious choice for regent?"

"You won't believe me, but no."

"Does a leopard change its spots?"

"A leopard can have a mate and cubs. I know how that changes everything. Rothgar's already shifted most of his attention from statecraft to domestic concerns. Now he awaits the birth of his first legitimate child in December. He truly does not want to run the country. Accept my word on this, Thorn."

"I can't stop being wary, Robin, but in this situation, I'll try. Very well, tonight."

Robin considered him. "In friendship?"

"I can't go that far, but I hope I'm rational."

"And you have a spare corner here for me?"

"A cupboard, perhaps." Thorn rang for a footman. "What of your nursery matters? Petra is well, I assume."

"Robust to a fault, but she wants to spend Christmas at Rothgar Abbey."

"Shouldn't you be at your own place for the season?"

"Mother can rule over the festivities. It will be Petra's first English Christmas, and she wants to spend it with her father and new family. And also greet her half brother or sister."

"How typical that Rothgar arrange for his child to be due at Christmas."

"Don't be an ass."

Thorn laughed. "That was meant to be amusing. Traveling will do Petra no harm if you take it slowly."

"I know, but I worry. I suppose any man does."

"Unfortunately no, but any loving husband must." He turned to the footman and asked for the housekeeper.

When the man had left, Robin said, "If you're in love, cousin, try very hard to make her your wife."

"Even if I know she'll be miserable?"

"With the man she loves? That must be the case or you wouldn't even consider it. She'll learn to be a duchess. If you've fallen in love with her, she has to be extraordinary."

"Leave it be, Robin. You above all people know love is not always eternal. You tumbled in and out of it. In a few weeks I'll have forgotten her name, especially if serious matters are in hand."

"What is her name?"

"Bella." *Damnation.* He'd not meant to say that.

The housekeeper came in.

"A room for Lord Huntersdown, if you please." To Robin he said, "Off you go. If I'm to fritter away the night, I need to work even harder."

Robin went, but in his room he immediately sat to write a letter to Christian in Devon.

485

Whom do we know called Bella? Thorn is smitten, but thinks her unsuitable. We need to act. He took a trip to Dover recently. Anyone come to mind?

He signed it, folded it, sealed it, and sent it off.

Bella returned to Lady Fowler's house that evening. Some of the ladies were in the parlor taking tea, but she found a few in the basement helping to print the sheets. Olivia glared at her, but had no excuse to order her away.

Bella was intrigued by the machine itself, which seemed quite simple. The typesetter had put all the letters into a kind of box in the middle of the wooden frame. Plump Betsy Abercrombie, who was always indiscriminately willing, was pressing ink onto the letters with a stuffed ball of cloth. Ellen Spencer, looking anxious as always, placed a sheet of paper in the frame, and Olivia heaved on a lever twice to squeeze a large flat surface down onto the paper. Then she raised the press and Ellen took the paper off, the text in place.

A page in a moment.

"How wonderful!" Bella exclaimed, and in a way it was. She went over as if to admire, but in fact to read.

Olivia stepped in her way. "Don't touch anything, Bellona. You don't know what you're doing."

Bella had caught a glimpse, however, and even though the sheet was upside down, she'd seen the words "Tyranny" and "Oppression," notable for the capital letters.

She let herself be turned back toward the press and watched the process again. After a little while, she said, "I see I'm not needed, so I'll return upstairs."

The press must definitely be disabled, but sheets were already being printed. She wished she'd tried harder to tamper with it earlier. Now she'd have to attempt to destroy the sheets as well.

Some ladies still sat in the parlor, worrying over tea. Above, she heard nothing but could sense the hot, malodorous room of death. Should she attempt to see Lady Fowler again? She knew she'd make no impression on the woman, and Helena Drummond would be there on guard.

If she was the leader here, she felt herself a weak and useless one. She needed to not just pretend she knew what to do; she needed a plan.

CHAPTER 26

Thorn knew it was unbalanced to feel wary as he and Robin climbed out of his coach in the front courtyard of Malloren House, but he couldn't believe that Rothgar's purposes were completely benign.

He was out of sorts anyway after having to run the gauntlet of petitioners at his door. He'd been tempted to slip out of his house quietly, as he often did to avoid notice, but after having shirked his duties for so long he hadn't permitted himself that luxury. In any case, when heading off to face Rothgar, it had seemed important to do so with due pomp, by the front door.

He knew some high aristocrats who enjoyed being the recipient of this kind of groveling, seeing it as proof of their importance. He disliked it, perhaps because he wasn't able to brush haughtily past them as such men did.

He made it his practice not just to take

the letters they thrust at him, but to listen for a moment or two. He was often tempted to give money then and there, but that would only encourage a horde of beggars to camp out on his doorstep. He passed the letters to Overstone, who would review them. Many would be cases of genuine hardship, for times were difficult. Some would want his help with matters before the courts, and it was true that influence could turn the direction of a case. He never did that, however, unless he saw grave injustice. He wanted to help every desperate one of them, but in truth it was in the hope that eventually there'd be no more. He might as well try to drain the Thames.

As he'd dealt with the petitioners, he'd even resented Robin, passing along untroubled in his wake. On his own doorstep, Robin would encounter similar, but not so many. An earl was not a duke.

Now, as he and Robin entered Malloren House, he felt wary and out of sorts. They passed over their hats and gloves, and were led to a room of modest size. It reminded him in some odd way of the inn parlor in Upstone. The walls were painted an ivory shade rather than being whitewashed, and the paintings were far finer, but the overall cozy look was the same. The fire burned merrily in a hearth enclosed in a marble mantelpiece, but a fire gave the same heat for king or peasant.

A settee and two chairs sat before the fire. On the other side of the room a modest table was laid for four.

Four?

Rothgar greeted them dressed in comfortable style, his only ornament his signet ring and a rather excessive diamond that Thorn gathered had been a gift from his wife. He seemed to wear it like a wedding ring. Thorn had thought that ridiculous, but now, with Bella haunting his mind, he wondered if he might be tempted to do the same.

Bella, however, would not be able to afford such a splendid sign of ownership. Rothgar's wife was Countess of Arradale in her own right, and rich enough to afford diamonds. She was exactly the right wife for the great marquess, and the Duke of Ithorne should marry a similar lady.

He gathered his wits and greeted his host, glad to have guessed correctly and dressed in the same plain style. Talk was instantly casual — of racehorses and artists, inventions and mechanicals. Thorn had wondered if Rothgar's enthusiasm for clocks was to forge a connection to the king, but it was clearly genuine. He'd taken a close interest in Mr. Harrison's chronometer.

So had Thorn, but because of the implications for navigation. He was unlikely to ever sail a ship far from a coastline, but being able to navigate accurately across oceans was a grand thing. He found himself truly enjoying the discussion and decided not to fight that.

A new arrival was announced.

The Duke of Bridgwater.

As everyone bowed, Thorn was intrigued. For one thing, Bridgwater was one of the young dukes, close in age to himself. A few years ago, he'd been a member of lively circles, but after a disappointment in love he'd retreated to his northern estates and turned his devotion to canals. That marked him as eccentric to the point of insanity, especially as he was known as the Poor Duke and had to scrimp and save to fund the work. His waterways, however, were now carrying his coal cheaply to market and beginning to revolutionize transport, and people viewed Bridgwater differently.

He was still an unprepossessing figure, slender, pale, and always looking sickly. He also had a diffident manner, but Thorn knew he'd never been as unsure of himself as he seemed, and his wits were keen on matters that interested him.

They sat to their meal, served by one presumably very discreet footman, and talked of politics, statecraft, and engineering. Thorn continued to enjoy himself and eventually realized it was because he was truly among equals.

Had Bridgwater been invited solely for that reason?

It wasn't a matter only of high rank, though that formed a common perspective, but a similarity of mind, despite the men's striking differences.

They were all knowledgeable, and if they lacked knowledge on any subject, they felt no need to pretend otherwise. On politics, they all understood how the complex machines of Parliament, influence, money, trade, and international connections operated. They all seemed to agree on what was important or unimportant.

Rothgar, however, was the clear leader here. He was a decade older, and that decade had been spent steeped in such matters under two kings.

"There are pivot points in history," he said as they sipped brandy, the footman having departed. "Europe's move into the eastern Mediterranean with the Crusades. The Renaissance. The Reformation. I believe we are on the brink of another such time, and though the consequences of these pivots were eventually good and necessary, none were pure pleasure for those who lived through them."

"The Renaissance?" Thorn questioned.

"Was mostly benign, but change destroys. It must. Many found that their traditional ways were no longer necessary. And thus it always is. Consider the spinning wheel."

Thorn hoped he hadn't shown that he missed the relevance of spinning wheels to the discussion.

It was Robin who said, "The spinning jenny. Soon there'll be no need for the cottage spinners."

"And the next thing you know," said Bridgwater, "no need for the cottage weavers, either. I don't approve. A whole way of life will be swept away."

Thorn said, "Your canals are going to affect the livelihood of carters and packhorse drovers."

"Ah, true."

"But like Canute, we are powerless to stop any tide," Rothgar said.

"But the tide can be affected," Thorn pointed out. "Groins and breakwaters. Sometimes even more substantial construction."

"Even so, the next big wave may sweep

man's work away."

"Not if it's properly engineered," Bridgwater stated.

"In any case," Thorn said, "it's often better to adjust to the power of the sea. To understand it and use it. Never any point in fighting winds."

"As in a windmill," Rothgar said. "Thus we must understand and use the new spirit of our age."

Thorn had the irritated feeling that Rothgar had been steering them to this point all along.

"We can look for causes, as in blaming our philosophers for asking troublesome questions, or our monarchs and politicians for creating injustices, but that will change nothing. Nor, in my opinion, will new, draconian laws. Better to understand our times and use the rising forces in the cause of peace and welfare. Are we agreed?"

Robin and Bridgwater said aye, but Thorn demurred.

"You state a theory of winds and waves. To what port do we steer?"

"A good sailor prepares his ship for whatever wind might blow. Especially for a storm."

"You expect one?"

"Yes," Rothgar said with certainty. "Possibly a hurricane."

They had not spoken of the king's sanity, of course. To do so would come close to treason. But the subject lay behind everything.

The king could be stubborn, especially when distressed. Though he was guided — even ruled, to a degree — by Parliament, he could seriously tamper with the sailing of the ship of state. If he were insane, he could sink them all, especially if faced with stormy seas.

All in all Thorn agreed that it would be wise to establish a means of preventing that. Devil take it, he was going to have to join forces with the Marquess of Rothgar.

Bella had asked Kitty to be sure to wake her early, and it was still dark outside when she went to take her breakfast in the kitchen. She needed to talk to Peg about future plans, and wanted to do so and still leave the house while the town around slept.

The kitchen was clean as always, with sparkling copper pots and aromatic herbs hanging from the ceiling. A big kettle was always by the edge of the fire, ready to be brought to the boil in a moment. Bella laid her own place at the plain wooden table and selected a bread roll from a basket, still warm from the nearby baker's.

"To what do we owe this pleasure?" Peg asked, but with a twinkle. She was at the table too, enjoying some bread and ham and a big pot of tea, Ed Grange and Kitty by her side. Annie was getting Bella's chocolate.

"Plans," Bella said, buttering her bread. "I'm going to become myself again."

"Well, thank the Lord for that."

"And probably move from London. How would you feel about that?"

Peg sipped her tea. Bella's mouth puckered because she knew how strong and stewed Peg liked it.

"I'm content enough here," she said at last, "but I've no objection to moving elsewhere. Only within the country, mind. I'm not going to foreign parts where I won't know what people are saying, or what I'm eating, either. Snails," she added with a shudder.

"I wouldn't care for that, either," Bella said.

"And we'll need to see to Ed," Peg said, putting a tender hand on the lad's shoulder.

Bella had almost forgotten Ed, but he and Peg were like mother and son.

"Certainly Ed will come with us," she said.

Annie brought over the chocolate pot.

"Kitty and I will stay with you a while, miss, if you need us."

Bella smiled at her. "You're very kind, but I have no intention of keeping you from your beaux. I hope to dance at your wedding before I leave."

Annie smiled, those stars in her eyes. "Then we'll make it soon, miss. We're agreed that we'll all live together for a while, so we can make do."

"What an excellent idea." Bella poured the chocolate and turned back to Peg. "I don't know where I'll go, but it won't be near Carscourt."

"That won't bother me, dear. As I said all along, I've a fancy to see a bit more of England. What of Dover?" she asked, eyeing Bella over the top of her cup.

"I went there on business, Peg." Bella prayed her expression gave nothing away.

"And then?" asked Peg.

"More business."

"With a man."

"Peg . . ."

"I'm not your mother, I know. But you're young, love, and have always had a bit of a March hare in you."

"A what? You think I'm mad?"

Peg chuckled. "No, but even as a child you'd rather run than walk, rather jump

497

than stand still. You were more like a lad in your restlessness. More like a lad than your brother," she said, with a twitch of distaste. "Anyway, that restlessness sent you off on that assignation that caused all the trouble, didn't it? You weren't smitten with that young man. You simply liked the adventure of it."

"You're right, of course, but I hope I learned by it."

Peg's brows went up.

"Yes, very well, there was a bit of March madness about my recent adventure, but it was also necessary. And very worthwhile."

Despite her aching heart, Bella still relished the satisfaction of Augustus's disgrace.

"Good thing, then. As for where, though, you'll have to decide on your own. Perhaps you should ask that nice Mr. Clatterford."

"He'd want me to go to Tunbridge Wells."

"And what's wrong with that?"

"I'm wary of a small, fashionable place. In truth, I don't know what I want, but as soon as Kitty and Annie are married, we'll be off. I think it would be best to be far away from Lady Fowler and her followers."

"Then why don't we leave now?"

Bella sighed. "Because I have to try to leave them safe."

She left and walked the short distance to

Lady Fowler's house, uneasy in the dark, deserted streets. She arrived safely, however, and entered at the back, through the kitchens, startling the servants.

"I was up early," she said carelessly, "so decided to come over. So much to do."

The cook and the maid looked at her blankly, so she left the room. Bella knew none of them would concern themselves in affairs upstairs. Servants never stayed here long. Lady Fowler had always been erratic, and there were many people to take care of, all of them too poor to give the little gifts of money that were the norm.

She slipped along to the printing room — and found it locked. When had that begun? Perhaps it was always locked at night. She went upstairs, furious and worried. Now she needed to create an excuse for turning up so early, or the Drummonds would become suspicious.

The house was quiet and also cold, for the fires had not yet been lit. Bella kept her cloak on as she went into the scriptorium. She put a sheet of paper on the table and checked a pen. She opened an inkpot and found it dry.

Had everyone ceased to copy out the letter now that they had the press? She found some ink and added it to the pot and started writing.

There was no need to fill the page, so she paused often to think of other things. How long would it be before she could be sure the women here were safe? Where should she go? What should she do with her life?

March hare. It was true, and she had to be very careful not to leap into danger. The March hare in her had been quashed during the four years at Carscourt, and she'd thought she'd left there a changed, sober woman.

When she considered her recent adventures, however, she could see the spring-maddened hare was still alive and well. She suspected that meant that she should find employment. Not for pay, for the positions open to women were tedious, but something to occupy her time and her brain. She couldn't imagine what. Perhaps she should forget her origins and run an inn, as Thorn's more-or-less aunt did.

She closed the door on memories, but when she looked at her sheet of paper she saw that she'd written, *Thorn.* It disappeared after the O because the nib had run out of ink, but she could see the word anyway.

"Oh, Bellona! What are you doing here so early, with the fires not lit?"

It was Clara Ormond, swathed in shawls. "I'll just go and get some hot coals," she said, and hurried out again. She returned with a bucket from the kitchen and placed the glowing coals on the tinder. Soon the flames were licking the coals laid the night before.

Wood was more pleasant, Bella thought, but there wasn't enough to heat the cities, so she should be grateful for coal, even though it made the air so dirty.

Did practicality always require compromise and some dirt?

Clara said, "There. Nice and cheerful. I do like to make myself useful." She was smiling, but her eyes were anxious, as always. "What were you writing?"

Bella had scribbled out the revealing word. "On my journey, I heard about some matters that might be suitable for the newsletter."

"Oh, we don't do that anymore. Lady Fowler is interested only in the news sheet, and Helena Drummond writes that. I do worry," she said. "Now that we're useless, will she let us live on here?"

Bella felt deeply sorry for the old woman. "I doubt there'll be any changes soon."

"No, I suppose not."

They were both referring to Lady Fowler's death.

"If you had to leave here," Bella asked, "where would you go?"

Clara's face crumpled, and she sat. "To the workhouse," she wailed.

Bella went to hug her. "Oh, surely not. You must have family."

Clara shook her head. "No, none. I had only one brother and one sister. Dear Algernon was a clerk for a merchant, but he was drowned while traveling to France. Dear Sarah went to be a governess. She lives on the charity of one of her charges, and mean charity it sounds too. I would not be welcome in any way. Sarah always resented me for marrying, and even more for being happy. Oh, but it is a terrible thing to be an old woman alone."

Bella held her closer and said the only thing she could: "I will not let you go to the workhouse, Clara. If necessary, you may live with me."

Clara's watery eyes stared. "Do you mean it? Is it true?" The tears spilled over, down her lined cheeks. "Oh, Bellona! You are the best of women. You are a saint!"

"No, no, and please don't speak of this. I don't have room for all."

"I see that," Clara whispered. "I will keep

our secret."

But Clara was unable to keep a secret, and in any case if she seemed cheerful, the others would plague her with questions. Bella simply didn't have room for all the flock, nor the income to support them, and she wanted to be Bella Barstowe.

What on earth was she going to do?

To crown the day, when she returned to the printing room and found it open, the printed sheets were gone. The press stood silent and the typesetter hadn't yet arrived, but the dangerous items had disappeared.

Bella looked at the press, trying to find some small item she could remove or break, but it all seemed very solid. Short of taking an ax to it, she couldn't see what to do. As she'd feared, she was a failure in all respects.

CHAPTER 27

Bella had promised to attend Kitty's and Annie's weddings and hence she couldn't leave London anyway, so she continued to go to Lady Fowler's house every day, always seeking some solution to the problems. She did manage to gain access to Lady Fowler's room once, but the poor woman's mind had gone. After that, she contented herself with asking Agnes Hoover for news on the rare occasions the faithful attendant left her mistress.

Clara tried to keep their secret, but it leaked out, and Bella had some other ladies beg for help. She had to agree, but she began to paint a grim picture of the future, claiming her income would provide only the simplest food and warmth. Slowly, members of the residential flock began to follow Elizabeth Shutton's example and decide that their family's charity might be preferable to this house of death and danger.

Eventually there were only eight of the flock left: the Drummond sisters and their adherents, Betsy Abercrombie and Ellen Spencer, Bella, and those who might see themselves as of her party — Mary Evesham, Clara Ormond, and strangely enough Hortensia Sprott. Bella had always thought Hortensia disliked her, but she now decided the woman gave the impression of disliking everyone.

The press continued to do its work, but the typesetter now had an assistant, an unpleasant young Irishman whom Bella decided was a guard. From Olivia Drummond's smirk, he was there expressly to prevent Bella from doing anything to disturb their work.

But what was the work?

Sheets were typeset and printed and then disappeared. Bella suspected they were in Lady Fowler's room, but she couldn't see how to retrieve the large stacks. She took some comfort from the fact that no news sheet had been distributed, but its existence hung over the house like the sword of Damocles.

The weddings hung in the air too. They hadn't happened. As October drew to an end, Bella summoned Kitty and Annie and demanded a date.

The sisters exchanged glances. "It's not quite convenient for us yet, miss," Kitty said. "We do hope you don't mind."

"Why is it not convenient?"

More shifty looks. "We're not sure we like the house!" Annie blurted.

"Two weeks ago, you said it was perfect."

"It's a bit dark," Annie said. "We're looking for others."

Bella sighed. "Are you delaying because of me?"

They both looked down. "We don't like to desert you, miss," Kitty said.

"It's more than we can bear!" Annie cried, looking at Bella with tears in her eyes. "After all you've done for us. Why aren't you leaving London, like you said?"

"Hush, Annie," said Kitty fiercely. "I'm sorry, miss. You take your time."

Bella looked to the heavens for guidance. It would be more than she could bear to abandon the remainder of the flock yet, but she couldn't have the girls putting off their wedding again and again like this.

"Two weeks," she said, using a Bellona voice. "Fix the date for two weeks hence, and no backsliding. Peg and I can manage perfectly. Yes?"

"Yes, miss," they muttered, but still reluctantly.

Bella went to hug them. "You are the dearest girls, and you've served me very well. I only want to see you happy. Promise me you'll marry in two weeks and be happy."

Both smiled, blushing pink. "No doubt of that, miss," Kitty said.

She sent them back to their work and contemplated. Eventually she saw a solution. This house had only three bedchambers. One was hers, one was Peg's, and the other was the sisters'. With them gone, she could move Clara and Hortensia into that room, and Mary could share her own big bed.

It would be a crush, but it would work, and at that point she'd end her association with Lady Fowler. She was doing no good, and could feel storm clouds gathering. She'd lingered only to help those she wanted to help. The Drummond sisters and those who'd chosen to support them could fend for themselves.

The wedding was a simple affair, but brimming over with happiness. Kitty and Annie had old friends from before their father's death and new ones among the servants at nearby houses. With the family and friends of the two brothers, about twenty people packed into Bella's house afterward for the wedding breakfast.

Bella was truly happy for the girls, but she had a hard time keeping a full smile. This only reminded her of what could never be.

She fought day and night not to think of Thorn, but the pain seemed to get worse rather than better. Daily she had to fight the urge to go to Dover and seek him out again. She'd not been able to stop herself from reading books about ships and navigation and even practicing knots.

She could be a good captain's wife; she knew she could. She would endure the long times apart when he was at sea and make a cozy home for him when he came ashore.

He clearly didn't think so, however, and she would not chase after him again. She would not.

When she thought about moving, however, about being somewhere he'd never been, she was tempted to let him know her new direction. He had given her a place to send a message: the Black Swan Inn, Stowting, Kent. Wouldn't it be simple courtesy to send a letter to him there, giving her new location? Just in case he had need to find her.

Folly, but such folly possessed her, even as she waved off Kitty and Annie to their new lives. That night, she couldn't help thinking of their marriage beds. She hoped their husbands were kind and able to show them the wonders Thorn had shown her.

Without the girls, the house felt empty, but she'd soon fill it. Before she could do so, she received notice that Mr. Clatterford was in London and would like to speak to her. She immediately invited him for tea, and took pleasure in becoming Bella for the occasion. She wore the pretty sprigged dress, and he took this as a sign that she'd ceased to be Bellona Flint. "I am most relieved, my dear. What I hear of Lady Fowler concerns me. A sad case. Lord Fowler was . . ." He shook his head. "All the same, I fear she may be connected with dangerous matters. I received a warning."

"A warning?"

But he shook his head again. "It was very oblique, my dear, offered only when I mentioned your connection. But you have no more connection?"

Bella almost lied, but wanted to have done with deception. Even so, she would omit the idea of the women coming to live here.

"I will want to say farewells, sir, when I move. But I don't know where I can live comfortably."

"And now there's your brother's behavior

to add to the pot," he said, shaking his head. "I'm not sure if you've heard. . . . Most unsavory. Most."

Bella's face went hot. She hoped it was taken for embarrassment or anger. "Peg heard gossip from Cars Green. Hard to believe."

"But true, my dear. I have that from most reliable sources. Quite shocking. Sir Augustus has always seemed so . . . otherwise." He shook his head. "Of course, such a salacious story, and involving three magistrates, has spread."

Bella had hoped it would be confined to one area, but as soon as Peg had received the gossip, she'd known that could not be. "I don't suppose it makes much difference." She sighed. "Dust on dirt."

He put down his cup. "I have been giving your situation considerable thought, my dear. Considerable thought. Your father made much of your sin, but he was known for his stern and unforgiving nature. Given how impeccable your behavior has been since, many may doubt that old story, given encouragement."

"My behavior was impeccable under duress, sir. And now there's my time as Bellona."

"We will forget Bellona Flint. You have

simply lived very quietly for the past six months, recovering your health and constitution."

"Will that be believed?"

"If there's no reason to doubt it. Consider, you never committed a sin or caused a scandal under the noses of those who matter."

Bella thought of the Olympian Revels, and of the Hart and Hare. But no one knew that had been Bella Barstowe.

"Most of the people who matter," he continued, "have never heard of you."

"They've probably heard of Augustus," she pointed out.

"But can be persuaded to pity you the connection rather than apply his dirt to you."

Bella wrinkled her brow. "Do you really think so?"

"I would not deceive you, my dear. Especially on such a matter. Lady Raddall would come back to haunt me. I do believe that if you present yourself to society again, and under the cloak of the right lady, you could be accepted."

"Could be?" Bella queried, wary of hoping.

"It will take courage, and some of the bold spirit that put you in peril all those years ago, but also the same spirit that rescued you then."

"Peg Gussage refers to that as my March-hare madness."

"Does she indeed? But I would like to see you frolic." He took more cake. "Delicious. Mistress Gussage is a treasure."

"Yes," Bella agreed. "But what lady would give her support to someone like me? Are you thinking of Athena? Her husband will never permit it."

"Even if your sister were willing, Miss Barstowe, she does not have the stature. I have already broached the matter discreetly to some ladies I know."

"Oh. Who?"

Perhaps he smirked. "The Trayce sisters. They were acquainted with your great-grandmother in Tunbridge Wells." Yes, he was very satisfied with himself for some reason.

"Trayce. I believe Lady Raddall did mention them, but they seemed somewhat odd. One wears a huge red wig and another is dotty?"

"Your great-grandmother was odd in the eyes of many," Mr. Clatterford pointed out. "The Trayce ladies are eccentric, to be sure, but not to be discounted. The very opposite. They are aunts of both the Marquess of

Ashart and the Marquess of Rothgar, and though they rarely travel, or even gad about the Wells, they are copious letter writers and wield great influence."

"But if they don't go into society, what can they do for me?"

"Their mere smile would work miracles."

"Really?" This was all sounding very unlikely to Bella, though something about the name was familiar. Then it came to her. "Trayce! They're on the subscription list for Lady Fowler's letter. Are they of her type?"

Mr. Clatterford chuckled. "Absolutely not, but I'm not surprised they receive the letter. They enjoy a juicy scandal sheet. You do realize that many of the subscribers to that letter do so for the enjoyment of the stories she shares?"

"I have come to, poor lady."

"She has no idea?"

"By now, I doubt she has any idea about anything, but she used to see the letter's growing popularity as proof that she was changing the world."

He shook his head. "A sad case, but I believe your situation can be improved. Are you willing to move to Tunbridge Wells? To live with the Trayce ladies for a while? You can act as a companion to them, but you would be treated as a guest."

Bella's instinct was to refuse. She'd determined to cope on her own, but another sanctuary was very tempting. Just for a little while. Especially if it might restore her reputation.

Hopes stirred.

She quashed them before she sank back into sorrow.

"What of Peg?" she asked. "And there's the boy, Ed Grange."

"Ah," he said. "I doubt it would be suitable to take them to your new home, my dear, but I would be loath to let Mistress Gussage go. She does have a wonderful way with cakes."

Bella smiled. "I'm sure she'll bake some for you whenever you visit, sir." Bella was thinking. "I could afford to keep up this house, could I not?"

"If you wish."

Bella didn't tell him about the other ladies, but that meant she could give them the use of this house and escape with an easy conscience.

"Then Peg and Ed can stay here for now, and if the Trayce ladies will befriend me, I will go."

"Excellent. Once you have spent some time with them, you will have entrée anywhere. Anyone of importance who visits the

Wells pays homage at their house, and Lady Thalia and Lady Urania do go about the town a little. Once people have accepted your acquaintance there, they must accept it elsewhere, and, of course, they will soon see what an estimable young lady you are."

Bella raised her brows.

"None of that. You are most estimable, my dear. There are also many eligible young men who visit the Wells," he added with a twinkle. "It is time you thought of marriage."

Bella blushed again. "I do," she replied honestly. "But I will marry only for love."

"Love joined with wisdom," he advised, "so please don't play the March hare in such matters. Consult me, Miss Barstowe, before commitment. There are many charming rascals about, and you do have a modest fortune."

"A comfortable annuity."

"But that ends at thirty, at which time you receive the complete inheritance."

"Do I?" Bella asked, startled. "Perhaps you told me at the first, but my head was spinning. How much will it be, do you think?"

"Still in the region of fifteen thousand, for the interest is paying your income. Enough to tempt a patient rascal, however, so you must have settlements to protect you."

Fifteen thousand, in her own hands, under her own control. It was alarming. "I promise you, Mr. Clatterford, I will only marry wisely."

That was easy to say, for at the moment Bella couldn't imagine marrying anyone other than Thorn.

"I return to the Wells in three days. Will you be able to travel with me?"

Bella would need to explain it all to Peg and arrange for the money to maintain the house. Then help the women to move here. "I have arrangements to make."

"I find myself impatient to see you a fashionable young lady in Tunbridge Wells, accepted by society, dancing at balls. Attending masquerades . . ."

Bella almost jumped in her chair, but she managed a smile. "It sounds delightful."

"You will come?"

Impulsively, Bella said, "Yes. In three days I will come."

Mr. Clatterford assisted Bella with the practical arrangements, and she made the house ready for the women to move into after she left. Because there'd be more room then, she found two foundling maids to serve them. The girls weren't as quick and clever as Kitty and Annie, but they were steady workers.

She claimed illness as reason for not visiting Lady Fowler's house, for there was nothing she could do there. She stayed inside, readying the house and also making small improvements to her gowns, being Bella, not Bellona, every delightful day.

It was seven o'clock at night and she was packing the last few items for the next day's journey when she heard the door knocker. She peered out of her window and saw a woman below. She knew the hat. It was Mary Evesham's.

She ran to the head of the stairs and caught Peg on her way across the hall. "Say I'm not home!" she hissed.

Peg opened the door. "Yes, ma'am?"

"Miss Flint. I need to speak to her."

"I'm sorry, ma'am. She's not at home."

"Not at home? I thought she was unwell."

"She's at the doctor's," Peg said.

"At this hour?"

Bella thought Peg might get flustered, but she should have known better.

"I can take a message, ma'am, and give it to her when she returns."

After a moment, Mary said, "Very well. Please tell her it's urgent. She's needed. If she's at all capable of it, will she please come to Lady Fowler's? Matters are so very,

very grave."

"I'm sorry to hear that, ma'am. I'll give her the message."

As soon as the door shut, Bella went downstairs. "What am I to do?"

"Ignore it," Peg said. "You've done all you can there, and tomorrow the ladies you want to help will be here and safe."

"She did sound distressed."

"You leave them be, Miss Bella. You've your own life to live."

Bella sighed. "You know I can't and have an easy conscience. I'll resume Bellona and go there one last time."

Peg sighed, shaking her head. "You'll do as you want. You always do."

"I'll simply see what the commotion is this time."

"You'll be dragged into staying and try to help."

"No, I promise. I vow. Tomorrow I leave for Tunbridge Wells and a respectable future."

Bella had no difficulty in looking flinty as she approached Lady Fowler's door. If this was a storm in a teacup, she'd give them all a piece of her mind.

She turned the knob, but the door was locked, so she rapped.

The door was opened so slightly she could see only anxious eyes, and then it was flung open. "Oh, Bellona! Thank heavens you're here."

It was Betsy Abercrombie, one of the Drummond faction, pink nose pinker, as if she'd been crying.

Bella went in, and women seeped out of nearby rooms. "What's happening?"

"Oh, Bellona!" Betsy started to cry again.

Clara and Ellen Spencer joined in. Bella saw no sign of the Drummonds. She was strongly tempted to turn around and leave, but instead reached for the universal panacea. "Tea!" she commanded. "Let us take tea and discuss matters."

The story began before she'd even sat down. Lady Fowler was at death's door and was attended solely by Agnes Hoover. Various ladies protested that they'd like to help, but the heat, the smell . . .

"What does the doctor say?" Bella asked.

"She won't have one anymore," said Mary. "Screams if a man touches her. Agnes provides laudanum."

"That's probably as much as can be done." Bella was sorry for the woman, but she'd lasted longer than seemed possible.

The tea arrived and the business of serving it distracted and calmed everyone. When each had her cup and was sipping, Bella asked, "Where are the Drummond sisters?"

Cups rattled.

"Gone!" Betsy declared.

"Fled!" exclaimed Hortensia.

"Stole the silver!"

"Left us in the lurch!"

"Why?" Bella demanded.

Silence answered. That and shifty eyes.

Then Mary said, "We think they distributed the news sheet."

"And it contained other things," said Hortensia.

"What other things?" But Bella thought she knew.

"Irish things."

Bella took a deep drink of tea, glad she'd put plenty of sugar in it. "Their main interest was always Ireland. Did any of you see what they printed?" She looked directly at Betsy.

"Mere mentions," Betsy said, but her eyes shifted. "Additions to the lists of the tyrannies and oppressions of men."

Bella kept on looking at her.

"Lately there have been more."

Bella looked at the six women. "Why didn't anyone stop them from distributing such material?"

"How?" bleated Ellen Spencer, who

looked as if she expected the hangman at the door.

It was a fair question. A good part of the reason Bella had avoided the house was to avoid a confrontation with the Drummonds, and she'd been more capable of it than anyone.

"If they're gone," she said, "the worst is over."

Shifty eyes again.

"Tell me," Bella said with a sigh.

Mary produced a folded sheet of paper. "We received this only an hour ago."

Bella unfolded it and read.

Be warned. Your work has come to the notice of the authorities. Flee while there is yet time.

There was no signature.

She swallowed. "This could be mere scaremongering. Or even a trick. It could even be from the Drummonds. I'd not put it past them."

"Oh," said Betsy, and looked brighter.

"That could be," said Mary, not quite reassured.

The others seemed to be. They drank tea and ate cake with more enthusiasm, as if the crisis were over.

Bella, however, was considering new problems. With the addition of Betsy and Ellen, and possibly even Agnes Hoover, the flock was now too large for her house. Would it be possible for them to continue to live here? If only she knew what was in Lady Fowler's will.

"Ladies," Bella said.

Eyes turned to her, some impatient at the interruption, some worried again.

"Is the press still in the house?"

"Yes, of course," Mary said.

"It would be wise to get rid of it. Tomorrow if possible."

"But it is very useful for printing copies of the newsletter," Hortensia said.

"If Lady Fowler dies, so does the letter."

Hortensia raised her chin. "I was thinking of continuing the work. The real work, reminding women of the vileness of men, and also proposing improvements in the laws."

On those matters, Hortensia's heart was in the right place, but anything written by her would be a rant. "That's very kind of you, Hortensia, but it would be wrong to use Lady Fowler's name, don't you think?"

"Lady Fowler would wish her work to live on. I'm sure she's made provision in her will."

Clara brightened. "You think we'll be able to continue to live here?"

"I don't see why not," said Hortensia, who was clearly envisioning herself as both scribe and leader of the flock. "If it would be inappropriate to call it the Fowler letter, we must find a new name."

That caused excited chatter among some of them — mainly Hortensia, Clara, and Betsy. Bella wanted to hold her head and scream. Had they forgotten the warning note? She'd tried to ease their anxieties, but not to wipe them away entirely.

The chatter was interrupted by a knock at the door.

"Whoever can that be?" Mary asked, but she rose to answer it.

She returned a moment later, ashen, followed by a stern gentleman. Behind him were other men, some solemn, but some leering.

In a thin, shaking voice, Mary said, "I . . . I think we're all under arrest."

CHAPTER 28

Thorn was taking breakfast when a foot-man brought a note. "A gentleman is below, sir, requesting urgent word with you. He asked me to present this letter."

Thorn took it, surprised. Petitioners didn't receive such care. Then he saw the seal.

But, no, his people wouldn't leave Roth-gar in a reception room.

He opened the letter.

My apologies, Ithorne,

But I fear I must impose on you, as I am committed to leaving Town today by matters that cannot be put off. I am sending my secretary, Carruthers, to explain a situation of some delicacy, in which I seek your assistance.

Rothgar

Rothgar seeking his assistance? Was this a sign of victory, or a subtle plot?

"Bring Mr. Carruthers up," Thorn said.

The man who entered and bowed was a well-dressed fifty or so, and could probably move comfortably at court in his own right. Thorn recognized another Overstone — brilliant, efficient, and knowledgeable. He waved Carruthers to a seat and offered refreshments, which were refused.

"Very well, sir," Thorn said. "Present your case."

Carruthers's lips twitched. "It is a matter of a Mistress Spencer, sir, Ellen Spencer, currently residing with Lady Fowler. I believe you may know of both, sir."

Thorn tried not to show surprise, and it was the name Ellen Spencer that startled him. After the scandal at the Olympian Revels between Christian and the lady who proved to be his wife, Caro, there'd been an attempt on Christian's life.

Caro's longtime governess companion — the said Ellen Spencer — had resolved to free Caro from what she saw as an oppressive marriage. It perhaps wasn't surprising that Mistress Spencer had also been an ardent admirer of the ridiculous Lady Fowler, but that connection had inspired her to attempt to kill Christian with foxglove baked in cakes.

A farcical attempt all around, but Thorn

would have liked to see the Spencer woman in an institution for the insane. Tender-hearted Caro had instead arranged for her companion to live with Lady Fowler. Perhaps that was punishment enough, but Rothgar had added to it by giving the Fowler woman responsibility for Ellen Spencer's future good behavior.

How had all that led to this?

"I am aware of both ladies," said Thorn, picking up his teapot, "though I'm surprised to have them served up with breakfast. What has the Spencer woman done now?"

"She is under arrest for treason."

Thorn put down the pot. "How in God's name did she manage that?"

"By association with Lady Fowler, sir, who acquired a printing press. A dangerous piece of equipment, as Wilkes demonstrated."

"The Fowler letter's a mere scandal sheet, providing amusement for the *haute volée.* What did they print? Some royal peccadillo?"

"Alas, no, sir." Thorn could tell Carruthers was about to enjoy himself. "They printed and distributed a call to arms. A call for women everywhere to rise up to end the monarchy and create a new commonwealth."

Thorn gave the man an appropriately

dramatic reaction, putting a hand to his face and regarding Carruthers through his fingers. To laugh or to curse? The last commonwealth had involved the monarch losing his head, so this call to revolution must have caused George to froth at the mouth. Perhaps literally. With the colonies restive, any stirrings at home would have to be crushed.

It was not, in fact, the slightest bit amusing.

"Mad," he said. "I warned that was the case."

"I don't believe Mistress Spencer took a leadership role, sir. That was two women called Drummond, already well-known to the authorities in Ireland." Carruthers took a newspaper out of his pocket and passed it over. "On the surface the document is about the oppression of women, but underneath it deals with Ireland."

"And thus is particularly treasonous," Thorn said, scanning the crude printing, "with France always poised to use Ireland as a back door."

"There are a number of women caught in this trap, almost certainly all dupes, but the law can chew indiscriminately once someone is in its jaws. Lord Rothgar hopes you will exert yourself to extricate Mistress

Spencer."

"Why?" Thorn asked bluntly, putting the rant aside.

"Primarily because she is innocent, sir, but also because the marquess had a part in establishing her at Lady Fowler's house. In his mind at the time it seemed a safe location and a minor punishment for both ladies. As you doubtless know, Lady Fowler had made him and his daughter a subject in her letters."

"Proof that she, at least, is insane."

"Definitely, sir. However, the marquess believes that a person is responsible for the consequences of his actions, even inadvertent ones."

"As do I."

Carruthers inclined his head. "Which is why he's approaching you."

"Yes?" Thorn asked, feeling a trap closing.

"The matter of a thousand guineas, sir?"

Thorn poured tea to cover a shocked moment. "How the devil does he know about that? And don't tell me omniscience."

Carruthers smiled. "Any omniscience is the result of a policy of being well-informed, sir. As I said, Lady Fowler became of interest to Lord Rothgar by offending against his family. When he learned that the Fowler Fund had received such a magnificent donation, he naturally wished to know more."

"Does he know I made the payment on behalf of Lord Huntersdown, and that it was only due because of his marriage to Rothgar's daughter?"

"Most appreciated, I'm sure."

And no admission of knowledge or ignorance. "What has that money to do with Mistress Spencer's downfall?"

"Some of it was used to purchase the printing press."

Thorn swore. Of course, he'd never imagined such a thing, but Robin had argued against keeping to their foolish vow on the grounds that it would be dangerous to give Lady Fowler so much money. It seemed he had played a part in this mess.

"Very well. I'll extricate Mistress Spencer from the lion's jaws. Where should I send her?"

"Alas, sir, that's a quandary. Lord and Lady Rothgar begin a slow progress to Rothgar Abbey, for the doctors think the child may arrive a little early. There are also some important meetings en route. Lord and Lady Grandiston are in Devon."

"I'll send her to Lord and Lady Huntersdown, then. The donation was originally his."

Carruthers shared his smile. "That does seem just, sir."

Carruthers rose and Thorn escorted him to the door. "The address of the Fowler house?" he asked.

"At the Hen and Chicks, Grafton Street."

"Does Lady Fowler have a sense of humor?"

"It would seem so, wouldn't it? Once, at least. I gather she's raving mad now and on her deathbed."

Thorn handed him to a footman and summoned Overstone.

"Lady Fowler. Bring me the details of her recent activities, especially illegal, and discover the exact cause of the arrest of herself and her chicks last night." Even Overstone showed mild surprise. "Who is the prime mover in the arrest, and who might best provide legal help. Also sources of irregular assistance. And anything else that occurs to you."

"We are seeking to assist Lady Fowler?" Overstone asked in a carefully bland voice.

"We are seeking to assist a Mistress Spencer, onetime companion to Lady Grandiston."

"Ah." Overstone knew all about the affair of the poisoned cakes.

"I'll have to go there." Thorn wrote a

quick note. "Send this to Fielding at Bow Street, asking him to authorize my entry and freedom to speak to the ladies."

When the secretary had left, Thorn contemplated his situation with annoyance. This was going to be tedious and might require asking assistance from people to whom he did not want to be obliged. He also had a sense of being put to the test. He did, however, accept some responsibility, so in that spirit, he would do his best for Mistress Spencer.

He sent for Joseph and returned to his bedchamber. "Correct dress for a sober intervention in the affairs of distressed gentlewomen, Joseph."

"Country wear, sir," said the valet confidently.

"What a gem you are. I would probably have terrified with soberest black. And breeches and boots mean I can ride. Have a horse and groom waiting."

By the time Thorn was ready, a letter had arrived from the chief magistrate to say his way was clear. It also mentioned that the Lord Chancellor was concerned with the matter.

Hell and damnation.

Thorn walked the gauntlet of the petitioners outside his front door, mounted, and rode off, accompanied by a groom who would know the way.

"Here we are, sir," the groom said sometime later, as they entered a quiet street of narrow houses.

Thorn felt a puzzling familiarity, but then he realized he was very close to Bella's home.

He could go there.

He wouldn't.

Time had passed and his feelings hadn't changed, but that made it even more impossible to drag Bella from her comfortable independence into his impossible life.

At first glance, Grafton Street seemed unaffected by drama, but then he spotted a man on guard outside one house. Discreetly dressed, but definitely on guard.

Thorn dismounted and approached. "Ithorne. I have admittance."

"Yes, Your Grace." The man used the brass knocker and then stepped aside. When the door opened a few inches, he said, "His Grace, the Duke of Ithorne."

The door opened fully and Thorn passed in.

Gads, foul as well as fowl, he thought at the smell.

The quietly dressed man who'd let him in

said, "Lady Fowler died in the night, Your Grace."

"And is putrefying already?"

"And was putrefying before, sir."

The man was about forty, stout but stiff, looking as if he wished to be anywhere but here.

"The devil of a job," Thorn said sympathetically. "Your name, sir?"

The man bowed. "Norman, Your Grace. Acting on behalf of Lord Northington."

Thorn lost sympathy. He sensed a minion who enjoyed playing God, but as minion to the Lord Chancellor he had the powers of at least a demigod.

Thorn stripped off his gloves. "Why is Lord Northington involved?"

"This is being regarded as a matter of national significance, sir."

"A bunch of women? And now only the chicks remain? Is it truly worth such weight?"

"That is not for me to say, sir."

A Pontius Pilate, enjoying power, probably particularly power over women, but distancing himself from blame. Thorn had hoped to use ducal power to extract Mistress Spencer immediately and be done with this, but Norman would hold on to his victims like a miser hoarding guineas.

"The ladies are still here?"

"Under house arrest, Your Grace. For now."

"Where are they? I have authority to talk to them."

The man hesitated, but ducal power triumphed. "Two are still in their beds, sir, having suffered distress. We have locked their doors, but a man is up there to let them out if they request it. The others have breakfasted and are in the small drawing room to your left."

"Names?"

"Mistress Abercrombie, Miss Sprott, Miss Flint, and Miss Evesham. She's the steadiest, and possibly the ringleader, though Miss Flint is very firm in her ways."

"And the distressed two?" Thorn didn't want to reveal his particular interest.

"Mistress Ormond and Mistress Spencer."

Thorn nodded. "Just six?"

"The numbers dwindled, Your Grace, when Lady Fowler fell ill. But there were two more — Miss Helena Drummond and Miss Olivia Drummond. Irish, and likely the ones to write the treasonous piece. They slipped away as soon as the item was distributed."

"Leaving the chickens for the hawks. I assume the hunt is on for them?"

"Of course, Your Grace. They won't get far."

Thorn wondered. They'd probably planned their escape, with new identities and disguises. The simplest solution for this would be their arrest. With a little encouragement, the law would content itself with them.

Thorn nodded his thanks, opened the door, and went in.

Anxious eyes fixed on him — as if, he thought, he were an executioner. Four ladies, and a general impression of middle years and dullness.

Someone gasped. One buried her face in her handkerchief, weeping. He applied a mildly charming smile as he bowed. "Ladies, you have my sympathy for your predicament. I am the Duke of Ithorne, and at the request of some well-wishers, I will do what I can for you."

"Oh!" declared one ruddy-faced woman, rising to her feet, her hands clasped to her ample bosom. "We're saved!"

A sensible-looking middle-aged woman said, "Thank God."

An angular one demanded, "May we leave, then. Immediately?"

The other still wept.

"I make no promises. You are involved in

very serious charges, ladies. May I be seated?"

The angular woman snapped, "Sit down, Betsy. Don't you see His Grace can't sit while you're standing there?" That must be Miss Flint — all sharp edges.

"Betsy" collapsed back into her chair, babbling apologies. She must be Miss Abercrombie, as she was neither middle-aged nor determined. The middle-aged one must be Miss Evesham, especially as she took the role of spokeswoman.

"May we offer you tea, Your Grace?" she said. "I believe we are still free to do that."

"Thank you, but no. Perhaps one of you can give me your account of events here?"

They all looked to one person, the one still dabbing her eyes. Miss Abercrombie whispered, "Bellona!"

The goddess of war, and presumably the lady named Sprott. He realized his guessing game was foolish. "May I have your names, ladies?"

Again the middle-aged one attended to the courtesies. "I'm Miss Evesham, Your Grace; this is Mistress Abercrombie" — she indicated the plump emotional one — "Miss Sprott" — she gestured to her right, and then opposite — "Miss Flint."

Interesting.

At least the soggy Flint lowered her handkerchief a little to acknowledge the introduction. Sallow skin, half-moon spectacles, and eyebrows that almost met in the middle. Her hair seemed scraped back off her face, but in any case it was concealed beneath the sort of nunnish cap that tied beneath the chin.

He didn't know why the others had so instinctively turned to her, for she looked dumbstruck. "Ah," she said, in almost a whisper. "I really don't think . . . After all, I wasn't here when things happened. Mary?"

She'd addressed Miss Evesham, so perhaps Norman had been correct about her being the leader.

Miss Evesham said, "Mistress Abercrombie and Miss Sprott have been with Lady Fowler for much longer than I, Your Grace, but I can speak to recent events. We are victims, I believe, of two snakes called Helena and Olivia Drummond."

"Why do you describe them as snakes, Miss Evesham?"

"Because they threw themselves on Lady Fowler's charity, and then used her shamefully. In parting, they did their best to destroy us all."

Succinct and probably accurate.

The Abercrombie woman began to sob,

and Flint's handkerchief rose again. Thorn concentrated on the admirably calm Miss Evesham. "Why would they do that?"

"Spite. They were — are — nasty, spiteful young women."

She went on to tell the tale. The donation of a thousand guineas had caused great excitement, and Lady Fowler had seen it as a sign of secret support among important people. It had raised her ambitions. There had been much discussion, but it was the Drummond sisters who'd put forward the idea of a printing press. They'd suggested it purely to assist with the production of the letter, claiming that Olivia Drummond knew how to operate it, which turned out to be true.

"Tell me more about them, if you please," Thorn said. "Where did they come from?"

"If what they told us was true, they are daughters of an Irish gentleman. When he died, the estate went to a cousin, leaving them only with small dowries. They decided to use their funds to fight for fairer laws for women rather than to buy themselves into the eternal slavery of marriage."

Thorn must have raised his brows, for Miss Evesham looked directly at him. "It is often the case, Your Grace, for what power of independence does a married woman have?"

"And yet most women choose marriage if they can," Thorn replied mildly.

"For lack of alternative. However, the Drummond girls knew of Lady Fowler and came to join us here."

"Did Lady Fowler welcome everyone?" he asked.

"Every supporter. There were natural limits to how many she could shelter in her house. The Drummonds, having their small income, took lodgings nearby, as did Miss Flint."

Thorn glanced at Miss Flint. If she had some income, why not buy a decent gown? And why such a watering pot? She'd never stopped dabbing at her eyes — and without taking off her spectacles. Odd. And that handkerchief had a dangling thread. Why didn't she mend it?

Miss Evesham cleared her throat and he dragged his attention back to her. There was, however, something about the watery Flint.

"Helena and Olivia Drummond arrived full of enthusiasm and praise," Miss Evesham said, "and offering some of their small dowries as contribution for the cause."

"Did Lady Fowler need the money? Had

her generosity stretched her income?"

"I don't believe so, Your Grace, but I am not privy to such information."

"Perhaps Miss Flint is," he said, turning back to her.

Some instinct told him she was the most important person here, though why, he couldn't imagine. Then he noticed a spot of blood on the handkerchief. He hadn't heard her cough, but was she consumptive?

She blinked at him over those spectacles, but even if she were dying of the disease, he wouldn't allow her to escape that way.

"Well?" he demanded.

"I know nothing of Lady Fowler's income and expenses," she mumbled.

She was a strange creature, but he was allowing irrelevancies to distract him. He was here to secure Ellen Spencer's release.

He addressed all four women. "Can you prove that the offensive publication was the work of the Drummonds alone?"

Miss Evesham answered. "Will anyone believe us, Your Grace?"

An excellent point. He considered options.

"Have you discussed this among yourselves?"

"Of course, Your Grace. We've spoken of little else."

"I mean, specifically of who printed and sent out this last edition."

He saw only anxious uncertainty and wanted to shake every one of them.

Miss Flint lowered her hands and handkerchief to her lap and spoke calmly. "I don't think so, Your Grace. I was asked to come here last night, when it was clear that Lady Fowler was dying and the Drummond sisters had left. No one was sure what to do."

"And they turned to you?"

She was almost a different woman now, calm and clear. And he felt a powerful sense of recognition. Surely he'd remember her. The poor woman even had a wart on her nose.

"They did, though I'm not sure why."

"But, Bellona," Miss Abercrombie said, "you have always had such a steady head, and are so confident. It comes from having an income, I'm sure," she said with a sigh. "And from never having been subject to the tyranny of a man. You stood up to the Drummonds when none of us would. You saw through them, in fact."

"No. I simply didn't like them."

"Another form of sound instinct," Thorn said, but he was struggling to maintain control.

For as she spoke, he'd realized the truth: Miss Bellona Flint was Bella Barstowe.

As she spoke again, he looked away, testing his outrageous idea by concentrating on her voice.

"Be that as it may, Your Grace," she said, "I was here for only an hour before the officials arrived to put us under arrest, and I have been here ever since. Though there has been much general discussion, I myself know nothing of the finer details."

Without sight to distract him, he had no doubt. He looked at her again, asking her some vague question as he put together the pieces.

Liberated from the cruelty of her family, she'd joined a woman who fought, however foolishly, to prevent such things. The disguise? Perhaps she simply hadn't wanted to be Bella Barstowe any longer. Having some income, she'd taken a house nearby.

His rather rudimentary interest in this matter had suddenly become saber-sharp.

Bellona Flint was his Bella, and clearly looked to as a leader, which put her in grave danger, especially lacking the Drummonds to blame. He should have brought Overstone and a lawyer or two, but that could be corrected. He also needed to speak to Bella alone, but that would have to wait. He mustn't single her out.

Ah, he saw a way.

"Very well," he said, rising. "We are going to attempt to establish the truth. I'm going to make some arrangements, and then each of you will privately give an account of recent events. I must ask you not to speak of them in the meantime, and it would be best to put one of the guards in here to be sure of it. Do you object?"

Someone, probably Sprott, began to object, but Mary Evesham overruled her. "No, Your Grace. I think we understand your purpose."

He bowed to the room, managing not to look at Bella in any special way, and went out, leaving the door ajar.

He found Norman hovering. "You are ready to leave, Your Grace?"

Clearly that would brighten his day.

"Not quite yet. Who is with Lady Fowler's remains?"

The man rolled his eyes. "Her maidservant, Agnes Hoover. Insists on laying her out, sir. Screeched that no man would touch her sweet lady. It's to be hoped she'll allow the undertakers to put her in her coffin."

The man irritated Thorn, but he tried not to show it. "If some of the ladies are willing to place Lady Fowler in the coffin, will you permit it?"

"I don't see why, Your Grace. My orders —"

"Do not rule out compassion. What harm can they do? It would oblige me," he added, trying not to snarl it. He always disliked wielding the ducal club.

Angry color touched the man's cheeks, but he gave in, as he must. "If you advise this, Your Grace."

In other words, *If you take all responsibility.*

"I do. Most firmly." But would any of the women be willing to take on such a task?

He returned to the room and asked, to be met with silence and shifting eyes.

Of course, it was Bella who spoke. "I will, and I'm sure some of you will help. We all know how Lady Fowler felt about men."

After that Miss Evesham and Miss Sprott agreed.

He remembered discussing leadership with Bella and her admitting she might be an unwilling leader. This was what she'd been talking about. Reluctantly, she was the leader of this pathetic flock, and it had dragged her into danger.

He left the room again, boiling over with admiration and exasperation.

CHAPTER 29

Bella was gathering her wits and trying to work out how to use this opportunity.

Thorn's half brother the duke was here, in some sort of official capacity!

When he'd entered, she'd thought him Thorn himself and instinctively hidden as best she could. She'd slowly realized that it had to be the duke, and then the subtle differences had shown themselves. The duke was haughtier, of course, and even though he was wearing country clothing, he was impeccable in every detail, and so closely shaved that hair on the ducal chin must be unthinkable.

The resemblance, however, was astonishing. No wonder Thorn had been sent away as a lad.

Now that she'd realized the truth, she had to find a way to use it to save them all. Would a direct plea work, claiming . . . Claiming what? That she was Captain

Rose's friend? Did she dare claim to be his lover? She wasn't sure that was true, but looking as she did, he couldn't possibly believe her.

Thorn kept informed about the duke's life. Did the duke do the same in reverse?

The duke had said a man would come to listen to be sure they didn't discuss things, and now a guard had joined them in the room, a grim-jawed fellow who stared at them suspiciously. Everyone fell silent, but then Betsy whispered, "The Duke of Ithorne! They must regard this so very, very seriously. Do . . . do you think we truly could hang?"

"No, no, I'm sure not," Bella said quickly. "We're innocent."

"They could make an example of some of us," said Hortensia, firing a glare at Betsy. "Those who were eager to help with the printing."

"I didn't mean any harm," Betsy wailed. "Olivia Drummond was so forceful!"

Bella tried to direct Betsy's attention to the listening man and succeeded all too well. Betsy began to wail again.

"None of us will hang," Mary said soothingly. "Ladies of good birth. It's unthinkable."

"Some of us may be transported, of

course," insisted Hortensia, who never let a grim fact go unfaced.

"This will all be cleared up," Bella insisted. "The duke has come to help us."

"You put great faith in dukes, Bellona," Hortensia sneered. "Simply because you frolicked at . . ."

Thank heavens she didn't complete that, but Bella's cheeks were hot beneath her paint.

"He does not have our interests truly at heart," Hortensia completed, and Bella feared she might be correct. What were they to the Duke of Ithorne?

"I suspect he is interested only in Ellen Spencer," said Mary.

Bella glanced at the listening man, but nothing about Ellen was likely to condemn them for treason. "Why?"

"Don't you remember? Before Ellen came here, she was companion to a lady who turned out to be a lord's unwilling wife." Mary was being careful not to name names.

"Oh, yes," Bella said. That had been about the time of the Olympian Revels, when Bella hadn't been paying much attention to daily events here. She flashed Mary a questioning look, for she still didn't grasp the point.

"I think her lady's husband is a connection of the duke's."

"Ah." Bella considered that and was cheered. "If he's here to save her, he must save us all."

"Do you think so?" Hortensia said. "You do not know the callous ways of his sort. And he's an arrant rake." She made no attempt to speak softly. "Don't you remember how heartlessly he treated the poor woman he'd been corrupting for years? Tempted her into adultery, but as soon as her husband died, cut the connection entirely."

Bella sent Hortensia a warning look. All this could be reported and this was no time to antagonize the duke. In any case, she'd encountered Lady Jessingham at the revels. The duke had been in the wrong, but the lady, in Bella's opinion, didn't appear to be an innocent victim.

Mary spoke the warning. "It will not advance our case to treat the duke with hostility, Hortensia."

Hortensia scowled, but said no more.

Betsy, however, whispered, "We should remember his reputation, though, ladies. A ravening rake. Did I understand aright that he will want to be alone with each of us?"

Bella doubted that even Signor Casanova, who was supposed to be the wickedest rake alive, would try his wiles on Betsy — on any of them, for that matter — but she didn't say so. She'd learned here that even ladies who claimed to have no interest in men became affronted if told their appearance made them safe from them.

They all fell silent, waiting as their fate was handled by others.

Bella smoothed out her handkerchief, grimacing at the blood spot it had gained when she'd held it to her face and pricked her finger. It needed salting immediately, but she doubted she'd be allowed to do it. In any case, she should finish the hem before she attempted to launder it. She rethreaded her needle, curled the hem, and set another stitch, trying to find a way to lead everyone out of this deadly maze.

Given their need, she would write to Thorn at that Stowting address, begging his influence with his brother, but she doubted she'd be allowed to send any message, and it would take days for him to respond. She feared they didn't have days before at least being taken to a prison. She knew enough of prisons to dread that fate. They were places of disorder, full of vice, cruelty, and disease.

If only she'd heeded Peg and not come here. She could be safely on her way to Tunbridge Wells. But the other women would still be in danger.

Her needle froze.

She was remembering the Trayce ladies in Tunbridge Wells. She should be on her way there now, and she wondered what Mr. Clatterford was doing. Perhaps he could help. The worrisome thought was that their names were on the subscription lists!

Had the lists been found? They were tucked away with a lot of other papers in a small room off the scriptorium. The door to that room was papered just like the walls, and so easily missed. She wanted to groan at another duty falling on her, but she must try to destroy those lists. The Trayce ladies wouldn't be the only innocents on them. In fact, all the women on the lists were innocent, but it was terrifyingly clear that the authorities didn't care.

Perhaps they would hang eight women.

Perhaps they would even drag hundreds into the courts.

Then she saw this from another side.

According to Mr. Clatterford, the Trayce ladies were aunts or great-aunts to the Marquess of Rothgar and the Marquess of Ashart. Could she use their jeopardy to gain their assistance?

Let's see, she thought, with grim amusement — *one duke, two marquesses.* She really should try to find three earls connected to this mess.

Thorn had summoned Norman again, and he'd arrived with a tight, resentful mouth but an obsequious bow.

"I think it advisable to question the ladies separately in order to establish some truths. If any are lying, it will become clear. Do you object?" When the man didn't immediately agree, he added, "I will discuss the matter with Lord Northington if you prefer."

He was aware of using a cannon to kill a gnat, but he wanted to kill something.

Norman blanched. "No, no, of course not, Your Grace. But *you* wish to question them? Alone?"

Thorn decided to ignore the insinuation. "One of the other ladies can sit in as chaperone." This was the important point. "I suggest Miss Flint, as she wasn't present at the crucial times. In fact, I see no reason for her to be held."

"My instructions were to prevent anyone from leaving, Your Grace." A modest attempt to fire back.

Thorn reminded himself that the man doubtless needed his post. In fact, he was bullying Norman for following his reasonable orders.

"You appear to be executing your responsibilities very well, Norman. Unless you have a clerk here with time, I will send for one of my own and then begin the questioning."

There was no need for Overstone, so Thorn sent a message to him to choose a suitable underling, and also to send a lawyer here to advise. He sent a brief report to Rothgar, in case he had not yet left Town, suggesting a word with Northington.

This was not the sort of work Thorn was accustomed to, and he'd intended to quickly place it in the hands of others, but that was unthinkable now, with Bella involved.

And soon he'd be alone with her.

He had to struggle not to smile. This situation wasn't amusing, but her extreme disguise was enough to make him laugh aloud.

Bella thought she had herself in hand, but when the duke returned, his words startled her.

"Miss Flint, may I speak to you in the room opposite?"

As she rose, folding her needlework, Betsy gasped. "Oh, Bellona . . . !"

"I'm not summoned to the gallows, Betsy. I'm sure I'll be completely safe."

"Completely," the duke said coldly. "The door will, of course, remain open. Ladies, you will all soon be asked to give your account of recent events, but to do so privately. Miss Flint, who wasn't here at the time, will be your chaperone."

Bella left the room with the duke, wondering if she might have an opportunity to get the lists. She would need only a few moments alone.

"We call this the scriptorium," she said as she led the way in. "We sat at the long table to write copies of the letter. Before the printing press, that is." She turned to face him.

As promised, he'd left the door ajar. He was looking at her strangely, and she wondered if he'd realized how much of her appearance was false. Any disguise could be seen as suspicious.

Or perhaps it was something about her manner. She realized that she wasn't behaving with enough awe, because it was hard not to see him as Thorn. They truly were almost identical. She longed to go to him, to touch him, to smile and expect a smile in return. She almost laughed at the Duke of Ithorne's reaction to such an assault by Bellona Flint.

"You are willing to play the chaperone,

Miss Flint?"

"I will do anything in my power to help the ladies here, Your Grace."

He grimaced slightly, glancing at the door. Bella looked that way, but no one was there. She turned back, wondering if the duke had an unfortunate twitch.

"But you would not lie," he said.

"Wouldn't anyone if it were that or the gallows?" He gave her such a fierce warning look that she realized the danger. "But no, Your Grace, I rarely lie, and there would be no point. I know nothing that need be concealed."

"Very well." He accompanied that with a nod.

Was he really so strongly on their side? Why?

"A clerk will arrive shortly," he said, moving around the long table. "He will record what is said. You will attend only to preserve the proprieties." He came to the end, the point farthest from the door, and twitched again, poor man. "You will not speak or prompt. Do you understand?"

Then he beckoned.

Lud, were Hortensia's fears valid? Were rakes so undiscriminating?

But then he said softly, almost mouthed, "Come over here, Bella."

By the stars, it was Thorn!

In some way he'd learned about her situation and come here to rescue her! But the danger. Impersonating a duke amid issues of treason? Here in London, where his brother was nearby?

He played the duke well, but this couldn't work.

She realized she was scowling as she went to him, to the spot farthest from the door and listening ears, and well out of sight. But then she smiled. She couldn't help it.

She remembered to respond to his latest words as Bellona should. "I will not speak or prompt, Your Grace. I wish to thank you most sincerely for coming here to assist us."

"I am here to establish the truth, Miss Flint." But Thorn had taken her hands and was returning her smile. Bella suddenly felt stronger, and no longer alone. "I hope to find all the ladies present in the house to be innocent."

"You will, sir." Bella realized she could achieve two very desirable things right now. She gently freed her hands. "There's a small room here," she said, opening the disguised door to the storeroom. "It mostly holds paper, ink, and such, but it has a collection of all the issues of Lady Fowler's letters. I'm sure they will stand as evidence that no one here had treasonous intentions."

She went in, powerfully aware of him following her, but then she realized something else — something that made her stomach lurch. Now Thorn knew all her folly, and in addition, he was seeing Bellona Flint — literally warts and all!

It took all her courage to turn and face him.

When she did, he was smiling. "Bella, you are a constant surprise."

"And you are mad!"

"Do not attempt to be sour with me. It seems I'm about to rescue you for the third time. Will I win a prize?"

"It's likely to be a hangman's rope."

"Why on earth am I in danger of that?"

"For impersonating your brother. Here, in London, in the midst of an investigation into treason!"

Thorn was dumbfounded — something that happened to him rarely. He'd been so shocked to find Bella here, so afraid for her, that he'd failed to understand that she would see Captain Rose. No. Probably she'd thought him the duke until he'd been so foolish as to reveal himself.

Whoever "himself" was at this moment.

Be Thorn and have her terrified on his behalf.

Be Ithorne, and reveal to her the deception he'd played, here and now, with no subtlety or preparation.

"You must have seen the risks," she said, frowning at him — which was quite alarming with the scraped-back hair, meeting eyebrows, and wart.

"Of course," he said mechanically. "But they're minor."

"Minor? I read in the papers only yesterday of Ithorne attending some event at a charity school in Cheapside. Someone has to notice there are two of you."

"But who is the real one?"

She rolled her eyes. "You can be useful, however," she said, astonishing him. "Keep giving Bellona instructions for a moment." She turned away and opened a drawer.

Thorn stared at her back, but then had to fight laughter. Bella Barstowe was truly the most amazing woman he'd ever known. He had to rack his brain for some rational patter. "Perhaps you should take out all these copies of Lady Fowler's letters, Miss Flint."

She pointed to a number of boxes on a shelf and continued riffling through the papers in the drawer.

Shaking his head, he took down a box and opened it. "How many are there?"

She took out a number of sheets and

looked at them as she replied, "I'm not sure, but Lady Fowler began the letter not long after her husband died, and that was ten years ago."

He saw that the box did indeed contain a single copy of each letter, written in a rather sharp hand. "Are these archived letters the originals, written by Lady Fowler herself?"

"I don't know, but I assume the older ones are." She came over, papers in hand, and looked at a letter. "Yes, that's her writing. From some time ago, I think. It's become wilder recently, and the last ones were dictated."

"What are they?" he asked quietly, glancing at the sheets she held.

"The addresses of those who received the letter. I have to destroy them."

He snatched them from her. "Better not. That would be a serious offense."

She grabbed the free end, hissing, "Most of these women are innocent of even the tiniest revolutionary inclination."

"Then they'll come to no harm."

"As with us?"

"Not quite so innocent . . ."

"Your Grace?"

They both froze at Norman's voice out in the other room.

Bella stared at him, begging him.

With only a second to decide, Thorn thrust the sheets down the back of his breeches under his coat. He'd only just finished when Norman came in, frowning suspiciously. "What is this place?"

"I've just learned of it myself," Thorn said, having trouble regaining his ducal hauteur. "Merely a storeroom, but Miss Flint was good enough to inform me that it contains originals of all Lady Fowler's letters. I assume they should be taken away in case they are evidence."

"Most certainly," said Norman, seizing the box from Thorn. "I think it would be best if you left the investigation of this room to my people, sir."

"You are quite correct. But I do feel thanks are due to Miss Flint. Without her voluntary assistance, it might have been some time before this room was found."

Norman's lips tightened, and he looked at Bella with a sneer that, as far as Thorn was concerned, put his life in danger, but he did say, "Your assistance will be noted, ma'am."

Bella was extremely flinty. "So it should be. I have told you, Mr. Norman, that if you would regard myself and the other ladies as your allies, this could all progress more smoothly."

"Kindly return to the parlor, Miss Flint,"

Norman snapped.

Bella, the naughty wench, looked at Thorn. "Does that accord with your wishes, Your Grace?"

He wanted to say no, partly to annoy Norman and partly to simply spend more time in her presence, but wisdom triumphed. "It does, Miss Flint." He accompanied it with a bow.

She dropped a curtsy that was both elegant and saucy, and swept away, back straight. He remembered that back. . . .

"A tricky one, that," Norman muttered. "There's more to her than it seems."

"More intelligence, you mean."

"Females are never intelligent."

"Sir, I fear you are in danger of a great many shocks in life, but for now I'm interested in the two women hiding away in their rooms."

"They were both very distressed, Your Grace."

"And you trust a distressed woman more than a clever one?"

Thorn saw Norman wanted to protest the word "clever" but decided against it. "It is only natural for a woman to collapse in a situation like this."

"All the same, I strongly recommend that they be told to join the others in the parlor."

Resentfully, the man said, "As you will, Your Grace."

Thorn nodded. "I must return to my house to put some measures in hand. I trust you to prevent all the ladies from discussing recent events."

He stalked away, hoping the slight rustle from his back wasn't audible a few feet away.

Bella returned to the parlor tempted to throw a fit so as to be allowed privacy in a bedchamber, but then the others would assume Thorn had treated her horribly. Assume the Duke of Ithorne had treated her horribly, which didn't concern her except that it might make one of them do something foolish, or even dangerous.

Her head was whirling with the extraordinary events, but beneath it hummed happiness. He'd come to help her. He cared. She'd seen him again. . . .

"Bellona, dear. What on earth has happened?"

Bella blinked at Mary Evesham, who seemed very worried. "Oh, nothing really. I mean . . . I think the duke does intend to help us."

"Never trust a man like him," snapped Hortensia.

"We need help from someone," Bella

snapped back.

"Oh, don't," bleated Betsy. "Please don't argue. I feel a megrim coming on."

Bella was saved from exploding by Ellen and Clara coming into the parlor. Clara merely looked worn down by worry, but Ellen Spencer was shaking, and her eyes darted around as if fearing danger in every corner.

"You too assisted the Drummonds!" Betsy declared, pointing directly at her. "If they hang me, they must hang you too!"

Ellen Spencer fainted.

CHAPTER 30

Thorn spread the crumpled but neatly written address lists on his desk. They were arranged alphabetically, though some of the less common letters were grouped together, with the lower entries in fresher ink, and the top ones faded. As he scanned the names, he recognized many fashionable ladies. He wasn't surprised. The Fowler letter had become a source of amusement.

Robin's mother's name was there, and Psyche Jessingham's. He saw Lady Arradale and raised his brows. Had Rothgar's wife been his conduit, or had she requested the letter on her own behalf? She was known to feel strongly on many matters to do with women.

He couldn't destroy them because they could be important. A few of the people on these lists could be dangerous, true advocates for revolution. He was pleased to have removed them from the house, however. He locked them away in his desk.

Another service done for his extraordinary lady. He felt uneasily sure he'd do even more dubious things if she asked them of him. He certainly had to remove her from her current danger. . . .

And then what?

Tabitha leapt onto his desk. *"Ai-o."*

"A sigh of resignation? I think so. I cannot possibly attempt to ignore her existence. I'd go gray overnight. But when am I to tell her the truth?"

"Tell who the truth?" Christian asked, walking in.

"Most people knock," Thorn said coldly.

Christian raised his brows, but he was singularly unimpressed. "I've been walking in on you most of our lives. Still talking to Tabby? And is she still talking back?"

"In the manner of an oracle. Thus, what is truth?"

Thorn watched in amusement as Tabitha disappeared under the desk. Clearly her dislike of Christian had not been forgotten. The kittens, now months old, romped out to scramble around Christian's boots.

"Are you staying?" Thorn asked.

"If it's convenient," Christian said, almost sarcastically.

Thorn shook his head. "I'm sorry. Of

course, this is your home. I've had the devil of a morning."

"Tell me," Christian said, so Thorn did.

"The Spencer woman!" Christian exploded. "I'm not having her under my roof."

"I thought of dumping her on Robin."

"Won't work for any length of time. What we need is convents for women like that. Enclose them, but treat 'em decently."

Thorn remembered discussing that with Bella.

"Why are you smiling?" Christian asked.

"Insanity."

"Can you get Ellen Spencer out of the mess?"

"I have to," Thorn said, suddenly able to tell his foster brother all about Bella.

When that tale was told, Christian was grinning. "She sounds just the woman for you."

"She has no more idea how to be a duchess than this cat has sense," Thorn said, rescuing Sable from the curtains.

"He has sense. Just isn't interested in behaving the way you expect. We said you needed a wife like that."

"The eccentric Duchess of Ithorne? I don't want her to be unhappy, Christian. You know how cruel our world can be, especially in the higher reaches."

"Yes, but she sounds as if she has the mettle. And as you say, you have no choice."

"No, I don't, do I? Whatever the strange force that compels people together despite logic or all the precepts of society, it has me in its toils, and it's ruled me far too long to believe it's a whim. Have you a purpose in Town other than advising me?"

"A few errands, and we thought we should relieve you of the cats."

Thorn looked at Tabitha and felt an unexpected pang. "But whom will I consult?"

"If you want to keep 'em all . . . ."

"Caro might object."

"Dozens of cats at home, and she's busy as the bees she's learning to manage." Christian smiled, dotingly. "She was made to be a country lady. She's also swelling with the next generation, Lord save England."

"Congratulations."

"Get to work on such matters yourself," Christian said cheerfully. "Keep the cats for now. When we have opportunity for you and Caro to be together, we'll put it to the test."

"Very well. I wish I could stay, but I must return to the foul den." He opened the door to come face-to-face with a footman, who stepped back, startled.

"Yes?"

"A gentleman to see you, sir. A Mr. Clatterford, in connection to the Fowler matter."

"Where is he?"

"The third reception room, sir."

Thorn went down and encountered a gentleman both stocky and plump, but at first glance, honest.

Thorn nodded. "Mr. Clatterford."

Mr. Clatterford bowed. "Your Grace."

Thorn waved him to a seat. "How may I assist you?"

"I apologize for intruding, sir, but I understand you have become involved in the unfortunate events at Lady Fowler's house. I have come to beg your assistance in helping one of the ladies there."

Thorn controlled impatience and disappointment. A petitioner, no more than that. "Which lady?"

"A Miss Flint."

Ah, now this was different. "What is your connection to Miss Flint, sir?"

"I am her solicitor, Your Grace. I was honored to handle the affairs of her great-grandmother, Lady Raddall, and when Lady Raddall left . . . Miss Flint a bequest, I was given charge of the matter."

So the lawyer knew the name was false.

"What can I do for you, Mr. Clatterford?"

"I hope you will assist me to remove her from the house. She had cut the acquaintance some weeks before the unpleasant events."

Had she? "Why?"

"Because, as you suspect, sir, she became uncomfortable with some of what was happening."

"Then why return?"

The man grimaced in agitation. "That I have only from her housekeeper, sir. Mistress Gussage sent to me in distress last night. When her mistress didn't return she walked to Lady Fowler's house and found it under guard. She was not allowed to speak to Miss Flint. She immediately sought me out, but it took some time for her and her son to find me, it being late. At the earliest possible time today I went to Lady Fowler's house. The people there are most officious, but one directed me to you. I assure you, sir, Miss Flint is incapable of any crime."

Then you don't know her as well as I do. Bella Barstowe would do whatever she felt necessary in a just cause. Thorn could only hope that she never felt it necessary to truly overthrow the monarchy. However, here was a sober, reputable gentleman willing to vouch for her, which could be useful.

"To the best of your knowledge, Clatterford, she has taken place in no treasonous activities?"

"Certainly not, sir."

"Are there others who will support her?"

The solicitor looked extremely uneasy, which wasn't surprising when he knew he was using a false name to refer to the lady in question. "I'm sure I can find some, Your Grace, but she has lived quietly."

Thorn rose. "Very well, sir, I'll do what I can. Where are your offices?"

"In Tunbridge Wells, Your Grace."

Thorn paused by the door and looked a question.

"I came to Town to persuade the lady to return with me to the Wells. We were to leave today."

"May I ask why?"

"To live, sir. I have arranged for her to come under the wing of some ladies there with the intention that she take her rightful place in society."

"And she has agreed?" Thorn asked, much interested.

His surprise was misinterpreted. The solicitor took offense. "I believe some improvement is possible, Your Grace."

Thorn decided he liked Clatterford. "I wish Miss Flint well in the Wells, and I assure you I will do all in my power to enable her to go there."

He meant it. If Bella was established in society, it would make many things easier, and there would be ways Thorn could help bring it about. He saw Clatterford out and was about to return to Lady Fowler's house when a courier arrived bearing a letter from Rothgar.

Dear Sir,

Written in haste. On the Fowler affair, I fear that if we leave the matter in the hands of spy catchers the ladies could suffer severely before any regular processes bring them ease. I suggest a direct appeal to the king. His Majesty is always kind to the weaker sex and may be willing to succor such ladies in their distress.

Your much obliged, etc.,

Rothgar

Thorn admired the vague obligation made possible by haste, and the words chosen in case the letter fell into the wrong hands. No man married to the Countess of Arradale could believe women to be universally weaker than men, but the king took that as the word of God.

Thorn considered Bella as a representative of the weaker sex and shook his head, but she could play a part. Evesham and Abercrombie would fit the king's standard. He knew nothing of the other women who'd taken to their beds, but that reaction seemed hopeful. The sticking point would be the thin and sour Miss Sprott. She seemed the type to insist on hanging for her principles.

Thorn set Overstone to compose the right missive to the king, and Joseph to devising exactly the right clothing for an eventual royal audience. When he set out to return to Grafton Street, at least he left two people happily employed.

Bella was sewing, having picked up an item from the basket of charity sewing kept in the parlor. She'd encouraged the others to do the same. They all needed something to occupy their minds, especially now that they were forbidden to discuss the important matters.

Her mind returned, as she knew it would, to the inn parlor in Upstone, and to Thorn reading to her as she sewed. It was probably unnatural of her to find that memory even sweeter than their time in the bed, but it had been so uncomplicated, which made it easier to visit.

What danger he was in, however. She wouldn't be able to bear it if he came to grief through helping her.

She was alerted by some inner sense, and looked up to see Thorn in the doorway. She worked very hard at not smiling at him and had to pray her blushes didn't show.

"We are ready to begin the recording of your accounts, ladies. Miss Flint and Mistress Evesham, please."

Bella rose, thankful that Mary was his first choice. Her account would probably be the most coherent and unbiased. They went to the scriptorium, where a young man stood beside the table on which he'd arranged a neat pile of paper, a number of fresh pens and three inkwells, one uncapped. Prepared for anything.

There was another clerk present, with his own supplies, though not so impressively ranked. Presumably he was to record everything for the Lord Chancellor. An elderly man sat in the corner, seemingly only to observe.

They all sat and the questions began.

All went well and Mary's account made it clear that most of the ladies had played no real part in the writing or printing of the treasonous paper. Betsy Abercrombie remained in danger, however.

Next, Thorn summoned Ellen Spencer.

Ellen arrived already protesting her innocence with a desperation that suggested she was being dragged up the steps of the gibbet and was guilty as the devil. When Thorn commanded her to calm down and simply give her account of the past few weeks, she burst into tears.

Thorn looked to Bella for help. She'd obeyed his instructions not to speak or react, but now she took Ellen into her arms. "Ellen, dear, you must not go on so. We all know you've done nothing."

Ellen looked at her. "But I have, Bellona! The worst possible thing." As if she might be able to keep it secret, she whispered, "Murder. And Helena Drummond knew of it."

Bella shot Thorn a look, but there was nothing he could do, and Norman's clerk was taking all this down — as was his own.

She thought to wonder where he'd found such an impeccably ducal clerk.

Someone had to ask, so Bella did. "Whom did you murder?"

Still whispering, Ellen said, "I didn't precisely. . . . Because he didn't eat the cake, you see. But I tried to. And they told Lady Fowler, so Helena knew. And she made me *do* things."

Bella refused to ask the next question, but

Thorn did. "What things, Mistress Spencer?"

"The news sheet. I wrote out fair copy." Ellen covered her face with her soggy handkerchief. "Such terrible things. Things against the king, who is such a good man."

"Get that down," Thorn said sharply. "Mistress Spencer, no one is going to take further action against you for the matter of attempted murder. You were in temporary distress because you thought your employer was in danger, and you attempted to save her in the only way you knew. Your character is vouched for by a number of people whose opinion is valued."

He knew all about that?

How?

"It is?" Ellen asked, emerging slightly from her soggy shield.

"On my honor, ma'am."

Bella took the sodden handkerchief and substituted her own, and Ellen blew her nose. Bella was still trying to make this new piece fit.

Ellen began a moderately coherent account of recent times. It turned out to be particularly useful, because Helena Drummond had known she had Ellen under her thumb and hadn't bothered to conceal anything from her. Bella suspected the Irishwoman had enjoyed forcing Ellen to hear and see things that distressed her.

Helena had pretended to consult with Lady Fowler, but as that poor woman was rarely capable of rational speech, it had been more a matter of telling her what was happening, but Ellen had been instructed to stand witness to Lady Fowler's agreement.

"And generally she did agree," Ellen said seriously. Now that she'd revealed the worst, a sensible woman was slowly emerging. "Lady Fowler wasn't in her right mind, so she agreed that having her name attached to a great revolution would be a memorable triumph. She did not fear death, but she feared being forgotten."

Thorn said, "But the plan and the news sheet proposing it, those were entirely a creation of Helena Drummond?"

"From what I heard, Your Grace, yes."

"Do you have anything else to add that you think might be of significance, Mistress Spencer?"

Ellen Spencer considered, almost a different person now in her neat composure. "Only that the ladies here cannot possibly be traitors, Your Grace. Some are silly and some are bitter, but all are honest and loyal."

A sensible woman, but unkind, Bella thought, glad to see Ellen Spencer's back.

Thorn looked at Bella. "Thank you for your assistance, Miss Flint. Do you agree with Mistress Spencer's assessment of innocence?"

"Completely, Your Grace."

He looked down at a list. "Whom do we have left? Miss Sprott, Mistress Ormond, and Miss Abercrombie. We'll see Miss Abercrombie next."

Bella was concerned about Betsy. She had been an enthusiastic supporter of the Drummonds, perhaps simply because she was a weak woman always attracted to the strong, but she was also silly, and might say something to incriminate herself. Thorn seemed to guess that, however, and asked her simple questions. Out of good sense or terror, Betsy volunteered nothing.

Hortensia was next and she exuded hostility, but she kept her words brief and to the point. As she'd detested the Drummonds, it came out well. Clara Ormond was so obviously just a sweet, elderly lady that no one could suspect her of anything.

When she left, Thorn said, "And there we have it."

"Not quite," said Bella. "There's Agnes Hoover, Lady Fowler's woman. Now her mistress's body is in its coffin she may be persuaded to speak with you, if someone else keeps vigil."

Thorn turned to Norman's clerk. "Can you attempt to find the substitute, sir? Perhaps Miss Evesham would be the most suitable, but whichever lady is willing."

The clerk bowed and left.

As soon as he was out of the room, Thorn said quietly, "This clerk is mine, as is Mr. Delibert, a solicitor. We can speak freely for a moment. We're attempting to interest the king in leniency. If this can be achieved, he may send someone to investigate on his behalf. It's crucial that each and every lady is clearly sober, righteous, and conventional."

Bella twitched her brows at him, but said, "I understand, Your Grace. I must thank you again for your efforts."

Lud! Was he going to find someone to impersonate an emissary of the king?

Norman's clerk returned then, and soon Agnes Hoover arrived. She was as stoical in bereavement as she'd been all along, but she gave a damningly caustic description of the Drummonds. Her opinion of the rest of the women wasn't kind, but it offered no basis for prosecution.

Once she'd left, Thorn said, "Thank you, Miss Flint."

Bella wanted an opportunity to speak to

him privately and persuade him to end this dangerous deception, but she had to stand, curtsy, and leave.

Thorn hated to have Bella out of his sight, and he hated to leave her worried about his safety. He could see no reasonable opportunity to reveal that he was, in fact, the duke. It could scatter her wits and she needed all her resources to get through the next days. As soon as the ladies were all safe, however, he would explain everything and hope for happiness.

The sooner, the better. He sent for Norman. "It's my opinion that all these ladies are innocent and should be set free."

"With respect, Your Grace, I do not agree. Clearly some were willing accomplices of the Drummond sisters, or more. In fact, that is what the Drummonds claim."

Damn him. He enjoyed exploding that without warning.

"You have the Drummonds?"

Norman smirked. "Yes, sir, and they claim Miss Abercrombie and Mistress Spencer were enthusiastic participants. My clerk informs me the Spencer woman admitted as much."

"She admitted to compulsion."

"Because she feared prosecution for murder."

"I can assure you, Norman, that no one died and no one is going to bring a case over that."

"The Drummonds also claim that Miss Flint was a supporter of their cause and often said as much to them."

Snakes indeed, Thorn thought. *Vipers.* They either were determined to destroy others with themselves, or were cunningly trying to link their fate to those who might be rescued.

He'd hoped not to have to try to interest the king, for George was unpredictable in such matters, but it was now the only course. Rothgar, of course, had been right.

He'd toss in an explosion of his own. "You should know that the king is interesting himself in this matter, Norman, and is inclined to leniency — apart from the Drummonds, of course."

Norman's lips tightened. "I understood that His Majesty was much incensed."

"But only against the true villains."

"I will await confirmation of that, sir."

"Of course. You have your duty to do. But I would advise a respectful approach. Some of these ladies, including Mistress Spencer, have powerful people concerned on their behalf. Even in addition to myself."

Thorn collected his clerk and returned home, working through the next moves of the dangerous game. He realized he'd never played for such high stakes before in his life, and hoped never to do so again. The stakes were high because Bella's very life was at risk.

CHAPTER 31

Thorn prepared carefully for the audience with the king. It would be private, so full court grandeur was inappropriate. However, the king had appointed St. James's Palace as the location, which made it extremely formal. It also warned that His Majesty was not necessarily kindly disposed.

Joseph had laid out velvet, dark blue but lightly embroidered. Thorn approved, exchanging only the waistcoat for a more ornate one. "We don't want to look funereal."

After careful consideration he decided not to wear a powdered wig, but that did mean summoning the coiffeur to arrange his hair more carefully. In the end, with subtle jewels and his orders, he felt he'd achieved the best possible appearance, but he intensely disliked feeling even slightly anxious.

He presented himself to Tabitha for comment. She blinked.

"No advice?"

"Eee-ah."

"Totally incomprehensible." Thorn looked into the basket. "Where, ma'am, are your offspring?" He looked around and saw Sable perched on the back of a chair, attempting to look ferocious. Georgie was sitting on the floor. Thorn picked him up and placed him beside the other kitten. "If only the other Georgie were as easily manipulated," he remarked, and left the room.

As Thorn had anticipated, King Georgie was on his high horse. He was offended, much offended, by the violent intentions of the women. It offended every law of man, God, and nature, and an example must be made.

"Of the Drummond sisters, indeed, sir, but these other ladies are not of the same type at all. We have a curate's sister, and a dean's widow, a gentle, elderly lady, and one who will sadly never find a husband. They gathered around Lady Fowler only because they had no other refuge."

Thorn was finding it hard to strike the right note. He was a petitioner, but the king would never believe any groveling and Thorn doubted he could stomach it. In general their relationship had been distant, especially as at one point they'd both been interested in pretty Lady Sarah Lennox.

George probably thought he looked severe, but to Thorn's eyes, his expression was closer to a pout. "They should accept the refuge of the head of their families, what?"

"Alas, in some cases that gentleman is very far removed from them, and they are wary of putting themselves entirely in his power. Being decent ladies, sir."

"I see, I see. Unfortunate, what?"

"Very, sir, especially as it has led to their predicament. Unthinkable, I'm sure you'll agree, that such decent ladies be thrown into a prison."

Thorn watched anxiously as the king took a turn around the room, hands clasped behind. George stopped and glared. "I did not think you the sort to be involved in such a matter, Ithorne."

Thorn had been prepared for that. "I wasn't, sir, but I was asked to interest myself. By Lord Rothgar, among others."

"Rothgar, eh? He sent a letter on the matter. Decent women, what? No rebellious tendencies?"

Thorn suppressed thoughts of Sprott, and possibly Bella herself. "Absolutely not, sir."

"Need to marry, what?"

Thorn realized that was addressed to

himself. "I do hope to do so soon, sir."

"Excellent. Sets a man's thoughts on his duty and posterity, what? Wipes away foolish days."

So you still think of Sarah Lennox, do you? "I do hope marriage will enrich my life, sire."

"Enrich, enrich. Excellent, what? And children. Many children, what?"

Fearing they were heading in a different direction, Thorn said, "So, may I set the ladies free, sir?"

The king stiffened, and then he twitched in an odd way. *'Struth, don't let him throw a fit over this.* At least they weren't alone. Lord Devoner was gentleman-in-waiting, looking bored, and a statuelike footman stood against the wall.

Thorn played his last card, the one he'd hoped not to have to use. "Perhaps I could present the ladies to you, sir, so you could assure yourself of their decency and loyalty."

The king twitched again, and he was frowning as if aware of the problem. But then he said, "Yes, yes! Splendid notion. But I will see them where they are. I will see this house. I will sense it. I will know it."

Thorn realized the concerns were valid: the king wasn't entirely sane. The ramifications of that were for later, however. Now, the main concern was Bella's safety and this odd decision. Thorn had expected George to summon them here, or to some other royal location, and had depended on that to cow the rebellious Sprott. There was no help for it, however, and he had no means to send a warning.

He tried one deflection. "Lady Fowler is recently dead, and some evidence of her illness lingers in the air, sir."

But the king glared at him. "Are you trying to conceal something, Ithorne?"

"Absolutely not, sir."

They left almost immediately, in a plain carriage without outriders, because the king wished to be incognito, but the grooms were armed, and two armed gentlemen rode not far away. They arrived in Grafton Street without incident, though the guard on the door looked in danger of an apoplexy when he saw who was approaching.

Norman went white, then red, and then began to sweat. Thorn enjoyed that.

"The ladies?" Thorn asked.

"In the parlor, Your Grace," Norman said, "having finished their dinner not long ago. An excellent dinner, I assure you."

The king was looking around at the very ordinary house. "Smells unclean," he said.

"Poor housekeeping, what?"

Thorn didn't remind him that he'd been warned. "Shall I summon the ladies before you, sire? There's an unused room over here."

"No, I shall brave the lionesses in their own den, what?" George had turned genial, which was a good sign. He liked to be a benefactor. "Which way?"

Norman sprang forward to open the parlor door and announce, "His Majesty, the king!" so Thorn didn't even see what the king saw.

When he followed, he smiled. Bella had done her work well, of course.

All six ladies were there, all rising to their feet, astonished. They'd been engaged in needlework, except for Mistress Abercrombie, who had been reading to them.

The king sat down.

Thorn was relieved that all the ladies realized they should remain standing.

"Read on!" George commanded.

Unsteadily, Mistress Abercrombie did. By chance or design, her choice of reading was some sort of sermon on humility. The king listened for a few minutes, nodding. Then he said, "Enough. Enough."

The room went silent, and all eyes fixed on him. Most were anxious, though Thorn could almost feel Miss Sprott strain at not being able to speak. Bella was the most composed, but even she was wary.

"You have all been very foolish," the king said. "It is never good for women to lack male guidance, and here we see evidence of that. Lady Fowler's peculiar behavior commenced only after the death of her husband."

A sound escaped Sprott, but was changed into a cough.

"I am told that none of you ladies has a gentleman of your family in a position to protect you, what?"

He was answered by murmurs and nods, but seemed to see that as appropriate incoherence.

"Very well, then. I take you under my wing. I will be as a tender father to you."

Thorn was having a great deal of trouble keeping a straight face, especially when he could see Bella's struggle to do the same thing.

But then it ceased to be amusing. "As my proxy, I appoint His Grace the Duke of Ithorne. You will submit to him, and he will keep you from such folly in the future."

The blank silence stretched dangerously, but then Ellen Spencer saved the day. She flung herself forward on her knees before the king, hands clasped in front. "Your Majesty! You are too kind, too noble! To do so much for foolish women such as we."

It was the kind of performance the king enjoyed, but Thorn thought it was completely honest. The others followed her example. Mistress Evesham looked extremely wry and Miss Sprott as if she were choking, but they went to their knees. Bella did so too, her head bowed low.

Thorn realized something then.

At some point since he'd entered this room, she would have realized the truth.

She'd held to the belief that he was Captain Rose, but no one would dare continue such an impersonation when it involved the king in person. His hands were clenched in the effort not to rush to her now to try to explain.

He had one clear ironic thought: Rothgar would have managed this better.

Bella was simply stunned.

She should have realized when he'd first mentioned involving the king, but she'd assumed yet more deception.

At first she'd seen no one but the king and been intent on presenting exactly the right appearance while keeping an eye on the others. It had only been the words

"Duke of Ithorne" that had driven home the fact that he was here. She'd looked and seen and known.

Quite apart from the fact that he was at the king's side, he was now every inch the court aristocrat, in velvet and jewels, the heels of his shoes high, his hair elaborately dressed. Impossible to imagine him facing down ruffians in the Black Rat.

That must have been the true Captain Rose, Ithorne's half brother.

This was the duke, but a while ago Thorn had been here. The man she'd traveled with, who'd helped her vanquish Augustus, couldn't be this one. Were the two so close in appearance they could work together in this?

She couldn't sort out what was what and who was who. As drama happened around her, she tried to do her bit whilst most of her mind struggled over who had been Rose and who had been Ithorne.

Whom had she confronted in that room at the Compass?

Who had read to her in the Hart?

Who had made devastating love to her?

She was hardly aware of the king and the Duke of Ithorne leaving the room, but then had to snap alert to deal with exclamations of relief and murmurs of new concerns. Apparently they were to immediately remove to the duke's house and had only a half hour to collect their possessions.

"Placed in his power!" declaimed Hortensia. "This is vile."

"Count your blessings," said Mary Evesham sharply. "Let us all do as we're told. I cannot wait to be out of this house."

"Oh, yes," said Clara, and hurried away.

The rest followed, but Bella said to Mr. Norman, "I have no possessions here. I had to borrow the essentials last night. May I go to my house to collect some items?"

He was losing people to bully and turned his spite on her. "You go nowhere, ma'am, except where you are sent. His Grace will decide the rest."

So Bella returned to the parlor and her needlework, but it lay idle as she continued to puzzle over identities.

The half-naked Rose in the Compass had seemed confused by her. She'd taken it for drunkenness, but perhaps he hadn't known what she was talking about. He must have been the real Captain Rose, but that would mean the Duke of Ithorne had rescued her in the Black Rat and staggered in apparent drunkenness through the Dover crowd.

Which meant Ithorne had been with her on that adventure to punish Augustus. No wonder he'd not been worried about dealing with Lord Fortescue. How amused he must have been at her alarm. No wonder he hadn't felt able to marry her. The whole idea was ridiculous.

Anger was welcome for it could cloak pain, but she made herself remember that he had come here to rescue her, and for that she would be grateful all her days. She wished he'd told her the truth in Upstone, but she'd lived enough lies and disguises herself to understand how they could entrap.

What to do now, however? She could only hope he would allow her to leave with Mr. Clatterford for Tunbridge Wells and agree that they should never see each other again. That would be painful, but to be in his home for long, knowing how impossible her dreams were, would be torture.

The impossibility of a future was nailed down when they arrived at Ithorne House. The ladies climbed out of the three carriages and were escorted into the grand entrance hall. Of course, Bella had been here before, but it had been a theater set, all unreality. Now it was very real, and very awe inspiring.

The walls were dark, divided by half columns of golden marble. The ceiling was painted with gods and goddesses ascending into impossibly high clouds, as if to assert that this place was not for ordinary mortals. The floor was marble tile, and she did remember that. It had looked simple amid the mock Italian square, but now looked luxurious.

Thorn was there. . . .

No, not Thorn. Ithorne. He put each lady into the care of a maidservant who would take them to their rooms. Bella, however, he asked to speak with. She supposed this had to be, but she wished she could disappear to some modest bedchamber and weep.

He gestured her into a reception room near the front door, one of the places where he would meet someone not quite suited to the parts of his house he would consider his home. She appreciated that, for it provided distance.

However, he closed the door.

"You permit?" he asked. "I don't think we wish to be overheard."

Bella shrugged. "I don't suppose anyone will think you wish to ravish me."

He inhaled, but then said, "I do, you know."

Bella turned away. "Don't. I can't imagine how all this has come about, but I understand now why you wanted no more to do with me after Upstone." She found the courage to turn back and face him. "I do understand. But I can't be your mistress, so there must be an end of this, now."

He was smiling slightly. "Kelano the Amazon, I see. But it is Bella I wish to marry."

So he had known all along that Bella Barstowe had been Kelano. Known and said nothing.

Then the second sentence registered.

"I'm sure I'm honored, Your Grace, but no."

"No?"

His shock almost amused her, but her anger and irritation were too strong. "It's impossible and you know it. That's why you've not tried to find me. You could have done. Deny it if you dare."

"I could," he admitted. He closed his eyes for a moment before saying, "I wasn't sure what was best."

"Nonsense. You knew precisely what was foolish. Look at you. Look at me."

"I know my mind now," he said steadily. "I can't live without you. Any minor problems can be dealt with." He stepped closer, his voice gentling to the one she remembered too well. "Bella, I love you. I love you to distraction."

She longed to surrender, but this wasn't Thorn. This perfectly polished man, this bejeweled aristocrat in his elegant setting, wasn't her lover, her friend, her dream husband in a cozy parlor.

"Listen to yourself!" she snapped. " 'To distraction.' This is a passing madness, Thom—" She cut off his name and turned away. "One day soon you will regain your sanity, Your Grace, and I do not want to be your wife when that happens."

"What sort of fool do you think I am?"

"A lovesick one, it would seem." But she winced at her own words. "I apologize. You've been all that is kind."

"Bella . . ."

"I have an invitation to move to Tunbridge Wells to live with some ladies there. I ask you to allow that."

Silence pressed at her, but she could not face him.

"I will give you whatever you want, of course," he said. "Even that."

She heard Thorn's voice and it made her turn back, but the man before her was still the duke.

"It is better this way," she said.

"Yes," he said. "I think it is." Her illogical hurt must have shown, for he made a sharp gesture. "I didn't mean that. I'm a lovesick

594

fool to attempt this now. I couldn't wait. But I will wait. For you to change your mind."

"Don't, please. If I weaken it will only lead to disaster down the road."

He took her hands, and his touch almost broke her will, but when she looked down she saw a sapphire ring and the deep froth of lace at his cuffs. Lace that must have cost a small fortune. She looked up and saw a sapphire at his earlobe.

She moved gently away and took out the handkerchief. The only folly she'd allowed herself all these months was to carry his skull earring around in her pocket. She unwrapped it and held it out to him.

He took it, considering the ruby eyes. "The whole idea of this and all the other oddities is to support the deception. Caleb and I are alike, but not perfectly so, but when people see the old-fashioned frock coat, the scarlet neckcloth, and the skull, they see Captain Rose." He looked at her. "Whenever I'm able, I steal some time to be Captain Rose, but that is not frequently. It was my half brother, Caleb, you spoke to at the Compass. He told me, and I traveled to Dover to find out what was going on. At some point, I should have told you all, but it never seemed the right time."

"I should have guessed when we met Fortescue."

"Caleb has impersonated me a time or two, but only if essential. The duke is the harder part."

He meant that literally and it tugged at her heart, but she must remain strong. To him it might seem possible that she be changeable as the sea and become part of his world, but she knew it was not.

"It would never work," she said.

He put the skull in a pocket. "Take your rest, Bella, after service nobly done. You can trust your ladies to me, and I will arrange for you to travel with the excellent Mr. Clatterford tomorrow." At her surprise, he said, "He came to me for help, but I'd already been recruited. If we're to be honest, I went to Lady Fowler's without any awareness of your presence, to rescue Ellen Spencer."

Suddenly Bella laughed. "Mary was right all along. I recommend her to you, Your Grace. She has the soundest head of all of us."

He just smiled at that, but he held out a hand. Bella felt compelled to put hers into it, even though she knew he'd kiss it, which he did.

"I wish I were a sea captain, for that is what you want. But I am what I am, and always have been. I will hope you can forgive me for it."

He let her go and went toward the door, but she asked a question.

"Why did you give a thousand guineas to Lady Fowler's fund?"

He turned, surprised. "How did you discover that? No, never mind," he said with a wry smile. "You are you. A piece of folly, Bella, nothing more. Did you imagine some plot? I paid it for a friend, and he owed it because of a foolish vow."

Bella met his eyes. "A piece of folly, but it almost destroyed a number of people. Bear that in mind, Your Grace."

She opened the door for herself and entered the magnificent hall.

One maidservant waited. Bella dropped a curtsy to the Duke of Ithorne and went up to a quite handsome bedchamber, where she was finally, finally allowed some privacy and could weep until she fell into an exhausted sleep.

CHAPTER 32

"Lord Youland, Bella, dear. Flirt with him."

"But I don't want to, Lady Thalia," Bella said amiably. "You know he's too easily encouraged."

"But you need practice, my dear. You rather frighten the gentlemen away."

They were walking, well swathed in fur-lined cloaks, along the Walks in Tunbridge Wells. In December those present were mostly residents of the Wells or hardy invalids, but it was still a sociable gathering.

Bella had emerged here two weeks earlier, once she had the complete new wardrobe the Trayce ladies insisted on. She'd protested that she needed only to rest a little and reclaim her identity as Bella Barstowe before finding some worthy purpose in life. However, Lady Thalia Trayce, a petite confection of a lady despite her years, had insisted almost tearfully that Mr. Clatter-

598

ford had promised that Bella would be their companion for a while.

How could she refuse?

"We had a young companion last year," Lady Thalia had explained, "and found it quite rejuvenating. Dear Genova. But then she married. We did try another young lady, but such a droopy creature, always assuming the worst would happen. We recommended her to Lady Vester, who is of the same inclination."

There were three Trayce sisters, all daughters of the Marquess of Ashart. A previous one, for the current one was young. In fact, he was one of the rakes Lady Fowler had followed most carefully. He had rewarded her with juicy morsels of debauchery, showing no sign of caring a jot for her rants.

He was married now, and to that Genova who had been the ladies' companion. She had been only a sea captain's daughter with no portion to speak of — a fact Lady Thalia produced whenever Bella said she was too ordinary for the grand gentlemen presented to her.

Lady Thalia was the youngest sister at a sprightly seventy. She'd never married, for her beloved had died in a war long ago. She still dressed in a youthful manner, because the only thing that seemed to worry her was what her beloved would think to see her so old when they met in heaven.

Lady Urania, a few years older, was calm, stately, and a widow. She had already left for the home of her oldest son to spend Christmas there.

The oldest of the Trayce sisters was Lady Calliope, a large and forceful lady who could manage only a few steps at a time. The ladies kept two stalwart footmen to carry her around in a special chair, and Lady Thalia shamelessly admired their muscles.

At first Lady Calliope had alarmed Bella, for she seemed sharp and angry about everything. But Bella had learned to look for the twinkle in the pouched eyes, and listen for the sardonic tone. By now, she knew to trust Lady Calliope above all. She was a rock. Lady Thalia, though delightful, was a butterfly.

Bella agreed to be presented to Sir Irwin Butterby, who looked somewhat lost, but as she approached with Lady Thalia, something like panic widened his eyes. Lady Thalia did have that effect on a number of people, for she was always attempting to devise love matches.

When Lady Thalia flitted away, Bella set to putting the baronet at his ease. She worked in a casual comment about Lady Thalia's ambitions as Cupid and a vague reference to a gentleman who was elsewhere.

He instantly settled and confessed to a similar situation. He was here as escort to his sickly mother, but the illness had meant delaying his marriage to his dearest Martha, who was a saint not to complain. After a quarter hour they had agreed to be each other's shield. Bella moved on, well pleased with that new friend, but sad in other ways.

Sadness lived in her these days, and she saw no help for it. She feared she would be perpetually sad over Thorn, but whenever she encountered starry-eyed lovers whose paths were smooth, her grief cut deep. Even Sir Irwin, suffering a delay out of duty to his mother, was in a much better case than she.

She cried too often. She'd never been quick to tears, but now they came too easily, threatening to embarrass her, for she didn't want anyone to know. At first she hadn't slept well, but at least insomnia had exhausted itself. Her dreams, however, were gloomy. It would not do. She was twenty-one years old and with most of her life in front of her. She would not spend it moping.

Come the spring. That was what she'd resolved. Come spring she would begin to establish her independent life, though how, she wasn't sure. Ed Grange had begun an apprenticeship in London, and she feared Peg wouldn't want to leave there, but Bella knew she could not live in London. She could not live anywhere where there was danger of meeting the Duke of Ithorne. Her will might prove too weak.

She lived in fear that he'd come here. She'd joined the Trayce ladies to mend her reputation, but not expected to be carried into the highest levels.

Perhaps she should join Mary and the others in their nunnery. That was what they laughingly called it, for the five ladies lived in a pleasant house on the fringes of London, sharing the management of it and undertaking charitable works in the neighborhood. Hortensia was still fiery, but she'd agreed to take on manageable reforms. Mary was unofficial mother superior, with Betsy as her earnest assistant. Once they were truly established, they planned to find other suitable ladies to join them.

Bella couldn't go there, however. It would be just another flock and it was under the patronage of the Duke of Ithorne, who had set it up and funded it.

Lucinda had suggested that they set up house together. Two miserable spinsters together — that had been the implication. Bella had felt a slight pull of pity, but she wouldn't weaken on that case.

To everyone's relief, she was sure, Augustus had managed to kill himself. So had Squire Thoroughgood, but he'd done just as he'd said — shot himself the day after the events at the Hart in Upstone. Sir Newleigh Dodd had fled abroad like the scared rabbit he was.

Augustus had attempted to recover from the scandal, certain he could somehow wriggle out of his shame. When that had failed and he'd suffered the ostracism he'd perpetuated for her, he'd taken to laudanum in increasing amounts. Eventually, accidentally or deliberately, he'd taken too much. Bella felt absolutely no guilt about that after the way he'd acted not just toward herself, but toward any who fell under his power. The world was better for his absence. Charlotte Langham was now betrothed to a pleasant, reliable man.

That part of Bella's life was over. Soon a new one must begin, and, despite temptation, without Thorn . . . but not until spring.

"Time to prepare for Christmas," said Lady

Thalia one evening as they sat in the small drawing room, made cozy by a large fire.

"Load of nonsense," grumbled Lady Calliope.

"Now, now, Callie, you know you wouldn't miss it for the world."

Miss Christmas? Bella wondered.

"I'm looking forward to it," Bella said. "My last four Christmases were spent at Carscourt and were stingy affairs."

"Then this will be very different!" declared Lady Thalia, "for we are to spend it at Rothgar Abbey."

Bella paused midstitch. "But isn't that quite far away?" Lady Thalia and Lady Calliope never traveled. Bella wasn't sure Lady Calliope was able to.

"Damnably long way," grumbled Lady Calliope.

"You know you want to go, Callie. Rothgar's baby!"

Ah. "Has Lady Rothgar had her child, then?" Bella asked. The event had been eagerly anticipated all the time she'd been here.

"Oh, no, not yet," Thalia said. "And not, I hope, before we arrive. Lady Elf — Rothgar's sister, Elfled — had her child right on Christmas Eve last year. Wouldn't that be perfect? To have another Christmas baby.

And Genova had her *presepe* — that's a delightful representation of the stable at Bethlehem, dear — and we sang that song she knew. About joy and bells. I do hope someone remembers it."

"Oh, stop your chattering, Thalia," Lady Calliope grumbled. "Not but what it wasn't pleasant enough once we arrived."

"Rothgar is to arrange everything, and you know he's promised some special seating to make it easier for you, dearest. And his daughter is to be there. I do so want to meet her. So romantic. A love affair in Venice," she said to Bella, without a hint of embarrassment. She was quite extraordinary.

"A scandal in Venice," Lady Calliope corrected. "He was scarce more than a lad."

"Young love!" exclaimed Lady Thalia. "And now Rothgar's daughter is married to Huntersdown — the Earl of Huntersdown, dear," she explained to Bella. "Such a merry rascal and a delightful flirt. You'll be enchanted by him, Bella, dear."

Bella was suddenly wary. From the Fowler letter she knew Lord Huntersdown was cousin to Ithorne. Might he be there?

"Will this be very grand?" she asked.

Thalia pouted. "Not this year, alas. Because of the baby, only close family are invited. But it will still have all the essentials, I'm sure. Wassail and feasting. Holly and ivy. The Yule log."

Bella's head was whirling, which was often the case around Lady Thalia, but now that she didn't need to fear another meeting with Thorn, she could be easy.

"Then I look forward to it, ma'am. Thank you for including me."

Thorn read the letter, recognizing pure temptation. It was from Rothgar, and it invited him to Rothgar Abbey for Christmas.

Damn the man. How had he learned about Bella?

That had to be it. The same post had brought a letter from Clatterford with the news that Bella herself was going to Rothgar Abbey for Christmas. That fact played havoc with his plans.

He'd purposefully given her a month to recover her equilibrium in the hope that time with the Trayce ladies would convince her that ducal splendor was tolerable. They were among the highest of the high, and though they didn't host grand events, she'd learn from them how to deal with the elite.

He would have liked to give her the opportunity to experience court circles, but his patience wouldn't stretch to January when the winter season began. He'd been planning a courtship visit to the Wells just before Christmas. If he won her, he'd carry her off to Ithorne Castle for Christmastide with some sort of chaperone.

Once he had her commitment, he'd give her as much time as she needed to adapt to his world and learn its ways, but he must have her commitment. He lived in fear of hearing that she'd married another man. She was capable of making a sensible marriage to prevent herself from surrendering to him.

He'd been waiting, keeping his sanity only because of the intelligence sent by Clatterford, but now the solicitor reported that the Trayce ladies were about to travel to Rothgar Abbey for Christmas, and they were taking Bella with them. Even if he raced there now, they would already be on their way.

He'd been attempting to resign himself to more patience, but now the unexpected invitation was hard to resist. It would mean taking what he wanted at Rothgar's hands, and neglecting his duty to celebrate Christmastide here at Ithorne Castle.

"Your judgment?" he asked Tabitha, who was sleek now that her kittens were less demanding of her. Instead, the kittens demanded a great deal of Thorn and his servants, for they were intrepid seekers of adventure.

The oracle remained silent.

"Dare I wait?" he asked.

"Ee-ah-a."

"No, no, you will like having her in residence."

"Ay-a."

"You will be obliged to like having her in residence."

"Ah-oo-ee-a!"

"No point in protesting, and I must settle the matter. I can't bear this torture much longer."

He considered Rothgar's letter again, but he could find no malice in it. It annoyed him that Rothgar had learned of his love, but to let that turn him from what he wanted would be folly.

His main obstacle, as always, was duty, damnable duty.

He paced to the window that looked out over the frosty grounds of Ithorne Castle, where he'd celebrated Christmas every year of his life, even in the cradle. Many a time he'd longed to go with Christian to his home, where there were a vast number of brothers and sisters, and merry celebrations for all ages.

He'd always done his duty, however, so as

not to disappoint the people here. Without him in residence, why bring in the greenery? Why prepare a grand feast for only the various family dependents who lived here on his charity? His tenants and other local people expected him to join in their celebrations. There were traditions and responsibilities that it seemed only he could perform.

Robin had a mother happy to be his proxy. He had no one.

Perhaps next year he would have a wife, and in time children.

Bella, and Bella's children.

His people could celebrate without him one year. This year. He sat to write to Rothgar accepting the invitation.

But then he crumpled it and threw it in the fire.

It would not do. Too many people would be disappointed.

He took another sheet of paper and wrote to Robin asking him to take care of Bella in his stead, and to ensure above all things that she did not form an attachment to anyone else.

Once his Christmastide obligations were over, however, he'd make haste to Bella, wherever she was. If she was still of the same mind, if she could not tolerate the Duke of Ithorne, he didn't know what he'd do.

Bella climbed down from the luxurious traveling chariot at Rothgar Abbey, full of anticipation. The journey had been good for her. In some way it had removed her from her treadwheel of unhappiness, and she felt fresh-made and ready to enjoy herself.

She'd never experienced a merry Christmas. Under her father's rule Christmas had been a sober affair marked for its religious significance. There'd been no hint of the older practices Lady Thalia had chattered of on the journey — a Yule log, a mistletoe bough, and the Lord of Misrule.

Augustus had added penny-pinching to the tradition. Of course, now she knew he'd needed those pinched pennies for his gaming debts. Bella was still amazed that no one had guessed, and she thought often of the secrets people kept. The Trayce ladies, for example, knew about her youthful scandal, but nothing of Bellona Flint, or of Bella's feelings for the Duke of Ithorne, and she'd keep it that way.

The dark-haired man awaiting them must be the marquess, but he was dressed very simply, and his smile was so warm Bella wondered why he was sometimes called the

Dark Marquess. She was introduced, and then he offered Thalia his arm up the stairs while Lady Calliope was extracted from the ingenious sling seat that had eased the journey for her. Despite his dress and easy manner, his power, his importance, were palpable.

And Thorn was of even higher status, she reminded herself.

It would not do.

It was a lovely golden day, as sometimes came in December, when the low sun struck warmly off bare branches. Bella paused at the top of the entrance steps to look out over the parkland, drawing pleasures into herself. There was so much beauty in the world if one cared to look. A person could make a good life without a husband, without children, without that special kind of love.

Lady Calliope was being carried up the steps now in her big chair. Bella waited and then entered the house with her, for she was still intimidated by this grand establishment.

The house was as splendid inside as out, but she saw no sign of the lavish Christmas ornamentation she'd been promised. She was introduced to the marchioness, who was unconcealably enormous, and who rubbed her belly with a wince. "I think the child's practicing a jig in there."

Her glow, her ripe contentment, gave Bella another pang. But then, nearly everything did. She curtsied and thanked Lady Rothgar for inviting her.

"You are most welcome, Miss Barstowe."

Lord Rothgar came to his wife's side. "You must excuse us for celebrating quietly this year, Miss Barstowe. We are all at the whim of the littlest Malloren."

He smiled at his wife.

Stars in the eyes again, even here among such people.

Might it be possible?

That was a question she'd forbidden herself, but it broke through. She shook it away. The Marchioness of Rothgar had been the Countess of Arradale before her marriage — a countess in her own right, having inherited the title from her father. Like should marry like. Wasn't that in the Bible?

She was given into the hands of a maidservant and taken upstairs, then led through a bewildering maze of corridors to a room that seemed too grand for a mere companion. Bella knew better than to say so, but she asked where Lady Thalia and Lady Calliope were.

"Just down this corridor, miss. You won't lose them, but everyone new here gets lost.

Don't you hesitate to ring for a footman to guide you. Here's the bell." She showed Bella a knob by the fireplace. "Just give it a good hard pull, miss, and it rings down below. I'll go and get you some hot water so you can freshen yourself after your journey, miss, and soon your luggage will be here. Is there anything else you'd like, miss?"

"No, thank you."

Bella absorbed the room, absorbed the great house around her, surprised to find that it wasn't as terrifying as she'd imagined. Despite its size and grandeur and the confusing warren of corridors, there was a comfortable, domestic feel to Rothgar Abbey.

The question poked at her again, and new thoughts began to stir, like seedlings unfurling from the ground in spring. She resisted for a moment, but then relaxed and allowed them.

The journey here had changed her in some peculiar way. Being in a new place, one without any associations, was also having an effect.

To fight her greatest desire would be insane, and if tiny plants could push aside stones, as she knew they could, she would let the seedlings in her mind do as they would.

CHAPTER 33

In no time at all, Bella felt at home at Rothgar Abbey.

Perhaps it was because this was, as said, a
small gathering, mostly of family. It being
the cold time of year, the dozen or so people
generally gathered in modestly sized rooms
that were easily kept warm.

She learned that in previous years, Lord
Rothgar's brothers and sisters had always
attended, but with their marriages patterns
were changing. They were beginning traditions in their own homes. If Lord Rothgar
minded, he showed no sign of it. He, after
all, was also changing patterns. He had a
grown daughter here for the first time in
Lady Huntersdown, a lively and lovely Italian lady.

Bella remembered how Lady Fowler had
tried to make Petra Huntersdown's existence a foul scandal and was ashamed of
having any association with it. She wished

she could apologize, but Bellona Flint was dead, taking all her deeds with her.

Soon Lord Rothgar would have a new child, probably the first of many, and in the future Christmas at Rothgar Abbey would take on a new tone.

There were a few more guests, whom Bella gathered were so accustomed to spending the season here that they'd been invited. A Miss Malloren, who was middle-aged and inclined to gossip. She knew all Bella's scandals, but must have been warned by someone, for after the first time, she didn't mention them. A Mr. Thomas Malloren was very quiet, and a Lieutenant Moresby was some family connection and home from sea with nowhere else to go. He was inclined to be pleased by everything, including Bella, which made him an excellent addition. She had no real interest in him, of course, but he became her partner and she enjoyed his company.

Lord Huntersdown seemed to sometimes compete for Bella's attention, which embarrassed her until she realized his wife didn't mind.

"Ah, Robin! He flirts as he breathes," Petra Huntersdown said in her delicious Italian accent, "and indeed, he does it so well. Is not the English Christmas odd? The heavy plum pudding. The gigantic log. Tomorrow the men must cut it. That will be amusing. We will walk down together, for we are the only two young ladies to hold the coats, which I gather is another tradition."

And so Bella walked with Petra on Christmas Eve to watch the younger men strip to their shirts to wield a huge saw and cut the Yule log. Even Lord Rothgar took part.

She went with Lieutenant Moresby to cut holly, ivy, and mistletoe, and later allowed him to steal a kiss under a branch of it. Or rather, she encouraged him. He was quite shy. Everyone worked together to decorate the hall with the greenery they'd cut, sometimes singing traditional songs.

This was not how she'd imagined the high aristocracy, and among them, she was aware of her small plant growing, of new leaves unfurling.

Oh, she knew the other side, the glitter and formality, the arrogance and distance, but now she knew this too. Simply a family celebrating Christmas — and awaiting, with some anxiety, the birth of an impatiently wanted child.

The doctors had said it might come early, but here it was Christmas Eve, and no sign of labor. A doctor and midwife were in residence, constantly observing Lady Rothgar, who now kept mostly to her room. Lord Rothgar played the host well, but tension grew in him.

"Because he can do nothing," Petra said to Bella. They were weaving bright ribbons around the railings of the stairs. Others were hanging tiny bells. They rang prettily, but the jingle was beginning to get on Bella's nerves.

"There is nothing anyone can do," Bella said. "But how terrible if anything were to go amiss."

Then she remembered that Petra carried a child, though there were some months before her lying-in, and wished she'd not said that.

"He is used to making things be as he wishes them to be. With a Malloren, he says, all things are possible. It is hard to love."

"Is it?" Bella asked, tying a holly sprig in with the ribbon. The berries were plentiful, which was held to mean good luck, but she remembered an old song that equated them with blood.

"But of course. When we love, we fear above all to lose our beloved."

"Perhaps it's better not to love, then."

"There is no choice. It is life. It visits us all." Petra looked at her. "You . . . you have never loved?"

"I'm not sure."

"Then you have not loved," Petra said with a dismissive flick of her hand.

"Yes, I have!" Bella protested, then sat on a step, despairing at herself.

Petra sat beside her, all eagerness. "Tell me!"

"No."

"Why not?"

Because to speak of it would turn a seedling into an oak in a moment, shattering everything.

"Are you all right, love?" It was Lord Huntersdown, all concern for his wife because she'd sat down.

"Of course." But then Petra admitted, "Just a little tired."

He helped her up, so tenderly, with such concern. Love, wondrous and terrible, and not to be denied, but the sweetest gift of a lifetime.

So, Bella thought, watching the couple move away, absorbed in each other. *Thus the tree grows, guard against it as one will.*

She sat on the stairs amid the greenery of hope and the ribbons of celebration, with the bells of joy tinkling all around her. Everything now seemed perfectly clear. So much so that she couldn't imagine why she'd ever seen it any other way.

Love was the key, and they had love. Captain Rose or the Duke of Ithorne — the man beneath was the same. He was the hero of the Black Rat and the generous traveling companion. He was her partner in revenge, her lover, and her friend.

Love glowed inside her. The same love he'd confessed to with perfect simplicity.

Such love was not delicate, to be crushed by trials and difficulties. It was like a plant, steady and strong, and able to move stones, even mountains. It was an oak.

Lady Thalia came to the bottom of the stairs. "Bella, dear, are you all right?"

Bella rose, smiling. "Perfectly." She picked up some ribbon and another holly branch.

Except that her blindness might have cost her everything.

What if he'd changed his mind? A month had passed.

No, that couldn't be, or their love was nothing.

But she'd rejected him. So definitively. If only she could go to him now, take back that rejection. It was impossible. She must wait. . . .

Why?

She dropped the greenery in her hands and hurried to the small drawing room, where she knew writing materials were kept.

March hare! she thought, and laughed, covering her mouth before anyone heard her. She was laughing for happiness, but a giddiness was bubbling up in her at thoughts of future bliss.

She could rush out to go to him — she could even steal a horse! — but she wasn't quite mad enough for that. He was too far away across wintry country. As it was, all she could do was try to put something coherent on paper.

She ruined five sheets, until she settled for absurdly simple words.

Thorn, my dearest,
    Forgive me. Yes. Please.

Yours,
Bella

She made a mess of folding and sealing it, and then, in some idiotic lingering resistance, didn't want anyone to know to whom she sent a letter. She forced her way through that and wrote the direction, then went in search of Lord Rothgar.

He was talking to Lady Calliope, and he turned a smiling face to Bella, but she saw the shadow of frightened love beneath.

The price of love.

One she'd pay, and willingly.

"I need to send this letter," she said. "I know it's Christmas, and I'm sorry to ask that a groom take it, but . . . but I must."

He saw the address on the letter and his smile warmed and perhaps the shadow shrank a little. "Of course you must. I'll see to it."

Then there was only waiting, as she, as everyone played their festive parts.

As midnight drew close, Lady Rothgar came down, smiling and seemingly relaxed, which eased the mood. She walked awkwardly, however, as if her burden were becoming too much. A large wooden box was carried in, and Lord Rothgar turned to Lady Thalia. "Would you care to open it?"

Thalia was like a child with a present. "May I? How exciting!"

She raised the lid to reveal straw, and then dug in it. She pulled out a painted donkey. "Oh," she said. "Is it a *presepe?* How wonderful. I was thinking how sad it was not to have one this year. Bella, dear, come help me. Genova brought one here last year. You remember Genova? Who married Ashart? Such games they played with each other last Christmas. Young love, young love. It never does run smooth, but that is part of the pleasure. Everyone help!" she called gaily. "We must have this set up so the baby can arrive exactly at midnight."

She seemed unaware of the looks that flickered around. Lady Rothgar seemed undisturbed. She simply sat, stroking her belly, and watched.

Petra was almost as excited as Lady Thalia, for this was an Italian tradition. She chattered to her husband about it, about other *presepes,* about other Christmases, and he grinned, entranced by her delight.

Love multiplies, Bella thought. *It multiplies pain, but also joy.*

A table had been set near the fireplace for the nativity scene, and it was put together with time to spare. The pieces were beautifully made, but there were only the major ones — Mary, Joseph, the ox, and the ass. There were three shepherds and some sheep, but Lady Thalia and Petra insisted on placing them some distance from the wooden structure that formed the stable. There were also three kings on their camels, but apparently they must wait for the Epiphany.

"Genova had many more pieces," Lady Thalia said, "but you will add more over time, as her parents did, as birthday presents for your child."

This time, her words carried a certainty

that soothed.

Then clocks chimed and distant bells rang, and it was Christmas Day. Thalia put the baby in the manger and they all sang carols.

The real baby hadn't arrived, however, and as everyone went to bed, Bella wondered how long it would take for Thorn to reply to her note.

The March madness was seeping away, leaving room for doubts. Could love fade? Could it die?

CHAPTER 34

Christmas Day brought sunshine, and after the service in the chapel Bella escaped outside. She needed to be alone for a little while.

Her prayers had mostly been selfish — *Let him still want me; let him say so quickly; let this agony of waiting be over.* But she'd remembered to pray for Lady Rothgar's baby to come soon and come easily, so the worry could be banished from the house.

She walked briskly along a frosty path between evergreen hedges, and she was unsure whether she was attempting to race toward something or run away from it. Love, she decided, was madness. She did not feel sane. She walked and walked around the paths as if she could truly walk to Kent, but then made herself stop.

She must return to the house for the Christmas feast.

They used a small dining room, but the

dishes were grand, and some were served on golden platters. Fine wine flowed and there were frequent toasts, but beneath it all, impatience and anxiety lurked. Bella began to think it would be better if they put aside festivity until the baby came.

Or did she mean, until Thorn came?

And then, just as the flaming plum pudding was carried in, Lady Rothgar said, "Ah."

All eyes turned to her, and no one needed explanation. She did not look afraid or in pain; she simply looked relieved. "I really do think . . . at last . . ."

Her husband was by her instantly, helping her to her feet and from the room. It left an awkward dislocation, but Lord Huntersdown took over. "Good news, and yet more reason to celebrate. Sit, my friends, and let us continue the feast."

They did so, but Bella suspected most people's attention was partly on what was happening elsewhere. The birth of a child did not always go smoothly. Sometimes babe or mother, or both, died. The celebration continued, however, moving to the drawing room for cards.

Bella was disconcerted to find herself at a large table, expected to play a gambling game. It made her think of Augustus, but the game was rather silly, and played for ivory fish. Everyone, even Lady Calliope, was soon exclaiming with excitement or disappointment, and enjoying themselves.

Bella couldn't help being aware of the birth, however. She wished someone would send reports, but all she could do was concentrate on the cards to distract her mind.

Someone said, "Bella?"

She looked up impatiently.

She stared, hardly able to believe what she saw, but then she rose to fling herself into Thorn's arms. At last, at last . . .

She emerged from a starving kiss, hearing cheers and happy laughter, and turned, blushing, to face the company. But they weren't looking at her. They looked at Lord Rothgar, with a bundle in his arms.

Starry eyes, she thought, bright with another kind of love. And with happiness. "I'm blessed with another daughter," he said. "And all is well."

Whatever the normal traditions of Christmas at Rothgar Abbey, they were shattered that day. More wine was brought out so they could all toast the baby, and then Petra and Thalia went upstairs with Lord Rothgar to visit the mother. The card game was abandoned for relieved chatter.

Bella and Thorn slipped out into the evening, hand in hand, wanting only to be alone. To press close, to kiss again and again, and again

He cradled her face, looking into her eyes. "You have a room?" he asked.

Bella knew what he asked and she knew she had stars in her eyes. "Come."

She got lost on the way, which made him laugh, which made her laugh, so they kissed there in a corridor; did more than kiss, so her low gown was lower and her hair was escaping its pins. Thank heavens there were so few people in the great house, and all were elsewhere.

She tried again, and at last found the right corridor, and her bedchamber.

He undressed her skillfully and she allowed it, enjoyed it, especially with all the interesting touches and kisses along the way. She was swaying on her feet, her knees scarcely strong enough to support her when he gathered her into his arms and carried her to the bed, to the sheets he'd already cleverly exposed.

Talent and training. As she watched him strip, she smiled. She felt she was all smiles, all happiness, all pure joy, brimming over with a kind of triumph that despite all, they were here; they were one. He came to her,

and she saw the same triumphant posses-
sion in his expression. It completed everything. This man, this hero, this duke, truly
did love, want, and need her as much as she
did him.

"I'm sorry for making us wait," she said.

He laughed. "At this moment, I am not."

He joined her in the bed to touch her in
that way he had, that skillful way, but she
sensed the difference, and saw it in his eyes.
When she recognized it, she caught her
breath. This time it would be complete.

"Make me yours," she said. "Seal this for
eternity."

And so he did, and whatever she'd thought
the final joining would be, it was not, for it
was beyond anything she could ever have
imagined, taking the searing pleasure he'd
given her before and carrying it, carrying
them both, impossibly higher.

Much later, she lay against him and had
to blink away tears that this could be hers,
would be hers. "I too will become skilled,"
she said.

Perhaps she expected that to be dismissed,
but he said, "How delightful." He turned
serious, however. "I should have been wiser
at the Hart. I should have accepted the gift
of you then."

She shifted to look at him, so beautiful in

all his disheveled glory. "Why didn't you?"

"Because I thought who I was was important. But this is it in the end, isn't it? We are our nakedness."

Bella chuckled. "I think not, for we'll have to put on our disguises again. Every stitch of clothing is a disguise. Perhaps I'll become Bellona."

He grinned. "I'll throw away your wart."

Much later, sometime in the middle of the night — and Bella didn't care that the whole household must know what they were doing — she said, "I'll learn to be a good duchess."

"You'll be a splendid duchess, my love, exactly as you are. You will not need to match other duchesses. You will set the pace."

"I'll be outrageous, you mean?" She still worried a little about that, but she'd pay the price.

But he said, "Oh, I do hope so."

He left the bed, as magnificent as a classical statue, and picked up his breeches from the floor. He took something from his pocket and turned. "You permit?"

It was a ring.

Bella found herself tongue-tied, which made no sense.

"You really must, you know," he said, and

she heard a touch of worry behind it.

The Duke of Ithorne was still just a little uncertain of her?

She jumped off the bed and into his arms, and he swung her around and around. Then he brought her to earth and slid the ring onto her finger. It was not particularly large, but held a single stone. A ruby.

"I thought of a skull design," he said, "but perhaps we don't want to be quite so outré."

"We don't?" she teased. "After this?"

He laughed again. "Undoubtedly we do. The outrageous Duke and Duchess of Ithorne." He kissed her again. "Outrageous, in particular, for their everlasting love and devotion." He led her back to the bed. "We'll fly high, you and I, but when the heights weary us, we'll be outrageous in another way. We'll run away to the *Black Swan* — Captain Rose and Buccaneer Bella, free on the high seas."

ABOUT THE AUTHOR

Jo Beverley is widely regarded as one of the most talented romance writers today. She is a five-time winner of Romance Writers of America's cherished RITA Award and one of only a handful of members of the RWA Hall of Fame. She has also twice received the *Romantic Times* Career Achievement Award. Born in England, she has two grown sons and lives with her husband in Victoria, British Columbia, just a ferry ride away from Seattle. You can visit her Web site at www.jobev.com.

The employees of Thorndike Press hope you have enjoyed this Large Print book. All our Thorndike, Wheeler, and Kennebec Large Print titles are designed for easy reading, and all our books are made to last. Other Thorndike Press Large Print books are available at your library, through selected bookstores, or directly from us.

For information about titles, please call:
  (800) 223-1244

or visit our Web site at:
  http://gale.cengage.com/thorndike

To share your comments, please write:
  Publisher
  Thorndike Press
  295 Kennedy Memorial Drive
  Waterville, ME 04901